KINGDOM

Tom Martin lives in Oxford.

Also by Tom Martin

PYRAMID

TOM MARTIN

KINGDOM

PAN BOOKS

First published 2009 by Pan Books
an imprint of Pan Macmillan Ltd
Pan Macmillan, 20 New Wharf Road, London N1 9RR
Basingstoke and Oxford
Associated companies throughout the world
www.panmacmillan.com

ISBN 978-0-330-45212-0

3 5 7 9 8 6 4 2

A CIP catalogue record for this book is available from
the British Library.

Typeset by SetSystems Ltd, Saffron Walden, Essex
Printed in the UK by CPI Mackays, Chatham ME5 8TD

Visit www.panmacmillan.com to read more about all our books
and to buy them. You will also find features, author interviews and
news of any author events, and you can sign up for e-newsletters
so that you're always first to hear about our new releases.

To Kuhn Sucharitakul

And to JK, il miglior fabbro

When everyone thinks something is good
it becomes evil.

Lao Tzu, Chinese sage, fourth century BC

1

Litang monastery, Pemako jungle, Tibet

No one knew the man's name. He had arrived at the monastery gate slung over the back of a mule, his hands and feet tied under the animal's belly. He was alone.

For three days now the rains had swept through the jungle, transforming it into a shining, living ocean that was forever attempting to wash over the sides of the monastery walls. A giant caterpillar rippled on the branch of a tree, its inch-long spines rising and falling as it flowed forward. Something stirred in the depths of the forest. But the slight noises, the sounds of something creeping, of shuffling through the under-growth, were drowned out by the persistent drumming of the rain. Even the hoots of the spider monkeys sounded ghostly and remote, smothered by the force of the water.

In the monastery's central courtyard Dorgen Trungpa, a novice monk, was splashing through the water. The Abbot had asked him to go to the village. His sodden robes clung to his limbs as he ran but he did not mind the rain, even as his bare feet sank deep into the mud.

Though he was young and strong, that day Dorgen Trungpa ran no further than the monastery gate. There he saw the man on the mule and terror fixed him to the spot. He had never seen a white man before. The pallor of his skin was strange enough to the young monk, but this alabaster skin was also covered in enormous leeches. For a moment Dorgen Trungpa simply stood in mute incomprehension, not knowing what to do. Then, his heart thumping and with a sense of foreboding, he slowly moved towards the stranger.

At first he thought he must be dead, so waxen and ghastly was the skin, and then there was the blood – the blood-coated hands and the blood across his ragged clothes. The rope had gouged deep into the man's wrists and ankles. His face was turned towards the belly of the mule, but Dorgen Trungpa did not dare to lift the man's head. He imagined his eyes, staring blankly, and the leeches sucking on his dead skin.

Dorgen Trungpa backed away slowly from the man, as if a sudden movement might disturb him, and then when he had retreated some distance he turned. He ran, gasping with fear, and didn't look round until he arrived back in the flooded courtyard.

A man, he told his fellow monks. A man with skin like alabaster. A terrible man, leeches sucking his skin, tied to a mule. Come quickly, he said, and two other monks followed him, shaking their heads and saying this would bring only evil.

In frightened silence, rain lashing at their thin robes, the monks struggled with the body, cutting it from the mule's back. A small sodden canvas bag was slung over the man's right shoulder, hooked tightly under his left armpit – it seemed to be the only possession he had.

Even now Dorgen Trungpa assumed they were bearing a corpse, that no man could be so waxen and terrible and yet living. With their heavy burden they wrestled their way up the cart track, sliding in the mud, their sweat mingling with rainwater.

In the courtyard they laid him on the stones. Somewhere in the ancient monastic complex a bell began to ring out over the rooftops with a slurred atonal sound, as if it was ringing underwater. And now a distant bellow of thunder rumbled across the mountains.

Tentatively, the three monks set to work tearing the leeches from the man's cheeks, leaving welts on his ashen skin. Dorgen Trungpa felt inside the man's mouth, and withdrew his hand holding a bloated monster. His gorge rising, he threw it into a puddle, where it squirmed violently.

Now the Abbot appeared in the doorway to the prayer hall. A man esteemed among his monks, the senior lama of Pemako. At seventy years of age, he was thin to the point of malnourishment and yet he glowed with energy. When they heard his footsteps approaching across the courtyard, the young monks ceased their activity and let the limp body slide to rest on the courtyard floor.

The Abbot held worry beads in his left hand. Click click, clack clack, the noise of the beads was steady though muffled by the rain. Behind him was a short, anxious man, with short black hair – the Abbot's deputy. At the ruined body the two lamas paused, and then crouched down. With the tips of his fingers, the deputy felt the white man's throat for any signs of a pulse. A second later, he looked up at the monks and muttered a single word.

'Doctor.'

One monk began running immediately he heard him, and vanished quickly through a low doorway in the far wall. Click click, clack clack, went the Abbot's worry beads, as he leaned towards the man, searching his face for signs. With his callused fingers the deputy delved under the flap of the bag and pulled out the contents: a pipe, some opium and a weatherbeaten, black-covered book, written in an unknown language. The two lamas inspected the items, mystified, and then returned them to their pouch and smoothed the sodden flap back into place. For a moment the Abbot held his hand suspended above the man's heart, as if seeking thereby to draw out his secret.

The deputy was the first to speak. He moved his mouth close to the ear of the Abbot so that neither of the younger monks would hear. His voice trembled as he whispered:

'His sherpas must have abandoned him at the gate when he caught a fever . . . He is on the verge of death . . .'

He glanced back down at the white man and then muttered almost to himself:

'. . . but how did a Westerner travel into Pemako in the first place? And why?'

When the Abbot spoke his voice was thin and resigned.

'This man brings a dark augury. His arrival signals the end of our monastery. By nightfall I will be dead and our gates will lie shattered.'

The rain pounded on the courtyard floor and gushed down the tiled roofs of the ancient stone buildings. Now the young monk reappeared with the doctor, who knelt before the stranger and began to examine his limp body. Water streamed down the Abbot's face but his unblinking eyes betrayed no hint of fear or panic.

'A terrible evil is coming from the forest . . .'

'But what can we do?' said the deputy, in a hoarse and frightened whisper. He was staring in horror at the stranger. The Abbot reached out and touched his arm.

'Do not be fearful. The devils that are coming are merely shadows sent to perplex you. Go immediately to the Cave of the Magicians. If you are pursued, then enter the tunnel network and go into Agarthi. Do not come back for seven days. Take everyone with you, this stranger included. We must care for this man who has found his way to our door, and protect him from danger.'

A look of grave concern crossed the face of the Abbot's deputy:

'But if he is a harbinger of evil, then surely we should have nothing to do with him?'

'No. That is against the vows of our order. He must be cared for. He must go with you. I will remain here. The forces of darkness must be met with compassion. Whilst the stranger lives, he is our responsibility – have the doctor do the best he can. Leave at once through the back gate into the jungle. You must go now.'

The Abbot took one last look at the stranger. Clad in rags and slick with rain, he seemed like a ship-wrecked sailor cast onto a lonely shore. The Abbot felt a profound sense of compassion for this man, who had been broken by the forest and the darkness he had found there. He nodded slowly to his deputy, who was still ashen-faced and hesitant. Then the Abbot turned and walked slowly away, bent under the force of the storm.

In the gloom of the prayer hall the Abbot's beads went clack clack clack. Slowly he walked into the ancient chamber. In front of the stone statue of the Saint Milarepa, the founder of his order, he settled into the lotus position and began the chant of compassion for the souls of those who, as surely as night follows day, were coming to destroy him.

Om Mane Padme Hum
The Jewel is in the Flower of the Lotus

How many minutes or hours passed the Abbot did not know. He chanted his prayer of forgiveness and compassion, and felt his soul grow light. He was deep in reverie when he felt a hand on his shoulder. Dorgen Trungpa was whispering in his ear.

'Abbot, please forgive me for disturbing your meditation . . .'

The old lama's eyes opened to the semi-darkness and his deep-throated chanting stopped. Dorgen Trungpa was shaking with fear. He could barely speak, and he struggled to explain:

'There are Chinese soldiers on the road outside. They will break down the gate.'

The Abbot stood up and shifted his damp robes over his shoulder. With a look of deep pity, he placed his hand on the young man's trembling shoulder.

'Why did you stay here? I told everyone they must leave.'

The novice said hoarsely, 'It was my doing. It was my karma. I found the stranger, I brought him in.'

The Abbot shook his head and sighed.

'You should feel no shame or guilt, my boy. But

perhaps this is the path you must follow. Remember today, then, that whatever they do to you, it is all merely an illusion. The thought forms that we mistake for reality are nothing more than dreams. All the devils of the world are in our imaginations and so is all the pain and suffering. Remember this today.'

And suddenly there was a sound, a terrible crash which echoed through the building, and made the walls shudder. Dorgen Trungpa, for all the teachings of the lama, could not repress a cry of surprise, and a surge of terror gripped his body.

'Remember my words and all will be well,' the Abbot was saying as Dorgen Trungpa struggled to gather himself. 'We must go outside now, my boy.'

Outside, they saw the ancient wooden gate hanging from its broken hinges. For hundreds of years it had kept the monastery safe, but now Chinese soldiers were filing into the courtyard. In the centre was an army jeep and in it stood a short, fat Chinese army officer. His filthy, ill-fitting, olive-green uniform was soaked through and rain was streaming over the peak of his cap and down his face.

Soldiers were filing into the prayer rooms and monks' quarters and the kitchen and dining hall. They swarmed through the silent abandoned rooms, as if they were searching for something. The Abbot stood in the doorway surveying the chaos before him, the troops that were ransacking his monastery. Yet his face was serene; he was almost smiling.

When the army officer saw the Abbot he raised a clipped cry, and a group of soldiers came forward, weapons raised. At their approach, Dorgen Trungpa flinched and wanted to turn, back into the shelter of the prayer hall. The Abbot made no effort to resist, and so Dorgen Trungpa stayed by his side, transfixed with fear. One soldier smashed the butt of his rifle into the Abbot's face, and the old man collapsed to the ground. They punched and kicked him and dragged him through the puddles over to the jeep. He collapsed again and again under the hail of blows, only to be lifted up again so that he could be beaten to the ground once more.

And Dorgen Trungpa found that now he had forgotten the teachings of the lama, and was retreating urgently through the hall, striving to escape even as the troops moved towards him. As he turned a corner he was met by soldiers coming the other way. They set upon him like a pack of dogs, pummelling and mauling him until he was inert with pain and bewilderment and offered no more resistance. Then they dragged him to the centre of the courtyard, and flung him down next to the Abbot.

My karma, thought Dorgen Trungpa. I brought this here. My actions have killed us both and destroyed the monastery. And he tried to contemplate his own death with equanimity, as the Chinese officer spat out orders to his soldiers. Then the officer stepped out of his jeep, his face ugly with rage, and addressed the Abbot.

'You understand Chinese, parasite?'

The Abbot, now on his hands and knees, raised his bruised and weary head and answered in Mandarin: 'Yes.'

The officer undid the button on the breast packet of his uniform and pulled out a piece of paper. The rain doused it as he held it up to read.

'On behalf of the peasants of Pemako and the government of the Tibet Autonomous Region of the People's Republic of China, we hereby charge you with feudalist practices.'

The officer looked up from the paper and spat on the ground in front of the old lama.

'You are guilty of systematic exploitation of the peasants, of enslaving them on your land, of taxing them in the form of tithes of butter and yak meat, of using them as unpaid labour in your monastery kitchens whilst you yourselves sit idle and do no work. You have continued these feudalist practices for generations and have sustained and justified this wicked system by scaring the people with stories of eternal hells that do not exist and threats that when they die they will be reborn as vermin if they do not obey you. In short, you have taken advantage of the common people's ignorance and used superstition and religion as tools of oppression. Furthermore, you are guilty of owning images of the Grand Parasite, the wicked dictator and leader of your feudal empire, the Dalai Lama, who has attempted to split the Motherland and sabotage China's relations with foreign nations – and of failing to recognize the supreme authority of the Communist Party of China. Furthermore, you are charged with harbouring a foreign spy. We demand that you hand over this man immediately.'

Now the officer snarled at the Abbot:

'What have you to say, parasite?'

The Abbot remained silent.

In a rage the officer threw the paper to the floor. He stepped towards the Abbot, and swinging his right foot back, he landed his army boot with all the force he could muster under the old man's chin. There was a sickening crack and the Abbot flipped over onto his back.

Dorgen Trungpa cried out in horror and tried to break free from the restraining grip of two Chinese soldiers but was beaten into submission.

The officer loomed over the broken body of the lama.

'Get up, parasite. Why are you lying in the wet?

Why don't you levitate? That's what you tell the peasants you can do.'

The Abbot's eyes opened slowly. The officer placed his foot on the old man's neck and shouted down at him:

'Where is the fugitive spy?'

The Abbot seemed now to be trying to speak, choking for breath. Perhaps expecting to hear an answer to his question, the officer lifted his foot. Gradually the Abbot's words became audible:

'Om Mane Padme Hum . . . Om Mane Padme . . .'

At the sound of the chant, the officer spun round and barked an order to the assembled soldiers. Two men stepped forward. The Abbot recognized them; they were fellow Tibetans, outcasts from the village. They had committed serious crimes in the past and so were forced to beg and live outside the community on the edge of the jungle. It was their job to clean the monastery toilets and bury the dead of the village. Their ill-fitting uniforms looked new. They must have been recruited only hours before.

The army officer smiled and said to the two Tibetans, 'I think the parasite has a headache. Cure him.'

One of the soldiers was carrying a hammer and a four-inch bronze nail in his hands. He had a gloating smirk on his face. The second of the new recruits sat down heavily on the Abbot's chest and grabbed the old man's head. The Abbot, as if oblivious to his circumstances, continued his mournful, low chant.

The soldier with the hammer knelt down beside the Abbot and carefully placed the bronze nail in the centre of his forehead. Pausing, he looked up at the officer. The officer briskly nodded his head and with a sickening crack the hammer fell. The nail sank into the Abbot's skull. Two more blows followed until not a single particle of the nail protruded. The Abbot's arms waved feebly in the air for a moment then fell limply by his side. Dorgen Trungpa cried out in agony and collapsed to the floor. Silence hung over the courtyard.

Then the officer spoke, and Dorgen Trungpa realized with a dull sense of dread that he was addressing him.

'So, boy, now that you have seen that justice is done, even in places such as Pemako that are far from Beijing, perhaps you can still be saved from the grip of these evil and insane old men. You are still young. Let us see . . .'

He turned towards the broken gates and shouted an order. Dorgen Trungpa gritted his teeth and cried out in rage and desolation. Two soldiers were dragging a young peasant girl along. She was the daughter of the village's biggest landowner. She was in her late teens, a beautiful girl, now emitting low moans of terror and struggling weakly against her captors. They marched her up to the young monk. The officer barked another order. The two soldiers holding her ripped off her clothes. Dorgen Trungpa averted his gaze from her naked form, as the soldiers held her upright before him.

'Now, monk, let's see you act like a real man. I order you to have sex with this peasant girl.'

The light had gone out in Dorgen Trungpa's eyes. Nothing in his eighteen years of life had prepared him for this. All he knew was the round of monastery ceremonies, the weeks of prayer and fasting and meditation, the festivals in the village and the order of a life maintained in unison with the forces of the universe. His breath came in short desperate gasps as the soldiers picked him up and thrust him towards the equally terrified girl. He would not look at her nakedness but he could hear her desperate low moans, like a dying animal. The officer shouted encouragement in a sardonic voice.

'Come on, boy! Forget the lies of these evil old men. Vows of celibacy are nonsense. You have been brainwashed, that is all ... Now my patience is running out ... I order you to have sex with this girl and when you have finished you will set fire to the monastery library.'

Before the monk's eyes, all the horrors that *The*

Tibetan Book of the Dead had described to him in rich detail seemed to be coming true: the soul afflicted by awful demons and unspeakable pain at the point of death. But this was life, an unspeakable sort of life, a life Dorgen Trungpa had no powers to comprehend. And he closed his eyes, calmed his breathing and tried, against all the odds, to free his mind.

2

It was daytime. That was all that Nancy Kelly knew. Where she was, or what time it was, she couldn't remember. The banging noise started again. Above her head an enormous fan hung from the ceiling, its giant blades turning morosely but failing to generate even the slightest whisper of a breeze. For a second she stared at the fan in confusion and then everything clicked into place: she was in India, in Delhi, in the company apartment. And there was someone knocking on the door.

Cursing no one in particular, Nancy groaned with exhaustion and rolled over in bed. The curtains were little more than diaphanous white sheets and the room was bathed in light. She felt disoriented and sick but she had only been in India for a few hours.

Surely I can't be ill already, she thought, that would be just too unfair.

She fumbled around on the bedside table, picked

up her phone and stared at its clock in confusion, uncertain whether she had changed the settings from New York to Delhi time. She remembered that her plane had landed in the middle of the night, that a driver had ushered her through the crowds of beggars and touts offering to change her dollars and find her cheap hotel rooms, to the safety of the waiting Mercedes. She had sunk back into the almost uncomfortably large leather seat and stared out of the window, watching the colour and chaos of the Delhi night drift by as if it was on a television screen until finally the car had slipped into the darkness of an empty street and deposited her outside the apartment building.

Nancy Kelly had come to Delhi to be the new *International Herald Tribune* South Asia Bureau Chief. She was thirty years old, which was young for the post, but she had been very fortunate with the timing. It was a new stage in her career and equally a new stage in her life. She hoped that it would allow her to put the recent past behind her and that the exoticism and excitements of India would help her forget her last few months in New York, months that had seemed at times to pass as slowly as whole years.

The knocking continued, but Nancy was still too groggy and confused to get out of bed. The message icon was flashing on her phone. Shouting weakly at the noise – 'Coming, just a minute' – she opened the message. It was a mail from her ex-boyfriend, James Long, the *Tribune*'s Buenos Aires correspondent. That made her heart sink; she could not help thinking that it was an inauspicious sign that the first message she should receive in India was from him. She had met him five years ago when they had been working together in the New York office; they had dated for three. She had been, unquestionably, in love – but their desires were so different. He wanted to settle down with a wife who stayed at home and looked after his children: that was never going to be her. Finally, he announced he had found someone else, someone he had met whilst she had been on one of her frequent trips abroad – a motherly stay-at-home type. She was from Argentina and James, it seemed, was very lucky: the Buenos Aires job came up the next day and James applied for the post and got it. Either that or he'd been seeing the woman for much longer than either he or Nancy wanted to admit. That was three months ago – she should have seen it coming but she took it very badly. She knew that they weren't suited but that didn't stop her being in love.

'My dearest Nancy, I am so sorry that I did not return your calls. As I explained to you when we last spoke, I felt it was better if . . .'

She stopped reading and then she weighed the phone in the palm of her hand before pressing Delete.

She exhaled with relief, as if she had just made the right decision about which wire to cut and had successfully defused a bomb. A few months ago, she observed with the fragility and hollowness that comes after grief, she would have been desperate to hear from him, but now that at last she had almost regained her equilibrium the very last thing she wanted to do was to re-establish contact.

'My dearest James,' she said out loud as the diaphanous white curtains stirred gently in the sultry Delhi breeze, 'I now understand that there will come a day, perhaps not too far in the future, when I will actually get over you . . .'

She managed a forced smile and then looked around the bedroom, almost hoping for encouragement from her new surroundings. Goddamn this knocking, she thought. 'OK OK,' she said, and really tried to move herself. She shifted her legs off the bed, rubbed her eyes. She was in one of the most fascinating countries in the world, with a challenging career break ahead of her, and the past was behind her.

Things had slipped into place, almost uncannily. The vacancy in India was announced the same morning that she made up her mind to go abroad. Or more accurately, Dan Fischer, the editor, who was over from Paris, had tapped her on the shoulder and invited her into his office. Anton Herzog, her hero, everybody's

hero at the *Trib* and the longest-ever-serving Delhi
Bureau Chief, had gone missing three months earlier.
After twenty years in the job, he had vanished without
a trace into the mountains of Tibet. Dan Fischer had
waited and waited but finally the board had put
pressure on him: someone had to be found to fill the
post; India was the biggest story in Asia and the paper
couldn't wait indefinitely for Herzog to return. Nancy
was offered the job on the spot. Dan didn't even
bother to advertise it on the paper's internal vacancies
board – a fact Nancy would have found far more
puzzling had she not been so glad of the opportunity
to leave New York. It was a big posting and she had
never even set foot in India, but Dan told her she had
powerful supporters on the paper, people who admired
her writing and her investigative skill. And, of course,
not having a partner might actually have been to her
advantage – people with partners always found it so
much more difficult to move. But she had big boots
to fill, Dan had quipped as he shook her warmly by
the hand. Anton was a legend – she would have to be
at the top of her game. She had smiled gratefully,
bewildered by the strange and fortunate turn of events,
but it was a huge opportunity and she certainly wasn't
going to quibble about the unorthodox hiring
procedure.

As for poor old Anton, the rugged, sixty-year-old

Argentine–American, everyone just hoped that he was off on one of his periodic jaunts and that sooner or later he would reappear. It was Anton who had first inspired Nancy to become a journalist, but despite her enormous admiration for him, she didn't know him well. She had always loved his stories, and whenever she picked up a copy of the paper she always searched for them first, but the truth was she had only ever had the chance to meet him on a couple of occasions. He was rarely in the office, and when he was, Dan Fischer treated him like royalty and hardly let anyone else get near to him. On the couple of occasions when she had got to speak to him he had always been so kind and encouraging – and so modest – but she had been tantalized rather than satisfied by their meetings. She hoped that he would walk back into the Delhi office before too long, no doubt with a few more prize-winning tales under his belt, and this time she would be the first to get to hear them.

But it was true that there were voices of disquiet. Some of Anton's close friends, the other old stagers back in the New York office, were getting steadily more and more worried that something else might have happened. Normally someone would get a call, or a postcard, or something, but this time they had received no word at all. Anton had been a fine moun-taineer in his youth, they said, and he was also a stubborn man. It wasn't too hard to imagine that he could have overextended himself on a climb somewhere, no doubt underequipped, relying on his notorious intelligence and strength. He was an old-school correspondent; he spoke several Asian languages and he had a huge knowledge of India and China and Tibet. On countless occasions he had turned down promotions and pay rises to continue to do what he loved: being out in the field on his own, chasing stories and taking risks that reporters half his age would shy away from. He was a legend, that was for certain, and maybe this was why everyone was so unwilling to contemplate the worst.

And now Nancy almost jumped out of her skin. The knocking had suddenly become much louder. An Indian voice was shouting her name through the letterbox. She tossed the phone onto the bed and stood up. Fumbling in her suitcase, she found a pair of khaki trousers and a clean shirt, which she slipped on. She grabbed a hairband and tied her thick shoulder-length brown hair into a loose ponytail. Glancing in a mirror, she noticed that she looked tired but that was hardly surprising, she thought.

Stepping into the hall, she suddenly had a view of the main sitting room. She'd been too worn out to look around when she arrived, but what she saw now amazed her. The room was overflowing with antique stone statues and figurines. Literally every surface of every table – and there were lots of antique tables of every size and shape – was crammed with carved statues. Some were huge life-size stone sculptures of Buddha's head, others were meticulous little carvings of merchants from the Silk Road mounted on camel back. The overall effect was astounding; it was like looking into a storeroom at Sotheby's. Clearly, Anton Herzog had been a connoisseur . . .

'Miss Kelly. If you are there can you please open the door?'

The voice was loud and impatient. She knelt down at the letterbox and saw a pair of brown eyes staring back at her through the slit.

'Yes?'

'This is the police. My name is Captain Hundalani. Please open the door.'

The eyes disappeared as Captain Hundalani stood up.

'Er . . . Yes . . .'

Nancy clicked open the three locks and opened the door a crack, and then seeing that two of the three Indian men in the hall were wearing police uniforms she swung the door open and let them in. The third man was wearing an impeccable dark suit. Captain

Hundalani was in his early thirties, clean-shaven except for a neatly trimmed moustache. Neither he nor the policemen were smiling. The Captain said, 'Miss Kelly, we are sorry to disturb you. However our business is urgent.'

'Er . . . OK,' said Nancy. 'Come in. Perhaps in here' – and she gestured towards the sitting room. 'Have a seat, wherever you like. It's not my apartment . . . It belongs to Mr Herzog, my colleague at the *Herald Tribune*. Or rather he lives here . . . Really it's the company's apartment. But Mr Herzog's away . . .'

Captain Hundalani cut in. His voice was cold and emotionless.

'Yes. We know all that, Miss Kelly. That is precisely the reason that we are here . . . Please, you will find it is best if you wait until we have explained.'

There was an unmistakable air of menace to his voice, Nancy thought. But she couldn't imagine what the problem was. She could hardly be in trouble for not registering with the police; she had only been in town for a few hours. With a feeling of panic rising in her belly she found a silk-covered chair, of an age and beauty she hardly had time to consider, and sat down. Mr Hundalani and the two policemen were still standing, glowering at her.

'We'd like you to come with us, Miss Kelly . . . To answer a few questions . . .'

There was not even a flicker of friendship on Captain Hundalani's face. A wave of adrenalin washed over her.

'What? Why? I've only been in India for a few hours. I only just woke. Surely I am allowed to change my clothes and have a shower before I register.'

Her voice sounded small and weak – she could hear herself speaking almost as if she wasn't saying the words herself. And then, suddenly, to her absolute horror and astonishment, it dawned on her what was really going on.

'Am I under arrest?'

Captain Hundalani paused for a second, choosing his words carefully.

'No, Miss Kelly. Not if you come with us.'

Her throat was dry:

'What are you talking about? I've been here only a few hours, and I've been asleep for most of those. How can I possibly have done anything illegal?'

'Our investigation concerns your colleague Mr Anton Herzog. It concerns his real reasons for being in India and Tibet.'

'I'm sure that's a very compelling subject, Anton's a fascinating man. But I don't see how I can help you. I've never been to India and I haven't seen him in months. I'm here to replace him, not to answer for his misdemeanours, whatever they were.' She looked nervously up and down the room, at the massed statues and antiques, all of them testifying to the personality of the absent Herzog. 'Anyway, you can't just march in here and take me away . . . Let me call the office; I need a lawyer.'

Out of the corner of her eye, she noticed that one of the policemen had placed his hand on the handcuffs that hung from his belt. Nancy could hardly believe what was happening, and what was most terrifying was that there seemed to be absolutely nothing she could do.

Paralysed by the course of events, she stood there as the policeman unhooked the handcuffs from his belt and then slipped them around her wrists.

'But I haven't done anything, I need a lawyer,' she repeated feebly, aware that she sounded just like a young child, unable to comprehend the logic by which her guilt had been arrived at, too naive to understand the transgressions she had committed. And then Captain Hundalani smiled: a cold smile, insincere and condescending.

He didn't even bother to argue.

'I'm afraid that won't be possible Miss Kelly. Now, if you have decided to cooperate, perhaps we can leave? Things will be much easier if we all remain friends.'

3

'Stop this at once.'

A loud voice with a Beijing accent rang out across the courtyard. Dorgen Trungpa's eyes opened in amazement, as if a god had spoken.

All heads turned from the naked girl to the monastery gates. There, between the broken gates, stood a tall, handsome, northern Chinese man, wearing a standard army-issue rain cape and the peaked cap of an officer. Behind him down the track other human shapes were visible, moving in the rain. Now that he had everyone's attention, the northerner spoke again – directly to the army officer.

'Order your men to stop vandalizing the monastery at once – and give the girl back her clothes. What do you think you are doing? The Cultural Revolution finished decades ago. And let the boy go.'

Dorgen Trungpa could hardly believe his ears. It was as if a guardian angel had materialized out of the jungle. A shadow of outrage passed across the army officer's face. 'How dare you march in here, barking orders? I am the senior officer in Pemako region. Who the hell do you think you are? Explain yourself or I'll have you shot at once.'

The northerner strode across the courtyard and as he approached, it became clear who he was from the insignia on his cap badge and the knee-length polished black leather boots that flashed under his raincoat as he walked. He was a Colonel in the notorious Public Security Bureau, or PSB as it was known, the Chinese equivalent of the CIA and the FBI all rolled in to one. Even the faithful supporters of the Communist Party lived in fear of the PSB. They were the thought police of the Chinese government, the guard dogs of the revolution.

The soldiers in the courtyard stiffened noticeably as they recognized the northerner's rank and affiliation. When he reached the centre of the courtyard he drew a letter from his pocket and held it out with a straight arm to the stunned army officer. The envelope was sealed shut with a single red star, wax seal.

'I am Colonel Wei Jen of the PSB. Orders from General Te of Southern Command in Chongqing. I am now the senior officer in Pemako, and henceforth all army units south of the Su La pass are under my command. And that includes you.'

The army officer stared in disbelief at Colonel Jen and then, like a petulant child, he snatched the envelope from the Colonel's grasp and tore it open. For a minute he studied the orders and then he turned back to his men with a look of angry humiliation on his face.

'Give the woman her clothes and assemble by the gates . . . And let the monk go.'

Dorgen Trungpa was roughly pushed forward. Released, he ran over to the body of the Abbot and flung himself onto the old man, weeping. Colonel Jen smiled at the army officer and nodded his approval.

'Good. These superstitious old monks are a tourist attraction and nothing more. The old Tibet is dead and gone – we can afford to be lenient on the last remaining savages.'

Colonel Jen slapped the army officer on the back and continued, not wanting the man to lose any more face than he had already done.

'In Lhasa, the capital, there are now twice as many Chinese as there are Tibetans. We do not need to persecute their absurd beliefs any longer – the young people are more interested in mobile phones than prayer wheels. The good sense of communism has replaced the foolish religion of the monks.'

Then he turned to survey the collection of bedraggled soldiers:

'Now, where are the rest of your men? I will need them all to report here in the courtyard at dusk. I want to organize a search party. Have them bring provisions for ten days. But first, treat this monk's injuries. And get rid of this corpse. When that's done I want to question the boy. Have him cleaned up and then bring him to me. I will set up my headquarters here, in the monastery's library . . .'

He glanced at the heavens in disgust. '. . . Surely at least that will be dry. And get a generator in here and some lights.'

With that, the Colonel marched briskly towards the door to the prayer hall and disappeared into the gloom.

4

The steel door slammed shut behind Nancy Kelly and she was led down a long, poorly lit brick corridor. As her footsteps echoed along the walls a feeling of dread engulfed her. It seemed that they would be questioning her about Anton Herzog. They were suspicious; or Herzog had already been condemned and simply had to be found. Either way, she was certain they had got the wrong woman for their interrogation. She would throw no light on their case. Despite worshipping Herzog as a journalist, she knew nothing about the man. She could picture him in her mind's eye holding court in the newsroom, back on one of his rare visits, mesmerizing all around him with his extraordinary tales. But as to his private life, the real personality behind the glittering façade, his motivations, his politics, she knew absolutely nothing, and her feeling of absolute ignorance only compounded her fear. She began to feel that she was falling into a nightmare world, that like Alice in Wonderland she was entering a realm where, precisely because she didn't know what she was being accused of, she would never be able to clear her name.

But what choice had she had? From Captain Hundalani's terse, hostile manner, it was quite clear that she was in very deep already, although her exact legal status was academic right now: she was being taken away against her will, without any chance to talk to a lawyer, and that was all that mattered. For all she knew she was about to disappear into some hellhole jail and no one would ever know . . . Perhaps that was exactly what had happened to Anton Herzog . . . Maybe he had been languishing for the past few months in an overcrowded stinking cell somewhere in the Delhi Central Prison, riddled with disease and wondering why no one had bothered to find him.

The corridor led to another corridor and then down some steps, through several doors and finally into a part of the police station that more resembled a normal office building than a penitentiary. The Sikh policeman knocked on a nondescript door and then opened it and motioned to her to go in.

Behind a desk sat a middle-aged, bland-looking Indian man. His nondescript face was featureless to the point of being completely forgettable. From nowhere, Nancy suddenly remembered something that one of her CIA contacts had once said while they were having coffee on Times Square, that all the best Intelligence operatives look like nobodies, like bank clerks, or people you see in a doctor's waiting room. 'They are so completely ordinary that they never ever stand out in a crowd; in fact even when they are on their own you don't notice them. They are our most prized assets; you can look right at them but your mind simply blanks them out.'

It was only the man's eyes that were in any way exceptional. There was a coldness about them that ran completely against the grain of his otherwise banal exterior. His voice surprised her. He snapped an order and there was an impatience and irritation to it that she hadn't expected.

'Take her handcuffs off, there's no need for those.'

While the policeman unlocked the cuffs, the man stood up and stepped round the desk and then quite unexpectedly he pulled out the chair for her.

'Please, Miss Kelly, have a seat.'

Nancy sat down, even more confused than before. He returned to his seat behind the desk.

'I'm so sorry that I had to ask you to come in . . .'

At this she bridled.

'I wasn't asked. I was ordered.' She rubbed her wrists. 'And the handcuffs were completely unnecessary . . .'

For a second the man appeared to be genuinely sympathetic:

'I'm sorry. These young officers, they sometimes have no idea. I will have a word with Captain Hundalani . . .'

The note of sympathy gave Nancy the hope that some measure of righteous indignation was justified. 'And what the hell do you think you are doing coming round and thumping on the door and waking me up like that and threatening me with arrest? Are you trying to intimidate me?'

Very suddenly the man's dark eyes flashed at her in anger. Quite instinctively, she realized that she would have to be more careful. When he spoke again, the man's voice was curt and uncompromising:

'Ms Kelly, this is not North America. India is not a rich country yet. In Delhi our police force is stretched to the limit. We do not have that much time. And I can assure you that the gravity of your situation more than justifies our actions.'

The man pushed away his chair and stood up and stared at her with dispassion verging on contempt.

'Besides, I won't have a North American criticizing our methods. I believe that one in every three black men has been in jail at some point in America. That doesn't sound to me like a fair and well-functioning system.'

Frightened though she was, Nancy was determined not to show it.

'I suggest you advance your complaints to the American Embassy. Much as I agree with your concerns about American justice, I'm a journalist not a judge.'

But whoever this man was he was clearly in no mood to discuss her arrest any further. As he glanced away, she had a second to collect her thoughts. Arguing with him wasn't going to help. He was clearly very senior and she suspected that he could do whatever he wanted with her. Before she could speak again, he said, 'I am Inspector Lall. You have been brought here because of the Herzog affair.'

Her heart sank. The Herzog affair – it sounded ever more serious, and worse, every time anyone mentioned Anton Herzog she got the distinct feeling that they assumed that she was on intimate terms with her predecessor and that she was already acquainted with the details of whatever it was that they were investigating.

She stammered, 'Listen, I've already told Captain Hundalani, I have no idea what you are talking about. I hardly even know Anton Herzog. I was sent to replace him. The *Trib* – the *International Herald Tribune* – is a massive international operation. Now you must allow me to see a lawyer or a representative from my Embassy.'

The man eyed her with his steady cold gaze before he turned to the policeman standing guard at the door and said, 'Please call in Mr Arumagum.'

The guard disappeared into the hall and the man returned to his seat. There was a coldness to his voice that frightened her to the core.

'A lawyer is on the way, Miss Kelly. May I suggest that you try to answer my questions when he arrives? I don't particularly want to ask them, but this is serious. Believe me, it is very serious. If you would rather go down to the cells and think things through, then that is your prerogative. We'll try not to forget about you. You'd be advised not to touch anyone down there. We wouldn't want you to contract leprosy.'

A chill ran down her spine. The door opened and the policeman re-entered the room, followed by a short, bald, tired-looking man in his fifties, with very dark skin and a pair of thick spectacles. Inspector Lall introduced him with a wave of his hand – a gesture that seemed to show that he thought the whole thing was a charade and a waste of time.

'Ms Kelly, this is your legal representative, Mr Arumagum. Please ask him any questions that you want.'

Nancy looked in despair at the tired old man who sat next to her. He inspired not one iota of hope, but he was all they would permit her. Barely concealing her desperation she asked, 'What's going on? Are they allowed to do this to me? You've got to help me . . .'

Mr Arumagum nodded his head and adjusted his spectacles and then, fumbling, he pulled a business card out of his pocket.

'Ms Kelly, here is my card.'

She almost screamed at him in frustration, 'I don't want your damn card. I want to get out of here. Just tell me what is going on . . .'

Flustered, the lawyer cleared his throat. Inspector Lall had folded his arms over his chest and was watching the exchange with a mixture of boredom and impatience. Mr Arumagum said, 'You are being held on suspicion of espionage. Consequently, all your usual rights are suspended under Article 3, section 7, of the Terrorism and Espionage Act of 2005. You can be detained without trial for a period of one hundred and thirty days, at which point a judge will assess whether you are still a significant enough danger to the state to warrant incarceration for a further one hundred and thirty days. You have no visiting rights, no rights of bail. The maximum sentence for espionage is the death penalty and for being an accessory to espionage it is twenty-five years. I believe you are being held under suspicion of being an accessory . . .'

It seemed to Nancy Kelly that Mr Arumagum's face had merged with the grey walls and the sound of his voice tailed off into the distance. For almost a minute her elbows rested heavily on the table top in front of her and she found she could only bury her face in the palms of her hands. Then she looked up again at Inspector Lall. Her voice was cracking: 'An accessory to espionage? This is insane . . .'

There was another deadening, terrifying silence, and then she said, trying not to let desperation creep into her voice, 'What about my Embassy? What about my paper? I demand you contact them immediately.'

'That will be done,' stated Mr Arumagum, in a flat voice which suggested he knew that would do no good either.

Inspector Lall nodded in reply, then said, in an unnerving, dry voice, 'Now, Miss Kelly, if we can begin.'

He opened the thick file that lay on the desk in front of him and peered through his glasses.

'You attended university in Paris, at the Sorbonne. Correct?'

Striving to maintain her sense of defiance, Nancy replied:

'Yes.'

'And you were there from 1997 to 2000. Correct?'

'Yes.'

'And you say that you barely know Mr Anton Herzog?'

Again she pleaded with him:

'Yes. I've met him a couple of times. That's all. In the office. He is not a friend, he's not even someone I work with . . .'

A note of impatience entered Inspector Lall's voice.

'Ms Kelly, it is really important that you are absolutely honest in your responses. I will ask the question one more time only. But first let me tell you that we already know that Anton Herzog taught at the Sorbonne for a year – 1998 to 1999; he was on sabbatical from the *International Herald Tribune* and he was allegedly teaching a writing course. Secondly, we also know that he was Chair of the committee that awarded you the cub reporter's scholarship when you first started on the newspaper. Now you have arrived to cover his job. You look more like a protégée to me, than someone who doesn't know him at all.'

Nancy Kelly shook her head in disbelief. Their case was thin; their assumptions broad. It was ludicrous, but Inspector Lall was staring at her, as if she must now confess everything. Trying to remain calm, she said, 'I never even met Herzog when I was at the

Sorbonne. I wasn't really switched on about top journalists in those days. I was just your average student – handing in papers late, going to bars. Anyway, even if I had known him there, what's the big deal? It wouldn't make me a protégée. Loads of people know Herzog. He's a rightly celebrated international journalist. And my getting this job, I mean likewise, what does that prove? I worked hard for this promotion and I got it on merit. I can't imagine what you're trying to suggest.'

The man looked at her almost pityingly, then he turned over the page in the file.

'Did you know what Mr Herzog was doing in India and Tibet, Miss Kelly?'

'Yes, of course I do. He was reporting for the *Tribune*. Most recently he was investigating a story about the melting of the glaciers on the Tibetan plateau . . . That was what he was doing when the newspaper last had contact with him . . .'

She dried up under Inspector Lall's scornful gaze.

'Do go on,' he said with a sneer.

'Well, the massive Tibetan glaciers are melting and they supply all the water to the seven holy rivers of Asia: the Yellow River, the Ganges, the Brahmaputra . . . And this means they also supply the drinking water for 50 per cent of the world's population. If the glaciers disappear the rivers will dry up and there will be no more water for people to drink. There will be drought and famine and war. It is a big story . . .'

'So this was Herzog's cover?'

'His cover? For what? This was what he was working on, as far as I know. And really that's all I know, that's what the editor of the *Trib* – Dan Fischer – told me. Why would my editor lie to me? This is what Herzog was doing when the *Trib* lost all trace of him. His whereabouts are now unknown, as far as I'm aware – though if you have any idea where he might be, then all of us at the *Trib* would love to know.'

Mr Lall turned the page again and said in a low voice:

'Believe me, Miss Kelly, we would dearly like to find Mr Herzog. We would dearly like to.'

For almost a minute, they sat in silence. Mr Lall slowly turned the pages in the file until he had worked his way through the entire folder, and then, abruptly, he shut it and looked up. 'This is pointless.'

Looking at the Sikh policeman he said, 'Please get the package for Miss Kelly.'

5

The orderly placed Colonel Jen's bags next to an old wooden desk in the monastery library. The Colonel did not even notice. He was walking slowly back down the gloomy book-lined stone hall, accompanied by a Captain from the PSB. As he walked, the heels of his boots clicked crisply on the flagstone floor. He shone the torch over the spines of ancient yak-skin books. Piles of books stood on the flagstone floor, having already been scrutinized and cast aside by the Colonel. Without taking his eyes off the shelves, Jen said to the Captain. 'If ever it was here, it's gone.'

Then turning suddenly to the Captain he asked, 'Are you sure you searched everywhere else?'

The Captain, his eyes also scanning the shelves, answered, 'Yes sir. Every last inch. We've checked every flagstone and every brick. I am quite sure.'

The Captain hauled down a heavy volume from the shelf in front of them and opened it at random. After flicking through the pages and glancing at the text, he shut it and replaced it.

The Colonel looked over his shoulder.

'Don't waste your time. It isn't here. That fat army idiot scared the monks off. If they ever had it, they took it with them. Or we've come to the wrong monastery.'

'But this is the only gompa in Pemako.'

'Correction: it is the only gompa that we know of. But there are stories which describe another.' Colonel Jen gave his colleague a strange look. 'You know of where I speak, Captain?'

'Yes sir, of course. But surely that is a myth. This whole region has been surveyed many times by aeroplane.'

'Captain, your confidence in our air force is touching – but I wouldn't be so sure. Flying in these parts of the world is exceptionally dangerous and even the best surveyors must sometimes be tempted to just draw their maps from the comfort of their barracks. Who, after all, is ever going to check? Besides, the ancient accounts of this other gompa are too numerous, and too persistent, to be casually ignored.'

Colonel Jen turned off his torch and sighed with frustration.

'Please excuse me for one moment, Captain. I would ask you to stand guard at the door. I must consult the Oracle and I can't have that foolish soldier interrupting me. The Oracle has successfully advised us thus far. Let's just hope it will help us one last time.'

'Yes sir.'

The Colonel picked up a small knapsack that had been brought in by the orderly and placed it on the desk.

'It is unfortunate that they murdered the Abbot,' he said as he undid the straps of his bag. 'He was a bodhisattva; an enlightened man. He had achieved Buddhahood but remained in the fallen world to help others follow the way. I could have talked to him for hours about the world. Perhaps he could have even been persuaded to help us . . . He might have shown us the way.'

Colonel Jen looked up at the Captain and concluded in a businesslike tone, 'That is all. The Oracle will advise.'

The Captain clicked his heels, saluted and marched out of the door, shutting it behind him.

Alone, Colonel Jen gazed up at the walls of books and allowed a frown to disfigure his face for a moment. Then he felt inside the bag and pulled out a small leather-bound tube and a well-worn book. Sitting down at the desk, he opened the tube and emptied forty-nine thin wooden sticks into the palm of his right hand. He closed his eyes and his lips moved silently, as if he was saying a prayer.

Then grasping the sticks in a bunch, he stood them on end on the desk and, opening his fist, let them fall at random onto the surface.

Sighing heavily, he began the painstaking process of sorting them and making sense of their unique pattern. As he picked the sticks up one by one, he began to draw a series of small dots and dashes on a piece of paper. The essence of the moment had been captured, now the Oracle would speak.

6

Inspector Lall was watching Nancy intently as he spoke. In front of them both, on the desk, lay a rolled-up cloth bundle. It was tied together with a piece of filthy string.

'This,' Lall was saying, 'was found a week ago on the body of a Yellow Hat Tibetan monk. The monk had frozen to death in a snowdrift, just north of Macleod Ganj in Dharamsala, on the border with Nepal. The autopsy concluded that he died eight or nine days ago. Macleod Ganj, as you may know, is the home of the head of the Tibetan government in exile: the Dalai Lama.'

Nancy put out her hands and received the bundle. It didn't weigh that much. She was expecting it to be heavier – but there was definitely something rolled up inside. Mr Lall continued:

'We can assume that the monk was trying to escape into India over the high passes. Like so many others, he perished in the attempt. We are fairly sure who the original owner was. It was your predecessor at the *Tribune*: Anton Herzog.' He paused and then added viciously, 'But it is addressed to you. Why don't you open it?'

Nancy stared at Mr Lall. Judging from his expression, she clearly didn't have any choice. But what did he mean, it was addressed to her? Nervously, she began to fumble with the ends of the string. She could feel Lall's penetrating gaze follow her every move. He sneered at her again. 'You already know what's inside, Miss Kelly, don't you?'

She fumbled with the string, ignoring his accusations. Perhaps they were simply trying to frame her, or hang something on her so they would be able to manipulate her later. The Sikh policeman stepped forward and produced a knife from his pocket. Carefully, he cut the string, letting the ends fall limply to the table.

Nancy laid the cloth bundle down on the table and then unrolled it. The first thing she saw was a thin strip of plastic, a little larger than a credit card. Nancy recognized it straight away, it was an *International Herald Tribune* ID card, and there in black and white, alongside a grainy photo, was the name, Anton Herzog.

She looked up. Mr Lall and his colleague were

staring fixedly at her, as if they thought she might give herself away in the slightest gesture. Very carefully, she continued to unroll the cloth bundle. As she did so she felt everyone lean forward, including the Sikh policeman who was still standing behind her. The cloth unravelled and there, to her astonishment, was an animal bone. It was about twenty inches long, she estimated. It must have been a thigh bone. It appeared to be extremely old. It was weathered and pockmarked and brownish in colour and at one end where it mushroomed into the shape of a ball that would have fitted into the socket of a hip, or a knee, it had what she could only describe as a mouthpiece, made of discoloured metal. The mouthpiece was just over an inch long. A simple but perfectly formed glyph was engraved on its side: a dagger emblazoned upon a swastika. She pondered what the glyph might mean. The swastika was a ubiquitous symbol throughout Asia, that much she knew. However, she had no idea what the significance of the dagger in combination with the swastika might be. Perhaps the symbol might belong to an ancient Tibetan Buddhist sect, or a Hindu royal house.

Beneath the glyph were six strange symbols, clearly letters from some long-dead alphabet. They were too primitive to be Tibetan letters, Nancy thought. Perhaps they were cuneiform or Sumerian? But that made no sense. They had to be from an Asian language – after all the bone was from Tibet.

The letters were crude in their design. They were made only from straight lines – no curves – as if they were designed to last for all eternity, to be chiselled into solid granite or hammered into gold and never committed to paper.

The mouthpiece itself reminded Nancy of a pipe, the kind that old men used to smoke when she was growing up. She shook her head in confusion, conscious all the time of the malevolent force of the stares of her interrogators. Not knowing what else to do, she picked the bone up in both hands and examined it more closely. It was a ghoulish object but it radiated a strange energy. Images flashed through Nancy's mind. She saw molten gold being poured in a cavern somewhere, a volcano erupting, a tower, a desolate plain, a famished child running along on an empty road. The clarity and immediacy of the images shocked her. She blinked hard to dispel them and then very gingerly she placed the bone on the table and turned her attention back to the cloth. As she carefully flattened out the last folds in the tired material her eyes fell on a small playing-card-sized picture of the Dalai Lama. She picked it up. On the back, in a spidery, faint hand, a few words had been written in English:

'To Nancy Kelly. Bone Trumpet. Found by Anton Herzog, Pemako, Tibet, 17th June.'

Nancy had stopped breathing. Her skin crawled with fear. It was only a conscious act of will that made her inhale again. She was gasping for air; she had to get out of the police station; she had to get away from Delhi, away from the ever-increasing claustrophobia of the Herzog affair. If she did not, she would never see the light of day again. Evil was at work; an evil beyond anything she had ever experienced, but she felt it now, close to her, coming for her.

The conclusion was inescapable: the bone and the rest of the contents of the cloth bundle must have been addressed to her before she was even offered the job. But this was ludicrous, it couldn't possibly be the case. She could feel Lall watching her, still waiting for a sign, for some confirmation of her guilt. But Nancy just shook her head in confusion. Twenty-four hours ago she had been waving goodbye to her friends in New York and now she was being held in a police station in Delhi, under the threat of imprisonment, and being asked to explain the significance of an ancient bone.

'Ms Kelly,' Inspector Lall needled steadily at her. 'Why has Mr Herzog sent this to you? This is his handwriting; we have checked it. And why would you be interested in an old bone? You are not an antiques collector, Miss Kelly, of that I am quite sure. So you will forgive me for thinking that it has some other value for you, some other meaning?'

Nancy shook her head in despair – she simply didn't know what she could say. This must be how interrogators wore people down, she thought; it must be why people cracked, confessed to crimes they had never committed. She felt exhausted and powerless. She had been in unpleasant stand-offs with policemen before – but that was back in America, where she knew her rights, and where, as a journalist for a powerful newspaper, she always knew that ultimately she would be supplied with the best legal representation. But out here in India, embroiled in an espionage investigation, she felt quite sure that she had absolutely no rights and that if things went against her, or if Inspector Lall decided it was necessary, she might not see the light of day again for a very long time.

Mr Lall pushed his chair back and stood up and began to walk slowly around the room. The second interrogator watched her through heavily lidded eyes. There was a long, horrible pause, while Nancy fidgeted and didn't know what to do. Then Lall began again, wearily:

'Ms Kelly, is this a message of some kind? Is it a signal? Everyone's life would be much simpler if you would just cooperate. Perhaps we can even help your friend Mr Herzog. You would like that wouldn't you? If you tell us how to contact him, or where he is, we will not only rescue him but we will also exempt you from further criminal investigation. How does that sound?'

Again he studied her. All she could do was bow her head.

'Ms Kelly, I will be honest with you. We think that your colleague is still alive in Tibet. We have good-quality intelligence that says Mr Herzog entered the Pemako valley system more than two months ago and still has not come out, and even as we sit here wasting time, the Chinese will be hunting him down. I can only hope for his sake that they don't catch him alive. The Geneva conventions don't apply over the other side of the Himalayas. I am quite sure that Mr Herzog would thank you from the bottom of his heart if he was allowed to face justice in India rather than in China. Now, if you don't help us, we can't help him. I will ask you one last time: what is the meaning of this bone trumpet and how do we make contact with Anton Herzog?'

The pressure was becoming unbearable, but still Nancy's instincts told her that despite her own fear and despite the perils of her situation, she should try at all costs to maintain a sense of outrage and injustice.

It was her only defence. Very slowly, as if she was spelling out the words for a child, she spoke. 'Look, Inspector Lall, I'm going to make this all very easy for you. I don't know what the hell any of this means. I have quite literally no idea at all. You've got the wrong journalist, and keeping me here all day isn't going to change that. So I suggest you either charge me right now, with whatever trumped-up meaningless charge you want to lay on me, or let me go at once. If you don't, then when I do get out of here, and you can be damn sure that I will get out of here, I will see that you and your bullying, useless excuse for police work are plastered all over the newspapers of the world for months to come . . .'

This time her outburst seemed to work. Inspector Lall paused for a minute and then inhaled sharply and with a look of disgust on his face he said, 'Very well. You are free to go – for now. But bear in mind, I am doing you a favour. I could hold you for one hundred and thirty days under the Terrorism Act. You are bailed indefinitely but you are obliged to remain in Delhi. Is that understood?'

She nodded without meeting his gaze, but inside she was screaming for joy. She looked across at the lawyer. Judging by his face, he was even more surprised than she was by the turn of events.

Mr Lall turned to the Sikh policeman. 'Take her up

to the front desk. Give her back her phone and wallet and have the bail forms written out. And give her the bone. It belongs to her office.'

Not daring to speak, in case Lall changed his mind, Nancy took the filthy rag bundle and allowed the policeman to lead her away.

Captain Hundalani re-entered the interrogation room, quietly shutting the door behind him. Before he could speak Lall addressed him.

'Hundalani, make sure we don't lose her.' The Inspector was rubbing his hands irritably over his eyes. 'She has our only piece of evidence. This is a risky strategy.'

'Yes sir.'

'The bone must be significant. She'll lead us to him in the end, I'm sure of that.'

Then abruptly Lall rose to his feet. He was tired and he wanted to get out of the stuffy interrogation room.

'Do you really think she is his accomplice, sir?' Captain Hundalani enquired nervously.

'Maybe, maybe not. But the bone means something to someone. Of that I am quite sure.'

Suddenly, for the first time in as long as Captain Hundalani could remember, Inspector Lall looked him full in the face and smiled. The smile was so unexpected and so very incongruous that it caused a shiver of terror to run down the young Captain's spine.

'Our own leads have now run dry, Captain. Let's see what our star journalist does next. Perhaps *she* can help us with our detective work.'

7

'How dare you send me out here?'

Nancy was almost shouting into the phone. The guards on the steps of the police station stared in fascination as she strode away along the pavement. The Delhi crowds parted before her; shoppers and businessmen turned and watched her marching down the street. Back in New York, on the other end of the line, Dan Fischer, the editor of the *Trib*, was trying to calm her down.

'Nancy, I had no idea. Listen, I had a visit from the CIA this morning as well. Just let me explain . . .'

'Well, I bet they didn't arrest you, take you to a police station and threaten you with twenty-five years in the black hole of Calcutta. Leprosy? Any threats of leprosy thrown in there?'

'No, but Nancy, listen . . .'

'How could you send me here? Perhaps next you would like to send me to North Korea? Perhaps you think this hasn't been enough of a challenge for me?'

'Nancy, please. Let me explain . . .'

Biting her tongue, Nancy waited to hear his excuses.

'I had no idea that this had all blown up until this morning. I was as much in the dark as you were. I would never have sent you had I known that the paper was going to get embroiled in an espionage row between India and China. And as for Anton, it's complete bullshit . . .'

'Tell that to the Gestapo over here.'

'Look, the Indians and the Chinese are totally paranoid. They are always giving each other the frights and finding excuses to get at each other . . .'

Nancy fell silent.

Dan Fischer continued: 'Now, I was woken this morning by two CIA officers who said that they were obliged to visit me as they had been asked by their opposite numbers in Indian Intelligence to investigate Herzog. They told me that they did not believe the charges and that as far as they know Herzog has never been involved with any Intelligence agencies. I told them that I also was certain that this was the case. Anton is a friend of mine, I've known him for years. It is the most ridiculous thing I've ever heard.'

'Well, if he's a friend of yours then why aren't you trying to find him?'

Nancy waved furiously at an approaching taxi that slid to a halt next to her on the road. She opened the door and got in.

'Hang on one sec, Dan. Can you take me to the office of the *International Herald Tribune* on Akhbar Street please . . .'

'Nancy – this is not the first time he's gone AWOL. It's his style . . .'

'Not for three months, Dan.'

'Listen, the CIA were very clear. The best course of action is just to do nothing.'

'That sounds very convenient for you.'

'Oh come on, Nancy, that's not fair.'

Suddenly Nancy became aware that she was still clutching the cloth bundle containing the grisly bone. This made her very confused. She realized that for some reason – God knows what it was – she didn't want to tell Dan Fischer about the bone trumpet. And then she was experiencing a profound urge to tell the driver to take her somewhere else, away from the office and away from the Herzog affair. Then she thought she just needed time to think; she needed to work out what on earth was going on.

'Listen, Dan, I'm going to the office, or somewhere I won't be hassled and arrested. I'll call you in a little while.'

'Sure Nancy – but are you OK?'

'Look, I'm about as OK as someone can be who's just been dragged from a jetlagged stupor, interrogated and then threatened with life imprisonment . . .'

'I am sorry – I really am. And please, just take it easy. We are pulling out all the stops this end to sort things out. The head of the Senate Foreign Relations committee is getting in touch with the Indian Ambassador. Just take it easy, do a local-colour story if you want to take your mind off things . . . something about elephants or farming . . . We'll have everything cleared up momentarily. I promise. It's important you stay there. Anton always wanted you to replace him if he ever went missing – so do it for him.'

For a second Nancy felt quite sick.

'What do you mean? He told you to send me here?'

'Yes. I always ask all my senior people who they think I should consider if regional vacancies come up . . . He always insisted you were perfect for the South Asia job . . .'

'But he didn't even know me; I met him so seldom . . . I hardly spoke to him . . .'

'Well, the man read the paper, you know. He did actually read your articles.'

'So he knew I was coming to Delhi?'

'Well, how would he? No one has been in touch with him since he disappeared. I just meant he always recommended you to me. But forcibly, with passion.

Like you were the only one he thought could do the job. That's why I was so delighted you wanted it so much when it came up.'

Nancy shook her head in confusion: Dan Fischer didn't know that the bone trumpet had been addressed to her and he hadn't been privy to Inspector Lall's insinuations. She had begun to accept that Herzog must have known – somehow, she didn't know precisely how – that she was coming to Delhi. Perhaps he was so certain of his influence with the editor that he just assumed she would be the one to replace him. Perhaps it was a deliberate gamble on his part, just in case. To surprise her, make her perplexed. But why, why would he do that? It made no sense. For a moment Nancy felt she might throw up; then she felt strangely passive and as if she was being manipulated by forces beyond her comprehension. She thought of her compulsion to go to India, her vivid recurring dreams of the high green valleys of Tibet, of the fact that Herzog had indeed selected her for the cub reporter's scholarship at the Sorbonne, and now – apparently – for this – but then a second later she remembered why she was newly released from the police station and her anger returned.

'Look, Dan, that's all very flattering. I don't know what the hell to make of it, but sure, I'm overwhelmed. Delighted. Now, hotshot hack that I am, the question

I'm running through my mind is why we don't just run a story on Anton's disappearance: tell the world that he's missing, tell them that the Indian police are completely out of control? Stir things up a little, see what happens?'

'Please, Nancy, have a little patience. Yes, eventually that might be a tactic. But at present, we need the help of these governments. Now is not the time to alienate them.'

'Believe me, Inspector Lall and his friends seem pretty damn alienated to me already. I don't understand you, Dan. He's a friend of yours and he's one of our team and you're hanging him out to dry.'

'Nancy, you have to let me call this one. I take your point, but I'm calling it and I believe I know what I'm doing. Just try to take it easy. Promise me you'll do that, at least.'

'Sure, I'll take it easy. I'll get myself straight to a Keralan yoga retreat and get myself busy comparing Ashtanga with Hatha, if that's what you want. Just please let me know if you get any further with this business. And if you don't hear from me, you know where I am – the black goddamn hole of Calcutta.'

Dan Fischer was probably more worried about headlines than anything else, she thought: 'Renegade *Herald Tribune* Journalist Arrested for Espionage' – that would hardly sell well with the shareholders.

Herzog had always been a tricky horse to back; she had a sense that Fischer had been fire-fighting for him for years. She liked Dan Fischer; on a good day she would have considered him a friend. He was a formidable journalist; a powerhouse of ambition and courage. He was only forty-two years old himself, not that much older than her, and they had plenty of mutual friends. He was hilarious, quick as a whip and exceptionally cunning. He threw monumental parties and charmed everyone. He picked his battles carefully, and he knew perfectly well that anyone was expendable – the brand came first and the shareholders certainly wouldn't want a big and very public row with the Chinese and Indian governments, she thought, with a mounting sense of revulsion; it might have a knock-on effect, it might cause other governments to withdraw support for the paper. It might hurt sales.

She sighed heavily and closed her eyes. The day was boiling, and she felt sweat trickling down the back of her neck. She had half a mind to do a story on Herzog herself, but what was the point? It would only get spiked by Dan. With all his cunning and political acumen, Dan realized that Herzog had become bad news. He had a plan, but it wasn't international exposure, that was for sure. As Nancy rested her head on the greasy leather seat, she felt tired and afraid, but most of all she was simply glad she wasn't Herzog right now; he seemed an increasingly lonely and abandoned figure; a man in dire need of friends. And whatever Dan Fischer said about not putting the authorities' backs up, her conscience was not going to allow her simply to ignore Anton Herzog's fate.

8

A young Tibetan woman hurried through the twilight across a jungle clearing, bowing her head from the relentless rain and clutching her shawl across her chest. She was a teacher from the village school who had trained as a nurse in Lhasa. Behind her on the jungle floor, on a makeshift stretcher, lay the body of the stranger. From the neck down he had been covered with a piece of blue plastic sheeting. His forehead was wrapped in a wet towel that shielded his eyes and the bridge of his nose. His white arms were folded across his chest, as if he were a fallen Viking warrior, awaiting the last rites of the funeral pyre. All around the clearing, little groups of monks were huddling beside makeshift fires, boiling up water for yak-butter tea.

The young woman ducked under a tarpaulin that had been strung between the branches of the trees to offer some protection from the endless rain. She bowed to the Abbot's deputy and then knelt on the yak-wool rug. The old lama motioned to the two monks who sat near him to leave. Hastily they picked themselves up and darted across the clearing to join the tea-drinkers. The lama leant towards her, his voice urgent, almost desperate:

'So, has he said anything?'

The girl had an anxious expression on her face.

'He is feverish. The doctor is very concerned.'

'But has he said anything?'

The girl hesitated. She was afraid she might get something wrong.

'Yes – but I'm not sure. I can't understand exactly. He is delirious. He sees things. Things that aren't there . . .'

'Well, tell me anything. What words has he said? His name?'

The girl looked confused.

'No, lama. Sometimes he says things in Tibetan. Words like the monks use at public prayers. Then he speaks sometimes in other languages, languages I have never heard before, and then sometimes in English. He is delirious. He is calling for people I think. He is in so much pain. But once, when we stopped by the waterfall, he smiled and looked at me as if he could see me. He was happy. He held my arm and then he kept saying one thing only, over and over again: Shangri-La. Shangri-La. Shangri-La . . .'

The monk felt his heart stop and then resume suddenly, with a massive thump and a terrible pain, as if someone had just pushed a blunt needle into it. Trying to regain his composure, he nodded and then, with a sickly look on his face, he said, 'Listen to him. Nurse him. Try to encourage him to speak.'

'Yes, lama. I will remain by his side at all times.'

She stood up to go and then stopped.

'Lama . . . what does it mean, Shangri-La?'

'Don't worry yourself girl,' said the old lama. 'Just stay by his side and tell me everything he says.'

She curtsied and left. The rain drummed on the tarpaulin. Shangri-La. The lama knew all too well what the word meant. It was the name that the Westerners gave to Shambala, the secret kingdom of the Himalayas that was hidden in the valleys to the west. Only a handful of lamas preserved the ancient secret knowledge of the precipitous route; even the Abbot himself was forbidden to approach.

He stared down at the stranger, as he lay like a corpse on the stretcher on the other side of the clearing, and then the lama shut his eyes and prepared to meditate.

Phantoms appeared in his mind's eye. Images of long-dead lamas came to him – great lamas who had taught him as a boy. He could hear conversations in his head, as if he was back there, all those years ago, sitting at their feet. Once, at Kailash monastery, a venerable old lama had told him that a terrible war had once been fought in the lands of the West, far beyond the Himalayas. It had seemed at the time that the whole world was on the point of going over to the dark side; that the sun was going to set for ever on the world. Some white men had come, seeking the kingdom of Shambala. They intended to go there and ask the King for help. The lamas had tried to aid them on their quest. It had been a terrible mistake. The lamas did not realize that the white men came from a different world, a world steeped in blood. They should not have trafficked with them. They should never have helped them. Such men brought only destruction.

The deputy thought of these things and tried to regulate his breathing, but every time he attempted to begin his meditation the word on the stranger's lips came back to haunt him: Shangri-La.

A desperate urge came over him to get up and run across the clearing and carry the dreaded stranger down to the river. There he could wade out into the middle of the stream, floating the stretcher and its cargo behind him, and then the ice-cold Himalayan waters would carry the nightmare away, off down to the great waterfall and on into India and beyond.

But the Abbot had specifically instructed them to care for this man. Against everything he had learned, he was to protect this white man, to save him if he could. And the lama shivered, and thought how much he wished the Abbot was with them now. If only the Abbot had heard the words himself . . .

9

The sun was long past its zenith by the time that Nancy Kelly arrived at the offices of the *International Herald Tribune* on Akhbar Street. The taxi had taken almost an hour to crawl around the rickshaws, cows, beggars and assorted broken-down vehicles that littered even Delhi's most important roads. The first thing she had done when she got off the phone with Dan was call ahead to the office.

Waiting for the phone to connect, Nancy had stared out of the window, frustrated at the slowness of the journey and wondering what she should do now. Beyond, the ragged inhabitants of Delhi, struggling to survive. An old man carrying thousands of crushed plastic bottles on his back shuffled past, his careworn face a map of his wretched life; a cow was standing at the entrance to the next street forcing the traffic to swerve, so some vehicles almost collided with an angry vegetable stallholder's stand. Nancy observed these incidents, but hardly registered them. All she could do was replay the interview again and again in her head and nervously finger the package on her lap. What could Herzog have done, she asked herself, that could so threaten the security of two powerful nations? Had he been interviewing the wrong people? Carrying political papers for Tibetan radicals? She couldn't imagine it; you had to be pretty green these days to get yourself caught doing things like that, and he of all people would have been alert to the pitfalls.

Another thought dogged her, a truth that Inspector Lall had planted in her mind: Herzog would be far better off explaining himself in India than in China. She dreaded to think what might happen to him if he was caught over the border, no matter whether he was innocent or not. She recalled an article that a colleague of hers had once written on the interrogation techniques used during the Cultural Revolution – it was enough to make you lose all faith in humanity.

Finally, Nancy had a connection. The phone was answered briskly by Krishna Murthi, a thirty-year-old Indian, famous throughout the *Trib*'s Asian correspondents for being better informed and better read than anyone else on staff. Back in New York, before she left for Delhi, Nancy had lunched with colleagues who had recently been through the Delhi office. When she asked who she needed to keep sweet, they all said that Krishna Murthi was the key to a successful stay. He was a miracle worker of the highest order, they told her. A fixer, in the old-fashioned sense. Now, holding the phone in a sweaty hand, the other still holding on to the bizarre package, Nancy told Krishna Murthi who she was and apologized for not having been in touch sooner. 'I'll explain everything when I get to the office,' she said, and rang off before the line cut out. Surely, she thought, Krishna Murthi would be able to shed some light on the mysterious activities of Anton Herzog.

Krishna Murthi was waiting for her when she pushed open the smoked-glass door of the office. Smartly dressed, slight of build, he put out a hand and said, 'Ms Kelly I am delighted to meet you. I was phoned shortly after your call by Dan Fischer.'

No doubt, thought Nancy, to instruct you to make sure I stay put in Delhi and don't do anything to rock the boat.

Krishna continued, 'He explained matters further. I am so sorry this has been your welcome to India.'

Krishna ushered her into the room. He had intelligent eyes and a kind face, and he was a calming element in an office which looked as if it had recently been ransacked. As well as hundreds more of the figurines and stone statues Nancy had admired in the living room of the company flat, there were two desks, covered in paperwork, several telephones and computers. In front of the desks was a large, well-worn leather sofa, covered in piles of magazines. Krishna rushed over and cleared a space for her. Nancy collapsed into the well-worn leather seat, briefly overwhelmed with tiredness and nerves. As she collected herself, Krishna weaved his way through the clutter and between the two desks and went over to an open doorway. Beyond was a second room. Speaking to someone in this room, he gave a quick order in Hindi and then turned back to Nancy.

'I've asked for some tea. Now, I called the head of the Foreign Press Corps to ask them to lodge a complaint with the government, and I have also made a further official complaint, on behalf of the newspaper, with the Minister of the Interior's office.'

'Thanks,' said Nancy. 'I'm just glad to be out of there.'

'Can we get you something to eat? You must be hungry. I doubt they gave you any sustenance in the police station after all . . .'

'I would love something, thanks . . . Just anything . . .'

Moments later, a woman appeared from the adjacent room carrying a tray with a large glass of water, a cup of chai and two fresh samozas. Nancy tucked in hungrily. Krishna had pulled up a chair and was watching her eat with an anxious look on his face, occasionally sipping his cup of tea. He waited for her to speak. She wiped her mouth with a napkin and tried to marshal her thoughts.

'Krishna, thanks so much. Sorry if I seem a little weird . . .'

'Don't be ridiculous. Do you want anything else?'

'No, no, that was perfect. What I would like to do is find out more about Anton Herzog.'

Krishna nodded cautiously. She continued.

'Can you help?'

He looked uncomfortable, as if he would much rather she had asked for a tour of Delhi, some advice on where to buy her groceries or where to eat out, or some other such triviality.

'Well, what exactly do you want to know?'

'You worked with him closely. Of everyone, you must know his habits, his predilections, what he was up to.'

'Not as well as you might think. Yes, it's true I've worked with him for years.' He paused, hoping that she would change the subject, she thought. But she didn't, instead she waited patiently for him to give her something more.

He shifted in his chair and muttered, 'Listen, Anton is a funny character.'

'How do you mean?'

'Well, he loves India, there's no question of that. He believes in India, he desperately wants to tell the world about India and make sure that we get a fair hearing . . . But he's not an easy man to get to know. He can be a little cold . . .'

'Cold?'

'No. Not cold. That's not the right word. I'm sorry – I'm not explaining myself very well. I don't mean he wasn't friendly – he was – I've lost count of the times I've enjoyed his hospitality, and it was he who trained me. I have nothing but praise for the man; he was an excellent boss. But there was something – well, you might say unknowable about him. That is the only way I can think of to express it.'

'Why do you think he's disappeared?'

'I don't know. That is what I'm trying to tell you. I don't really know him that well, despite all his kindness and despite having sat only a few yards away from him for all these years.'

'Didn't he ever talk about his private life?'

'No. Not his feelings, not his past, not his family. I can tell you his hobbies, where he drank, which section of the *Trib* he read first each morning, how he would abandon coffee for three months and then drink it constantly for another three. All his foibles and rituals. But his inner self was closed to me. Right at the beginning of his time here, just after I arrived at the office, was the only time that he ever mentioned his family to me at all. He said his father had died before he was born – that he had been killed at the battle of Stalingrad towards the end of the Second World War and that his mother had emigrated from their home-town of Munich to Argentina. After that, he never mentioned anything further, and certainly I never felt I could press him.'

Krishna rearranged some of the piled-up papers on the desk, revealing a tarnished silver frame containing a pale black and white portrait photo of a woman.

'That's his mother there: Anna Herzog.'

Nancy leaned forward and studied the photo in fascination. The woman's blonde hair was in a bun. She had a white shirt done up to her neck. She was middle-aged in the photo: beautiful with dark eyes and high cheekbones, and very pale, translucent skin. Nancy took the photo from Krishna.

Bad luck to lose your husband before your child is even born, she thought. What must it have been like to be looking after a tiny baby, with your husband gone and the whole of Europe on fire? She must have been tough, that was for sure. She looked it, under her delicate beauty and pearly skin. But then so many people were in the same position; people's expectations of life must have just become much more modest:

survival and retreat from the horrors of war. One day at a time. The greatest victory was to live. Nancy put the photo back down on the table.

Krishna continued. 'The funny thing was that even though he had no memories of Germany at all and had only spent the first few weeks of his life there, he was still German really . . .'

Krishna got up and walked over to Herzog's desk, which was farcically strewn with papers, as if he had tipped his files everywhere shortly before his most recent departure.

'Here: Goethe, *The Complete Poems*. Schiller: *The Complete Poems*. Nietzsche, *Thus Spake Zarathustra*.'

Nancy stood up and took a closer look. It was true: well-worn copies of the German classics littered the desk. It looked like the desk of someone who was homesick – she could imagine him listening to Bach's cello suites and reading Goethe's *Faust*, sitting at this desk late into the night, imagining himself far away from the heat and dust of India.

Krishna continued, warming to his task, as if he had momentarily forgotten whatever it was that Dan Fischer had told him. 'And it wasn't just the books – I suspect he had a German soul and a German temperament. In fact I think that Anton had all the good qualities associated with Germans: passion, rigour and such enthusiasm – he was like a force of nature when he was discussing something he believed in. And when he spoke about the universe and mankind's place in the world, he sounded like a Hindu guru.' Krishna looked up and smiled at her: 'Only a German can do that! And he was musical, very musical. He was a concert-standard pianist.'

Nancy was nodding to herself. Life could be so hard on people, she thought, constantly displacing them and their families and forcing them to leave their roots far behind. Herzog was so many people's hero, not just her own, but looking at his cluttered desk, with the sad photo of his mother and the collection of German books, she saw the human side of the myth, and she had the growing feeling that he might have been a deeply troubled man.

'Did he have a partner?' It was strange asking these questions about someone she had always revered.

'No. I don't know. No one serious.'

She waited for a moment, but Krishna didn't seem to want to go further than that.

'Never?'

'He wasn't gay if that's what you mean. He had girlfriends, sometimes – no one special. I wouldn't say they were intellectual companions. And there were other women too.'

She sighed heavily. It was all perplexing enough. Anyway, what had Anton's Germanness or otherwise got to do with the fact that she had been dragged off to a cell and accused of being in league with him, accused of spying? A sad old man, a loner with a passion for Tibet; what more was there to learn? Perhaps nothing. Then suddenly her eyes fell on a particularly well-worn book that took pride of place in the centre of the desk. It looked as if it had been thumbed with almost religious regularity.

'What's that one?'

Krishna looked at her:

'That is the *I-Ching – The Book of Changes* as it is called in English. He used it every day without fail.'

'I've heard of it, it's a book of riddles isn't it?'

'No. It's certainly not just a book of riddles. It's more like the bible of Asia.'

Now Nancy was embarrassed. She was painfully aware of her relative ignorance of Indian and Asian culture.

'Really?'

'Yes. It's a seminal book.'

'How? What's it about?'

Krishna paused for a moment and then said definitively:

'Its not "about" anything. It's the Oracle.'

She could scarcely hide her scepticism:

'The Oracle? So it helps you see into the future? Is it like a horoscope?'

Krishna was clicking his tongue in disapproval, and Nancy realized it was clearly held in far higher esteem than horoscopes were in the West.

'I'm sorry,' she said quickly. 'Forgive my questions.'

Krishna smiled:

'Well, those who use it swear by it. It is a very powerful force in contemporary Eastern life. The Japanese government often consult it in times of difficulty and all the leading businessmen in Hong Kong and Singapore use it all the time. I think it is even becoming more popular in the West.'

'But that's extraordinary.'

It was incongruous to imagine successful, besuited businessmen and politicians using a fortune-teller – but then again there were plenty of politicians in the West who did just that, though they normally didn't advertise the fact.

'May I have a look?'

Krishna picked the book up and passed it to her. Trying to suppress her scepticism, Nancy flicked it open at a random page. At the top was a strange diagram made of six straight lines, stacked on top of each other, each about two inches long. Some of the lines were unbroken; some had a small gap in the middle. Beneath the diagram was a name and beneath the name was a passage of cryptic text that reminded her of riddles she had learned as a child. Krishna leaned forward and pointed at the diagram.

'That is called a hexagram. There are sixty-four possible combinations of six broken and unbroken lines, which makes a total of sixty-four possible hexagrams in the universe. Each one has a name. Each hexagram represents one of the sixty-four stages in the endless cycle of change that affects all things in the cosmos. At any point in time, you can determine what point in the cycle of change we are at by creating a hexagram and consulting the oracle for its definition. You see, the text printed underneath the picture of the hexagram explains the meaning of the hexagram. If you want to consult the Oracle, first you ask it a question then you create a hexagram. In the old days, this was always done by tossing forty-nine yarrow stalks onto the floor. Depending on how they fall, they represent one of the sixty-four possible hexagrams. But nowadays people often just toss a coin six times; that's what Anton would do, every morning: a head is a broken line and a tail is an unbroken line. It's much easier.'

'But I wonder why he used it. It's a strange thing to do if it is not part of your own culture. And where did he come across it?'

'I don't know. But he wouldn't do anything without first consulting it. People find its guidance very reassuring.'

'But its guidance is based on random patterns, isn't it?'

'Well, that's not really true. Nothing in nature is truly random. If you think of the flow of water, or of the pattern in the grain in a plank of wood, it appears to be random but in fact it is ordered in a way that is beyond our perception. It is "ordered chaos" – its rules escape us but they do not escape the Oracle. The ancient Chinese called this underlying order within disorder "Li". Some people say that the Oracle simply translates "Li" into words, so that you can then understand where you are in the constant process of cosmic change and then act accordingly. So in a way, when you listen to the Oracle, you are listening to the voice of the universe. Or at least that's what the sages say . . .'

Krishna shut the book and then looked up at her.

'Anton is very knowledgeable about oriental culture, particularly Tibetan and Chinese. He would have known about "Li" and so the Oracle would have made sense to him. I suppose someone must have introduced him to it on his travels.'

A truly strange man, thought Nancy. Strange, but also quite intriguing; her own self-identity was so clear-cut, she had no doubts about where she came from or what culture she was at home in, but Herzog seemed to be a composite. One might put such a magpie-like tendency down as a sign of insecurity or lack of innate character if it wasn't for the fact that he was the very opposite of that: he was hugely charismatic; he had a massive, powerful, dominating personality that made an instant impression on everyone he met. But did anyone at the *Trib* know what he was really like? She studied the hexagram before her. Could it tell her what the future held? Could there be any truth in its utterances?

Nancy frowned.

'And Anton really used it every day?'

Krishna nodded. Nancy looked down and studied the worn-out leather cover of the strange book. In silence, she returned the Oracle to its place in the middle of Herzog's desk as if she was putting down a sleeping animal and she was afraid that it might wake up. When she had replaced the book, Krishna stood up.

'There is something I can show you that might help you understand Anton a bit better. It's a piece of video footage that he shot some time ago. I have it next door on DVD. Let me get it . . .'

As soon as Krishna had stepped out of the room, Nancy's gaze was drawn back to the book. It had somehow captured her imagination – she was sorely in need of help in working out what to do next. The idea that the Oracle would give her access to some inherent voice of the universe was incredible to her, yet compelling. At that moment, she had forgotten about her ordeal with the police and she wasn't even thinking about the fate of Anton Herzog. All she wanted to know was whether or not the Oracle might really work. What harm could it do? she thought to herself as she sat down in Herzog's chair and placed the *I-Ching* in the middle of the desk. She laid her left hand on the front cover of the book as if she was sitting in the witness box of a courtroom and she was taking an oath on the Bible. Very slowly she thought out her question in her head.

Oracle, do you really work? Do you really have access to the truth of the world?

Then she proceeded to follow Krishna's instructions, flipping the coin six times and then marking the results on a piece of paper until she had created her first hexagram. She studied it for a minute. It meant nothing to her, just a little stack of broken and unbroken lines. So she turned to the chart and studied it carefully until she found her hexagram.

It was Hexagram 50: 'Ting' – the cauldron.

Next, she read through the cryptic judgement that was written beneath.

50 – Ting – The Cauldron

There is food in the cauldron still,
My comrades are envious,
But they cannot harm me,
Good fortune.

But the handle of the cauldron is misused
Its proper functioning is prevented
The fat of the pheasant is not eaten
Once rain falls, remorse is spent
Good fortune returns.

Nancy read the verse several times, a frown deepening on her face.

10

'Here, I've found it.' Krishna said, bustling back into the office and squeezing round the tables, overflowing with magazines and books.

Nancy was still scrutinizing the cryptic definition and the hexagram. Without looking up she said, 'Krishna, can you look at this?'

'What?'

'Here. Hexagram number fifty.'

Krishna came over to the desk, his head tilted to see what she was looking at.

'So you asked the Oracle a question?' He eyed her suspiciously and turned the book round so he could read it: 'Let me see.'

First, he flicked through the pages to the back of the book and carefully checked that she had numbered the hexagram correctly.

'Yes – it is hexagram fifty. That is correct. "Ting". The Cauldron.'

Then he found the hexagram and read through the definition. As he did so his eyebrows rose in interest and he looked at her accusingly:

'Nancy, what exactly did you ask the Oracle?'

She could feel herself blushing.

'I asked it if it really worked.'

Krishna looked at her with the glint of a smile in his eyes.

'Well then, let me tell you how it answered. The Oracle describes itself as a cauldron.'

'Yes – I worked that part out. But I don't understand what it means, let alone the rest of it.'

'Wait, be patient and think a little. In ancient China, a cauldron was a communal vessel used for cooking food to nourish the whole village. Nowadays, no one uses cauldrons any more. This means the Oracle is telling you that in the old days everyone used it all the time and benefited from it but now it has fallen into disuse.'

Nancy listened in fascination. Krishna continued.

'Now listen carefully, this is the important bit.'

He read the definition aloud:

> *There is food in the cauldron still,*
> *My comrades are envious,*
> *But they cannot harm me,*
> *Good fortune.'*

Nancy shrugged her incomprehension, but Krishna continued.

'The Oracle is saying that it still contains food, which means it still contains wisdom and nourishment: it still contains the truth. Then it says that its comrades are envious. By "comrades" it means people who we turn to today as oracles, for example doctors or politicians or priests. It says that these modern-day oracles are envious of the *I-Ching*'s power but their envy is in vain for the *I-Ching* alone has access to the truth.'

'Then the next lines:

> *'The handle of the cauldron is misused*
> *Its proper functioning is prevented*
> *The fat of the pheasant is not eaten*
> *Once rain falls, remorse is spent*
> *Good fortune returns.'*

Krishna laughed out loud.

'What?' Nancy said impatiently. 'What does it mean?'

'The Oracle says that no one knows how to use it properly these days and that its real wisdom, the fat of the pheasant, isn't touched any more. Finally it finishes by saying that when these dark times pass, and when the rain has gone, then people will recognize that it speaks the truth and good times will return again.'

'That is pretty extraordinary. It seems to make sense. But I wonder how it works.'

Krishna smiled mysteriously.

'Well, now you know why the Japanese governments consult it in moments of crisis. Be very careful when passing judgement on the so-called superstitions of the East. And be careful in future not to ask the Oracle such cheeky questions. It has been known to play nasty tricks.'

He shut the book firmly but respectfully and slid it to one side. His expression had become serious again.

'But here – enough of that. Let me show you this. It will help you understand Herzog and Tibet.'

11

The television screen flickered for a moment; Krishna was fiddling with the cable that joined the DVD player to the back of the TV. Now a picture sprang into life.

It was a street scene, a scene of chaos. It looked like it was somewhere in Delhi. The picture quality was poor. She could tell from working with old news footage that it must have been shot more than a decade ago. The cameraman was filming amongst a crowd of people; monks mainly, and some normal Tibetan people as well. They were protesting in the streets somewhere; there was a large government building in the background, a Victorian-looking structure typical of the government areas of Delhi. Armed Indian policemen had formed a protective cordon around the gate, which was shut. Their faces were tense as they stared at the crowds.

And the protesters in turn were very agitated. They were holding up clenched fists, and waving their placards towards the gate. Some of these were in Tibetan and some were in Hindi but some were written in English. 'Free Tibet.' 'The World Must Help.' The cameraman must have turned the sound on, for suddenly a wave of noise emanated from the television. People were shouting and screaming and there were police sirens and orders barked in Hindi.

Then Nancy heard another voice. It was breathless and close; very loud compared with the other noises. The incongruity of the setting made her hesitate for a moment, but then she knew it was Herzog's voice. His accent was distinctive – American but with undertones of both Spanish and German, so that he always sounded almost like a European aristocrat speaking English.

'. . . I am now going to walk over to the gates . . . and film the crowd from there . . . the police are beating the hunger strikers . . .'

Nancy watched as the camera wobbled one way and another. Herzog was clearly being knocked into, buffeted by the tidal surge of the crowds. Yet he must have reached the gates, for he stopped and turned around and the picture steadied and she was better able to study the faces of some of the people in the crowd. They were so sad, she thought, so desperate, so full of anguish and pain and frustration. She could scarcely bear to watch. She felt tears welling up in her eyes. Krishna leaned forwards and pointed urgently at the television, touching his right index finger on the screen.

'Watch him,' he said.

Nancy leaned closer in. Krishna's finger had singled out the face of a man. He was clearly Tibetan, he had the characteristic rosy cheeks and round face. He was dressed in jeans and a T-shirt. He must have been about forty-five, she thought. His face was a mask of anguish. She watched him as he walked aimlessly amongst the crowd. He clutched his head in despair and then he set to beating his breast. There were tears in his eyes. Like a silent ghost he weaved around the picture and then suddenly he disappeared out of the shot. Nancy looked in alarm at Krishna and was about to ask where he had gone and who he was, but Krishna stopped her, abruptly raising his hand, his eyes still fixed on the screen. A second later the man reappeared. He was soaking wet. How had he got so wet? Were the police using a water cannon to control the crowd?

He seemed to be muttering to himself, perhaps he was praying. The crowd began to part around him, and then started to run, looking back over their shoulders at him. The devastated man sat down on the road, adopting the lotus position. The cameraman began to walk towards the man. Even as everyone else ran in the other direction, the cameraman was walking right at him.

And then it happened. The poor man took a box of matches in his hands. Holding them close to his chest, he struck a match and suddenly, in an explosion of light that turned the television screen completely white for a second, he was engulfed in a ball of flame. The man had set himself on fire. The water had been petrol.

Like a straw doll, the man burnt, a great cone of flame engulfing him. Herzog must have dropped the camera to the floor.

He could be heard shouting:

'Oh my God . . . Oh no . . . No . . . Help. Someone help. Stop him . . .'

And then the screen went black. Krishna had turned off the television. He stood up and wiped tears from the corners of his eyes.

'I'm sorry. It is very upsetting. But you have to see it. If you want to understand Herzog and Tibet, it is the only way. People have to be shocked into realizing the truth.'

Nancy was still staring at the blank television screen in shock.

'Is he dead?'

She felt foolish for asking.

'Gyurme Dorge? The man in the film? Yes – he's dead all right. They poured water on him, but it was too late. He survived in hospital for a few days. The Dalai Lama visited him and urged him to be compassionate towards the Chinese. He was happy. He was in high spirits when he died.'

They fell into silence for a minute, then Krishna began again slowly.

'He was a herder from western Tibet. He had walked over the passes many years ago into India so that he could finally live as a Tibetan, near his beloved Dalai Lama. He lived at Macleod Ganj, where the Dalai Lama lives. He was, by all accounts, a gentle and light-hearted man.'

'Was he a monk?'

'No. He was a layperson. He began life as a herder and served for a time in the army. He had made it to India. He lived in a tin shack on the hillside just down the road from the Dalai Lama's bungalow. All he wanted was to be near the Dalai Lama, amongst other Tibetans, living a religious life. He worked as a waiter and chef at a café when he wasn't fasting, or walking in the hills.'

'So, how did he end up there – in Delhi?'

'That was in 1989. It was the year of a brutal crackdown in Lhasa. So many people were tortured and murdered. And many of the last remaining monasteries and shrines were destroyed. You cannot imagine the pain for the Tibetans. It was as if the Chinese were destroying their soul. Gyurme went down to Delhi to protest. He was so upset, he wanted to do something. Lots of Tibetans were hunger-striking, others were sitting in the road. The army moved in to remove them – the Indian government had buckled to Chinese complaints. None of the other countries round the world did anything. No one had done anything in 1959, when the Chinese destroyed four thousand monasteries and smashed the lamas and forced the Dalai Lama to flee to India. The Americans and the British and the French all just stood by and watched. It is a shameful period of history . . .'

Nancy sighed heavily. She had read about it and it was a sad, sad day for the world. But what could any of the world powers have done? China considered Tibet to be her own sovereign territory. The Chinese government made it quite clear: if they were left to do what they wanted in Tibet, they would never use their veto in the United Nations. It was a cynical trade-off. So the great powers of the time just sat by and did nothing about Tibet; they had other priorities around the world for which they needed China's cooperation. Tibet was a long way down the list.

Nancy looked up at Krishna and said, 'Why was Anton filming it?'

Krishna looked over at Herzog's chair out of habit.

'Oh, he was always interested in Tibet, but after

that day he changed. He had been something of a playboy before then. He was always a great journalist of course, and even then he was a voracious reader, but after seeing that he was a different man.'

'In what way?'

'Well, he went up to Macleod Ganj for the cremation of Gyurme Dorge. I spoke to him about it only once. The other times he dismissed my questions, simply wouldn't be drawn. But on that one occasion he said that after the ceremony, which was attended by great crowds of Tibetans in the exile community, he went for a walk. He didn't know where he was going so he just wandered at random until he found himself standing in front of a small tin-roofed hut down a quiet back alley. An old man who was sitting near by told him that it was Gyurme Dorge's home. Anton said he already knew that, that he had just walked straight there. He didn't know how he had managed to do this but he had. The hut was tiny, no bigger than eight feet by six feet, and he had to bow his head when he was inside to avoid scraping the corrugated iron roof. Outside, the garden had been carefully maintained. There were bright red snapdragons and beautiful pansies in the little flower beds and there was even a small hedge that Gyurme Dorge had clearly tried to carve into the shape of a bird – a symbol of freedom.

'Inside the hut, there were several shelves that served as altars – they had three Tibetan flags on them and an image of the Dalai Lama. On the bed were two neatly folded and perfectly ironed shirts. Apart from that there was really nothing there. Anton said that seeing the hut and understanding how this man must have lived had a profound effect on him. Anton was a great scholar and he had read of the tea masters and poets of old who cultivated a "refined poverty", but he had never actually understood it until then. Gyurme Dorge wasn't a lama, after all, he wasn't a practising monk or anything like that.

'Anyway, Anton changed after he went to Macleod Ganj. Tibet became his personal cause. And it wasn't just a political obsession – he had been affected at a much deeper level too. He stopped going out so often in the evenings, he became more serious. I mean he was always rather serious, but even his irony, his dry levity went . . .'

'I'm not surprised.'

'He started to work all the time . . .'

'On what? I mean news journalism is finite – it's limited by the events that are going on . . .'

'He worked on his own things, in the evenings. He studied and read and collected antiques and old books. He developed his theories. He would regularly work until one or two in the morning, listening to Mozart and Bach, and then go to sleep on the sofa here in the office. I'd arrive in the morning, or Lakshmi would come in, and find him back at his desk . . .'

'But what was he working on?'

'Lots of things. To do with Tibet and India. I was never sure . . . He wouldn't discuss them with me.' Krishna shrugged. 'He got all his work done. He was my boss. It wasn't appropriate to ask, and he didn't volunteer the information.'

As Nancy listened to Krishna, for the first time since the police had questioned her she began to wonder if Anton Herzog had actually been engaged in illicit activities in Tibet. It was beginning to sound as though he had the absolutely perfect profile. Paranoia gripped her for a second: perhaps even Dan Fischer was involved.

'Krishna, do you think Anton could have been a spy? Could he have been recruited by some agency that recognized his sympathies and talents?'

Krishna snorted in derision.

'I think that's completely impossible. He loathed the American government for its failure to act on Tibet, and you should have heard him speak about politicians in general. He thought the whole world was guilty of selling the Tibetan people down the river. Everyone was to blame: the Americans, the British, the French, the Germans, the Italians, even the Indians

... The Tibetan culture that was destroyed in 1959 was probably the world's first government of peace. As far as Anton was concerned, by letting it get trampled on by its militaristic neighbour, the whole world was guilty, the whole world could go and hang . . .'

Nancy sank into her thoughts. It was true, who would Herzog have wanted to work for? He must have regarded all the governments of the world as complicit in Tibet's tragedy. But then what was he doing all those years, beavering away? And what was he really doing in Tibet?

12

There was no path through the jungle to the Cave of the Magicians – just the endless forest, seething with life and noise.

The Abbot's deputy, staff in hand, led the way, passing methodically over fallen branches and ducking under the overhanging limbs of the tropical vegetation. He knew the route. Colourful birds darted from branch to branch in the tree cover far above the long line of rain-soaked monks. The line moved slowly between the dripping vines and massive tree trunks of the ancient forest.

Occasionally, a monk would stop in his tracks and reach up and take hold of a large paddle-like leaf, common in this part of Pemako. He would angle the tip of the leaf into his mouth and quench his thirst with rainwater before wiping his brow and beginning again to labour up the incline of the jungle floor.

And every few minutes the Abbot's deputy paused

and looked back at the extended line weaving its way through the trees behind him. In the middle of the procession was the stranger, tied to the stretcher, carried along by four monks. The mere sight of the strange cargo filled him with dread. Ever the question tormented him: could this ruined man actually have been to Shangri-La? He would tell himself it was not possible. Shangri-La was like the land of death itself: no one who had been there had returned to tell the tale. He must have wandered off course, been somewhere else – there were many other strange places in the mountains, many ways in which a man's life could come undone. He was trying to convince himself, but the question dogged him all the same.

With an anxious look on his face, the deputy willed them to increase their speed. He was a bad omen, this stranger; a harbinger of doom. He would dearly like more time to interrogate him, to find out who he was. But that luxury was not available.

The soldiers would be coming. That was certain. The Abbot's deputy imagined that they had already departed. Under normal circumstances his monks would have had the advantage; their native knowledge of the jungle would have made their progress faster than the lumbering military men. But progress with the stretcher was painstakingly slow – they were travelling at a fraction of their normal speed.

And there was another fear at the back of his mind – another danger, of which he did not even want to think. His eyes narrowed as he scanned the jungle. Somewhere out there, beyond the monkey calls and the relentless seething of the insects, another enemy was stirring. Silently the old man prayed.

13

Nancy was scanning Herzog's CV, which she had just found on the *Trib* intranet.

'Interesting,' she said, and Krishna turned to face her. 'It seems from this that, after winning the Pulitzer journalism prize for a piece on the Dalai Lama and Macleod Ganj, he's turned down no less than nine offers of promotion, including the top jobs in London and Tokyo.'

She looked up at Krishna.

'I know that he liked his job, but refusing those big posts is quite extraordinary. He doesn't even have a family to slow him down.'

Her forehead was wrinkled by a frown. Almost to herself, she formed the question: 'So what's the reason?'

Krishna smiled and shrugged.

'I'm not really the person to ask. I've turned down promotions as well. I guess he wanted to stay in Delhi, to stay near his beloved Tibet . . . I don't know . . .'

Nancy scrolled through the CV again. A man's life, condensed into professional achievements. Despite the neat diligence of the *Tribune*'s scrupulous record-keeping, what did it really tell her about Herzog?

'There's simply nothing here that helps explain anything . . . I mean I'm not expecting him to put "spy" under work experience, but this résumé doesn't really give us any leads at all. There has to be some reason the Chinese and Indians have gone completely mad. And he is, after all, still AWOL.'

Krishna leant back in his chair.

'Well, for what it's worth, my theory is that he must have accidentally wandered too close to a military base. That sort of thing always sets the Chinese off . . .'

'Surely it can't be as simple as that. I know that in places like China they always go crazy if you acciden-tally photograph an airport or something, but this seems much bigger. I mean, as far as I could gather from my experience this morning, the Indians seem to agree that he was up to something and they also believe that he is on the run in the Pemako region of Tibet and that the Chinese are hunting him. That is quite different from him being arrested for photo-graphing a military site and getting expelled from the country – that is quite routine, isn't it?'

Krishna nodded and answered quietly: 'Yes – it is – that's true . . .'

Nancy fell silent for a moment and then turned to look directly at Krishna, who was deep in thought.

'Did you do the regular database searches as well?'

Krishna nodded without making eye contact.

'Yes. Nothing much of interest came up.'

Then he glanced at her in a way that made her feel that he wasn't at all comfortable with what she had asked him to do. He looked down at his desk. 'I must say it feels funny investigating our own colleague.'

'Krishna, I'm sorry to keep asking questions about Anton like this. And I'm sure Dan Fischer has given you strict instructions not to encourage me in any way. And I know what you mean, it does feel funny. But I'm sure we are doing the right thing. We are trying to help him. Judging from my experience in the police station, he is in real trouble, and HQ don't seem to be doing very much to help him, to put it mildly. We've got to try to do something, no one else is going to.'

They fell into silence. Nancy didn't feel that she was making any headway at all into the mystery of Anton Herzog. She stood up and suddenly felt utterly exhausted; a wave of almost unmanageable jetlag rolled over her. If she had rested her head on the desk she would have fallen straight asleep.

But she didn't want to go back to the apartment to sleep – in fact she didn't really want to go back there at all. What if the police came back and took her away for a second time? Maybe this time they would just chuck her in a cell and forget about her for good. She could suddenly see why the threat of the four a.m. knock on the door, the secret police coming to drag you forcibly away, was such a potent way to control people. It was a terrible burden to carry around in the daylight hours and then at night: instead of thinking that your bed was the safest place in the world to be, you became afraid to go to sleep. She wanted to call Dan Fischer and get some sort of reassurance that the paper would protect her, but she didn't want to reveal her thoughts to him.

And worst of all, she speculated, it was quite possible that the day's events were all beginning to affect her judgement: the fatigue, the unpleasant trip to the police station, the oppressive heat. She kept wondering whether, if she had slept properly and not had the threat of a jail sentence upon her, she would be pursuing her inquiries at all.

She was beginning to wonder if it might just be best to go back to the apartment and get some rest, when her eyes fell on the package containing the gruesome bone trumpet lying discarded on the sofa. She thought for a second of showing it to Krishna, asking if it meant anything to him, or if he could read the script. But it would be pointless; it needed an expert – someone like Herzog, she reminded herself, aware of the irony.

'Krishna,' she said slowly, 'is there anyone else in Delhi that Anton would have spoken to about his work on Tibetan antiquities?'

This remark seemed to dismay Krishna, and at first he stayed silent, and merely furrowed his brow as if she was prying too far. But Nancy had no choice; she had to pry, and Krishna was the best lead she had at that moment. So she persisted. 'Is there anyone you know who has even been to Pemako?'

Reluctantly, Krishna began to speak. 'To my knowledge, apart from Anton only a handful of foreigners have ever been there.'

He paused and then quite casually, as if he did not think the information would be of any use, he added:

'There is one man. His name is Jack Adams. He's an American. Anton knew him quite well – but I don't think they got on.'

Nancy studied his anxious face. She could see that he was beginning to wonder where this was all going. His life has been terribly disrupted, she thought. Twice in fact: first Herzog disappeared, and now she had turned up and started nosing around into the private affairs of his colleague and friend. It made her feel sorry for him. She could see that he was a good man, a well-meaning man, and she suspected part of the reason he never wanted promotion was because he found the responsibilities of management slightly sordid and the Herzog affair was precisely the kind of thing that he hoped never to be drawn into. It was a breach of his contract with life. He had chosen a humble station; he had refused all offers of passing glory on the understanding that he would never have to get involved in the politics of the newspaper. She watched him shift position in his seat. He was uncomfortable and it upset her.

'Krishna, I am sorry if I just seem crass and over-inquisitive but it really is because I want to do something for our colleague. I want Anton to come back alive – if it was you or me out there I'd like to think someone would be trying to work out what had happened to us.'

That sounded hollow; it was hard for her to explain how compelled she felt to act; how she was beginning to feel that something was driving her, some force beyond her control. So then she didn't know how to proceed. She was being inquisitive. She would have to continue to be so, if she were to discover anything else. So she waited, feeling a little awkward, and eventually Krishna shrugged and said, 'Nancy, I don't really know Jack Adams. He's an American antiques dealer and anthropologist. I only know that he's been into Pemako because he once left a message for Anton here at the office that said that he had just come back from there.'

For the first time since he had welcomed her into the office, he was looking completely despairing. He slumped back in his chair.

'I can't answer all these questions. I don't know what to say. I'm sorry Anton has gone. It's so awful. I want to help find him, but Dan Fischer says the best thing we can do is do nothing and leave it to the police. I just don't know what to do . . .'

'Why have so few foreigners ever been to Pemako?' Nancy asked.

It was a question that she knew Krishna would be more comfortable with – she had to get off the subject of Anton's private life or he would withdraw altogether into his shell. She was sure he didn't mind talking in the abstract, sharing his knowledge of places and things. She suspected he just had a fear of being drawn into other people's lives, other people's problems.

'It has been off-limits to foreigners for decades. Very occasionally, people manage to sneak in: botanists or mountaineers. But most of the time the PSB refuse the permits, and if you do get a permit it is only for the peripheral areas, never for the interior . . .'

'Who are the PSB?'

'The Public Security Bureau. The Chinese Intelligence Service – or one branch of it. The PSB are very active in Tibet. If it's true that Anton is still there and that he is being hunted, then it will be the PSB who are looking for him. They are not a very nice bunch of people – to put it mildly.'

'I see. It sounds like an interesting place.'

'It is. It would get more visitors, many more, if it weren't for its location. It's fantastically beautiful, lots of rare orchids and strange animals, but it shares a disputed border with India and it's cut off from the rest of Tibet, in fact it's another country really. It's also the home of the Bon religion.'

He was warming to the task, she thought. He was relaxing again. She asked another harmless question:

'I didn't realize they practised other religions in Tibet. I thought the whole point about it was that it was an ancient theocracy.'

Krishna nodded thoughtfully.

'Tibet is more complicated than that. Bon is old. Older than Buddhism. It's been around long before the lamas. They persecuted it and tried to stamp it out and called it black magic, but it clings on in places like Pemako. Anton knew a lot about it. To hear him speak about Tibet was an unforgettable experience – he's such an eloquent man.'

'So there are no Buddhists in Pemako then?'

'I don't know about that. Pemako is certainly a sacred area in Tibetan Buddhism. Anton has joined lamas on their pilgrimages there. It is one of the most important "beyuls" or hidden paradise lands. The beyuls are supposed to serve as refuges when the world succumbs to darkness. But I don't know if they have any lamaseries there.

'If Anton were here, he could talk all day about these things. He would know all the answers. He said that once you get down into the tropical valleys of this region, the boundaries between the material and the spirit worlds become very blurred. It is easier to pass back and forth between the two . . .'

'I see,' said Nancy, though she wasn't really sure she saw anything at all. Krishna seemed entirely serious. She trusted Herzog's intellect. And yet all this talk of spirit worlds was certainly unusual. It wasn't what she had expected to be discussing on her first day in Delhi. 'How come Adams is such an expert?'

To her surprise, Krishna suddenly looked embarrassed.

'Well, this is going to sound bizarre but he runs a company called "Yeti Tours". He takes rich Americans and Europeans on yeti-tracking expeditions in the Himalayas . . .'

'What? How absurd . . .'

So he's a crank, she thought, or just a cynic. She was feeling somewhat disappointed. He was probably just one of the many gin-soaked foreign fantasists who inhabit the fringes of expatriate life in the cities of the East. She imagined him: single, or leading a tawdry life with local girls that he strung along, too flattered by the hierarchies of his state to return to the West. This unappealing image of Adams appeared to Nancy, though she tried to dismiss it.

Krishna was smiling faintly at her reaction. 'You shouldn't be so dismissive. Maybe in America the yeti is a bit of a joke, but that isn't the case in India or Tibet. There are plenty of very convincing accounts of man-like creatures being spotted in the Himalayas. There is a lot of evidence nowadays.'

He hesitated for a second, then continued. 'I've only met Adams a couple of times, with Anton, and to be honest, I find him a little annoying. And I don't think Anton liked him much either. They had shared interests, that was all. They would meet every few months. They are very different people.'

'Why is he annoying?'

Krishna paused, frowning at her and then answered:

'. . . He's brash, loud, always talking and boasting. He's like the stereotype of the overconfident American abroad. Forgive me, but it's true.'

Nancy found this funny, despite its rudeness.

'Not all Americans are like that.'

'No. Of course not. I mean he's very macho. He's in his mid- to late thirties, I'd say, and very fit and strong from mountaineering. I'm sure you have met the type. Anton once told me that Adams got himself kicked out of Yale for some kind of terrible faux pas, something very public and excruciating, but not before he managed to acquire two PhDs, one in genetics and one in palaeoanthropology. He had lots of theories about mankind being far older than we currently believe, and before his final disgrace he was always telling the professors that they were a bunch of old buzzards . . .'

'So Anton thought he was a nut?'

'No, not at all. That is precisely my point. I don't think that Anton knows him very well, but he certainly doesn't think he is a nut. He actually thinks that Adams really knows his stuff. In fact he would probably say Adams is a world authority and it's certainly not out of the question that modern man is in fact much much older than we presently believe. Anton used to point out how absurd our current theories are, how they are all based on a handful of old bones dug up in East Africa. But Anton can also see why Yale threw him out. And I agree. He's abrasive and I am quite sure that he can be very rude when he wants to be.'

'So why's he running "Yeti Tours"?'

'He's broke. Anton once told me that Adams would never make a good antiques dealer because he can't bear to part with anything in his collection and, anyway, half the stuff he buys has no proof of origin. You can't sell anything on the international market without being able to prove its provenance – in fact you can't even give it away. It's to stop people tomb-raiding and robbing monasteries and so on. Adams buys this stuff because he likes it and because he's sure that one day, he'll stumble across the big one.'

'What does he think of as "the big one"?'

'You know: a Maltese Falcon, or a Topkapi dia-mond, or maybe a Buddhist equivalent of the Dead Sea Scrolls. He's always being suckered by smugglers who've got a good story. Anton says he's got a wild imagination – he's too credulous. But what he really wants to find, what he really believes he will find in fact, is some firm, hard evidence that anthropologically modern man, the same as you and me, walked the earth a million years ago.'

'What about evolution?'

'There are plenty of examples of animals that don't evolve over hundreds of millions of years, and Adams maintains that human beings are just the same. All the fossil remains of other hominids that have been dug up over the years, all the Lucys and other missing links that you read about in the newspapers, aren't our predecessors at all. They're our contemporaries because our ancestors were alive back then as well. And one day someone will find an intact skeleton of *Homo sapiens*, dating from one million BC, that will prove all our ideas of history and evolution wrong. Adams reckons the Himalayas are the place to look because they are so high up. People up there would have survived the floods and cataclysms that have buffeted the earth for millennia.'

'But it's crazy isn't it?'

'Maybe. I don't know. Anton had time for him. Anton used to say that if in a hundred thousand years' time archaeologists only investigated the area in the Congo basin where the pygmy tribes live, then they might think that pygmies were the only humans alive today. You see, the dating of mankind is all about fossil evidence, and if you look at the fossil remains that we have, you could fit them all on one large dining table. That's hardly a worthwhile statistical sample of early hominid life. Adams reckons we've only found the remains of other hominid species that lived contemporaneously to our ancestors – we haven't found the bones of our ancestors at all. He believes that one day we will.'

'Well, he certainly sounds like an original.'

'Anyway, he originally came to India not to deal in antiques but to continue his research. He's been in Delhi for ten years now – he's part of the furniture. But he ran out of money pretty early on. He is always buying antiques and old bits of bones and other such junk. He is a collector, like Anton – an enthusiast. But he doesn't have a salary so he had to start "Yeti Tours".'

'Do you think I can get a meeting with him today?' Krishna didn't smile.

'He lives here in Delhi and he's always short of cash. If you told him you were interested in going to Pemako on an expedition and were willing to pay good money, then I'd say he would be delighted to meet you.'

14

'Eat! Don't worry; it is vegetarian. I am vegetarian too. I hope you like Chinese food.'

Colonel Jen was seated in a high-backed chair at one of the long library tables. He was smiling warmly as he spoke in fluent Tibetan. Opposite him, in a clean and dry orange robe, sat the monk Dorgen Trungpa. His bruises had been tended to and the blood had been washed from his nose and ears, but still he was consumed by fear and suspicion.

The Colonel took a swig of water, without taking his eyes off the monk. Before them on the table was a great spread of dishes, freshly prepared in the monastery kitchen by the Colonel's chef. In gentle tones, the Colonel said, 'I am very, very sorry about what has happened here today. I just wish that I had arrived a few minutes earlier . . .'

Dorgen Trungpa was staring at the food in front of them. The Colonel smiled at him and urged him on:

'Go on. Eat! You must be hungry. This isn't a trick. Please eat. I beg you. It is for your own good.'

Not taking his eyes off the Colonel for a moment, the monk took a spoonful of one of the dishes and hungrily swallowed the food down. Then he took another. He began to eat steadily; he was very hungry.

The Colonel watched the young monk's every move and then, when he felt that the moment was right, he began again to speak. 'When I was a boy, my grandfather, a senior Communist Party official, took me to the Zhongshan mountains in southern China. This is where the Taoist poets lived in the old days, when China was a land of wisdom, before it was destroyed by communism.'

The boy had stopped chewing and was listening in surprise to the Colonel.

'. . . It is such a beautiful place,' Jen continued. 'White clouds pile up around the mountain tops and the valleys are filled with misty rain. The tiny houses of the woodcutters are the only human habitations and the distant sound of an axe echoing through the mountains is the only sound of civilization . . .'

The Colonel paused for a moment, lost in a reverie, and then continued.

'The paths of the old poets lead through long gorges choked with scree and boulders; wild rivers tumble alongside them and mist-laden grass covers the canyon sides. Moss clings to the rocks of the path, and the pines murmur, and the water is always trickling. The paths lead between the vines and rocky caves, to hidden huts deep in the mountains, where the white clouds touch the snow. It is another world.'

Now the Colonel was speaking in an urgent whisper, as if afraid that even his own orderly might hear.

'We walked for days through this beautiful scenery and finally we came to a halt at a ruined shrine. There we camped for seven days and my grandfather spoke to me about the world and about China and about our past – things that we cannot speak about any more in Beijing. Forbidden things. He taught me about Taoism, he taught me about alchemy, he taught me about The Way.

'My grandfather came from an aristocratic family. My forefathers were landowners and poets and served at the court of the emperors. After Chairman Mao's Cultural Revolution, they were stripped of their property and wealth and either murdered or sent to work the land. My grandfather survived by joining the Communist Party and renouncing his past life. He became a senior official in Beijing, but in his heart he never gave up The Way. He taught me and introduced me to the ancient brotherhoods that still survive in China in secret, despite the purges.'

The Colonel stopped for a moment and then he

leaned towards the terrified monk and whispered, 'If my senior officers knew one word of what I have just told you over this table, I would not live to see the end of the day. I am risking my life and the lives of my family. I know that your lama was a bodhisattva. I know that he was a wise man. We are on the same side. I work for the PSB – but that is just a front. I really work for my secret brotherhood. There is a tiny handful of us who have come together. We operate in continual fear of our lives – our desire is to throw off the communist yoke and return China to the path of wisdom. I believe that your high lamas may know of the whereabouts of the lost kingdom of Shangri-La. In the ancient library of Shangri-La we hope to find the most powerful artefact in all the world: the long-lost Book of Dzyan. With the knowledge contained in the Book of Dzyan, we will finally be able to set China free and return her to the old ways of the Tao; for whoever holds the Book of Dzyan controls mankind's destiny. Genghis Khan possessed it, Alexander the Great and Charlemagne and Napoleon have all possessed it and, each time it has been used, it always mysteriously returns to the library of Shangri-La. The Book of Dzyan represents our last and final hope. I beg you to help me, we have to find Shangri-La – we have to make contact with your lamas . . .'

Silence fell in the great library. The rain drummed relentlessly on the roof. Dorgen Trungpa stared in awe at the Colonel, paralysed by all he had heard, with no clue what to do or say.

15

Night had fallen over Delhi. The hot and crowded bazaar was lit up by fires and lanterns. Beggars and yogis, in the thick of the scrum and yet apart from it, collected alms from passers-by. Jostling for right of way with the people were the animals and vehicles. Camels, horses, donkeys and the sacred cows that wandered where they chose, protected by law and allowed to pass unmolested throughout the streets of India. Huge trucks, laden with boxes and draped with tarpaulins, lurched through the crowds, belching diesel fumes, their loads wobbling above the heads of the throng.

Krishna scuttled ahead, leading the way through the chaos. It had taken some persuading to get him to take Nancy to meet Adams. Yet ultimately she was his boss and, besides, he could hardly let her disappear alone into one of Delhi's busiest markets on her first night in India.

With every hour that had passed since her interrogation by the police, Nancy's indignation and self-confidence grew. Bullied by the police on the one hand and, as she saw it, given no assistance by Dan Fischer on the other, her journalist's natural instinct was to take things into her own hands. And besides, she was thinking, with a nervous attempt to be mischievous, Dan Fischer had told her to do a local-colour piece, and where better to look for it than the teeming market by night?

She watched Krishna marching ahead. There was a stiffness and tension to his body that was most uncharacteristic of almost everyone else in the crowd. He didn't look very comfortable in the thick of the market; he was too delicate, too well educated and too used to moving within the powerful elite of India. Then again, it was no different from her wandering around the rough parts of DC – she was never very comfortable there, but she liked to think she would have made a better attempt at masking her distaste for the environment.

They passed under the old gate to the Kashmir Serai, the main Bazaar, which was seething with people from all across central Asia: camel-herders from Baluchistan, Pashtuns from Kabul with their orange beards, Sikkimese in their short red garments and conical feathered hats. Men argued and struck deals. Boys kicked the caravan dogs and shovelled hay into the mouths of the horses or lugged plastic petrol cans on their backs. The Bazaar was in an old British-built Victorian square by the railway station. Around the square, up flights of steps, were shaded cloisters, and within the cloisters the more prosperous merchants had set up shop. Each arched cloister had been bricked up and a door had been installed, more or less durable, depending on the success of the merchant. In these shadowy lairs, all kinds of trades and crafts were being practised: money-lending, cobbling, horseshoe manufacture, key-cutting.

Nancy had never imagined that a place like this could exist. She was marvelling at the colour and density around her, while Krishna tugged her sleeve and dragged her past a gang of bickering Tajik truck-drivers who were arguing with their Hindu overlord about how much money they were owed for their most recent journey.

Smiling at it all, she leaned forward and shouted towards Krishna, 'What on earth is an American doing in a place like this?'

He yelled back at her, still with his eyes on the melee around them, 'It's a good place for the illegal antiques trade. Lots of stuff still comes down from Afghanistan over the Khyber Pass and the Karakoram highway from China. The old merchants can get anything through ... If you try to fly it out and get caught, you can spend a very long time in jail ...'

She shook her head, not bothering to respond above the din. What am I doing? she thought suddenly. A wave of tiredness washed over her and her confidence suddenly began to ebb away again. Surely I should just go home and get some sleep? Dan Fischer's advice was perfectly sensible and she was supposed to be a journalist, not a private detective. Her mood swings were becoming disorienting; for a second she had the distinct feeling that she was walking out over an abyss and beneath her there was nothing but a cold dark chasm, stretching infinitely away. But she tried to shrug off the thought. It was too late now. Krishna was climbing up a flight of stairs, and she watched him moving through a wooden doorway and into one of the mysterious cloisters. She followed behind him, and at the top of the steps she paused and glanced down briefly at the frenetic business of the market.

You could spend months here, she thought, just exploring this place, let alone the rest of Delhi. It was exactly what she'd hoped for when she had decided to pack her bags and leave her old life behind with its over-familiar routines, those rituals that had grown dull and eventually sapped her energy: buying a cup of coffee from the store on the corner on the way to work, the bland expanse of the newsroom with its trading floor-like rows of desks, lunch in the canteen or on the lawn when it was sunny. Now she was here and a huge continent lay waiting to be explored, another world, full of novelty and fascination. If only things hadn't started like this, she thought wistfully, if only Herzog would just walk back in off the dusty streets, it could all be so much fun. But that was never going to happen, Herzog was gone, and she had a horrible feeling he might never be coming back.

16

Inside, the cloister looked like a cross between a Turkish seraglio and a natural history museum. Two large fabulous lamps hung from a vaulted ceiling that arched over a space about twenty-five yards square. They illuminated a vast collection of antiques and ancient fossils and bones of all shapes and sizes and descriptions. Beautiful multicoloured Persian rugs hung from the walls and covered the floors; antique tables and cabinets from China and Japan were scattered everywhere, and on every surface imaginable lay the thousands of items that made up what Nancy assumed was Jack Adams's Tibetan collection.

The sight was breathtaking. In the middle of the room, in the only clear space available, Krishna was sitting on a pile of cushions, talking to a small Indian boy who appeared to be about twelve years old. The boy was dressed in shalwar kameez, the long baggy trousers of the Pashtuns, a pair of worn leather slippers and a grubby white skullcap. His expression was alert and as soon as Nancy entered the den he stood and made a small bow.

'Come over,' said Krishna to Nancy. 'This is Kim, Jack's assistant. Kim, this is Nancy Kelly of the *Herald Tribune* newspaper.'

Krishna turned back to the boy and continued to speak to him in Hindi. Nancy picked her way through the chaos and stepped on to the rug.

'Kim will get Mr Adams,' said Krishna to her as she approached.

The boy bowed again to both of them and then wriggled his way to the back of the room and disappeared through a doorway that Nancy hadn't noticed before, into the back of the cloister.

Krishna nodded at her. He looked a little nervous. 'Adams is here – which is lucky. I suddenly thought he might be away on one of his trips. Ask him about going to Pemako and then, once you've got him interested, ask him about Anton . . . I'm sure you know what to do, with your journalistic credentials . . .'

There was a noise from the darkness beyond and out stepped a tall, deeply bronzed white man. He had short-cropped blond hair and sky-blue eyes. He moved with a nonchalant swagger and with a compressed energy, the line of his muscles visible through his thin shirt. Nancy saw at once what Krishna had meant about his macho arrogance, though all he was doing was wiping his hands on a rag that he tossed to the floor as he came forward. Arrogant and requiring careful handling, she thought, with her journalist's instinct for a tricky customer. Charming if it pleased him, but given to treachery, or outbursts – certainly he looked like a man who played his own game and no one else's.

'So you want to go to Tibet?' he said, coming towards her with his hand extended.

As she shook the proffered hand, Nancy wondered about the best way to proceed. He was shrewd; she suspected he would see through her soon enough. Was it better to be honest with him from the start? As Krishna added his own wary greeting, Nancy thought that this image of the rugged explorer looked carefully calculated. Adams had fitted himself up with a wonderfully scenic office location, a great collection of antiques, and then he had his own physical appearance to draw on: the tough mountaineer-cum-adventurer. It was all a crucial part of his sales pitch no doubt, but she wasn't interested in that. He was handsome though, she conceded, and he must be used to women falling at his feet, mistaking what was probably quite a hard, ambivalent way of life for glamour and adventure.

She stopped herself: people can always sense what you think of them on some level, she thought. Particularly when they've fixed you with glittering eyes, as if they're speculating about your motives even as you try to analyse theirs. She should be more circumspect; he might after all know something about the bone trumpet. She had brought it with her, slung over her shoulder. As Adams released her hand, Nancy tried to get into her part, and said, in a breezy, interested way, 'Yes. That's right – I need to get into Pemako. As soon as possible.'

'I see,' he said, rubbing a hand over his chin.

Even his speech was slightly theatrical – probably born of dealing with tourists straight off the plane from the States. Naturally she was also straight off the plane, but she had travelled widely in her career and hoped she had learned a little about the many ways travellers could be exploited. Charismatic, certainly, she was thinking, but overdone, this posturing as an explorer.

As they all sat together on the cushions, Kim bringing in some cups of tea, Adams was saying, 'I was in Pemako only last summer, I went in over the Su La pass. It's a treacherous place – there are no accurate maps, none of the bridges are standing any more, and these days there are hundreds of Chinese soldiers, all trying to extract money from you. And then there are the witches . . .'

Krishna, fidgeting impatiently by her side, interrupted:

'What witches?'

'The poison witches. Pemako is famous for them. They are the old ladies who live in the villages. They poison strangers in order to take their "chi", their vital power.'

Nancy raised an eyebrow. 'Tell me,' she said, 'how much will it cost?'

'So, I see, we have an intrepid explorer in our midst?' Adams seemed to be sneering at her, and Nancy bridled, though she tried to tell herself this was all part of the pitch; nothing to really concern herself with.

'Not really,' she said briskly. 'Pemako is hardly the jungles of Borneo, is it?'

A shadow passed across Adams's face. He turned his head and spotting a large bone lying on the table top next to them, he picked it up. When he spoke, his demeanour had changed; he was no longer smiling.

'You see this? This is the thigh bone of a yak.' He slapped it into the palm of his left hand. 'The yak is a relative of the camel but it is skinny, lazy and even more bad-tempered. The Tibetans rely on the yak just as the Bedouin do on the camel. They get their milk from it, they eat its meat, they eat its eyeballs, they eat its testicles and they even light their lamps using its butter.'

He weighed the bone in his hand as if it were a club. Then, still unsmiling, he fixed her with a stony look. 'Perhaps, Miss Kelly, you believe all the propaganda about old Tibet? That it was a peaceful, happy place, where the Dalai Lamas presided over a contented population until the wicked Chinese arrived?'

He handed her the bone. She took it, unwillingly, transfixed by his mood change. This guy is getting curiouser by the minute, she thought. Adams was speaking again.

'That bone that you are holding was used as a tool. If a peasant committed a crime, even something as trivial as stealing a small amount of gruel to feed his starving family, he would be held down whilst the round ends of two such thigh bones were pressed into his temples. When enough pressure was applied, the peasant's eyes would pop out. And justice would be done in the feudal kingdom of the great lamas.'

Nancy dropped the bone onto the rug in disgust. He picked it up and replaced it carefully on the table and flicked his head up to fix her with a condescending stare.

'The bromides that are passed around at American

dinner parties about the magical, spiritual East are a long way from the truth. Tibet has always been a violent and dangerous place for those who don't understand it. And I would go so far as to say it is scarcely even Buddhist, it is an occult kingdom where black magic has always reigned supreme. It is not and never was a Buddhist land of peace . . .'

Krishna could contain himself no longer.

'OK, Adams, enough of your opinions. Do you want the job or not? We didn't come here for a lecture and I very seldom attend any American dinner parties.'

Adams turned to look at him and in a businesslike tone replied, 'It will cost you.'

'How much?'

'When do you want to go, how many people and what is the purpose of the trip?'

Krishna glanced at Nancy.

'Just me,' she said quickly. 'And I want to go without alerting the Chinese or Indian authorities. The exact purpose will be revealed when we get to Pemako.'

Adams smiled, as if none of this was surprising to him.

'I see. Well, then, let's say fifty thousand dollars for a ten-day trip, all sherpas and equipment included. And I need all the money up front.'

Nancy gasped:

'What? I don't know much about travelling in Tibet, but that really sounds totally outrageous. Surely we could hire an army of sherpas for that price?'

'You could, and you could even bribe the Chinese immigration officials – but if you went into Pemako without me, no one would ever see you again . . .'

Krishna interjected, 'I simply don't see how you run any sort of business with those prices. You and I know they're ridiculous . . .'

'Sure, if you think that, then good luck finding someone else to take you,' Adams replied, in a dry, nonchalant voice. He drank down his tea and looked as if he was about to conclude the meeting. Indeed Krishna was beginning to rise, when Nancy said, 'Listen Mr Adams, maybe we can do a deal. I don't have that kind of money. I'm a journalist, not a millionaire.'

Adams looked hard at her and then after a long pause said, 'I'll think about it. When do you want to go?'

Krishna was looking at Nancy in complete confusion. She realized he had suggested the enquiry as a ruse, to draw Adams out. She had thought of it differently – or had she? She wasn't sure whether she had intended to go from the start. Her motives were becoming cloudy to her; she felt driven by a deep prevailing purpose, but she couldn't disentangle the elements. If he can take me, why not go? she was thinking. But she couldn't afford his fee, that was for sure. She would have to find a way of haggling him down – quite how she didn't know.

'As soon as possible. I'm in something of a hurry.'

For a moment no one said anything. Krishna was looking incredulous and appalled, and Nancy and Adams were staring at each other. Nancy acknowledged once more that the man was irritatingly handsome, though his were unsubtle, over-brawny good looks that didn't much appeal to her. Now Adams was saying, 'Well, then you have a choice. An associate of mine is flying up tonight – it might just be possible to get on his flight. If not, then you'll have to wait at least another fortnight. Commercials are out – if you want to go in under the radar then you have to arrive by private aircraft.'

'What time tonight?'

'Midnight. From Indira Gandhi airport light aircraft terminal.'

She was flushed with adrenalin, and for the first time since the interrogation she felt she was taking control again of her own destiny. This was what she had wanted: adventure and a chance to make her name. Perhaps she could actually find Herzog. If only she had more money. All she had was five thousand dollars' worth of travellers' cheques which she had brought with her to India and then her savings – but she would have to wire those from the States and that might take days or even weeks and even then they only amounted to about fifteen thousand dollars. She could sense Krishna's mounting panic, but now she didn't care at all.

'What's your best price?'

'I'll think about it,' said Adams. And he fixed her again with his condescending eyes. What am I doing? Nancy wondered with excitement and mounting trepidation. It was certain that she was getting carried away. And to what end? He would never lower his price enough to make the trip affordable, and more importantly, none of this was exactly necessary. She had been harassed by the Indian police, that was a fact, but why was she now running off on a wild goose chase with a man who seemed part macho cliché and part something she couldn't quite understand? She sensed once more Krishna's discomfort, and knew he wanted to tell her to forget the business. A formal complaint, strong words from the editor, that was more in his line; he was firmly in the Dan Fischer camp. Absconding with this eminently untrustworthy man, he couldn't possibly approve. But then she didn't want to stay in Delhi, creeping around, waiting to be rearrested, or ordered back to New York – an unattractive prospect for different reasons. And she was quite certain that there would be no Indian police going into Tibet to look for Anton Herzog, nor any Americans either.

But what is it really that is driving me to do this? she thought again. She really couldn't understand this yearning she had to get on the flight, to get over the Himalayas to the magical realm beyond. She shrugged it off. All of a sudden, reality took hold of her again and the fantasy deflated. It was a crazy idea. She had only just got to Delhi. Both Dan and the police had ordered her to stay put. Time to consider it later, she thought.

'Let me see what funds I can come up with,' she said curtly to Adams. Then, in a more conversational tone, she added, 'There's one more thing you might be able to advise me on, if you don't mind. I want to know the origins of an old bone that a friend of mine gave me. Could you take a look at it?'

Adams nodded briskly.

'Sure.'

Krishna seemed heartily relieved that the talk of a journey had abated. Nancy took the cloth bundle out of her bag and laid it on the rug. She had already removed Herzog's *Trib* ID and stashed it in her bag. Adams knelt forward, his attitude expectant, perhaps even eager. She fiddled with the string and then slowly unrolled the dirty cloth, until she had revealed the strange bone with its metal mouthpiece.

'May I?' Jack Adams's salesman's swagger had gone altogether. A new guise, thought Nancy: the professional archaeologist. She nodded at him. As if it were a priceless vase, or other valuable antique, he reached down. He held it in his hands and examined it from all angles, slowly turning it this way and that. Then he paused and examined the mouthpiece more closely. He called over to Kim in Hindi and the boy trotted over with a small magnifying glass. Adams popped this into his right eye socket and proceeded to further scrutinize the metal mouthpiece. Finally, he let the eyepiece drop into the palm of his hand and with an expression of great earnestness, he gave the bone back to Nancy.

'Do you know what this is?' There was deep suspicion in his voice.

'I think it's called a bone trumpet . . .' she replied with little conviction.

'Put it to your lips and blow gently through the mouthpiece.'

Very tentatively she placed the mouthpiece in her mouth and blew. An eerie, haunting cry emanated from the old bone. Adams nodded slowly.

'It's used in Tibetan Tantric ceremonies. But bone

trumpets are older than that. They were used in the Bronze Age and probably before then as well. Judging by the state of the bone, I'd say this one is very, very old.'

'How can you tell?'

'Taphonomy. The study of the dating and decay of old bones. It's my field of expertise. I would have to check of course, but just looking at it I can tell it is at least twenty thousand years old, possibly much, much older.'

Then, almost absentmindedly, he added, 'It is made from the femur of a dead man.'

Nancy shivered with disgust.

'Euugh! What next!'

Hurriedly she placed the bone back onto the cloth and wiped her hands on the carpet. Adams seemed genuinely surprised by her squeamishness.

'Don't worry. I doubt the previous owner misses it. Do you know what a sky burial is?'

She shook her head.

'In many parts of the Himalayas, they don't bury their dead and there isn't enough wood on the barren mountain slopes to cremate them, so instead they leave them on the mountain tops. In Tibet the priests cut up the corpses and the vultures devour them so that the soul can pass quickly through the Bardo – the world between life and death. When the birds have done their work, the priests come and break up the remaining bones and scatter them like dust. Sometimes bones are left over.'

He gestured at the bone, lying on the carpet.

'Ancient sky burial sites, high in the mountains, are where we find most bones in the Himalayas. But this one might have come from a chieftain's burial mound in central Asia, or somewhere further west, in Europe perhaps.'

He looked up at her suspiciously.

'Can you tell me precisely where you got it? It's not from the region is it?'

Nancy paused. For a moment she gazed at the bone, then she decided:

'Why do you ask? Do you recognize the symbols?'

He paused for a second, long enough for her to be absolutely certain that he was not telling her the whole truth.

'Yes and no. The dagger and the swastika are Aryan I would guess. The Aryans were the original conquerors of India. They swept down from the plains of central Asia four or five millennia ago, and at about the same time they also migrated westwards into Europe. They brought their own religion to the subcontinent, a sort of proto-Hinduism. The swastika which you see everywhere in this part of the world is an archetypal Aryan symbol.'

His voice trailed off as he studied the mouthpiece again.

'And the letters?' asked Nancy.

Adams deliberately ignored her question and instead, fixing her with his penetrating gaze, he said:

'Where did you get this?'

'From Anton Herzog. He sent it to my office.'

Her answer produced a complex reaction in Jack Adams. He bridled visibly. Krishna had said that Anton didn't much like Adams, and she felt from his immediate response that the feeling was mutual. Yet there was something else: he was looking more carefully at the bone, as if it was weighted with further significance. Seeing his eager eyes upon it, his gaze somehow incontinent, almost ravenous, Nancy felt nervous again. So she began to rewrap the bone in the cloth, watching Adams closely. And, under her scrutiny, Adams forced a smile, though his eyes were still glued to the bone.

'Listen. I know Herzog. I can help,' he said. 'I can identify it for you – if you just let me have it . . .'

Nancy paused.

'But what about the letters? Do they mean anything? Do you know where they're from?'

'No.'

He was lying, of that she was certain. He continued urgently, desperate now to persuade her.

'Listen, let me take it to the Delhi museum.' He gestured to the back of the room, towards the doorway. 'They have all the equipment. We can date it by measuring the state of decay of its radioactive isotopes ... It's not perfect and this bone will have been polluted a lot but it's worth trying ... and I can check the letters – find out where they're from. And I can compare the design on the mouthpiece to others in my collection – and at the museum. I know everyone there.'

'First, tell me why you think Anton might have had this bone.'

She could see he was confused – perhaps he was wondering why on earth she would be asking such a question if she really knew Herzog, or indeed, if Herzog really had given it to her.

Cautiously he said, 'Herzog has certain ideas, about Tibet, and the history of mankind ...'

She waited for him to continue.

'For our own different reasons, we are both looking for evidence ...'

She glanced at Krishna and then back at Adams and said, 'Evidence that proves that Charles Darwin was wrong?'

Adams was being cagey. 'In my case, something like that.'

'And Anton? He's not an archaeologist or a palaeontologist.'

Adams paused then said, 'No. Our interests coincide, that's all. We discuss our research from time to time.'

Nancy's brow furrowed.

'What research?'

Again he paused; he seemed reluctant to be more forthcoming. She needed something more, some small thread she might follow, some clue as to what Herzog had really been up to all these years.

'Listen, Mr Adams,' she said urgently, 'I need your help. I've just arrived and Anton's out of town at the moment. Tell me what Anton was researching and maybe I will let you test the bone.'

His eyes scanned her suspiciously, as if it was she who was the renegade, and then he slowly nodded his head.

'OK. I'll tell you what I know, but it isn't much.' He paused, clearly working out where to begin, how to make sense of Anton Herzog to someone who knew nothing of Tibet.

'Anton has some strange ideas.' He glanced down at the bone trumpet. 'He's a sort of treasure hunter.'

'I thought you said he wasn't an archaeologist.'

'He's not. The treasure he's looking for is quite

different from all this stuff.' He waved his hand around the room. 'He's after ancient carriers of secret knowledge. The lamas call them "Terma".'

'What are they?'

'Listen, I don't really know. Temples, sacred texts, beautiful valleys, gates to other worlds – who knows? The lamas have written whole books about the "termas", but you can never be sure if you are understanding them on the right level or if you are taking them too literally. It's all always so vague. That's the way with esoteric traditions. I certainly don't understand any of it, and to be frank it doesn't interest me. Apparently there are still lamas alive today who know the locations of these things, know how to find them and bring them back into this world.'

She was staring at him in disbelief. Now it was Herzog who sounded like the crank and the mystery surrounding him seemed to deepen by the hour.

Clearly wanting to distance himself from Herzog's strange interests, Jack Adams continued. 'Listen, Anton had some kooky ideas that I don't go in for. We didn't really discuss them . . . Sometimes, the way he talks, he sounds more like a lama than the lamas themselves. He brought bones to me and asked me to date them or he brought ancient prayer wheels or other sacred objects. I'm always glad for the evidence and he wanted me to check to see if he was looking in the right parts of the Himalayas. He wanted to know if he was on the right track, archaeologically speaking. In order to find what he was looking for he needed to be near the areas of oldest human habitation. The termas that he was looking for dated from many millennia ago; they were vastly old.'

Nancy was thinking out loud. 'It's all extraordinary. It just sounds so crazy and I don't understand it. Everyone says that he was such an intelligent man.' Her brow was knitted in incomprehension. Adams answered curtly.

'He is. Listening to him speak is a pleasure in itself. No one knows as much as he does about Tibet, but he's equally knowledgeable about dozens of other subjects. He's an old guy; he's read a lot and thought a lot. He's a polymath – it's really pretty incredible.'

'But he really believed he would find these "termas" in Tibet?'

'Sure in Tibet. He's not the first intelligent man to go hunting for secret paradises or lost founts of knowledge up there, and I'm sure he won't be the last . . . Tibet's got a great tradition of explorers who've had esoteric interests: Sven Hedin, Aurel Stein, even the Nazis sent expeditions to Tibet, looking for God knows what.'

'I see. And that's all you know?'

He answered without looking her in the eye:

'I told you: we hardly ever spoke about the details. I hunt for old bones and worked flints and the locations of ancient settlements, things like that. That's quite different from Anton. He's not interested in proving anyone wrong – in looking for evidence that ancient man existed. He takes that as read. He needs to locate the lost kingdoms because he believes they will lead him to his ultimate goal. And he doesn't give a damn what other people think.'

Suddenly Adams laughed. 'And you wouldn't bet against him, he's the cleverest person I've ever met.'

Nancy sighed unhappily.

'Thanks for your help.'

She stood up. Adams scrambled to his feet.

'And the bone? May I borrow it?'

'I'll think about it.'

A change had come over Jack Adams. He was beginning to look desperate. He didn't want the conversation to end. How the tables had turned, she thought, from when she first walked in to his strange office, overflowing with antiques and pieces of human and animal skeletons.

In what was clearly a bid to sound relaxed he said, 'So where is Anton anyway? Gone off with Maya to a hill station for a few days' R and R?'

Out of the corner of her eye Nancy saw Krishna blanch guiltily. She tried to stay composed and not to let on that she had no idea who Maya was. She looked at Adams and replied as flatly as she could, 'No – he's just out of town. Doing a story.'

She walked over to the doorway.

Adams was shadowing her every move, and now he even put his arm on her shoulder, too heavily for her liking, and made a last attempt: 'Listen, I'll do the trip to Pemako for $10,000, all in, if you let me examine the bone and tell me where Anton got it.'

'I'll think about it and call you later,' Nancy stuttered, pulling herself away from his heavy grasp and slipping through the doorway into the sweltering Delhi night.

17

'The Cave of the Magicians.'

With a glint of triumph in his eyes, Colonel Jen prodded the Chinese military map with his finger. The Captain craned his neck – they were alone in the old library. On the map, the Himalayas ran from left to right. In between the majestic mountains flowed the river Tsangpo, rising near the Holy Mountain of Kailash in the west and then winding its way eastwards through the high valleys, filling with glacial meltwater as it went. Halfway along the Himalayan chain, the river turned abruptly south and crashed down through the cliffs of the Tsangpo gorge, gushing out into the valleys of Pemako. It fell from 17,000 feet to 5,000 feet in eleven miles. In Pemako, it continued at a more sedate pace through the forest until it disappeared again down into another impenetrable gorge. Twenty miles further south, and 3,000 feet further down, it transformed itself into the sacred Indian river, the Brahmaputra.

Colonel Jen acknowledged that the route would be arduous. Mountains, a river and a green patch that marked Pemako jungle. The rest of China, even the rest of Tibet, was well mapped by comparison. There were roads, villages, possible landing sites for helicopters and so on. But this map of Pemako was hopeless – it might as well have come from a children's fairytale book. Colonel Jen shook his head.

'The monk tells me that they are heading with the stranger for the Cave of the Magicians – the entrance to the cave system is supposed to be here.'

He prodded at an area on the map close to where he had marked the location of Litang gompa.

'If we do not get there before they do then we've lost our chance of catching them. I cannot tell you how frustrating this is. We only missed them by a few hours.'

The Captain said quietly, 'Sir, I have thirty-one men ready to go. And as you requested, I have told the army officer that you want him to stand guard here at the gompa, so we should have no more interference from him. I have ordered the men to leave all their kit here. We can move quickly. The monks only have a six- or seven-hour start at most on us. We will soon catch them.'

Colonel Jen shook his head again and stared in dissatisfaction at the map. The little that was on it was inaccurate. On the way down the river to the gompa from the Su La pass, they had followed the east bank of the Tsangpo, heading for a rope bridge. It had long since collapsed into the raging torrent. They had had to rely on a single rusted steel cable that wasn't on the map at all and that was a further eleven miles further downstream beyond the gompa. If the rope bridge had still been intact, they would have reached the monastery before the soldiers had swarmed in and ruined everything.

These sorts of unlucky and unpredictable events made Colonel Jen very nervous. He looked up and said, 'Monks travel fast. They do not need to eat and rest as much as our soldiers. I have seen lone monks travelling in the high Himalayas with nothing but a satchel of barley flour to sustain them. I have seen them perform feats of endurance that would make Olympic marathon runners wince. They can move at high speed for two or three weeks, day and night, without sleeping. Anyone else would freeze to death up there, or die of exhaustion, but these monks can generate their own heat and energy through their knowledge of yoga. Do not doubt their powers. We have to get to the caves before they do, or we will lose them for good.'

The Captain did not see the problem.

'But can't we follow them into the caves? We can take dynamite, or smoke them out . . .'

Colonel Jen looked up at the Captain – his face was grave.

'Captain, no one knows where those caves go. The Himalayas are riddled with tales of whole cities that exist below ground. Once, in Shigatse, in western Tibet, I met an Old Believer from Moscow, one of those Russian Christians that wear black robes and have long beards. He told me of the lost city of the Chud. Do you know about the Chud?'

'No, sir.'

'The Old Believer told me that you can still hear them singing in their underground cathedrals – you can hear their bells at festival time under your feet . . . Mark my words, Captain, we know little of the Himalayas – it is our job merely to steal into Shangri-La and take what we need. We are burglars and that is all. We do not want to disturb the sleeping kings – if we do, we will never get out alive. No dynamite, no smoke. We must catch the monks, force them if necessary to show us the way, and then leave as silently as possible.'

The Captain looked doubtful. Colonel Jen pushed the useless map to one side.

'You are sceptical, Captain. But I have seen things

up here in the mountains and in the wild west of China that would astound you. I have ridden across the steppes of Sichuan and heard the horseshoes echo through the tunnel systems beneath. I have seen strange figures at the bazaars in Kashgar – figures who have walked right out of the depths of the Gobi desert, dressed in clothes from long ago, carrying unrecognizable coins from the days before Duke Chou. I have approached them, with all the skills that I was taught as a young intelligence officer, and I have seen them literally vanish before my eyes. Don't underestimate the monks – they may not have weapons or army trucks but they have other knowledge . . .'

Decisively, the Colonel put his peaked cap on and folded up the map.

'We must leave at once. If anyone falls behind they will be left to the mercy of the jungle.'

18

Neither Nancy nor Krishna said a word to each other until they were both sitting comfortably in the back of the *Herald Tribune*'s chauffeur-driven car. The Bazaar was too noisy for conversation and Nancy had had to keep her wits about her to avoid being knocked over by passing camels or robbed by mischievous smiling street children, and in any case she was too busy trying to work out the implications of everything that she had just learned.

Herzog was clearly on to something, something that he had been working on for years, she suspected, and Jack Adams was being economical with the truth. He had a far better idea of what Herzog was up to than he was letting on, and Nancy was convinced that he recognized the letters on the mouthpiece of the bone trumpet. She had clearly intuited that he was not telling the truth and she was sure that it had something to do with his initial hunch that the trumpet might come from as far west as Europe and not from Tibet at all. However, what was even stranger was that once he had learned that Herzog had sent the bone from Tibet, he had suddenly dropped his price just so that he could find out more. And then, of course, there was Maya.

Nancy had navigated her way through the scrum in silence, following Krishna back to the main street. Goodness only knows what he was thinking. Perhaps he was now even more worried about her plans, she thought. 'So who's Maya?' she asked as soon as the car pulled out. Krishna turned to look out of the window:

'Nancy, please. I think we've done enough for one day.'

'Krishna, why are you being evasive?'

She was beginning to get angry. Why did no one want her to find out anything about Anton Herzog? She was frustrated with Krishna and furious with Dan Fischer for giving her Indian colleague carte blanche not to cooperate. That was obviously what had happened. And yet she suspected that any display of her true feelings would only succeed in alienating Krishna even further.

'Listen, Krishna, you have to help me. Maya is Anton's fiancée isn't she?'

He turned back to look at her, but he said nothing.

'Then she must be worried too. I know that you don't want me poking my nose into Anton's affairs but I really think you should be less secretive. We're colleagues, remember, and all I want to do is help Anton.' She studied the expression on Krishna's face – was there any sign of him softening?

'We should help her if we can. She must be very worried too. Have you been in touch with her?'

After a pause Krishna stirred from his silence.

'No.'

'Well, perhaps we should. We might be able to reassure her. Who else has she got to talk to?'

Keenly she waited for him to open up and give her a little more information, their body language mimicking their respective attitudes: Nancy alert, poised and receptive, Krishna hunched over, his eyes narrowed with worry. Then suddenly his reserve broke down.

Speaking hurriedly, he said, 'I don't know what to say to her. That is why I haven't returned her calls. I don't know what to tell her.'

Poor woman, thought Nancy. And poor Krishna too. He was entirely the wrong person to act as a counsellor to a grieving loved one.

'She called the office?'

Krishna shrank again into himself and muttered, 'A couple of times.'

'That doesn't matter, we can call her back now . . . it's not too late.' Then she had an idea. 'Or visit her. Do you know where she lives?'

'I don't think that's a good idea.'

'Krishna, she must be worried sick and terribly isolated. What's her address? Do you know?'

Silence again. Nancy pressed on urgently. 'Krishna, Anton would have wanted you to help her, wouldn't he? Surely he would hope that you would at least reassure her and console her? We don't need to take things any further. I agree, let's forget about Tibet and Jack Adams and the bone trumpet – but we really can't just leave her to grieve alone.'

She held her breath as Krishna continued his own private debate, until finally he sighed and looked up.

'Rumeli Street in Old Delhi. She lives on Rumeli Street. But this is the end of our investigation isn't it? No more playing the detective. We will go to help her and that is all.'

Trying hard to look as if she meant it, Nancy nodded her head.

19

Nancy stepped back from the low doorway and glanced up and down the deserted street. Still no answer. Krishna was waiting in the car twenty yards further down the street; he had declined to come to the door with her. They had hardly spoken after she persuaded him to visit Maya. She assumed that he was very worried about everything, and for her part she was terrified that if she opened her mouth he might change his mind about taking her to Maya's address.

At last, she heard a noise, then the door opened a fraction. She could see a woman's face peering out at her from the gloom within. If this was Maya then she was younger than Nancy had expected; in her mid-thirties, she guessed, with soft features and beautiful dark eyes. But she looked afraid. Nancy stuck out her hand.

'Hello, my name is Nancy Kelly, I'm from the *Tribune*, I'm a colleague of Anton's. Are you Maya?'

The woman said nothing, and did not extend her own hand. Nancy fumbled in her pocket for her *Trib* ID and held it up so that the woman could read it and see her picture. But did she speak English? thought Nancy suddenly. Did she even know what Anton Herzog did for a living? Faced with the woman's silence, Nancy realized that she was making a whole series of assumptions. Perhaps the woman knew nothing of Herzog's professional life, perhaps they conversed in Hindi, or an Indian dialect. Perhaps Krishna's instincts were entirely right and it was better to leave her alone in her grief. Or perhaps even, she wasn't grieving at all, and was used to long periods alone whilst Herzog indulged his love of adventure – perhaps she even knew exactly where he was. For the first time Nancy feared that her eagerness to find Herzog had become presumptuous – and then the woman spoke.

'What do you want?' Her voice was soft and sad.

'I've come to see you about Anton.'

'What do you know of him?' she asked, her voice cracking with emotion.

Suddenly, Nancy felt quite sick. What on earth did she think she was doing intruding on this woman's life, a woman she knew nothing about, with her own private hopes and dreads?

'I think he's in Tibet. I am worried about him.'

Maya – Nancy was certain now it must be she – hesitated and then she said, 'Come inside.' She threw open the door, and Nancy followed her. As soon as they were inside, Maya turned and locked the door behind them. Nancy saw her hands were trembling as she turned the key. Then she saw something else, which made her gasp with surprise. Maya was pregnant.

'Please, take a seat in here,' she was saying, moving slowly into the house.

They entered a darkened living room. The blinds were drawn. The room contained two chairs and a sofa. Awkwardly Nancy sat down on one of the chairs. Maya perched on the edge of the sofa, waiting for Nancy to speak.

'I'm sorry to surprise you like this . . .' she began. 'My colleague told me to leave you in peace. But I couldn't.'

'Is he dead, are you here to tell me that?' Maya said sharply, her face contorted with what Nancy assumed must be fear. Quickly, Nancy shook her head.

'You have not heard anything from him?' Maya asked.

'No.'

'Then why have you come?'

Nancy took a deep breath.

'Because I am trying to find him and I thought you might know why he went to Tibet.'

Maya looked crestfallen. She must have expected some news either way – that Herzog was alive and well or that he was in hospital in Tibet, or that he was dead. Any news was better than nothing and Nancy knew nothing at all.

'I'm sorry, we didn't have your phone number . . .'

Maya was staring dejectedly at the floor, one hand gently massaging her belly. She must be six or seven months pregnant, thought Nancy: but was it Anton Herzog's baby? Now Maya looked up at her.

'I don't know what to do,' she said, her voice so full of misery that Nancy could not stop herself from getting up and putting her arm around her.

Of course it was Herzog's child. And now that he was gone how would this woman support the baby? As Nancy stroked Maya's back and muttered soothing words, she glanced down to see if the woman was wearing a wedding ring, but her fingers were bare. She did not even stand to gain a newspaper pension.

'Don't give up hope, I'm sure he will be OK,' Nancy said helplessly.

Maya shook her head, her face unchanged despite Nancy's expressions of hope.

'No. He's not coming back.'

'What do you mean?'

Tears were rolling down Maya's cheeks.

'He said it was the biggest story of his life. The biggest story the world has ever known – but most probably he would never make it back. He said he had to try. He said the world has to know the truth . . .' She stopped, overwhelmed.

'What story? What do you mean? What are you talking about? You mean the story about the glaciers melting?'

Maya wiped her eyes and regained her composure enough to speak:

'No. It was nothing to do with glaciers – that was just his normal work. It was far, far bigger than that.'

She stood and walked over to the chest of drawers that leaned against the far wall of the room. In mounting confusion, Nancy looked on as Maya knelt down and pulled open the bottom drawer. It was stuffed with neatly folded and ironed linen. She carefully removed several layers of napkins and table-cloths and placed them on the top of the chest of drawers, and then she pulled out a medium-sized brown envelope.

'He left me this. He said if he wasn't back within two months then I should open it. He said if he wasn't back by then, then I should forget all about him – I should get on with my life.'

She laid the envelope reverentially on the sofa.

'Have you opened it?'

'No. I was afraid, afraid that if I opened it he would never come back. I was afraid that I would curse him.'

A thousand thoughts rushed through Nancy's brain, all her attention focused on the innocuous-looking manila envelope.

'But what could be inside?' she said, thinking aloud.

'I don't know.'

Nancy looked up at Maya. But the woman would not meet her gaze. 'Maya – we have to look. You have to open it. Anton's been gone more than three months now. There might be something here that can help us find him.'

As Maya began once more to sob, Nancy put her arm around her and tried again to console her.

'Please don't cry. We will find him. I promise. That is why I have come to see you; I am trying to help. But we must look inside in case there is anything that might help us.'

Maya's sobbing slowly ceased. Very delicately Nancy pressed the case again:

'Maya, listen to me. You have to open it for Anton's sake.'

There was a long pause and then finally Maya spoke again. 'Please, you open it. I can't.'

Nancy didn't need a second invitation. She swept

up the envelope, carefully opened it and pulled out the contents. A letter several pages long, and then a photograph and some small metal objects.

She unfolded the letter. At the top were written the fateful words 'Last Will and Testament of Anton Herzog'. Her heart pounding, Nancy glanced down the page. An Indian solicitor was the executor and a second solicitor from the same firm had witnessed Herzog's signature. It was brief and to the point. All the statues and antiques were to be left to the Delhi museum, while the contents of Herzog's Indian and US bank account, which came to just under $70,000, were to be left to Maya. That at least was good news, if good news could ever come from the pages of a will. The remainder of the letter was an inventory of the antiques that Herzog kept at the office and the flat. Nancy swiftly turned her attention to the photograph. It was faded and dog-eared, and in black and white. A man, tall, slim, handsome, in his fifties, was standing on the steps of a building. He supported himself with a walking stick. He was smiling. At the top of the steps, above the building entrance, were the words, 'Buenos Aires Hotel'. Nothing else. She turned the photo over. On the back in pen was written 'Felix at mother's birthday, B.A. 1957'.

Happier days in Buenos Aires thought Nancy. But who was Felix? She fished into the envelope again.

Medals. Two old war medals. She pulled them out, and to her horror she recognized one instantly and it made her recoil in fright. It was an Iron Cross, the distinctive award given to soldiers in the German army. But it was only when she saw the design of the second medal that she lost her composure altogether. It was a simple design, and yet she felt suddenly as if ice had been poured into her veins: it was a dagger emblazoned on a swastika, the exact same design as the one on the mouthpiece of the ancient bone trumpet. Quickly, she tried to pull herself together, but Maya had noticed her momentary panic.

'What's wrong? What have you seen?'

'Nothing. I'm sorry.'

'What does the letter say?'

'It's Anton's will. He has left money for you, to look after you.'

'But he's dead then?'

'No. We don't know that. He must have done this as insurance. In case something happened to him. But it doesn't mean he's dead. You mustn't give up hope.'

She could see that Maya was about to burst into tears again. Quickly she handed her the photograph.

'Do you know this man?'

She studied it for a moment.

'No.'

'Does the name Felix mean anything to you?'

'No.'

'And these?'

She looked at the medals and nodded.

'Yes. Anton used to keep them in his desk drawer. I once asked him what they were and he said they were family heirlooms, that was all. He said one day he would give them to our child.'

She blushed and fell silent, her hand still caressing her swollen belly. Nancy's heart was pounding. She was certain the swastika and dagger medal was identical to the design on the mouthpiece of the bone trumpet, but she could not imagine why this was so. And who was the old man in the photograph and was he connected to the medals? Had they once belonged to him? Clearly he was someone enormously significant – but not Herzog's father – surely it would have been too odd for Herzog to call his father by his forename if in the same sentence he referred to his mother as 'mother'.

But what was she thinking? Krishna had said Herzog's father was killed at the Battle of Stalingrad in 1944. Perhaps it was Herzog's stepfather, or uncle.

Carefully she replaced the letter and the fateful medals in the envelope and laid it back down on the sofa.

'Maya, I beg you: please try to remember. Did Anton ever mention anything at all about the story that he was working on?'

'No. He hardly spoke about his work. Sometimes he'd talk about it a little bit, but this time he did not even tell me he was going till the last minute, and then he was so different from normal. He told me he had to go – for mankind's sake. He felt very bad but it had to be done.'

A chill ran down Nancy's spine. It sounded like the journalist's holy grail. Anton Herzog's biggest-ever story – surely it could be her story too, if she just had the courage to seize the opportunity? She became aware that her pulse was racing as the two conflicting sides of her character battled with each other. The risk-taking, ruthless side, the side that had made her an excellent journalist, was already dreaming of the glory; this could make her name for ever, she could rescue Anton Herzog and sweep the international prizes as well. But the more sensible, conservative side tried desperately to rein in her ambition, aware of her near-total ignorance of what was really going on, except that Herzog was a wanted man accused of espionage and that only hours earlier she had been sitting in a police station being threatened with decades in jail.

As ever she reached a compromise with herself, the

same compromise that she always ended up making, that perpetually tipped her life towards further adventure, that allowed her to pretend that she was not about to make any rash moves. She would continue to investigate the Herzog affair. There was too much now to ignore, too many bizarre coincidences and tantalizing leads. She could not abandon him to his fate, even if that was what Dan Fischer wanted her to do, particularly now she had met Maya – she had to find out more for her. But she would not leave Delhi, not yet anyway – she would not yet ignore the police. The mere thought of seeing the interior of the police station again filled her with dread. If she was taken in for a second time, she knew that she wouldn't see the light of day for a very long time.

'Maya, you mustn't worry. I am going to find out what's happened to Anton one way or another.'

Someone had turned a radio on, somewhere in the courtyard beyond. Soothing strains of Indian classical music intruded on the sepulchral atmosphere – Nancy was glad of it. Maya picked up the envelope and they walked into the hall. Nancy opened the door and stepped back out onto the street. The air was hot and thick. She was glad to have escaped the oppressive dusty interior of the house, a place reeking of anxiety and pain.

She was just about to say her farewells when Maya

spoke in a whisper, 'Don't turn your head. They're following you as well.'

Panic flooded through Nancy's body.

'What? Who?' she whispered back, looking deep into the woman's eyes.

Maya cast her eyes up the street, barely moving her head. Now, trying to appear as if she was simply looking for her driver, Nancy scanned the street. A smart-looking station wagon with blacked-out windows was parked thirty yards down the road. It hadn't been there when she first arrived. It looked completely out of place in such a poor neighbourhood. All her confidence and recklessness of only moments before melted away in an instant. She turned back to Maya, aware that she was now deeply afraid.

The Indian woman spoke again, her head bowed. 'I don't know who they are, but they follow me too. Goodbye.'

20

They had hardly spoken to each other the entire way back from the Bazaar. Nancy assumed she looked rattled by her experience at Maya's house, but she hoped that Krishna would put this down to her meeting with Maya and not to the fact that some unknown agency was now shadowing her every move. Discreetly, as their car nosed its way through the Delhi traffic, she had checked to see if they were still being tailed. Every time she sneaked a look, she could see the black station wagon just behind them.

Krishna was content to let her be silent, she thought. He was perhaps relieved she had stopped asking questions. For her part, Nancy chose not to tell him about the will and the medals, or indeed the details of the conversation: the suggestion that Anton Herzog had knowingly left Delhi on a do-or-die mission from which he had not expected to return. If she told Krishna all this, she knew it would only make him more nervous about what she was going to try next – and maybe he would even call Dan Fischer and report back that she was disobeying orders. It was hardly the ideal working relationship to have with her new colleague, but in truth, what else could she do? And so the burden of worry – worry about what was really going on, worry about who was trailing her, worry about the whole wretched business – all had to fall on her shoulders alone.

Back at the office, Krishna paced around the untidy room. Nancy was sitting at Herzog's desk, her head in her hands, wondering what on earth she should do next and who was monitoring her every move. In one sense, she even hoped that it was the police: that seemed the best of a series of dark possibilities, and she preferred it to the thought of an unknown enemy. But either way it made her life more difficult, for she had no doubt that in the eyes of the police her activities would be construed as guilt, attempts to make contact with what they thought was her fellow spy.

Krishna had slumped onto the sofa, looking exhausted. She looked up at him through her inter-laced fingertips. What did he expect her to do? Just forget the whole thing? Involuntarily, for the hundredth time, she turned over everything in her mind.

Now her eyes fell on the photo of Anna Herzog, widowed within a year of her marriage, forced to flee to Argentina before her child was three years old. She wondered suddenly why this young woman had gone to Argentina, of all the places she might have chosen. Maybe she had relatives there. Maybe she just wanted to leave the war behind. But perhaps there was something else. Her journalist's mind could not help worrying away at these matters. An idea flickered into her head.

'Krishna, is "Herzog" Anton's mother's maiden name?'

He sighed and looked up.

'I don't understand your meaning.'

She saw his reluctance, the awkward way he turned to speak to her, but she couldn't stop herself:

'Was Anton Herzog given his father's surname or his mother's surname when he was born? Sometimes, if a woman loses her husband before their child is born, she gives it her own surname – her maiden name – the name she had before she was married. Or perhaps they were never even married? I guess in the Second World War things could be tough to arrange, even finding time to tie the knot.'

'Funnily enough, Nancy,' responded Krishna tersely, 'it's never occurred to me to investigate the marital status of Anton's parents.'

The irritation was plain in Krishna's voice. Nancy regretted the fact that she had blasted into his life, and made him so uncomfortable. He was eyeing her with something that might even be dislike, she thought. As if her approach, her personality, were somehow distasteful to him. The visit to Maya had clearly been the final straw. He had obviously thought that it was hugely insensitive, no matter how she had tried to dress it up as being a mercy mission to help Anton's fiancée.

She was sorry about that. But there was something dogged in her, some elemental tenacity which meant she had to know. The truth compelled her. Always she had to hunt it out, piece everything together. She had been in tricky situations before: she had been threatened on several occasions by people that she was investigating for stories. Danger was part of the job of being a good investigative journalist. Though, she had to admit to herself, getting embroiled in suspected international espionage was a much, much bigger deal, and as for the ever-expanding collection of bizarre and utterly unnerving clues – the medals, the bone trumpet, the talk of the greatest story ever – she had never come across anything like it before.

But this bloody-mindedness – she supposed it was that – had stood her in good stead as a journalist so far. No matter how tedious and irrelevant a line of inquiry might seem to be, sometimes you would get lucky and some priceless pearl would fall into your lap. Ninety-nine per cent of the time, fretting at the minor details would get you nowhere, but there was always the one time when tediously checking someone's story would suddenly reveal a crucial inconsistency or biographical detail that would reveal their real motives or true nature. She needed any clue she could find; she was like a climber on a rock face, searching for handholds, feeling about on the smooth surface of her ignorance.

Reluctantly, Krishna got up and turned on Herzog's computer for her. As soon as it had booted up she began the process of logging on to the digital foreign cuttings databases that the *Trib* subscribed to. As she worked she thought out loud, aware all the time of Krishna's demoralized presence beside her.

'I think the *Süd-Deutsche Zeitung* is the newspaper of record in Munich nowadays. It probably was back then as well. Let's search their digital archive and see if there is any record of the Herzog family in there.'

She began to type.

'So, if Anton's father died in Stalingrad that would have been in 1944. We can assume then that his parents were married in '43 and that Anton was born in '43 or '44. So let's take a guess and search the Births, Marriages and Deaths announcements in the digital archive for the summer months of 1943. People married and had children in a hurry in those days, you never knew if the father was going to come home again . . .'

Nancy entered her keyword search and pressed Return: 'Herzog, marriage' she had typed in German. Nothing for May. Nothing for June. Then: jackpot.

'Here! This must be them. Engagements: "Anna Herzog, daughter of Karl Heinz and Maria Herzog, to Felix Koenig, August 12th, 1943."'

She could hardly believe what she was reading. So the old man in the photo *was* Anton's father after all – his name was Felix Koenig. That's why Anton had kept the photo all those years, guarded it jealously along with the medals. But it made no sense at all. Anton's father was supposed to have died in Stalingrad in 1944 and yet the photo had definitely been dated Buenos Aires 1957. She was shaking her head, thinking out loud now, her voice filled with uncertainty as she reread the notice.

'That must be her – there can't be two Anna Herzogs getting married. So, Anton's father was called Felix Koenig. Herzog was his mother's maiden name.'

Krishna chipped in. 'Good, well now you know that, can you content yourself with research from Delhi and some local stories while we deal with the police?'

'Yes, yes, whatever you say.' But Nancy was hardly listening to Krishna's entreaties. She had no idea quite how any of this was meant to help, but experience told her she was on the right track. She had found a sore spot and she should keep pressing. She continued: 'Now the next question is: who was Felix Koenig?'

She fell silent as she scanned through the search results. There were plenty of Felix Koenigs knocking around in cyberspace – academics with their dour pages, an artist, a chef from Hamburg. But there was no one who could plausibly be Anton's father. She felt Krishna waiting, and she knew he was hoping that the trail would be cold.

Finally, she turned to him. 'Nothing. There's absolutely nothing.'

21

The monks had paused again, under a vast, lichen-covered overhang of rock in the depths of the jungle. It was a relief to be out of the rain that was still teeming down on the forest canopy, its noise on the lush foliage so great that they had almost to shout at each other to be heard at all.

Exhausted, they lay like casualties on a battlefield, contorted this way and that into strange postures, resting as best they could. Only the Abbot's deputy remained standing, his suspicious eyes still scanning the forest. The schoolteacher was also still alert, patiently squatting on her haunches, studying the slow rise and fall of the white man's chest, expecting every exhalation to be his last. Just as the Abbot's deputy had instructed, she had not left his side throughout the march, even as the monks had carried him slipping and tripping their way across the tangled forest floor.

Gingerly she removed the wet towel that covered his forehead and his eyes and began to dab tenderly at his forehead. Just then, a mosquito landed on his collarbone and began to walk in circles around the man's Adam's apple. She gently placed the towel to one side and very gingerly tried to brush the fly off.

Suddenly, as she leaned forward, the man's eyes opened wide. She froze. She had never seen blue eyes before, and these eyes were the blue of precious living coral, the blue of the Tibetan sky in cloudless midsummer when not a drop of moisture taints the crystalline atmosphere. She screamed in terror, but even as she did so she felt his huge bony hands grip her shoulders, causing her to scream even louder. Within a second four monks sprang to their feet and grabbed hold of the white man's arms. The schoolteacher was thrown backwards to the floor, where she lay whimpering whilst the young monks grappled to subdue the ghoulish figure. A second later the Abbot's deputy was there. The white man had calmed down, though he was hyperventilating. He had the glassy thousand-yard stare of someone in the grip of delirium. With fear and extreme anxiety in his voice, the Abbot's deputy attempted to regain control of the situation. 'Who are you?'

No response. The white man's chest rose and fell. Then, slowly, he turned his head so that he could look straight up at his questioner. There seemed to be tears in his eyes but he was smiling. With ecstasy in his voice, he said, 'I have been to Shangri-La.'

The doctor, who was standing next to the Abbot's deputy, leaned towards him and whispered, 'He is out of his mind.'

A look of fury crossed the white man's face – he seemed to have heard the doctor's words, or at the very least intuited his doubts.

'I *have* been there.'

Then he fell back, exhausted. His eyes closed and he said almost in a whisper, 'I followed Felix Koenig.'

The Abbot's deputy leaned forward, praying the man would not slip into unconsciousness again, and asked:

'Who is Felix Koenig? Is he another of your companions? Is he dead?'

The piercing blue eyes opened again, and though the head remained still, the dazzling pupils flickered and turned to deliver the full force of their gaze. The man smiled weakly.

'Felix Koenig did not die . . . he was captured.'

'By who?'

'By the Russians. They took him to Siberia . . .'

The Abbot's deputy thought that the white man was mad or delirious, that was for sure: there were certainly no Russians in Tibet. He studied the man a moment longer and then, speaking very slowly, he made one last attempt.

'Tell me: who are you and what are you doing in Pemako?'

'We have been to Shangri-La. We have seen the Book of Dzyan.'

The man fell silent. The Abbot's deputy turned to the doctor monk and said quietly under his breath, 'What do you think?'

The doctor frowned.

'He is fantasizing. He is delirious. We have to get him to eat and drink.'

'Can you give him something for the fever?'

'Yes. But let me ask him a question.'

The Abbot's deputy nodded. The doctor knelt down so as to be closer to the stranger's ear.

'Do you know where you are now?'

The man's eyes had closed again, but the lips moved and in a barely audible whisper he said, 'Of course. Germany. Before the Second World War. Felix Koenig was at the university, in Munich ... Professor of oriental languages. He was such a good student ... he spoke all the languages of the East ... he was not a soldier ...'

The two Tibetans stared at each other in bafflement as the voice trailed off to nothing. The Abbot, unsure what else to do, said:

'Prepare him a pipe.'

The doctor glanced at the Abbot's deputy.

'Deputy, a pipe will ease the pain and help him to speak, but it may also make him dream.'

'It is a risk we will have to take.'

The doctor reached into his satchel and pulled out a long pipe and a little rolled-up leather case containing tobacco, matches, metal pins and small, greasy balls of yellowy brown opium. The Abbot's deputy leaned over the white man and whispered in his ear the one question that any human being can always answer if they have a grain of sanity left, 'What is your name?'

Too late. He had gone, slipped away into a private reverie. The Abbot's deputy shook his head and then turned to survey the rain-lashed jungle, a feeling of nausea rising up from the pit of his stomach. Then he looked down at the corpselike figure again. He could see the great bony chest rise and fall. Where was this troubled man now? Of what was he dreaming in his delirious sleep?

Anton Herzog, for that was the name of the cadaverous blue-eyed man who lay on the damp earth beneath the rocky overhang, dreamed of a great city. He could smell and see and hear Munich before him: the wide boulevards, the elegant pre-war bridges that spanned the Isar, the streets thronged with unemployed people in their dark clothes. He had never been to Munich, but Felix Koenig had described it to him a thousand times, and so it was through Felix's eyes that he was transported now. It was Munich in the Thirties that Felix had always described for that was when, at the height of his powers, he had lived and worked there, a world-famous scholar. It had been a dark city then, down on its luck, no jobs, no money for new clothes, no money even to fix the roads – the world was in the grip of the Great Depression.

Anton Herzog left the jungle and the monks far behind and in his dream he walked the musty corridors of Munich university until he came to Felix Koenig's door. There he was now, sitting at his desk surrounded by dusty books in Sanskrit, Tibetan, Bhutanese, Chinese and a host of lesser-known dialects. In Herzog's mind's eye, Felix Koenig was a muscular young man with curly blond hair and boyish good looks, poring over the ancient books. His intellect was legendary – even at the Gymnasium in Vienna, the teachers had marvelled at his concentration and mental stamina. He had once told Herzog that these powers were earned in the harvest fields of his native village, where as a boy he would toil for whole days in the sunshine.

In his dream Herzog could see over the rooftops of

the city. A storm was gathering to the south, over the Alps. Wotan, the ancient German god of war, was awakening from a long sleep; a second great war was brewing, a war that would transport Felix Koenig to hell and back. Poor Felix Koenig worked on in his library, oblivious, content to pursue his private interest in the history and origins of the Germanic peoples, deeply fascinated by old mysteries such as the dream of Atlantis. The young scholar sat at his desk, poring over the ancient texts of long-dead civilizations.

But then Anton Herzog felt the rain on his face. Where was he? In Munich or Tibet? His eyes opened again and he felt the Tibetan doctor again, sponging him gently with the wet towel, and he saw the dark rock of the overhang above, the jungle all around and the endless rain. He did not want to be drawn away from his visions and his dreams; he did not want to leave. He wanted to go up to Koenig's door. He moaned and protested and tried to roll his face away, but the doctor would not leave him alone and then he felt hands grasping his shoulders and back and he was hauled into a sitting position. The doctor forced a pipe between his lips and urged him to breathe. He did as commanded; the delicious smoke filled his lungs and seemed to coil up into his brain, covering up the pain and hiding all possibility of sadness.

He smoked the pipe through until it was empty and then the monks allowed him to lie down again. He could hear the doctor's voice, asking him questions. He wanted to speak; he wanted to help the monks, to tell them what he had seen, to tell them who he was and why he had followed Felix Koenig. He tried to focus on the doctor's face but all he could now see was a soft blur.

Yet now he could clearly see Felix Koenig in the Munich university faculty cafeteria, talking to two men. He began to describe the scene to the doctor, or at least, that is what he thought he was doing – but perhaps he was not speaking at all, perhaps he dreamed the phrases he was saying. He knew who the two men were, for Felix had described the scene so many times: Karl Haushofer and his student assistant Rudolf Hess. Haushofer – a senior professor, a man of strange occult leanings and enormous intellect, a highly decorated soldier, a prophet for the German people; and Hess – one of the demons who would drag his beloved Germany over the abyss and into war, one of Hitler's closest henchmen.

It was too early for Koenig to know all this, and even as Herzog thought he was speaking to the doctor, he wanted to cry out to warn the young man, to tell him to beware. Shun them! he wanted to cry. But they were speaking calmly, these man-devils, explaining to Koenig that they needed manuscripts translated from Tibetan and Chinese and, in the near future, they planned to send expeditions to Tibet. If Koenig liked the work he could perhaps accompany Haushofer on one of his expeditions there. Young Felix was examining the documents, manuscripts never seen before, written in long-forgotten tongues, which explained the origins of the Aryan race and the myth of Shangri-La, the paradise in the clouds. Never before had Felix Koenig seen source documents like these. It was a treasure trove. With these he could make his academic name – he would be immortalized for all time. And now Herzog was trying to tell the doctor that this was where it all started, that within a month Koenig had attended his first meeting of the Thule Society, an esoteric group of men with a thirst for true knowledge of the past. Visions floated before Herzog's eyes: the *I-Ching*, the Oracle that Koenig was introduced to at the Thule Society.

Then Herzog could see the doctor's face clearly again for the first time. He was leaning towards him, his voice laden with anxiety.

'What were these men hoping to find in Tibet?'

The Abbot's deputy was squatting at the doctor's

shoulder, listening in horror. Anton Herzog, lifted high on the wings of opium, began to speak with ever more fluency:

'They believed that many thousands of years ago there existed in the Far East a highly developed civilization – a civilization that was the work of the people who had fled the collapse of ancient Mu, or Lemuria as it was also known, the great continent that used to exist somewhere in the middle of the Pacific, inside the Ring of Fire. These refugees from Mu were the ancient Aryans, the forefathers of the German peoples, and they made their new home in what is now the Gobi desert many aeons ago and established a thriving civilization, gloriously distinct from the fallen races of lesser men who eked out a turbulent existence across the rest of the globe . . .'

The Abbot's deputy listened with a baleful expression on his face as Anton Herzog spoke. On several occasions, he had tried to interrupt the sickly Westerner, to ask questions, in an attempt to make sense of the deluge of strange information. But it was only now that the ravaged man seemed to hear him; only now did he turn to listen as the deputy asked, 'Why did this Pacific civilization collapse beneath the waves?'

Anton Herzog did not know, or could not remember. But he knew of the belief in the cyclical winnowing of the human races that was slowly but surely refining mankind until one day the superman would be reborn, the Aryan superman who would be a world Messiah – a German Jesus. Then he said that in accordance with this theory of the alchemical purification of the master race through successive tests, this second civilization was itself destroyed later by a massive cataclysm that was suspected to have been of atomic origin. The lush homeland of the master race was turned into the present-day Gobi desert, and the survivors, the Aryan kings, fled west and south and created a new capital – a vast underground kingdom beneath the Himalayas from where they could continue to rule the world. The name of this new capital was Shangri-La. Some said that it lay south-west of present-day Lhasa, near Shigatse monastery. Other sources claimed that it lay beneath the great mountain of Kanchenjunga, still others that it was in Afghanistan or Nepal. Finally, said Herzog, in May 1935 Koenig joined his first Thule Society expedition to Tibet.

The Abbot's deputy listened in horror.

'So Shangri-La was their goal.'

'Yes,' replied Herzog. 'They were to locate Shangri-La and attempt to establish contact with the Masters, and most important of all, they were to retrieve the lost wisdom of the Aryan race: wisdom from Lemuria itself that would explain how to turn any human into the superman, part of the perfected master race, destined to rule the world. They went first to Mount Kailash and Shigatse in the west and then to the mountains north of Lhasa before finally ending up in the east, in the little-explored region of Pemako. There they disappeared . . .'

'Where did they go?' asked the Abbot's deputy.

'Five months later,' said Herzog, and now sweat was running down his face, so that the doctor tried to cool him with the wet rag again, 'Felix Koenig walked into the German Consulate in Bombay, alone and seemingly out of his mind. He could not explain what had happened to the other members of the expedition and he refused to talk about where he had been, but he made a statement that Germany was heading in the wrong direction and that the German people was being misled. He was put aboard a ship to Hamburg, arrested on his arrival, sent to an asylum in the Alps, discharged from the army and relieved of all his privileges, a broken and exhausted man. Then a ray of light: Anna, a beautiful, vivacious twenty-two-year-old girl who was – alone of all people – able to distract and console him. They were married in '44.'

And now Herzog was in tears, mingling with the sweat, and he turned his half-seeing eyes upwards. There, the jungle canopy. Or was it the firs of the Bavarian Alps? He did not know. The doctor wiped his brow again, and Herzog said, 'It is true, what I say, everything is true. You do believe me?'

The Abbot's deputy looked grimly at the doctor, who looked back at him. For a moment nobody spoke. Herzog sweated and wept in the fit of his delirium, though in a sense, thought the Abbot's deputy, he was sounding more and more lucid, even though what he actually said was so strange.

'We believe you,' said the Abbot's deputy softly, and Herzog turned his eyes towards him – bright blue but filmy with moisture.

'Then I must tell you that Koenig became implicated in a plot to murder Hitler. When the secret police arrived at his house, he had been married for only three days. They had not even had time to register their marriage at the town hall; the policemen had literally to tear him from the arms of his Anna. He was given an unholy choice: either Auschwitz or the Russian Front. The following day Koenig was parachuted into the *Kessel*, the besieged triangle of German-occupied territory to the west of Stalingrad, in November 1944, with the rank of lieutenant. In charge of eleven young men, none of whom was over the age of eighteen, he was last seen leading his troops on a dawn raid, in an attempt to capture the ground floor of a derelict department store – just one more soldier lost in the brutal fighting on the Eastern Front . . .'

Now at last, Anton Herzog had exhausted himself. The Abbot's deputy managed to stutter out a question. 'So Felix Koenig died and that was the end of the dream of finding Shangri-La?'

Herzog sighed long and hard. Wearily, he struggled to say, 'No, you don't understand. He told all this to me, he taught me the *I-Ching*. I promised him I too would go to Shangri-La. Felix Koenig was my father.'

22

What on earth to do? So much had happened, and so quickly. Nancy's world had been turned upside down. Everywhere she looked, more and more mysteries seemed to be emerging. And yet she felt more energetic and focused at this moment than she had ever felt in her old monotonous life in New York.

She looked at her watch: eight p.m. The flight she could catch if she wanted to get to Tibet unnoticed by the authorities left in four hours. There was no point pretending to herself that she wasn't very tempted. The injustice of her arrest, the lack of support given to Herzog by Dan Fischer and the paper, the chance of getting in on the greatest story of all time, and now the tragic plight of Herzog's fiancée, all motivated her to go in search of him – and yet still she prevaricated, still she couldn't decide. Krishna's arguments were perfectly sensible and his logic was overwhelming. Quite simply it was reckless to pursue Anton Herzog into Tibet, if indeed he was in Tibet at all. Dan had given her clear instructions to stay in Delhi and do some local-colour stories; the police had bailed her on condition that she stayed put. She had made snap decisions throughout her life, but she had never before been drawn to a course of action so clearly fraught with danger.

Krishna had gone to make a phone call, and she could hear him in his office, though his words were indistinct. She felt helpless and alone.

For some reason she could not entirely unfurl, she could not just forget about Anton Herzog. It perplexed her that he had been abandoned, but it perplexed her too that she felt such a significant sense of loyalty to him – it would be so much simpler just to leave his fate in the hands of Dan and the police. He was a colleague she admired, but he was not a friend after all and, in a way, he hardly needed more people searching for him; he already had an array of spooks combing the mountains and plains of the Far East to find him. Admire him, she told herself, but don't charge in there and imagine you can save him.

For all she knew, Anton Herzog wanted to be lost. That was a whole other strand she hadn't really considered. And perhaps he wanted no part of Maya's life. Perhaps he had wanted to escape before the child was born. She had always heard him spoken of as a confirmed bachelor, after all. But despite the urgings of her reason, something was still drawing her in. The unresolved questions, turning in her brain: what had Herzog really been doing all these years in India? What was he really doing in Tibet? Why had he watched over her career? What in his past had propelled him to these extremities, to such obsessions and dangerous acts? Most of all she wanted to know what was the great story that had caused Herzog to disappear into Tibet like a great hunter in search of a mythical beast?

Despite all these questions, all the caveats she rehearsed to herself, she knew she had to try – nothing else would do. And if she did, something told her that all the threads of the last twenty-four hours would be drawn together: the inconsistent family history, the disturbing fact that the second medal had the same design as the ancient bone trumpet – even Jack Adams's sudden enthusiasm to take her to Tibet: all would make sense, all would become clear.

Then, by chance, her eyes fell on the Oracle. A wave of adrenalin flooded through her body. It somehow seemed utterly appropriate. She reached out for the book and with the noise of Krishna murmuring on the phone in the other room she asked the question and tossed the coin six times.

Oracle, please help me. You have to tell me what to do.
Hexagram 42, Increase. She looked it up.

Hexagram 42 Increase turns into Hexagram 43 The Judgement. Increase leads to The Judgement. The answer to your question includes both definitions.

Two definitions for the price of one, she thought. She flicked to the back of the book and looked up 'Increase', number 42. Uncertainly, she scanned the text, trying to fathom the cryptic meaning. Gradually, like fog clearing on a sunny day, the advice became absolutely clear. It made the hairs on her arms stand up, to perceive that it actually made sense, that the Oracle was offering her lucid suggestions about how she should act. It read:

42 – Increase

> *It furthers one*
> *To undertake something.*
> *It furthers one to cross a great obstacle.*

The Himalayas! She almost cried out loud. Surely the Oracle was telling her to cross the Himalayas and go to Tibet.

> *Ten pairs of tortoises cannot oppose him.*
> *Constant perseverance brings good fortune.*
> *The King presents him before God.*

The King? She almost fell off her chair. 'Koenig' was the German word for King. It could not be a coincidence.

One is enriched through unfortunate events
If you walk in the middle
And report to the Prince.

The Oracle knew that she had suffered unfortunate events but that she felt enlivened by her new situation. How? How did it know that? Was the Prince the same as the King? She did not know. She turned from the definition of Hexagram 42 to the definition of Hexagram 43. It had the ominous name of 'The Judgement'.

The Judgement

One must resolutely make the matter known
At the court of the King.
It must be announced truthfully. Danger.
It is necessary to notify one's own city.
It does not further to resort to arms.
It furthers one to undertake something.

My God! she thought. Unless she was lurching into over-interpretation, finding significance where there was none, it seemed as if the Oracle was telling her to go. She was almost certain of it – the message was: Get up, go to Tibet and find the King. Find Koenig–Herzog. There would be danger, it was necessary to notify one's own city – and she wondered if that meant she should make her peace with Dan Fischer, explain everything, or perhaps with Krishna – but the urging seemed insistent. She should go at once.

It was incredible. She exhaled in amazement and relief. She closed the book and sat there for a moment, trying to gather her thoughts. As soon as the book shut she was plagued with doubts. Perhaps she was reading way too much into the ancient definitions. Perhaps it was just coincidence that it spoke of a King and great obstacles. But then she wondered if that mattered. The fact she interpreted it thus was compelling anyway. Clearly she wanted to go to Tibet. The cryptic words of the ancient book had pushed her over the edge, had forced her to make up her mind: she was going to Tibet. She was going to find Anton Herzog and – she could not disguise the thrill this gave her – she was going to unearth an immense story.

Krishna walked back into the room with a tea tray. Nancy watched him place it on his desk and then carefully transfer the two cups. He thinks he's persuaded me, she thought, he thinks I'm giving up, the poor man.

'Krishna?'

'Yes.'

'Can you please call me a cab? I'm going back to the apartment.'

There was something in her tone of voice that

betrayed her at once, she could tell. His head hanging dejectedly, Krishna set down his cup of tea. She saw his hands were trembling and she regretted once more that she was causing him such anxiety.

'Nancy,' he said, quietly, 'you are not thinking of getting in contact with that man Jack Adams again, are you? You're not going to take all this nonsense any further?'

'You've already made your opinion perfectly clear and I promise I will make it absolutely clear to anyone that you were totally opposed. I haven't yet decided what I'm going to do. If you can bear to, it would be great if you could just help me a little. There must be more we can find out about Anton and his family. Call our German office and get them to help, try anything.'

But Krishna was shaking his head. 'Nancy, I am not having anything more to do with this. Dan Fischer has expressly said you should stay in Delhi and he has given no indication that he wants us spending our time looking into Anton's disappearance. The *Trib* isn't a private detective agency, we've got a paper to write.'

'Do you actually believe what you're saying, Krishna, or are you just trying to save your ass?' said Nancy in a sharper tone, which made Krishna face her directly and stare at her in silence for a moment.

Then he said, no longer trying to suppress his anger, 'With respect, you know very little about this region. I know you have an excellent reputation as a journalist, but you are not a regional expert. You do not speak the languages. You have never even been to Tibet. I was advised that you are brilliant but impulsive, and that you would need a lot of advice about local detail,' he said bluntly. 'I didn't quite realize I would be spending the first day trying to persuade you out of a crazy scheme like this, but if that comes within the remit of advising you then that is what I have to do.'

'And I appreciate your advice,' said Nancy, speaking more quietly now, though she too felt a surge of rage. 'I have been listening to your advice. You've given me nothing but advice since I arrived. Thank you. Now, as an intelligent free-thinking person, equipped with all your advice, I have made up my mind. I'm going and that's that. If you feel like helping, then please find everything you can about Felix Koenig. I'll be on my cell if you get any leads.'

'You'll be on your cell until you vanish too, most likely,' said Krishna.

'Did you argue like this with Anton? Or was he too much of a myth? Too much of a character? Too much of a man? Is it only young female journalists who get this kind of treatment from you?'

'That is out of order,' Krishna shouted back. 'Anton knew the region better than I do. It would have been inappropriate to question his judgement. You are simply being arrogant.'

'Well that's interesting,' said Nancy. 'In men, I find this sort of behaviour is more often called determination. In women, it always gets called arrogance.'

Krishna shrugged as she said this. 'It is pointless defending myself against such a ridiculous charge,' he said.

'I agree, it's pointless, our whole discussion,' said Nancy. 'I'm sorry I can't persuade you to see things my way. But I will assure Dan Fischer that you have done everything to explain to me what a bad idea this is. You will not be reproached in any way, I promise you.' Now Nancy picked up Herzog's copy of the Oracle and grabbed her jacket from the back of the chair.

'I just hope you can live with your conscience,' she said. And then she marched out of the office, not looking back.

23

Nancy knelt on the floor of the apartment bedroom and stuffed some clothes from her suitcase into her small knapsack. Whatever she did next, whether she stayed in India or not, she wanted to leave this place. It was the scene of her arrest and it was filled to overflowing with memories of Anton Herzog. She wanted to disappear, to throw her pursuers off her trail, get space to think.

The interior of the flat was dark; she had chosen not to turn the lights on. She was almost certain that her cab had been followed back to the apartment, though perhaps it was just that the strain was beginning to make her paranoid. But she preferred now to be in the semi-darkness. If they were watching her – whoever they might be – at least it would be harder for them to see what she was doing.

What should she pack? And where was she going to go? To a hotel? To the mountains? To Tibet? It would be cold there, she guessed. The truth was she didn't know what she was doing. As she threw a sweater and a fleece into her bag, her stomach tightened, as if her body was tensing up, becoming more alert as danger approached. She rolled up a set of thermals and stuffed them into a side pocket. Then there was the Oracle. She flicked through its pages and then carefully slid it down the back of the bag. Herzog must be missing it, she decided. She would give it to him when they finally met. If they ever met – but she couldn't contemplate failure, not when the odds were so clearly stacked against her.

A siren in the night jolted her and she stood up. She left the suitcase, still lying on the floor of the bedroom, exactly where she had dumped it when she first arrived from the airport. It had been roughly disembowelled by her frantic repacking, clothes spilling everywhere. She stepped into the hall and glanced for a second into the living room, glancing briefly at Herzog's fantastic hoard of antiques again. The apartment would be a lovely place to live, she thought – a great place for parties, elegant soirées. She felt a spasm of regret for the glamorous expat life she might have had in Delhi – but now she was preparing to become a fugitive, and she dismissed such musings before they ran on and sapped her resolve.

Before she left the apartment she had one more line of inquiry that she wanted to pursue. She hadn't wanted to make this particular call in front of Krishna, but now she was all alone she felt she could do it. She walked across the cluttered living room and took a seat at Herzog's writing desk, then turned on his computer and logged on as a visitor. In a second she had the number she was looking for. She paused briefly to collect her thoughts and then, inhaling deeply, she dialled. The phone rang for a minute and she was just about to give up when it was answered by a male voice with an American accent. For a split second she dithered and almost deciding to hang up. She had not been sure how she would respond when she heard the voice, and now she knew: she felt incredibly confused.

'Hi, James, it's me, Nancy. Sorry to call so early.'

'Nancy – I thought we'd agreed not to talk.'

She could hear the tension and anxiety in his voice and she knew exactly what he was thinking.

'Listen, James – I'm not calling about us. This is a professional call. Our relationship is over – I know that too.'

But even as she said the words she knew he'd never believe her. She could picture him holding the phone, his handsome face wearing a frown, his green eyes narrowing with doubt. He was already worried about her state of mind. She had taken the break-up very badly at first and he was bound to doubt her words.

'Listen, James, I'm serious. I need your help. I need to ask you something about South America.'

She could hear the suspicion creeping into his voice. 'I thought you were off to Delhi.'

'I'm there now.'

'What? Then why are you doing a South American piece?'

'I need some information about a person in Buenos Aires. Can you help?'

Silence, followed by a terse question:

'Who?'

'Anton. Anton Herzog. You probably know already – he's gone missing, in Tibet. I need you to find out all you can about his family and his early days in Buenos Aires.'

'What! You want me to investigate Anton's family? Nancy, are you serious?'

'Yes. Absolutely serious.'

'Look, I don't know what you mean by this. I just think this might not be a good idea. Perhaps we should stop this conversation.'

Now she was furious. 'James, I agree, we shouldn't speak. But you're the only person I know in the right place, with the necessary expertise. And you're the only person I can trust in this. So I'm begging you to do this. Do it for me, for whatever we were. Please.'

There was another pause, and when he spoke his voice was softer.

'OK. OK, I'll have a look. What exactly do you want to know?'

'Anything. Anything you can find. I'm convinced Anton's background will throw light on his disappearance. But his background might be more complicated than it first appears. I can't explain, I haven't much time. I need the information now. Or some information. Something.'

She was calmer now and she could hear that James was relieved by this.

'OK. I'll see what I can do. But it's early here – some people don't come in until later in the morning. I'll make some initial calls and get back to you in twenty minutes or so. But I might not have much to report.'

'That's great, James, just get me anything you can. Thank you.'

24

Silently Nancy paced the room, waiting for the call. Twenty minutes passed, then thirty. It seemed like an eternity. At one point she went over to the street-side window and lifting one slat on the blinds saw the ominous black car, waiting patiently below. A shiver of terror ran down her spine. If it was indeed the police they would surely be tapping her calls. She would have to be careful what she said if she wanted to stay out of prison. But then again, she thought, surely her conversations would demonstrate her innocence? She didn't want to put this theory to the test. She doubted very much she'd be given the benefit of the doubt.

Finally the phone rang.

'Nancy.'

'James. Thank God.'

She wondered for a second if he was going to say he'd had second thoughts.

'I found some stuff on Anton . . .'

He sounded as though he was in a state of shock.

'Go on.'

With immaculate timing an ambulance passed slowly down the road beneath the apartment window, sirens blaring. James said something, but she couldn't hear his words.

'One second, James, hang on . . .'

She walked through into Herzog's spotlessly clean kitchen, which overlooked a quiet courtyard.

'What were you saying?'

'I did some searches on Anna Herzog. Hang on, where are my notes?'

There was a pause. She shut her eyes in frustration. She could picture him in the cluttered office, sitting at his untidy desk, digging through piles of paper. She wished that he would hurry. After a few seconds, he began again:

'Anna Herzog of Boulevard de Recoleta, Buenos Aires, married a man called Gustav Deutsch in 1954. He was a German émigré who arrived in Buenos Aires that same year.'

'So Deutsch was Anton's stepfather?'

But what about the photo then, she thought to herself; the mysterious photo of Felix Koenig on the steps of a hotel in BA, back from the dead – allegedly taken in 1957?

'Wait, not so fast,' James said. 'I couldn't get anything more from the usual sources. There are no photos anywhere of either Anna Herzog or Gustav Deutsch. So I called our contact at the Simon Wiesenthal Centre: you know, the Nazi-hunters. They have an office in Buenos Aires. It's always a long shot, but with stories about German émigrés of that age it's always worth trying; lots of Nazis ended up in Argentina. Now and then something comes up. To cut a long story short, I've just got off the phone with this man – one of the most prolific Nazi-hunters of them all. He says they have a record for Deutsch. He's dead now – he died in 1972 – but back in the Fifties they opened a file on him because there was a suspicion that he was in reality a man named Felix Koenig, an eminent academic and a member of something called the Thule Gesellschaft, a sort of occult society with links to the Nazi regime.'

'My God.'

'Extraordinary, isn't it? I never knew Anton had such a dark past.'

'But why did the Wiesenthal Centre even suspect that Felix Koenig survived the war? Anton always claimed he'd died at Stalingrad.'

'Well, yes – but this is where it starts to get really strange. The Wiesenthal Centre knows about Felix Koenig's war record and it's true that officially he is down as "missing in action, presumed dead". He was last seen leading a platoon of men into a derelict building on the front line. Hundreds of thousands of Germans died at Stalingrad. But war records for Stalingrad are a bit of a waste of time – either you made it back to Germany, or you were killed in the battle, or you were taken prisoner by the Russians. Since being taken prisoner was as good as being dead, the soldiers who didn't make it home were routinely described in the war records as "missing presumed dead", just like Felix Koenig. Now, Herr Deutsch, on the other hand, arrived in Argentina in 1954, having served nine years in a Siberian gulag. There is no war record for him but that is not completely unusual. The story he gave was that he'd been one of the hundred thousand German soldiers who had been captured at Stalingrad and that he was one of the very few lucky ones who were ever seen again – most prisoners disappeared into the gulag and vanished for ever. At the time of Deutsch's arrival in 1954 Anna Herzog was living with another German man named Freddie Klaus, who worked as a mechanic in a garage in Recoleta. But here comes the important bit: as soon as Deutsch turned up on the scene, Anna Herzog kicked Klaus out and married Deutsch. That's why the Wiesenthal Centre suspected that Deutsch was really Felix Koenig, Anna Herzog's original husband . . .'

Nancy could hardly believe what she was hearing. She stared out through the kitchen window, across the rooftops of Delhi. The lights of the city lit up the sky to the south. There wasn't a star to be seen, just an orange cape of pollution and then, far above it, the black night.

'It's almost romantic,' she said. 'She still loved him all those years later. She had been waiting for him.'

What a thought – love even there, pure love, amidst the criminals and the lost souls of the Nazi revolution. And what did that mean for the world? That love was prepared to forgive absolutely anything; that it could turn a blind eye to anything; that it was in the end essentially – even diabolically – amoral? She could see the lights of an aeroplane in the distance, gradually rising up above the distant Delhi rooftops. Any second now, it would begin its ponderous journey to the clouds.

'But do they have any other proof?'

'Yes – you're not going to believe it. "Deutsch", or perhaps I should say Koenig, ended his life as a librarian at Buenos Aires library. He was in charge of the oriental languages section. He could read and write Chinese and Tibetan, and this is why the Simon Wiesenthal Centre was so sure that Deutsch and Koenig were the same man. You see the Thule Gesellschaft, the Nazi organization that Felix Koenig was a member of, sent expeditions to Tibet in search of lost Aryan knowledge. Felix Koenig was chosen to join the expeditions because he could read and write Tibetan – a rare skill, I think you would agree.'

'Incredible. So Anton's lifelong interest in Tibet—'

'Must be bound up with his relationship with his father, I should think, yes,' said James, finishing a sentence Nancy was hesitating over. She was in a state of complete shock. Anton's own father had been a member of a strange esoteric cult and a Tibetologist – esteemed by his deranged peers. She wasn't sure if she wanted to learn any more and now she was far from certain that she wanted to step on to the plane, now that the night seemed to be filling up with dark shadows and horrible ghosts from Europe's past.

For a second neither of them spoke. Finally, she said, 'But what on earth were the Nazis doing in Tibet looking for lost Aryan knowledge – and what does that really mean? What the hell was the Thule Gesellschaft?'

'I don't know but I'll try to find out. Our guy at the Simon Wiesenthal Centre is pretty dismissive; all he said was that it was just one of the many crackpot occult societies that flourished in Europe between the wars. I haven't had a chance to have a proper snoop around. I wanted to call you straight away. I typed it into the Internet and got millions of links and articles but I haven't had time to check them out. I had no idea that anything like this would ever come up . . . What's going on, Nancy? What is Anton doing?'

Nancy was already struggling to make sense of all the new information. She was too busy even to enjoy the fact that James's tone had changed from pitying scepticism to eager curiosity.

'James, I just don't know yet.'

Then suddenly she heard a noise outside the flat. It was coming from the communal staircase, a knock or a bang of some kind, then silence again. She was petrified with fear.

'I've got to go.'

'Nancy, what's going on? Are you all right?'

'I can't talk. Something's come up. Thanks for your help.'

She dropped the phone into its cradle, then tiptoed across the room into the corridor and over to the front door of the apartment. There was a spyhole that looked on to the stairwell. She peered through, her pulse racing. Nothing. Perhaps it was just a neighbour coming home. But then again, perhaps someone was lying in wait, pressed against the wall, right next to the door, just out of sight. She couldn't believe she had been so short with James; a few months ago she would have done anything to talk to him on the phone. But she didn't have time to think about that now. She wanted desperately to get away from the apartment.

She inhaled deeply and steeled her resolve. She had one more thing to do, then she would be gone.

She went straight back and sat down at the computer. As her fingers traced the keys, she wondered if anyone else in India had ever typed in the words 'Thule Gesellschaft', the name of what the man at the Wiesenthal Centre had described as a bizarre cult; a cult from halfway round the other side of the world no less, and half a century ago. Anyone else except Anton Herzog, that is. She waited as the painstakingly slow connection froze for a second and then began to click and hum.

Finally, a page of assorted links appeared on the screen. There were, as James had said, thousands of sites to choose from. But that in itself meant nothing. You could type anything into the Internet and you would almost be guaranteed a couple of thousand links. Nancy needed a reputable source, not just any old article. She scanned the links, clicked through to a few, and then finally her eyes fell on an old *Guardian* article – a reliable British newspaper.

To the left of the story was an accompanying image, titled, 'Symbol of the Thule Gesellschaft'. It was a dagger emblazoned on a swastika, identical to the medal and the detail on the bone trumpet. Nancy's throat tightened. It was as if a previously distant evil was beginning to pour into her world, and this was her own doing, and with every step she took to investigate the Herzog affair the evil was rising all around her. She wanted to turn off the computer and run away. But in a state of horrified fascination she read though the article to the end:

FEATURES. JUNE 1979

The Thule Gesellschaft, or Thule Society in English, was founded on August 17th 1918 in the Four Seasons Hotel in Munich, by Rudolf von Sebottendorff, a German occultist. Its aim was to promote ideas about the origins of the blue-eyed, blond-haired Aryan race. Thule was the name of what the members believed was the mythical Aryan homeland.

At the time of the society's foundation, the First World War had just finished and Communist revolutionaries were plotting to overthrow the German government. Adolf Hitler was one of the one million defeated and angry soldiers who had returned from the front. He had recently been awarded the Iron Cross, the German army's highest honour for bravery, and like many other soldiers, his patriotism burned brightly despite the defeat.

The Thule Gesellschaft decided to capitalize on this unstable situation, and in 1919 they started something called the German Workers' Party. This was created in order to disseminate the society's ideas of German and

Aryan supremacy amongst Germany's general population. In the following year, the German Workers' Party became the NSDAP, the political vehicle through which Hitler would ascend to power. In due course, the NSDAP became known as the Nazi Party.

Among the early members of the Thule Society was Dietrich Eckart. He was a wealthy German publisher and a master of black magic. It was Eckart who spotted Adolf Hitler's potential, after he saw him speak in a Munich beer hall. He took Hitler under his wing and trained him in the occult arts of charismatic projection, mass persuasion and oratory.

Hitler's talents for rhetoric and propaganda far surpassed Eckart's, as history attests. Eckart died in 1923, from damage to his lungs caused by mustard gas in the trenches, but before he died he told the other Thule Society members: 'Follow Hitler. He will dance but it is I who have called the tune. We have given him the means of communicating with Them. Do not mourn for me: I shall have influenced history more than any other German.'

Before his final ascent to power, Hitler spent some time in jail. During his stay in jail he was visited many times by General Karl Haushofer, another Thule Society member. Haushofer, a Professor at Munich University, had long conversations with Hitler in which he told Hitler how he had travelled to Tibet and studied under the highest Tibetan lamas. The

Thule Society thought that the Aryan race had its homeland in Iceland but that it had also been forced to spend time in the high Himalayas, after the last world had been destroyed in a cataclysm. Haushofer knew this, but he was less interested in history and more in power.

Haushofer believed that the secret mystical lodges of Tibet possessed the knowledge of the 'superman', which they had been entrusted to look after by the Aryan kings. He was convinced that, using ancient Aryan occult practices, the Tibetan holy men could somehow transform normal men into supermen. It was this power and knowledge that the Nazis sought. The powers of mass hypnosis and mass suggestion that Eckart had taught to Hitler were as nothing compared to the powers of the superman. As soon as Hitler's Nazi Party had enough money, it organized expeditions to Tibet to locate the hidden Kingdom of Shangri-La, which was supposed to be the seat of the grand lodge of the High Masters.

The chief object of their searching, and what they thought of as the work containing the secrets of the superman, was 'Das Buch des Ringes' – The Book of the Ring. This was the name that the Nazis gave to what had always been known in Western esoteric traditions as 'The Book of Dzyan'. It was the Russian occultist Madame Blavatsky who called it that.

But the Nazis did not consider this book to be a

Tibetan creation at all, and so refused to use the Tibetan name. They thought that it was the ancient Aryans who had made the book. Its cover was rumoured to be made of jet-black leather that came from the skin of a now extinct animal, and on its front was a picture of a gold ring with a serpent twined around it, swallowing its tail.

The Nazis never found the book. In the modern era the Tibetan lamas, including the Dalai Lama himself, have denied its existence altogether, and since the Chinese invasion of Tibet in 1959 so many monasteries and libraries have been destroyed that we will probably never learn the truth about the mythical book. But it is worth noting that the Chinese Communist Party has acknowledged the existence of the book and voiced a desire to bring it for so-called safe keeping to Beijing. In official Party doctrine the Book is referred to simply as 'The Black Book', and it is considered to be an object of ill-omen and superstition capable of seeding counter-revolutionary activity.

Nancy read in mounting horror, at first unable to grasp the implications of what she was learning. In desperation, she clicked some of the other links, but they only verified the story, giving different takes on the same information.

If all this was true, she thought, then the Nazi movement had essentially grown out of an occult society, or at the very least had its roots firmly in the occult, and specifically in the Thule Society, of which Anton's father had been a member. Nancy had never heard about this before, and the thought of it chilled her to the bone. This same society had sent expeditions to Tibet hunting for an ancient Aryan relic, *Das Buch des Ringes*, or the Book of Dzyan, which they believed contained the secret of the superman. It was madness, complete madness; but she began to wonder if the Book of Dzyan might not have been the focus of Herzog's journey to Tibet.

Nancy logged off feeling sick and confused. She found she was deeply disturbed by the thought not merely of occultists forging paths through Tibet searching for Aryan relics, but also of Anton Herzog embarking on his own version of this quest. For whatever reasons, and she couldn't gauge what they might be, he had followed his father back through a particularly dark and sinister story. Surely he believed that the Book of Dzyan really existed, or perhaps he just wanted to understand his own origins, the strange heritage he had been born into. She didn't know. She sat in the darkness, reeling from what she had learned.

Now what should she do? Where could she turn for advice? She had no experience that she could draw on; she had only ever known the kind of blameless life that is led by the vast majority of people throughout the Western world. All she thought, all her opinions, coincided perfectly with the version of reality that was presented in schools and universities. She was dimly aware that there were other ways of seeing life and history, but she had never really had to imagine what that might mean. But now, here in India and Tibet, new experiences and new ways of looking at the world were tumbling in on her every hour. Her former life in New York suddenly seemed like a daydream; she began to wonder if she had been sleepwalking all these years.

And she was remembering something Herzog had once written, an op-ed piece that had caused something of a stir at the time. When was it? A decade ago, perhaps – she couldn't be certain. He had railed against materialism, the materialist view of reality and history. He had proposed – she was remembering now – that myth and magic coursed through all the seismic moments of history, that almost all the great turning points in history were reached by a handful of people acting on higher urges: revolutionaries, religious maniacs, crusaders and their descendants, the empire-builders. At the time everyone had admired his eloquence – he was overstating the case, they thought, but so beautifully, so richly – the guy could certainly write. It had caused a debate in the letters page: some eminent scholars, a few pundits, all of them swirling around each other, talking learnedly about 'the real'. Now Nancy began to wonder if Herzog had been more in touch with reality than anyone else. Perhaps it was just that she had been in ignorance of the real driving forces of history. She had been living her life in the dark.

Then she remembered that she had to move. She had to get out of the apartment as quickly as possible. She remembered also the Oracle and its insistent, almost shrill advice that she go to Tibet. There was only one person she could think of to whom all this madness might make some kind of sense. She fumbled in her pocket for Jack Adams's card and then punched the number into her cell phone. He had recognized the symbol on the bone trumpet and had even recognized the script, she was sure of that. And he had been prepared to drop his price to find out more. She was quite certain that he knew more than he was letting on, and in any case he was the one person who could take her into Pemako. The phone was answered after only one ring. She could barely hear anything though, there was so much noise in the background. He must be in a bar, she thought. She could go there and find him, then she wouldn't have to mention the fact that she wanted to catch the flight. If the phone was being tapped, she could keep her plans from the police.

'Mr Adams?'

'Yes.'

'I need to talk to you about what we were speaking about earlier – but I can't talk on the phone. I need to meet you face to face. I need to meet now.'

Surely an unreasonable request, she thought to herself, though she was desperate for him to agree. She could hear the noise of the bar diminish; he must have walked away to somewhere quieter. His reply was immediate and deadly serious.

'Come to Rick's Bar at the Taj Mahal Hotel on Mansingh Road, I'll be waiting for you there.'

25

The car pulled slowly out onto the road that ran up the side of the Lhodi Gardens. The Gardens were quiet; a few lonely figures could be seen in the darkness, making their beds or chatting amongst the sparse trees. Beyond, somewhere in the night, lay the dejected gothic ruins of Humayun's tomb. She gazed at the empty scene, all thoughts, all emotion in abeyance. Her experience of life in those seconds was little more than a mood, a hollowness, a feeling of disengagement, as if she was not really in India at all, as if it was all a dream.

She thought again of the Oracle, Anton Herzog's guiding light. Perhaps what the Oracle really means is that you get precisely what you wish for in this life, she pondered, as the car pulled up behind a goods lorry and the night-time traffic began to gather all around. She had longed for more excitement in her life, and more recently she had yearned for distractions that would stop her brooding on her past, would take away her heartbreak, and now she had them in abundance. You get precisely what you wish for, she thought, but you are never able to foresee what that will really mean until it is too late. She still could not believe she had just spoken to James and that she'd felt so little pain. She had been too intrigued by the mystery of Herzog's origins to wallow in their past. But did she really no longer care about him? There was a price to pay for this new perspective on life.

The traffic began to move forward again, in fits and starts, like blood in a clogged artery. She drifted into sleep, dreaming of the Book of Dzyan, the black covers decorated with the snake-entwined ring. There it was before her, resting amid burning ruins of a long-lost city. She stretched her arm out to hold it but it remained out of reach. All around flames rose higher and higher. She was forced back by the heat. The Book of Dzyan alone in the inferno did not burn.

She awoke to the sound of the driver's voice. 'Memsahib, we're here. Please wake up.'

With an effort she opened her eyes; she would gladly have paid him to let her sleep all night. Stiff and tired, she stretched her neck and looked ahead through the windscreen. Here lay the magnificent front entrance to the Taj Mahal Hotel, clearly a six- or seven-star establishment, she thought, judging by the marble and gold atrium and the row of Bentleys waiting in line in front of her cab, taking it in turns to disgorge beautiful young Indian couples on to the glittering forecourt. It reminded her of a movie pre-miere or a fashion shoot.

A minute later it was her turn. With a great effort of will she sat up and grabbed her bag. She was just about to open the door when it was opened for her by a liveried footman. Feeling completely underdressed in khaki trousers and a white shirt, she got out of the car, paid the driver and scuttled into the air-conditioned lobby through a pair of huge double doors that opened before her as she approached.

The cool lobby was a vast expanse of marble and at its centre was a tulip-shaped fountain made of smoked crystal glass. Chairs and tables were scattered around, filled with elegant Indian society, at ease amidst this luxury. The high ceiling was decorated with huge three-yard-wide upturned bowls of light that were covered in elaborate Mughal designs; they reminded Nancy of the exquisite Persian carpets that hang in the Metropolitan Museum in New York.

A smartly dressed Sikh doorman pointed the way to Rick's Bar and she joined a horde of fashionable young Indians, the sons and daughters of fabulously wealthy oligarchs, heading in the same direction. As she walked, she looked at her watch. Nine thirty p.m.;

clearly these people were coming from dinner. What on earth was Jack Adams doing in a place like this?

She passed a group of young Indian women dressed in beautiful saris, and hurried along one more white marble corridor. At Rick's Bar she was greeted by a scene out of a Bollywood movie. To the right was a long green-glass bar top that ran the length of the room, and perched on leather stools all along the bar and draped on each other were yet more exquisitely dressed young Indians. To the right there were sofas and chairs filled with people and everywhere waiters were coming and going, reaching with outstretched arms to collect the empties before ducking out of the way of the guests.

This was the last thing Nancy had been expecting to see after the day's harrowing events. The room was brightly lit and the noise so loud that she could barely hear the waiter. 'Memsahib, may I help you? Would you like a drink? Or are you looking for someone?'

'Yes. Mr Adams. Do you know him?' She was already scanning the room.

'Yes, Memsahib. Please, follow me.'

She struggled to keep up as the waiter weaved through the crowd, until finally they reached the far side of the room. There in the corner, sitting on the edge of a comfortable armchair, looking slightly ill at ease, was Jack Adams. He was talking to a plump-looking Indian man, who appeared to be in his late twenties. The Indian man was lounging back in his chair, and from their body language alone it was quite clear what their relationship was. Adams was trying to sell him antiques, thought Nancy. The waiter bowed to the lounging man and then whispered into Adams's ear. Adams turned and she nodded at him. He nodded back without smiling. Perhaps he was in the middle of an important deal, she thought. He rose to his feet and then bowed to his companion, whose head moved almost imperceptibly in response, and then walked briskly over. He seemed to be very stressed.

'So, you made it. What's the story?'

She took a deep breath.

'I want to catch the plane tonight. I've got $5,000 in travellers' cheques. I'll cash them with the concierge and you can borrow the bone. That's all I can afford – but you get the bone, like you wanted. I just have to be on that plane tonight.'

Jack Adams glanced back at the plump Indian man and then turned to her. If he felt any sense of conflict, he seemed to resolve it quickly.

'Fine,' he said. 'I'll meet you at the concierge desk in two minutes.'

*

Five minutes later a well-manicured hotel employee finished counting out the fresh banknotes and slid them across the marble counter top into Nancy's waiting hands. My nest egg for my new life in Delhi, she thought ruefully. And I'm about to hand it over to this extremely untrustworthy man, all for the pleasure of being flown to Tibet so that I can put myself in even greater danger.

Suddenly she felt Adams's hand clasp her elbow. With a hiss he whispered in her ear. 'Go straight to the elevator and take it down to floor minus one. Then turn right and take the second door on the right marked "Staff only". Then wait in the corridor.'

Urgently, he pushed her towards the bank of elevators on the far side of the marble corridor, then he marched briskly up the grand flight of steps that led to the Marchan Restaurant. In a state of confusion Nancy followed his bizarre command and instructed the bell-boy to take her to floor minus one. The doors opened and she turned right as instructed and found the second door on the right marked 'Staff Only'. Her heart pounding, she pushed open the door and went through to the corridor beyond. It was spotlessly clean like the rest of the hotel, but featureless apart from a door at the far end and two other doors on the right-hand side marked 'Housekeeping'. She was contemplating what to do next when Jack Adams burst through the door at the far end.

'Quick, follow me. Hurry.'

She ran down the corridor towards him and through the open door and into the corner of a noisy underground kitchen.

'Where are we going?' she shouted as they hurried along.

'We're taking the scenic route.'

He grabbed her by the hand and marched her past a smiling cook, dressed in immaculate whites.

'Why?' she cried out.

'Because there's someone up there who seems to want to know where we're going.'

Her heart skipped a beat, but Adams was moving too fast to notice her panic. He dragged her onwards, past a row of gleaming steel workbenches that were covered in neat, identical plates of food, waiting to be taken out to the hotel guests. A chef smiled at them from behind a steaming broiler and shouted to them in Hindi. Adams shouted something back and the chef laughed.

He must have spotted one of the people who was following her – perhaps someone had been standing in the lobby watching her and she hadn't noticed. But then why didn't he ask her who it was? Why didn't he want to find out what was really going on? Surely he must be alarmed to find that she was being trailed? They reached a pair of swing doors. Jack barged through, dragging her along behind him, and they came out into a large underground loading area. A pair of vegetable delivery vans were parked side by side with their doors open, a kitchen porter was examining the contents of a pallet of lettuces that lay on the floor.

'Here,' said Adams before marching her past the delivery vans and over to a beaten-up old car that was waiting with its engine running.

'Right,' he continued, 'we'll leave my own car out front. Let's get a move on, eh, Kim?'

She glanced through the window and now recognized the driver as Adams's helper Kim. Mystified as to what all this meant, she ducked her head and climbed into the cramped and dusty back seat. Kim shifted over into the front passenger seat as Jack took the wheel and gunned the car up the delivery ramp and on to the hotel's service access road. They passed through the back gates and out into the busy evening traffic.

'I'm sorry about that,' Adams said. 'We just had to get out of there as quickly as possible. I saw someone watching you change your travellers' cheques and I was concerned someone had seen us talking in Rick's Bar.'

'I admire your quick thinking,' said Nancy, drily.

'Well, I've had some practice. It's easy to make enemies in the antiques business.'

He swerved around a slow-moving lorry. Stunned into silence, Nancy sank back into the uncomfortable seat, marvelling at the good fortune of this particular case of mistaken identity: Adams had assumed that her pursuers were his own, and she had no intention of disabusing him of his mistake. He turned round one last time, his forehead dripping with sweat.

'We're on our way now. We'll be at Indira Gandhi airport in half an hour, in time for the flight . . .'

26

As the monks carried him aloft through the jungle, Anton Herzog dreamed of his youth in Argentina. Deep in the grip of opium, in a trance-state that dimmed his pain and fear and plunged him deep into his past, the forest dimmed to a blur and then vanished. He was in dusty, sunlit Buenos Aires, in 1954. His mother, Anna, was getting him ready for school when a tall, gaunt, blond-haired man walked through the front door of the house and came straight into the kitchen. Anton was ten years old, playing with his breakfast and being scolded for it by his mother as she prepared him a packed lunch. He was a child again, it seemed, and he was watching his mother with the confusion and adoration of the child. He watched her from below, far below her lofty greatness, as she turned and stared at the man as if she was seeing a ghost, and then Herzog was hearing the man – he was whispering 'Anna, Anna' over and over again, as if he could not believe what he was seeing. There was a crash – and in the jungle Herzog twitched in his stupor, and tried to put out his hands – and now he saw that his mother had dropped everything – the cup she was holding in one hand, the plate from the other. She was oblivious; she did not mind at all. Instead she stepped over to the strange man and embraced him and clasped him to her as if she was afraid that if she didn't he would disappear into thin air.

In the jungle Herzog's mouth twitched, and he said, 'Gustav Deutsch.' The stretcher carrying him wobbled as the monks below stepped over a huge fallen tree trunk. His head lolled crazily but his body was tied in place, he could not fall. One of the monks tried to hear what he was saying – strange words, guttural sounds in a language he did not know.

His head lolling and his body tied, Herzog's thoughts wandered across the globe, over the glittering pampas of Argentina, and now he remembered his eighteenth birthday, when Gustav had taken him away for the weekend on a short walking trip to celebrate his birthday. They were sitting on the side of a mountain overlooking a pine forest and Gustav said that the view reminded him very much of his native Austria, a land he hadn't seen for eighteen years and which he doubted he would ever see again. With the peaceful forest below as a backdrop, Gustav Deutsch had told him for the first time, 'I am your father. My real name is Felix Koenig.'

And Herzog remembered how he had stood up and walked into the woods and cried and cried until night began to fall. He did not know precisely why he was crying. He was young and overwhelmed. He could not understand. And as his head lolled and his body was carried high on a stretcher, tears coursed down Herzog's shattered face; filling the deep hollows of his skull. He remembered how when he finally returned, when the gathering darkness frightened him back to his father again – this man who was now his father, and had ever been, though he had not known – Felix Koenig was still sitting exactly where he had left him, staring at the darkening pine forests below, looking weary and old. They went back to the campsite and lit a fire, and his father told him stories about the fabulous Himalayas, about India and the spice markets of Bombay, and about the holy rivers of Asia and the ancient lamaseries of Tibet.

As the monks carried him along – and he thought that he did not know where they were taking him, and that it no longer mattered – Herzog's whole life passed before his eyes. He remembered his days studying oriental languages at Harvard, his youthful joy when he was offered the job as a cub reporter on the *Washington Post*. His days in Shanghai when he was a stringer, the happiest days of his life; his many journeys to explore the lands of the Chinese wild west: the fabulous cities of the old Silk Road, the vast Gobi and the endless sand sea of the Takla Makan desert; and his annual trips home to Argentina to spend the month with his parents. They had retired to Pilar – the air was better and they had managed to scrape together enough money to buy a small plot of land in the Pampas. There were woods and rivers and mountains in the distance. He remembered how he was taught the *I-Ching* by his father, how they had long conversations about Germany and the war. He had always been obsessed with the war, and what had happened in Germany that had allowed it to come about. An entire civilization had seemingly vanished overnight from the banks of the Rhine to be replaced by a new ethics, a new world order, a new morality. He remembered the endless circular conversations and his father's complete incomprehension of his own motives.

And now one of the monks saw that the white man's face was clenched into a grimace, and his hands were locked into fists, and he was trying to cry out. The skeletal body was tensed, as if anticipating an attack. Where are they taking me? Herzog wondered, but he could not think. He was not sure where he was, and sometimes the rolling motion of the stretcher made him think of a ship in a storm. He was on a ceaseless rolling ocean, and then he was flying – flying in a storm – and then he was sitting in the shade, in the garden in Buenos Aires. The rattling ceased, or he no longer noticed it. His father was beside him, telling him of Shangri-La. 'I have seen it,' he was saying. 'I have seen cities and fabulous oases. I have seen Shangri-La.' He was telling his son how they travelled with Reichsbank notes padding the linings of their fleece coats and bars of bullion, stamped with the swastika, weighing down their mules. In Koenig's memories, Munich and Stalingrad mingled with Bombay and Tibet. His past poured out until it threatened to drown all sense of reality. Herzog had clung to hints and clues, a word here, a sentence there, as a shipwrecked sailor clings to a piece of driftwood, hoping that, if he could just hold on to one thing, then at some future point he would be thrown up on dry land – within touching distance of what had now become his obsession and his dream.

Finally, his father had spoken of a place of unrivalled tranquillity; a valley where the pagodas clung to the precipitous mountain sides like beautiful rare orchids. Such a place as exists only in dreams. He said they arrived there over the mountains and through steep gorges. It had taken them months and cost them the lives of three of their sherpas. They had been on the point of turning back when, early one morning, they awoke to find an emissary from the kingdom waiting up ahead on the path. The emissary was an old Chinese man, who spoke a quaint type of antiquated English and promised them hospitality and rest. They accepted the emissary's invitation and followed him over a treacherous route – a route they would never have found on their own. Finally after two more days' hard climbing among cloud-covered heights, they arrived. Among the pagodas, a deep silence reigned. Through focused meditation, a select brotherhood of Masters guided the world. They were kings of the subconscious mind, their writ extended into the darkest depths of the human soul.

Now Herzog knew he was alert, that he was not dreaming, this was lucid recall – he was struggling through the opium haze to remember everything. A select brotherhood, he was remembering. Through practices developed in former times, they have so improved their minds that they can leave their own egos behind and descend into this communal pool of being and thereby manipulate the fears and desires of the human race. For they are like gods, and all that we witness in our narrow lifetimes, be it war and destruction or peace and plenty, are but tiny fragments of their gigantic schemes. Their psychic machinery turns and empires rise and fall; for we are not the authors of our own destiny. We are but unknowing mortals, tumbling from love to hate and back again, believing in our state of delusion that we control events, that we are the active agents of our own destiny. Rather, we are owned; we are farmed in a sense; we are nurtured and developed, whilst these kings live in splendid glory, in palaces that cling to the walls of heaven itself. And there, in the heart of the palace, in the innermost sanctum, on a lectern where the walls were burnished gold, his father had held in his hands the most sacred and sought-after Aryan relic of all time.

And what was it? Herzog had asked him, and in the jungle his dry mouth framed the question. Inaudibly, and no one turned towards him. There came no answer. What did it look like? No answer. Had Felix Koenig seen these Masters? Yes. And why had he left? What had happened to his compatriots? How could he get to this wonderful land? Silence. Forgetfulness. No memories at all. Something had happened that had caused him to be ejected from this paradise, or he had ejected himself.

A splash of brilliant emerald green. Herzog saw it and believed it was in the past, or in the story his father had told him. But it might have been the forest cover shining in the sun. Then he was dreaming again, a dream within a dream; of high roads, golden highways, fields of beautiful flowers, a stone, a statue, a crystal, a Master, a King, a Queen, a palace, a lover, on an island somewhere in the clouds . . .

'The clouds,' he was muttering, as the monks carried him through the forest. And Herzog knew he was lost, and that he was alone.

27

They parked at a lonely gate in the airport perimeter fence. All around was darkness, except for the lights of aeroplanes rising into the night sky. Nancy walked quickly behind Jack Adams towards a small sentry box where the guard was slumped in his chair, watching television. She wasn't sure if she was supposed to simply ignore the guard or whether she should dig into her bag and present her passport.

Jack turned as she hesitated, and said, 'I've taken care of all that. Just come straight through.'

Surely, she thought, it couldn't be that easy to leave a country without alerting the authorities. Yet when she looked back over her shoulder the guard was still watching television, as if she had never been there.

'How did you do that?' she hissed to Jack Adams, or to his back, as he was setting such a pace she could scarcely keep up with him.

'Are you happy to do this my way?' he said, not turning round.

'I guess I have to be.'

'Great, now let's hurry. The plane has to leave any minute.'

He could make a vague effort to be a little friendlier, she thought. Yet as she came alongside him, she wondered if he was nervous, or just focused on the job in hand. She looked ahead. The tarmac of the airport stretched out into the darkness, a great lake of black. There were lights in the distance, scattered aircraft waiting to take off. Beyond them, the control tower and the low roof of the passenger terminal glowed with artificial light.

'Whose plane is it anyway?'

'A friend. Khaled Hussein.'

She glanced at Jack, expecting him to say something else, perhaps tell her something more about Khaled Hussein, but his lips were pursed. A small airport vehicle towing half a dozen trolleys laden with baggage motored past, an orange light flashing on its roof. Jack barely paused as it passed right in front of them. After another minute of walking, it became obvious which aeroplane they were heading for. She could see the refuelling vehicle packing up and a man in shalwar kameez waiting at the foot of the steps. Jack waved at him.

The aircraft engine was making so much noise that it was impossible to hear anything, so when they reached the steps the man simply gestured to them to board the plane.

Once inside, Nancy did as she was told and strapped herself in next to Jack Adams. The engines were humming noisily; the main door was still open. She nodded briskly when Jack asked if she was ready to go. He seemed less tense now they were on the plane; she acknowledged that to herself, and then she found her thoughts returning to what James had told her and what she had learned on the Internet and from Maya. She could scarcely take it all on board, and so many questions were going round in her head that she found it impossible to gain any distance on it all. The biggest story the world had ever known? What did Herzog mean by that – or was it just a strange boast he had made to his impressionable fiancée? And did the Book of Dzyan really exist? Was there any truth in the old myths? And what about the strange glyph, the symbol on the medal, the hallmark of the Thule Gesellschaft?

She shook her head in despair. And what about Anton, how did he carry the burden of knowing that his father had been a member of a strange esoteric sect, allegedly involved in some of the Nazis' more arcane activities? No one on the *Trib* had ever known about any of this: but then why should they? Herzog had every right to his privacy and it should make no difference whether his father was a pillar of the community or a notorious serial killer. He was his own man; everyone deserved to be judged on their own merits. Nancy had no belief in genetic predetermination, that an evil man would breed an evil son. She would never condemn someone for their parents' sins. But she was aware that while acknowledging the logic of this statement, she was thinking of Herzog differently already.

It was perhaps because of how Anton had behaved. Rather than wanting to forget his father's dubious activities, he appeared to have been reaching back into Felix Koenig's past, trying to draw it into the light. Thousands of Germans, tens of thousands, hundreds of thousands, had family members who were intimately involved in the sins of the Nazi regime. But to resurrect their obsessions, indeed to make this resurrection the driving focus of your own life: that was highly abnormal, not to say dangerous. Perhaps Anton was just taking a historian's interest in his father's work; that would be the generous thing to think. But then he was apparently prepared to abandon his pregnant partner in pursuit of his dream.

The idea that the ancient Aryans, the forefathers of

the Germans, had anything to do with this part of the world seemed far-fetched to Nancy, though she knew she was no expert. Still she kept coming back to her central question: why would an intelligent man such as Herzog – and everyone was in agreement on that point – be chasing Nazi myths? From the little she knew of Nazi mythology it was a hotchpotch of old Norse gods and Wagner's Ring cycle, with a little bit of Satanism thrown in for good measure. In much of the history she had read about this period, the Nazi emphasis on Germanic mythology was treated as pure propaganda, window dressing for the party's lust for power. But the Thule Gesellschaft was no mere window dressing. If the article in the *Guardian* could be trusted, it was the fount from which the entire evil ideology had sprung. And deluded as the Nazis were, the region had a genuine lure, for at least some of them, beyond fetishism and ritual performance. Perhaps there was some truth in what they believed? Anton Herzog clearly thought so; that was the inescapable conclusion.

The aeroplane had begun to taxi, and Jack finally smiled and said to her, 'Cat got your tongue?'

She smiled grimly back at him.

'No. I'm just a little tired. Is everything OK?'

'I hope so,' he said, his smile ebbing away.

'How did we evade all the security people?'

'I have friends if not in high places then at least in the right places,' Jack said, with a shrug.

'Well, it's always nice to take a trip, get to know the region,' said Nancy, trying to make light of the situation. Jack didn't bother to reply.

Nancy was just wondering why his moods seemed to shift around so much, why he was almost debonair one moment and then profoundly charmless the next. But her musings on the compelling subject of Jack's personality disorder were interrupted when Khaled Hussein appeared through the door to the cockpit. He was dressed in shalwar kameez trousers and a small pakul hat. He was handsome, almost feminine with his high cheekbones and delicate features, and he had a neatly clipped beard that framed a wide smile. A quite different prospect from Jack, she thought, though he was probably as inscrutable in his own way.

Khaled sat down in the pilot's seat in front of her and shouted over his shoulder, 'So Jack tells me you are going walkabout in Tibet – you'd better watch out for those crafty old lamas.'

'What do you mean?' Nancy yelled back.

'They'll rip you off. A nice girl like you – full of naive ideas about Tibetan Buddhism. They might even try to buy you as their wife . . .' He was still smiling, though Nancy was not sure if he was being entirely jovial.

'You seem to have a very low opinion of them,' she said.

Khaled put his seatbelt on and tapped the co-pilot on the shoulder in a friendly manner. The co-pilot, who was already wearing headphones, gave him the thumbs-up sign. Hussein turned round in his seat again and leaned towards her so that he could speak at a more normal volume.

'Well, that's probably because I have spent so much time up there. I know what you Westerners think . . . and I know what the lamas are like too.'

Nancy glanced at Jack. He was smiling to himself now, a snide, quite ugly smirk, which made him look like a fox.

Meanwhile, Khaled was continuing. 'I've seen lamas using their rosaries as abacuses, to calculate profit and loss. I've seen some of them attach their prayer wheels to water mills, so that they don't have to turn them themselves. And I've been into monasteries where in public they've denounced the killing of animals but the kitchen storerooms are piled high with mutton and yak meat. And do you know how they kill the animals?'

'No.'

'They are driven over the edge of a cliff – so they kill themselves!' Now Khaled slapped his thigh with grim amusement. 'You see, they are great theologians, those lamas! They know how to get around the word of Buddha!'

Now Jack interrupted. 'I suspect you're boring our guest with your travel tales, Khaled ... And she doesn't believe you anyway.'

Khaled ignored him.

'And the best thing of all are the nunneries! Once I was travelling in the Kongpa region, I was going through a valley, and the nuns were all in the fields, bringing in the wheat. And you know what? They were all topless, toiling away in the hot sunshine! I can tell you, it was quite a sight. About one hundred beautiful young maidens all in the peak of physical condition, and as I passed by the field, every single one made eyes at me. It was incredible! You see they get locked away in nunneries at the age of sixteen – but they are only human. Anyway, that night the Abbess invited me to the nunnery to see them perform a rare Tantric ceremony . . .'

Jack Adams had started to laugh.

'Now, Khaled, you've just lost any credibility you might have had. What kind of young maiden would so much as even look at you, you lecherous old Pashtun?'

Just then the co-pilot said something to Khaled in a language Nancy didn't understand. Khaled snapped his headphones over his ears and said, in a more businesslike tone of voice, 'OK – I'll finish this story later . . .'

'I'm sure Ms Kelly will be on tenterhooks,' said Jack, patting him on the back.

As they turned towards the runway, Nancy said between her teeth, 'Nice friend.'

'He's just trying to entertain you,' said Jack, with a sardonic smile.

'Interesting idea of entertainment. Is there any truth in what he was saying?'

'Sure. There's some truth. You get bad priests in any religion, Buddhism is no exception.'

'It sounds medieval.'

'It's not that bad – he's exaggerating, or talking about how it used to be. Nowadays it's different. Tibet is under attack. Nothing like a bit of oppression to focus the mind; even the Bon seem to be behaving themselves and getting behind the Dalai Lama . . .'

'Are the Bon animists?'

'No, not at all. They're not primitive – it's a sophisticated religion. They're a sort of mirror image of the Tibetan Buddhists. You'll have to ask Herzog when we find him – he knows all about them. I think they are all equally weird: the Bon and the Buddhists.

They all wear the same robes and their gompas look exactly the same as the Buddhist gompas from the outside. But, apparently, in the gompa rituals everything is reversed.'

'What, they literally do all the rituals backwards?'

'Yes. Or maybe the Dalai Lama and his gang are all doing it backwards and the Bon have got it the right way round. Who knows? Ask Anton. Even their swastikas turn in the opposite direction to the Buddhists – the same way as the Nazis' swastikas.'

At this she started.

'So there are swastikas in Tibet – I thought it was a Hindu symbol?'

'Everyone uses swastikas. It's a Hindu and Buddhist symbol. The *Trib* must be going downhill if its correspondents don't even know that . . .'

And now he was smirking at her again, that accusatory, almost hostile expression which made her pause and wonder: what was with this guy? She was wondering if it had something to do with institutions, if he despised her for being a company woman, a journalist within a big corporate newspaper. He had been rampaging around on his own, a lone creature, taking inconceivable risks for whatever he thought of as his work, for so many years, she wondered if he had got to loathing those who toed an official line, who yoked themselves to a particular organization. There was no doubting it, Jack Adams was a maverick, and she could see precisely why Krishna didn't much like him. He was just so changeable. Sometimes he was quite the action hero, suave, confident, and then he became – well, like a drunkard, or a lost soul – clearly self-destructive, or destructive of everything. Everything and most likely everyone, she thought, and shivered in her seat.

Jack took the cushion from his seat and jammed it behind his head.

'Right, I'm going to get some rest ... In a few hours the sun will be up ... Remember to wear your seatbelt at all times. Over the Himalayas, there are lots of air pockets – a small plane like this can drop a hundred feet in a couple of seconds. I've seen people break their necks on the ceiling ...'

'Kind of you to be concerned,' she said.

'Well, if you break your neck, I don't get paid,' he said, roughly, but again with a creeping sort of humour, and then he shut his eyes.

Nancy stared out the window into the darkness as the engines roared, and the lights of Delhi spread out beneath her.

28

In the darkness of the jungle, the Abbot's deputy studied Anton Herzog with suspicion in his eyes and asked the question again, to make sure the white man understood.

'You flew to Lhasa four months ago?'

Herzog nodded. He was calmer now, and he had opened his eyes. His dreams had receded. He saw the jungle all around, heard the clicking of prayer beads and the murmuring of the monks. And this old man before him, he knew him to be a lama, and he sensed he was afraid.

'Yes,' Herzog said quietly. 'If you say we are in the Seventh month now, then yes, it was four months ago.'

The Abbot's deputy breathed a sigh of relief. Finally, the white man was making some sense. He had taken a little food and water and his voice was stronger now, his train of thought more cogent. And yet, his claim was preposterous: he could not have been to Shangri-La. Speaking loudly and slowly, aware of the fragility of the white man's reason, the Abbot's deputy said, 'Why did you go to Pemako?'

'Everything that I have been working on led me to believe that, at last, I had a clear idea of where I ought to look.' The white man broke into a fit of coughing before recommencing. 'Through a process of triangulation, involving my father's stories, and my own decades of research in the dusty libraries of a hundred Himalayan lamaseries and the thousands upon thousands of hours I have spent talking to gurus and monks, I had narrowed down my search to the high southern valleys of Pemako that open out on to the Tsangpo valley floor.'

'How could you be so sure?'

'All the evidence pointed to Pemako, but in the end, just to be certain, I consulted the Oracle. In one of the least ambiguous readings I have ever received from it in all my years of practice, it ordered me to go . . .'

The Abbot's deputy looked sceptical.

'And you left everything – your job – you say you are a journalist?'

'It is my job to travel and research stories. I never planned to be away this long. Besides, my past life is trivial, it is nothing more than preparation for this final journey. I don't care what they think – this is the end. I don't give a damn about the newspaper, I don't give a damn about my former life.'

'You were travelling alone?'

'No. I was travelling with a terton, a lama by the name of Thupten Jinpa. I had hired him to aid me in finding the gate. I had decided against sherpas, so we were carrying our own supplies. I have studied the Tantric practices, I can survive on a handful of tsampa a day, even when undertaking strenuous exercise . . .'

The white man paused to cough violently again. He is dying, thought the Abbot's deputy. He thought this quite calmly, and wondered how much longer this shattered body could remain alive. Perhaps only until his story is told, he thought. Perhaps then, he will journey to the Bar Thodal. He would never make it into the Caves, he would never survive the descent.

'We descended into the Tsangpo valley,' the man was saying in a low voice. 'We crossed the river by the metal cable just below Litang monastery – your monastery. We did not want to draw attention to ourselves so we avoided contact with your monks and headed through the jungle, navigating by the surrounding peaks. Finally, we reached our first destination: a small abandoned hermitage two days' walk from Litang gompa. It was our plan to undergo the Tantric practice of metok chulen. You are familiar with it?'

'No. I know of it but our order does not permit its use.'

'Well, it is good for purifying the mind, and Terton Jinpa was convinced it would show us the way to the hidden path that my father spoke of. The hermitage was nothing more than four stone walls with a roof that just managed to keep out the rain. It was situated on a small hill, surrounded by fields of rhododendrons that eventually gave way to the vegetation of the forest. Just in front of the hut was a small patch of earth, where one could meditate with a fine view over the surrounding fields and into the edges of the lush forest. Terton Jinpa began by making a paste from crushed flower petals. His recipe used eighteen different species of wild flowers, some of them unique to Pemako valley and all containing rare phyto-chemicals that stimulate particular elements of the brain or body.

'We fasted for twenty-one days, during which time we ate nothing and only drank one cup of water a day, infused with the terton's flower extract. By the fifth day I thought that I was going to die. My head was aching as if it was being crushed in a vice and my eyes were throbbing in their sockets. My tongue seemed to be glued to the roof of my mouth; my cheeks stuck to my gums. We could barely lift our limbs, and simply sat cross-legged outside the hermitage day and night, unless it rained, in which case we would retreat into the dark of the hut. When I closed my eyes all I could see, hear and feel was water; the rolling waves of an endless freshwater ocean. By the fifteenth day, a strange transformation came over me. All the pain began to subside. At first it was replaced by a feeling of fatigue and light-headedness, but then that too passed and I felt as if my mind had expanded to take in the entire valley. When I opened my eyes and looked at the multicoloured butterflies and birds that moved from flower to flower in front of the hermitage, I felt as if I was floating with them and sucking the nectar from among the petals of the wildly beautiful orchids. When I saw the deadly green and red diamond vipers crawl past me on the ground, I was not afraid. I felt as if I was at peace with the snakes and they would do me no harm. The monkeys came up to us and gently stroked us, and once a jaguar appeared from the forest and crossed the field and licked my cheek. The metok chulen was successful, we had left our bodies behind and entered the valley.

'On the twenty-first day, I awoke and the terton had prepared flower tea, into which he mixed a very small amount of tsampa. I hardly wanted to take it, so keen was I to maintain my state of blissful union with the surrounding nature, but he pressed it on to me and insisted that I drain every last drop. We then collected our meagre belongings and without exchanging a word set off in a direction that both was and was not of our choosing. Even though we stuck to no path but gently meandered through the jungle, we never once hesitated and we never once turned back or changed our course. Some other instinct or intelligence led us on our way.

'This went on for three days, with brief pauses every five hours or so for more flower tea and tsampa. Finally on the evening of the third day we had climbed out of the forest and were scrambling along a scree path towards a pass that we had not noticed before and which was not marked on any of the lamas' maps. The path seemed to go on for ever and in my weakened state, not having eaten now for almost a month, I became delirious and was barely able to put one foot in front of another. It was then that disaster struck. The terton, who was just ahead of me on the path, slipped on the scree and in a second vanished from sight down the side of a gorge. In a state of acute despair, I came a hair's breadth from throwing myself after him. Somehow, I managed to retain the last vestiges of my senses and step by step I picked a tortuous path down to the bottom of the gorge. The terton was dead.'

Anton Herzog had paused. If he was expecting a reaction from the Abbot's deputy, none came. There was just the rain and the background noise of the forest: the animals hooting, the birds calling from their perches in the branches. The Abbot's deputy was staring in horror and confusion at the man before him. He did not know what to think; he certainly could find nothing to say. After a minute's silence, Herzog began again.

'Starved and with my sensitivities heightened by the disciplines of recent weeks, I stood for a long time at the bottom of this gorge, wailing my grief. Somehow, I managed to drag the terton's body into the sunlight of the scree slope. There, in the cool, crystalline air of the mountains, I prepared his corpse for sky-burial. I was so weakened I could barely do this, even though I had an Indian army knife. Once I had chopped him up and the beastly griffin vultures had massed and were impatiently awaiting their feast, I retired to a rock higher up the hill and lay down in terrible exhaustion.

'In this state I must have lain for two days and two nights, wrapped in a yak's-wool coat, a chuba, starved to the point of madness. With no more flower tea to maintain my psychic functions, my mind and body began to shut down. Gazing up into the darkness, I floated over the Himalayas and visited the stars and the moon. I journeyed with the terton to the abyss and saw the sea of eternity below. I was slipping from this realm and I began to feel that this would not be so grave, that I had far to travel . . .

'And then, a hand touched my shoulder. When I managed to focus my weary eyes I saw a Chinese man, of sixty or so years. He was speaking to me and pressing a water bottle to my lips. It contained a sweet liquid that warmed me to the core. Revived a little, I sat up and discovered that this man was accompanied by several sherpas. He himself travelled in a curtained chair, carried by four of the sherpas. He spoke to me in Chinese, and when I explained where I was from he addressed me in precise and perfectly accented English. "Welcome. You are very lucky. We only pass this way once every ten years. We have little need of contact with the outside world. You must come with us to our lamasery and we will help you to regain your strength."

I could scarcely believe my ears. I was indeed lucky. But I had questions. "I am most grateful for your offer and willing to accept it. But perhaps you can help me? Am I far from Shangri-La? Is that the name of you lamasery?'

'No,' said the Chinese man. 'You are not far. Stay with us. You will find our hospitality to be most generous.'

'I could hardly contain my joy. In my father's tale of his own visit, he had described how he had been invited to visit Shangri-La by an old Chinese man who spoke beautiful English. So, not only had I been saved from death but I suspected I was about to be led into the heart of the sacred kingdom. The coyness of the Chinese man as to whether or not Shangri-La was the name of his lamasery did not surprise me at all; it was all quite in keeping with the mythology of the place.

'He helped me into his chair, and for the next five hours he walked beside me whilst the sherpas climbed ever higher up until finally, eventually, we crossed over the pass and the path began to descend steeply . . .'

Now a thickset monk had stepped over to the side of the Abbot's deputy and was whispering in his ear. Herzog heard a rustling, like leaves, as the monks conferred. And in the jungle, something was stirring; he felt it deeply. A force, something was coming for him. He knew they would find him; it was simply a matter of time. He had no fear. There was little he could do now; the time when he might have exerted some control over events had long gone. Something urgent was being said. Though Herzog could not lift his head to see it, the Abbot's deputy was looking anxious, and now he said, 'We cannot stay here any longer. There are dark tidings; we have to leave at once. We are taking you to safety.'

'To safety?' asked Herzog, with hope in his voice.

'Yes. To the holy city of Agarthi. But we must leave at once.'

With that the Abbot's deputy gave an order and the entire company of monks sprang to their feet. The youngest monks lifted Herzog on his stretcher once more; he felt his head tipping backwards, and then the familiar rolling motion began again. Aloft, he thought, drifting like a leaf in the wind, or bark on a storm-lashed sea. And below him, his face set grimly, the old lama began to lead the sodden and bedraggled collection of monks through the darkness of the night, through the cloying embrace of the ever-moving forest.

29

'Chomolongma! Chomolongma!'

The shouting woke Nancy with a start. She could not recall when she had dozed off – she remembered the take-off and for some time she had watched Hussein and the co-pilot as the plane rose through the night towards the Himalayas and Tibet. Then her jetlag had overwhelmed her, and now she had no idea how much time had passed. She saw the co-pilot grinning at her and pointing at the window with his gloved hand. Khaled Hussein was nowhere to be seen. The sun was up and for a moment, because of the way the sunlight was being refracted through the glass of the windscreen, Nancy couldn't see anything but the crystalline blue of the sky. She rubbed her bleary eyes and twisted her neck from side to side and then leaned forward to take in the view.

'Chomolongma! Mother Goddess of the Universe!' the co-pilot said.

It was the most breathtaking sight she had ever seen. Level with the aeroplane, off to the right, was the most enormous and beautiful white mountain.

'Mount Everest?'

The pilot made the thumbs-up sign. The snow-covered slopes of the mountain rose up to a crinkled peak that looked like a fabulous Arabian headdress, pleated and folded to hide the modesty of the Goddess's face. Below, an infinite distance further down, a river curled like an azure necklace around the mountain's base. In all directions, snowy peaks extended towards the horizon – like a thousand worshippers reaching upwards to touch the Heavens, thought Nancy. The vastness of the mountain suggested a realm completely beyond the human, something scarcely comprehensible to the brain. She glanced briefly to her side and saw that Jack Adams was awake – he was staring down at the seemingly endless depths of the valleys below. In a low voice, he said, 'It reminds me of something Anton once said: "Hell is the mould for heaven." The way the valleys are like the mountains except upside down.'

Nancy stared in wonder at the bottomless crevasses and ravines that opened up in all directions below. It was true; they looked like plaster of Paris moulds she had played with as a child. The valleys were the mirror image of the mountains, she thought, or their natural opposite. Yin and Yang. Occasionally, she could pick out an alpine valley, a splash of emerald green in the white and grey of the massive mountains.

'Such a beautiful hell, though, just as lovely as heaven,' she said. 'I wouldn't mind which one I ended up in.'

She peered forwards so that she could almost look straight down: were those tiny dwellings that she could see, clinging to the green slopes of a valley? Half to herself, she said:

'I wonder what the people who live down there know of us. I bet they're happier than we are.'

Jack laughed, and she imagined he was once more mocking her for her ignorance. But then he said, 'Now that really sounds like Anton. I've heard him going on about the perfect isolation of the valleys – how people who lived here would be able to survive anything, even nuclear war and the end of civilization. He thought that these valleys were the best hiding places that you could ever dream of.'

'Have they all been surveyed?'

'No. Far from it. It's an impossible task. They can't even be surveyed from the air. Who knows what is down there? I know sherpas who swear on their souls that there are other mountains higher than Everest and that there are kingdoms and peoples that we know nothing about. And the lamas take it as historical fact that some of the valleys were used as refuges during the last Ice Age. The seeds of civilization have been kept alive here many times over, while the rest of the world has frozen or burnt . . .'

Nancy laughed nervously, struggling to process what he was saying.

'Now who's sounding like Anton?'

Just then, the co-pilot motioned with his right hand down towards a gorge that splintered at the base of the great mountain.

'Lhasa – Gongkar airport!'

The plane banked in a graceful arc, turning towards the gorge.

On the tarmac at the airport, 12,000 feet above sea level, Jack and Hussein were talking earnestly to a pair of Chinese soldiers. Nancy waited by the aeroplane steps, breathing the thin, cold Himalayan air for the first time. The purity of the atmosphere seemed to heighten the brilliance of the light, so that she squinted in the glare. Two hundred yards away, a fuel truck trundled slowly across the tarmac towards a waiting plane. Everything was swimming in this clear, blinding light. It made Nancy feel ecstatic and at the same time slightly dizzy.

A package was pushed into the hands of one of the Chinese soldiers. The other smoked, and looked bored. Something seemed to have been resolved among them. Now Jack motioned to Nancy to join them, and she followed him into a waiting army jeep. Khaled had vanished silently away, without saying goodbye. On the jeep, no one was smiling. Jack was looking around the airport, as if he feared a threat might emerge from any direction. She sensed the tension and anxiety. If they were caught attempting to bribe the Chinese soldiers, who knows what would happen – to them, to the soldiers themselves. They passed through a gate in the perimeter fence, and turned onto a dusty road, clouds of dust pierced by sunlight. With a sputter, the truck paused and the soldiers nodded to Jack.

'Here's where we get out,' said Jack to Nancy. She stepped down from the truck. As soon as they were on the ground, the truck turned and roared back through the gate. As they stood in a cloud of dust, coughing out their relief, Jack said:

'Jesus, that gets worse every time. Now, let's see if we can get a lift down to Lhasa . . .'

Their furtive progress, thought Nancy. Bribing guards, sneaking past security gates, and naturally it was all entirely illegal. She had never done this sort of work before. She sensed this was only the beginning, that she would break many more rules before this was all over.

'Come along,' Jack was saying. 'We'll admire the view later.'

30

She walked past oxblood-red and white walls, up zigzag
flights of steps, until finally there it was before her: the
Potala Palace, floating like a lone ship in the sea of
clouds high above Lhasa's main square. It dwarfed all
the other buildings in the capital. The biggest temples
and lamaseries of western Tibet would fit inside it
many times over. But it was a sad sight, thought
Nancy. For centuries it had buzzed with life: home to
thousands of monks, it had housed vast libraries and
enormous dining halls that could feed hundreds at a
sitting. Now it was deserted, as empty and echoing as
an abandoned city. There were no lamas filing in and
out of the great doors, on pilgrimages from far-flung
corners of the Tibetan empire. No monks tended the
tens of thousands of butter lamps that lined the
interior corridors; there was no need. Masses were no
longer chanted night and day to crowded rooms and
in the dark recesses and quiet cloisters.

No, it was clear to Nancy that the Palace was nothing but an empty husk, a memorial to former greatness. There was something grave about its unsymmetrical white and red walls – it reminded her of a photo she had once seen of the *Ark Royal* aircraft carrier, after it was retired from service and put into dry dock before being dismantled. From the very top, on the highest golden tower, a Chinese flag fluttered in the breeze. A handful of monks kept up a semblance of activity, but in reality the heart of the fortress–cathedral had long since stopped beating. The main visitors to the place were aged caretakers, carrying juniper broomsticks, or monks in the pay of the Chinese secret police, come to sniff around. Outside, soldiers were keeping careful watch. Chinese tourists were milling around having their photos taken. Some of them had purchased traditional Tibetan chubas, and were posing for the camera.

Nancy and Jack stood in silence, until eventually Jack said, 'The first time I saw it, it wasn't like this at all. It had a different feel.'

He sounds almost distressed, thought Nancy, as if he cares passionately. She glanced at him, but he was staring up at the Palace, his face impassive.

He continued, in a harder tone, 'Which is odd, because even then it was pretty much disused. I think that people still believed that Tibet would be free, and so when they looked at the building it was still a symbol of hope, whereas now it is a reminder of failure – failure to throw off the Chinese.'

'When was that?'

'Oh – years ago now. It was when Tibet was virtually impossible to get into – unless you had masses of cash and came in on a guided tour. I didn't – I was a student, so I hitch-hiked in from Sichuan province. It was quite a journey. Eleven days in the back of a lorry that was carrying flour up to Lhasa. I had to sit in the back the whole way because the driver was so terrified of being stopped. I slept on the bags of flour – quite comfortable actually. By the end I was completely white – the flour got into every pore of my skin and every inch of my clothes. The only window was a tiny little gap just above the lorry cab. I had to stand on tiptoes on the bags of flour to see out of it. On the eleventh day, we were driving across the Lhasa plateau and I looked out and on the horizon I could see the white walls and gold stupas of the Potala Palace. It was the closest I've ever come to a religious experience . . .'

He lapsed into silence. Curious, thought Nancy. He seems completely sincere. In the depths of his ragged and compromised soul, there is still something, something almost pure, almost meditative, she thought. And then the hardened exterior, all the cynicism and toughness – she wondered what the balance was, how much softness there remained within him. Not so much, she suspected, just a tiny kernel. But she didn't know. Now Jack leaned close to her – she thought he might be about to reveal something else, some further aspect of his inner life, but instead he whispered, 'Let's get going to Balkhor market and the Jokhang Temple, that's where the Tibetan quarter is. But don't discuss anything to do with the trip while we are in public. Half these so-called tourists will be spies. They are paid to walk around and eavesdrop on people's conversations . . . Stay close to me and don't discuss anything till we get inside the Blue Lantern tea house.'

She glanced around at the little groups of Chinese, photographing one another. They didn't look like spies, but then what did she know? She shifted the weight of her bag on her shoulder, and turned for one last glimpse of the unhappy palace. Then she followed Jack across the square.

31

They walked through streets filled with beggars and pilgrims, confused-looking nomads from the steppes and ambling tourists, until they came to Jokhang Temple, its thick stone walls reminiscent of a medieval European castle. As an aside, Jack explained to Nancy that this similarity was often pointed out by the Chinese in their anti-Lamaist propaganda. The reason for these massively sturdy walls was that like all of the gompas in Tibet, the Jokhang monastery was designed to double up as a fortress.

'Tibet was a wild and dangerous land,' he told her, 'and before the Chinese came, the Dalai Lama's remit often didn't extend that far beyond the gates of Lhasa. Tales abound of his emissaries to western and eastern Tibet being thrown into ditches and laughed at. Outposts of Lamaism had to be able to defend themselves, from Chinese and Mongol invaders but also from recalcitrant Tibetan lords.'

Jokhang Temple was fronted by a cobbled square and a cobbled lane that ran right around the perimeter of its great stone walls. This lane, sandwiched between the massive walls and the stout Tibetan houses that made up the native quarter, was the home of an immense market. Glancing at the stalls, Nancy noticed that the market seemed to be more exclusively Tibetan than those in other streets they had been through. There were no Chinese stalls selling roasted nuts and chicken feet, as she had seen nearer to the Potala Palace.

And now Nancy watched in amazement as a man walked to the centre of the cobbled square. He seemed to be a young monk, lean as a whip, his face bronzed the colour of teak by the elements. He stood and flung his arms towards the heavens and then he collapsed onto his knees before finally lying flat on his front on the ground. Then, after a brief pause he picked his weary body from the street, took a step forward and then the cycle began again. Surely he must be in enormous pain each time he knelt on the ground, though the look on his face was of pure bliss. How far has he come, she wondered, advancing like a centipede, and almost as slowly? A level of religious devotion almost unimaginable in the West these days.

Where is Jack? she thought suddenly. She had been distracted by the bizarre and moving sight. Turning frantically a few times, she managed to locate him: he had marched off down the lane into the depths of the market. Had it not been for his height and shock of blond hair, he would have been lost to sight. Cursing him under her breath, Nancy shot after him, struggling through the crowds. Fifty yards up ahead he suddenly stopped and turned and ducked under a low doorway and into what she assumed must be the Blue Lantern.

32

The walls of the tea house were black from the centuries of butter-lamp smoke. The floor was made of flagstones, the furniture primitive but sturdy: low wooden benches and stout three-legged stools. There were half a dozen tables around which sat young men, some in cheap Chinese suits, others in casual sportswear. A couple of the men were wearing trilbies, and all of them seemed to be smoking. The tea house had an atmosphere of gangland menace, thought Nancy, and she kept her head down as she passed among the benches. At the far end of the room was a small bar and beyond it a doorway opened onto what was clearly the kitchen. The small windows were nothing more than grey smudges in the unhealthy dark.

Jack was talking to the man behind the bar. Self-consciously, Nancy crossed the room to join him, and for all the gloom she was aware that she was nonetheless being scrutinized as she walked. They turned unsmiling faces on her, and she tried not to meet their eyes. Jack was speaking in Tibetan, so when she reached him she was obliged to wait, uncomprehending, all the time thinking of what she had discovered and what it might mean.

Indeed, she had to admit to herself that she was regretting her impetuousness. She had thought that finding Herzog would be a useful thing to do, somehow honourable, that she would be doing a good turn for a colleague she had always admired, even hero-worshipped. She had not imagined he would emerge as such an ambiguous and troubling figure. Nancy wondered if she should tell Jack what she had discovered, about her confusion, her apprehension. He and Anton Herzog had never been great friends, but at least he knew something of Herzog's ambitions. He might be able to help her process the information. Or perhaps she should just announce that she had decided to leave. Jack wouldn't care at all. He would take the money and she would never hear from him again. She looked across at him as he talked, and wondered at his rudeness, that he failed even to acknowledge her as she stood there. She was, after all, his employer. Perhaps he was finding out useful information, or perhaps he was just playing another of his bizarre power games, or generally acting up: it made her click her tongue impatiently, and she rolled her eyes and hoped he was noticing how bored she was.

Perhaps it worked. After a minute or so, the barman flipped open a section of the bar top and led them to the last remaining table, all the while talking to Jack in a low voice. A young red-cheeked Tibetan girl appeared, carrying two big steaming bowls of food, and a second girl came from the kitchen clutching a large samovar of tea, from which she poured out two thimble-sized cups.

'Momos,' said Jack, smiling and nodding at the steaming bowls of food, 'Tibetan dumplings. Eat them. They'll keep your energy up. And the Blue Lantern has never poisoned me yet . . .'

Jack nodded to the waitresses. Then he leaned over the narrow table and whispered, 'You are about to meet Gunn Lobsang, he is a friend of mine and my fixer in Lhasa. Please don't do or say anything that will make him nervous.'

'Sure,' said Nancy. 'I know this isn't my element exactly, but I'm not a complete fool.'

'I'm glad to hear it,' said Jack, with a slight edge to his voice. 'Just remember he's taking a major risk in talking to us.'

'Of course,' she said, bridling anew, and he subsided and took a spoonful of his dumplings. Nancy sighed in exasperation and began to eat her food. Hot, tasty, it was exactly what she needed, and she felt her spirits palpably reviving as she ate.

She was just feeling improved enough to think again about explaining things to Jack, when the door opened and a tall young Tibetan walked in. He was wearing a leather cowboy hat that he didn't remove, and a tough-looking tweed jacket. He glanced around the room, clearly registering who was there, and then walked over to Nancy and Jack's table.

'Tashi Delek, Jack. Long time no see.'

The two men embraced each other briefly.

'Who's your friend?'

'Nancy Kelly. We came by the usual route . . .'

The Tibetan put his hands together in prayer and bowed briefly to her.

'Pleased to meet you, Miss Kelly.'

Then he turned straight back to Jack and said something in Tibetan.

Jack responded in English, 'She's trustworthy, Gunn. I can vouch for her.'

Gunn flashed a glance at her and then with a flick of his hand he ordered tea from one of the girls who hovered behind the bar. Then he turned to Jack again.

'What are you doing back in Tibet my friend? You know things have got much worse? Tenzin was thrown in jail last month. The police are arresting anyone they feel like nowadays – even the Tibetan police. And young people are just interested in money – they don't care about freedom any more . . .'

'Well, that's capitalism for you – it makes people selfish and only interested in feathering their own nests. I don't think Marx realized quite how effective this can be at preventing revolution – but maybe the Chinese do . . .' said Jack, shrugging expansively.

The girl returned with the samovar and a thimble cup for Gunn. He took out a packet of cigarettes, tapped it on the table and then offered them to Nancy and Jack, who both refused.

When he had lit his cigarette and enjoyed a long drag, he said, 'The only good thing is that it's getting easier to move around. Nowadays anyone can be bought, for a price . . .'

He drew on his cigarette again. Nancy studied his handsome face, momentarily distracted from her inner turmoil by his presence. Handsome and yet prematurely aged. As a rule Tibetans aged very well, better than Caucasians, but Gunn Lobsang's face carried the scars of a dangerous and stressful life. Jack nodded.

'So, you can get us into Pemako?'

The Tibetan blew two huge plumes of smoke through his nostrils, and watched them drift across the dumpling bowls.

'Sure. If you really want to go to that hellhole.

Lorry to Pome and then walk over the Su La from the Bhaka gompa. I can get you to Pome but you're on your own from there.'

Now Gunn broke into Tibetan again. After listening for a few moments, Jack looked at Nancy and smiled.

'Gunn is concerned about whether you are fit enough to get over the Su La. It's a reasonable question, as if you fail then we might all die.'

Nancy turned to the Tibetan. He nodded at her; he didn't seem at all abashed.

'You don't have to worry about me,' she said flatly. But Gunn continued to stare at her, assessing her, she supposed. Then he said:

'Why do you want to go to Pemako anyway, Miss Kelly?'

The question surprised her. She didn't know what to say and before she could formulate an answer, Jack butted in.

'We're looking for Anton Herzog – he went into Pemako and hasn't come back out.' He shrugged across at Nancy. 'I'm sorry, Ms Kelly, but I am not telling lies to Gunn, or any of my other friends in Tibet. Besides, Gunn knows Anton.'

Now Gunn took a drag on his cigarette, and looked from Jack to Nancy.

'So you're a friend of Anton's?' he asked her.

'Not a friend, a concerned colleague. We both work for the *International Herald Tribune*.'

'And why do you want to find him?'

'Because he's lost.'

'Many people are lost, Ms Kelly. Why him?'

'I have to confess that my motives are quite complicated,' said Nancy. If the guy was going to take a major risk for her, she too should be as honest as possible. Besides, if she wasn't, Jack would be anyway, it seemed. 'That is, perhaps I am not entirely sure of them myself. But throughout this I have had a strong sense that Anton Herzog is in terrible danger. He is a danger to himself, perhaps. I think he is lost both physically, but also there is something else, something worse: I can't really explain it. He needs help.'

'That wasn't what you said to me in Delhi,' said Jack. Now he was staring hard at her.

'Well, I've been thinking more about it since we arrived.' She met his gaze, felt the force of his scepticism, and tried to weather it.

Then the Tibetan began to speak, and Jack turned to face him.

'He passed through here last year – December I think. Herzog is a strange man; a powerful man. We Tibetans call him a white magician. I saw him here, in the Blue Lantern, talking to people.'

So he had been here, Nancy thought. He sat here,

only three months ago. Doing what? Relaxing, before he embarked on his crazy quest. Or he was in search of leads. He would have been nervous perhaps, or maybe he was so beguiled by thoughts of what he would find that he wasn't thinking about the risks at all. She thought of him, this man she had always regarded fundamentally – for all his brilliance – as just another journalist with the same fears and desires and professional ambitions as herself. And to think that back then she had been on the other side of the world, knowing nothing of the Thule Society or the Book of Dzyan.

'Why don't you wait until he comes back? Pemako is not a holiday destination,' said Gunn.

Jack interjected drily, 'My thoughts entirely.'

Nancy didn't even bother to respond to Jack's comment. Instead, her eyes fixed on the Tibetan, she replied, 'It's not that simple. If I just thought he was on some journey and had been delayed, then I wouldn't bother. But as I said, I'm convinced something has gone dreadfully wrong. He sent a sort of message, I think it was a cry for help. It felt at the time like a summons. As I said before, I am not entirely sure.'

Gunn looked at her pityingly.

'If something's happened to Anton Herzog, I don't see what you can do about it. I doubt very much you are as good a climber as he is, and he also speaks fluent Tibetan – and he knows how to live down there. He has studied Tantric yoga. He can go native if he needs to, reappear in a few years' time . . .'

She brushed him off. Though she had faltered, had even recently thought of giving up the venture, she found that his pessimism was only galvanizing her again.

'Do you know where he was going – did he tell you when you saw him?' she asked.

Gunn paused for a moment and stroked his beard. As he did so, Nancy noticed that the back of his hand had two painful-looking scars on it, as if he had once been burned by a cigarette. The idea sprang into her head that perhaps he had been tortured at some point. By the Chinese, she assumed, and for what? What had he done to attract their attention?

Speaking slowly, Gunn answered, 'No. I can't remember what he said – but everyone's pretty secretive these days. He just wanted me to help him find a lift to Pome. He was travelling with a companion . . .'

Now Jack and Nancy spoke at the same time: 'Who?'

It had never occurred to Nancy that Herzog might not be travelling alone, or that someone else might be involved in his research. Nancy had always thought of him as a loner. Gunn Lobsang exhaled another enormous plume of cigarette smoke that entirely hid his face in the darkness of the tea house. Then he leaned close in to them and said in a hoarse whisper, 'He was travelling with the Terton Thupten Jinpa.'

33

'My God,' whispered Jack in horror. 'What on earth was he doing with a terton?'

Gunn Lobsang shook his head and sighed heavily.

'I have no idea. As you know, I keep away from people like that. I think Thupten Jinpa is a Bon master, though he is supposed to belong to the Geluk order, the same as the Dalai Lama. I think he is a sorcerer.'

Nancy couldn't contain herself any longer.

'What the hell is a terton?'

The two men stared at her as if she was mad. Then, with a pained expression, Jack began, 'A terton is a treasure hunter ... He or she can find the terma. Or at least they say they can ... They use Tantric practices, very esoteric ones, to help bring the termas back from the upper worlds ...'

'And you were saying that a terma is some kind of gateway to another world?'

Gunn's eyes flicked on to Jack, and again the Tibetan muttered in his native language.

Jack waved him away with his hand and answered in English, 'Gunn, she's only been in town for two hours, give her a break. Besides, the Dalai Lama says it's good to know nothing of sorcery ... She is pure in heart – she knows nothing of the Black Bon and their magic ...'

Angrily the Tibetan cut in, this time in English, 'You can call it pure in heart, but you know as well as I do that there are grave risks attached to such innocence, or ignorance you could call it instead.'

Desperate not to lose the single thread that linked her to Anton Herzog, Nancy tried to mollify Gunn Lobsang.

'Listen, I'm sorry – I don't know much about what you talk of but I'm on a kind of pilgrimage all the same, and I heard that in Tibet pilgrims are supposed to be helped and respected.'

Gunn fell into a brooding silence. Jack spoke again, and this time Nancy felt grateful to him. He was defending her; he was trying to bring the Tibetan on board. He said, 'Look, I said before – it's a difficult thing to define. Let's say a terma is sacred knowledge that has been hidden in former times so that, if dark days come, it can be rediscovered and brought back to help us. The tertons are the monks that can find the terma and bring them back to us. That's right, isn't it, Gunn?'

The Tibetan was still looking a little surly.

'Yes.'

He lit another cigarette and then his eyes flashed at Nancy.

'But there are a lot of black magicians who want to acquire the power of the terma . . . that is why people are always suspicious of those who try to seek them out.'

'So tertons are black magicians?' said Nancy.

'No. Not necessarily. In the past there have been white monks who were tertons as well. Some of the greatest lamas were tertons. But nowadays, most people want the terma to remain hidden. What if they fell into the wrong hands?'

Nancy was desperately trying to follow the conversation. The correspondences with the Book of Dzyan were too obvious to ignore.

'So the Book of Dzyan must be a terma then?'

The change in Gunn Lobsang's expression was instantaneous and complete. Before he had been irritated and lofty, now he was thunderstruck. With his mouth ajar, he said, 'How do you know about the Book of Dzyan?'

'I read about it – in a newspaper article. It just sounded a bit like a terma.'

'The Book of Dzyan would be a terma if it existed – which is highly unlikely,' Gunn Lobsang answered, without taking his eyes off Nancy. 'If it existed, it would be the most valuable antique in the entire world. It would be a terma containing specific knowledge from very, very ancient times – from one or two yugas ago. Knowledge of how to make the superman . . . Some lamas say that it might be a black book – but not all.'

The Black Book, thought Nancy, immediately remembering that that was the Chinese name for the Book of Dzyan.

'You mean its covers are black?'

'No. I mean it is evil. It is a black terma. A terma from the dark side – that only a Bon master or a black monk can bring down from the upper worlds.'

Jack Adams let out a theatrical sigh.

'Right – I need a beer. This is getting way too heavy for my liking. Waiter, beer please! Over here.'

34

'That's all I can tell you. What Anton was actually doing with the Terton Thupten Jinpa I have no idea . . .'

Looking hard at Nancy, Gunn added, 'But one thing I can tell you for sure is that even a sorcerer like him wouldn't be stupid enough to try to find the Book of Dzyan.'

Nancy Kelly was not so sure. She would much rather Gunn had told her things that had contradicted all that she had learnt about the history of the Thule Gesellschaft's involvement with Tibet, but that wasn't to be. The gossamer-like threads that had seemed to possibly link the dark world of Second World War Europe to modern-day Tibet were turning into heavy and unbreakable chains. Although she could not yet make sense of it all, she felt as if her journey was in the grip of an unstoppable momentum.

'Is there anyone else who might know where they were headed once they got over the Su La?'

Gunn Lobsang tilted his head and thought for a moment.

'Here in Lhasa, I don't think so. But once you get to the Bhaka gompa you can ask there. In fact you might be able to track down some of Anton's sherpas when you get there . . .'

Gunn shifted on the stool then added:

'OK, look, I'll do this thing. I'll take a risk on you being fit enough' – and Nancy nodded her thanks. 'If you want to leave today then I have to get to work. I'll come back and pick you up once I've found out about who's heading east on the Sichuan road. I think there are some Khampa lorry-drivers going to Ambo this morning. For a price they'll take you.'

'Thanks, my friend,' said Jack, shaking him vigorously by the hand.

Gunn stood up and tipped his cowboy hat at them and left. The waitress arrived at the table, delivering a bottle of Snows beer for Jack. He thanked her in Tibetan, then smiled at Nancy and said, 'Are you sure you don't want one?'

'It's a little early for me. By about nine hours . . .'

'Suit yourself. I find it helps with the altitude sickness.'

'So tell me Mr Jack Adams, all that stuff about tertons and termas, do you really believe it?' said Nancy.

Jack took several long gulps from the beer bottle, wiped his mouth on his sleeve and then said, 'It depends what you mean by believe. What do you call the ability to stop your own breathing, your own heart and even your brain activity? Do you call it magic? This is what lamas can do in advanced states of meditation. When you rig them up to Western medical equipment and monitor them for signs of life, there aren't any. Not even on the electroencephalogram. They are clinically dead. Then, after an allotted amount of time – bang. They wake up again, open their eyes and stand up. Is that magic? Or how about the ability to levitate? Or the ability to cause someone to suffer a brain haemorrhage at one hundred yards, or the ability to become invisible? Magic? Or just physical actions that we can't currently explain using science . . .'

'So are you saying you think it's real, all of it?'

'No, that's not the point. I wouldn't presume to define reality for anyone. But I don't say it doesn't happen: the levitation, the stopping of the life functions and all the other extraordinary things that the high lamas can achieve. I just think science can't explain it all yet – but we will be able to one day. And as for hidden knowledge that is drawn down from higher worlds, well I don't know any culture where artists or seers don't rely on knowledge or skill that comes from somewhere else. So termas might be the like of that, I suppose. Who knows? I don't dismiss the results of Tantric Buddhism – I just dispute the theory behind it. But one thing is for sure . . .' Jack leaned across the table to make absolutely sure that no one else in the smoky tea house could hear him. In a husky whisper, his mouth close to Nancy's ear, he said, 'It's all the goddamn dark side if you ask me.'

In an even quieter voice he continued, 'And you know what? I would never say it to Gunn, but I can't help finding myself slightly agreeing with the Chinese . . .' He glanced quickly around the room. 'Not with their techniques, of course, not with their violence and oppression. But the distaste – I understand their distaste and unease. The whole of Tibet is a flaming madhouse. When the Chinese first invaded, they found some truly horrifying things. About a third of the entire Tibetan population was wrapped up in this mumbo-jumbo one way or another, as priests or nuns or lamas, and the rest of the population lived in feudal bondage, doing the donkey work for this bunch of superstitious magicians. The lamas controlled the minds of the peasants just as successfully as the communists control the minds of the people.'

Jack looked nervously around the room again, leaving Nancy with the distinct impression that they would be in grave danger if anyone else heard so much as a single word of what he was saying:

'. . . And when they broke into the monasteries, it's rumoured that the Chinese found hidden cellars filled with ancient occult manuals and monks who were practising all sorts of deviant black arts. The Chinese soldiers who fought their way into Shigatse monastery past two thousand monks told stories of animal and human sacrifices and flesh-eating rituals in the caves beneath . . .'

Nancy baulked. 'Come on, Jack! That's just propaganda. I can't believe you swallow it.'

'Well, it may well be exaggerated, but I'll bet you there's some truth in there too. You have to ask yourself, how can a massively hierarchical priesthood be properly Buddhist? It can't, and that's the truth. Buddhism is supposed to be about the dissolution of the ego and the renunciation of worldly affairs. What I see in Tibetan religion is a sort of military theocracy, lots of different ranks and privileges, lots of secrets and knowledge withheld from the people. And I really don't see what secrets have to do with the Buddha's teachings, or with magic for that matter. There's one hell of a lot of power or energy or mana or whatever you want to call it, all being controlled from the top. So something else must have been going on in Tibet all these years – something other than just plain old Buddhism. The only problem is that as outsiders we will never learn what. The lamas are doing their own propaganda job too – you can be sure about that – with the old boy trotting round the world, smiling at everyone, looking so cuddly and cute . . .'

'I'm surprised that you're adopting such an extreme position,' said Nancy. 'I've seen the Dalai Lama speak when he came to Central Park in New York. He was clearly a peaceful, enlightened man. He's the epitome of the Buddhist, as I understand it.'

'Well, I can see he's worked his magic on you. Doesn't it bother you that he's related to the last Dalai Lama and the one before that? It's hardly democracy, is it? More like hereditary privilege, or that's what it sounds like to me. I mean, I'm just a simple country boy from Oregon, but as far as I can see the whole religion is built on black magic and superstition. Would you believe it if a Western monk said that he was the incarnation of Jesus? No! So why the suspension of disbelief just because we're in Tibet? Would you revere any Western monk as a deity in the way that the Dalai Lama is revered? It's mass hypnosis if you ask me; or if we're calling it magic, then it looks a lot more like black magic than any other sort.'

Jack tipped his beer bottle back, emptied the last

few inches down his throat and then slammed it on the table.

'Don't get me wrong. I said from the start, it's pretty clear these guys are capable of things that we in the West can't even begin to understand – and I suspect they are way more advanced than us in their knowledge of the human mind – but the whole lot of them give me the creeps – big time. And you know what? That's why I think there's something of the dark side about all of them.'

They fell into silence, Jack nursing the empty bottle in his weatherbeaten mountaineer's hands. After a minute he said, 'But enough of my thoughts. What I want to know is what you're really up to, Nancy Kelly.'

She felt a rush of adrenalin.

'What do you mean?'

'You know perfectly well what I mean. How come you know about the Book of Dzyan? And why did you need to come into Tibet on the quiet – without the normal immigration procedures? You're not an antiques smuggler. And what was Anton really doing in Pemako? You know, don't you? Or at least you suspect something. And the man in the lobby of the Taj – he wasn't after me at all, was he? I want to know what's really going on.'

He was looking hard at her, with his unblinking blue eyes. She had to respond.

'Listen, Jack, the truth is I don't know.'

'You know a lot more than you're letting on, that's what I think.'

Everything was so confused in her own mind that it was hard to know where to begin. But she felt he deserved a better explanation than she had so far given him, if she could just disentangle her motives, make something coherent of them.

'Well, OK. Let's see,' she said, while Jack stared expectantly at her. 'The police in India and in China are after Anton. They are accusing him of spying. No one at the *Trib* believes it. I think it's absurd as well, for what it's worth. I got arrested as soon as I arrived in Delhi because he sent me that bone I showed you. They interrogated me about my connection with Herzog. They were clutching at straws, but I could see he was in big trouble. They let me go. I assume they have been following me and tapping all my calls, which is why I didn't want to discuss the flight on the phone. At first I was angry, angry about my arrest and about the fact that no one seemed to be doing anything to find Anton – he's been gone for three months already – it was all so odd. But at least then I thought it was pretty simple – journalist doing his job, repressive forces trying to stop him, that kind of story. But when I started to look into it, everything started to get really weird . . .'

Jack raised his eyebrows, but said nothing.

'I discovered that Anton's father – Felix Koenig – was a Tibetologist and a member of an esoteric German sect called the Thule Society, which conducted research into the history of the Aryans and sent expeditions to Tibet. It seems that Koenig went to Tibet, possibly more than once, on trips sponsored by the Nazis, in order to enlist the lamas on the side of Germany . . .'

She looked at Jack almost pleadingly – she was aware how strange her whole story sounded and she was waiting for the moment where he would tell her that she had lost her mind. But he remained silent, watching her; his expression impossible to interpret.

She pressed on. 'The Nazis thought that the lamas of Tibet – or some secret lodge in Tibet – had knowledge of the superman, that they knew how to transform an ordinary human being into a more advanced evolutionary type, a sort of higher order of man, born to rule the world. The Nazis thought that this knowledge belonged to them because it was really ancient Aryan knowledge . . . and that it would help them win the war. I know this all sounds far-fetched, but when I went to see Maya, she showed me some old medals that Anton had left with her and one of them was a Thule Gesellschaft medal which clearly belonged to Anton's father, Felix Koenig. It had the exact same design as the one on the mouthpiece of the bone trumpet.'

Jack Adams's eyes widened in amazement.

'Are you sure? That trumpet is massively old.'

'Yes. Absolutely certain. A dagger emblazoned on a swastika. But it was knowledge of the superman they desperately wanted, and they believed the Book of Dzyan held all this knowledge – they called it *Das Buch des Ringes*, the Book of the Ring – and they became obsessed with finding it, hence the expeditions. Anton's research must have been related to this. It simply must've been. This was the story that Anton was trying to research – he told Maya it was the biggest story the world has ever known . . .'

Nancy's voice trailed off. A dark shadow had passed over Jack's face.

'Jesus, Nancy – why didn't you tell me all this before we left?'

'Well, I've been finding out as we went along. Then for a while I just thought it was too weird and couldn't quite process it. Then I thought I'd give up, abandon the whole thing, that I was out of my depth and I should just pay you and go home.'

They fell silent for a moment, but then Nancy turned her gaze on him once again.

'But what about you Jack? Why were you prepared to take me to Tibet at such a knock-down price? And what does the symbol on the bone trumpet mean, and what about the letters – where are they from? You've known all along, haven't you?'

Jack sighed heavily and shook his head:

'Yes and no. I have no idea about the origins of the dagger and swastika symbol. I don't recognize it at all – but yes, it's true, I do recognize the letters.'

'And what are they?'

'They are the Elder Futhark.'

'The what?'

'Runes. They're the first six magical letters of the oldest known runic alphabet: F, U, Th, A, R, K. It's known as the Elder Futhark.'

'How could a bone trumpet that is more than twenty thousand years old have a European script on it? And what on earth is it doing turning up in the middle of the Himalayas?'

'Exactly. Now you know why I am so desperate to find where it came from. It's what I've been looking for all these years. It supplies categorical – to my mind – proof that humanity is vastly older than people think, that developed civilizations existed more than fifteen thousand years ago. To find an ancient bone with runes written on it, thousands of miles from northern Europe, is simply incredible. I am now absolutely certain that Herzog must have found the Aryan kingdom that he was looking for all these years, and I intend to go there and bring back its treasures and its relics. I want to show the world that I am right. And I can tell you something else – it will more than clear my debts if I can get my hands on even one decent piece of proof.'

There was a glint in his eye when he said this. Of course, thought Nancy, it would be a giant treasure trove; it would make the Tomb of Tutankhamun look positively modern. Jack Adams was frowning:

'How sure are you about all this stuff about Anton's dad?'

'Almost certain. The Simon Wiesenthal Centre corroborated it, pretty much. I mean, they confirmed that Anton's father is suspected to have been Felix Koenig, and that Koenig was an expert adviser to the Nazis on Tibetan culture, that he travelled to Tibet and so on. But the idea that Anton is after the Book of Dzyan is just speculation. Maybe he's just interested in Tibet for other reasons, though the fact that he is travelling with the Terton Thupten Jinpa only makes me more suspicious, given that the Book of Dzyan is a terma and it seems that tertons are the only people who know how to find the lost termas. One thing is for sure though, Koenig made several trips to Lhasa, in the pay of the Nazi regime, and it's on the record that he went there specifically to look for lost Aryan knowledge and the origins of the Aryan race.'

They fell into silence. Nancy watched Jack expectantly. Now she had poured everything out, she felt relieved to have shared her tentative speculation about Herzog's activities. Jack Adams might now join her in puzzling over what was true and what were simply the fantasies of Second World War occultists and crazy lamas. She studied him; his head was bowed now and he appeared to be deep in thought. After a minute or so, he began to scratch nervously at the label on his beer bottle. Finally, he looked up.

'Well, Nancy Kelly, this really is an interesting case. I'm not saying I believe in a lot of this esoteric hokum. I think the Nazis are even more nuts than the lamas, but I do know what the Nazis were looking for. Or at least I think I do. They must have been trying to get in contact with the Great White Brotherhood . . .'

35

'I haven't thought about the Great White Brotherhood in years. When I was younger, in my early twenties, I was doing some doctoral research in Kathmandu . . .'

The waitress clinked down more bottles on the table. Jack thanked her and then handed one to Nancy, who took it gratefully.

'I don't know if you've been to Kathmandu, but it attracts a lot of weirdos: seekers of the truth and so on, people who believe that there are gurus out there who know the secrets of life and people who think that they are gurus themselves. They traffic in a whole bunch of well-worn myths and give each other the heebie-jeebies about secret societies, evil curses and so on. At the top of the tree of all these myths and stories about gurus and secret lodges stands the Great White Brotherhood. It's supposed to be a mystical secret society of Masters who control the world from their underground kingdom, or valley in the high

Himalayas. Some people say the name of their kingdom is Shangri-La, others say that Shangri-La is a good place and that it could never be home to such a brotherhood, but either way, to be fair, there are very thorough accounts of them all across Asia – it's not just hippies making up stories.'

He took a slug of his beer.

'It must have been the Brotherhood that the Nazis were trying to contact. If you go to Kathmandu you will even meet people who claim to have found their way to Shangri-La and met the Brotherhood, but it's a pack of lies. The Brotherhood come to you and invite you – you don't find them . . . and I doubt anyone who has been invited would tell any tales . . .'

Nancy replaced her bottle on the table.

'But who on earth are these people?'

'Some say it is a sort of university for the enlightened. That they possess great libraries, filled with esoteric knowledge. If the Book of Dzyan really does exist, then maybe it's kept in one of those. Others say that, despite its name, the Brotherhood is under the influence of the forces of darkness.'

Nancy interjected:

'And what do you think?'

'Well, as I think I've made clear, I have a slightly sceptical approach to all of this. So, personally, I reckon that if the Brotherhood does exist, then it's probably more of a cave community of Indian and Tibetan occultists, up to no good. But that doesn't mean they aren't powerful. In fact, I'd go so far as to say that if it's true that the Nazis really did come to Tibet, then it could just as easily have been the case that it was the Brotherhood who summoned them, in order to draw them into some crazy scheme of their own making. I don't know, perhaps the whole idea of the Second World War was cooked up by the Great White Brotherhood itself...'

Nancy choked on her beer.

'What! You've got to be kidding me. I thought you didn't believe in all this black magic.'

Jack put his finger to his lips and looked around the room anxiously.

'Sshh! Keep your voice down. There are informers everywhere, even in the Blue Lantern. Now listen. You're not understanding me: I told you before, it's not that I don't believe that there are weird things going on in the world – it's just that I'm not convinced they've got anything to do with magic. Tibetan Tantric practices don't stop at party tricks like levitation, I can assure you of that. Telepathic mind control is a speciality of these guys.'

Nancy's face was screwed into an anxious frown. She was struggling to decide if Jack was being entirely serious. His urgent expression, his furtive air, suggested he was genuine, but it was hard to tell.

'OK,' she said, taking a deep breath. 'Even if there is a grain of truth in what you're saying and the Great White Brotherhood does actually exist somewhere, surely it must be a force for good. It's the Great *White* Brotherhood, right? Not the Great *Black* Brotherhood. In which case, why would they have anything to do with the Nazis? Surely in their great white wisdom they would have perceived that the Nazis were an evil force, that no good could come of the union . . .'

Jack shrugged.

'Well, it would be nice if that were true, but life isn't that simple. The Brotherhood is *supposed* to be white and they are meant to be furthering the cause of good in the world. But who knows. Maybe they have lost their way? Legend has it that Masters of the Brotherhood are themselves in telepathic contact with other Masters who exist on higher planes of existence. These higher Masters are meant to be like good angels, but maybe they're not who they say they are. Maybe they aren't telling the truth. Maybe the Brotherhood itself is being misled?'

Jack took a swig on his beer bottle and scanned the room to check again that no one was listening, then continued.

'You contact non-terrestrial forces at your peril. Whenever I hear stories of people who claim to have been contacted by divine forces, or UFOs, or Masters in Tibet, I can't help thinking to myself, "OK maybe it's true, maybe they have been in touch, but also maybe the forces that have contacted you are only pretending to be good, only pretending to help the world, and in reality they are actually trying to do evil – they are using you" . . .'

What the hell? thought Nancy. What on earth had she got herself into? Even Jack Adams, who she had assumed was – despite the eccentricities of his lifestyle – fundamentally rational, invested with degrees from prestigious universities, an ordinary sceptic like herself, seemed to be quite happy to contemplate the most outlandish conspiracy theories that she'd ever heard of. In fact, that was precisely why she was so freaked out: Jack Adams *was* a man of learning, and yet still he was willing to entertain ideas of telepathic Masters and Nazis in search of the secret of the superman. His brand of scepticism was the most peculiar non-belief she'd ever met. He was so sceptical that he wouldn't say for certain that anything was true; but neither would he say that it was untrue.

But then again, Nancy was thinking, who was she to blame him? Were telepathic Masters that much stranger, if you thought about it, than the world she knew already? The world of global wars and religious conflicts – and nuclear arms races inspired by differing visions of world government? Was contemporary Western life more or less insane than the world of the high Himalayas? She found she was echoing Jack's words: who was she to say what was probable and what was impossible? She was rapidly losing all sense of perspective; in danger of losing her ability to distinguish between truth and fiction. Or perhaps the terms were no longer meaningful to her. She had lost her faith in such convenient distinctions.

'Jack,' she said, in a desperate attempt to cling on to some sort of order, 'just tell me plainly what you think. Was Anton trying to follow up his father's Nazi research and find the Brotherhood? Was he after the Book of Dzyan and the secret of the superman, whatever that's supposed to be?'

The questions sounded absurdly simplistic even as she spoke them, and Jack wouldn't give her the reassurance she craved. He shrugged across at her. 'Maybe, maybe not. Given everything you've just told me about his father – and given what Gunn just said about the Book of Dzyan being a terma – it's quite possible – particularly, as he was last seen travelling with a terton.'

He paused for a second as if marshalling his thoughts.

'You know what, Nancy? Sometimes, even if you are a disillusioned guy like me, it pays to believe in the craziest theories.'

'What do you mean by that?'

'Well, if the entire population of Tibet, plus the Nazis, plus Anton, all believe in the Book of Dzyan or the Great White Brotherhood or reincarnation or flying pigs for that matter, and I am the only one who doesn't, then I guess I should just shut up. If we want to find Anton, we have to think like Anton – which probably does mean believing in all of the above. Besides, there's another thing: if the Book of Dzyan does exist, then it will be worth a million times more than the Koh-i-noor diamond. It will be the greatest antique find of all time.' And he nearly licked his lips; she saw the adventurer in him rising to the challenge, suddenly enticed by the prospect of treasure.

Of course, Nancy thought to herself, he thinks he can make money out of this. It's not just academic glory. For a fleeting second she was disappointed, disappointed that his response was not the same as hers, that the quest for Anton and the truth about what he had been doing all these years in Tibet had no greater significance for Jack than as a possible money-making venture. But if greed got him hooked, then greed would have to do. She had come this far and she discovered that all she wanted to do was go further. And if she was being brutal with herself, she knew that there was a kernel of self-interest in her quest: she wanted that story, the great story Anton had gone in search of.

'So you'll still come to Pemako then?' she asked cautiously. Jack Adams smiled.

'Sure, let's do it.'

'Do you think something terrible has happened to Anton?'

'Who knows? One thing's certain, Anton's one of those wiry indestructible types. The luck of the devil, that sort of thing. Could be, he's just pottering around old monasteries having a wonderful time . . .'

'Or maybe he's finally just gone totally insane . . .' Nancy added in a subdued voice.

Jack threw his head back and drained the last drops from the beer bottle, placed it heavily on the table and then looked over at the door.

'Or both. But, there's only one way to find out. Where's Gunn Lobsang when you need him?'

36

High on the mountainside, nearly at the edge of the treeline, the party of monks had stopped again. Under a ragged cluster of acacia trees they sought shelter from the rain. Below, the valley was filled with lingering bulky cloud.

For all his fear, his sense that something was pursuing them, Anton Herzog was relieved that they had stopped. When the monks moved him, the straps that held his emaciated body in place on the stretcher rubbed his skin, so it was raw and bleeding, and he was tired of trying to keep his head still as it was jerked around. He was pleased to have a respite from this; he tried to breathe more slowly, to relax his limbs. Perhaps they were almost there. Perhaps Agarthi was only one more march away. He hoped so; he knew he would not last much longer.

The Abbot's deputy came over and, squatting down, offered Herzog a fresh pipe. As he drew down the sweet smoke, Herzog could hear the old lama stand up and begin a conversation with another of the monks. With effort, Herzog forced his eyes to open. They were studying a map. After a minute the Abbot's deputy squatted down again and held the map before Herzog's eyes and pointed with a dirty fingernail to the top left corner of the bedraggled page.

'Here – is this where you were discovered by the Chinese man? Is this where you had given up?'

Herzog felt the thick honey-tar of the opium filling his throat. Under the effects of the drug, his urge to speak had returned. His neck no longer ached, the tearing sensation in his lungs had diminished, and a sense of peace and contentment had come over him again. But the Chinese man? What did the lama mean? What did the lama know of the strange Chinese man? Had he already progressed so far in his account of his journey that he had told the lama of the strange Chinese man? He couldn't remember. The opium was stealing away the last vestiges of his powers of deliberate concentration. It took away none of the vividness of his thoughts, but his mind now wandered where it wanted, he had been robbed of the power to direct it on its course.

'Yes,' he said, softly, visions of the elegant Chinese man appearing in his mind's eye. 'The Chinese man. That is right.'

With a renewed urgency the deputy interrupted him:

'Please, I ask you to concentrate and look at where I'm pointing on the map. Is this where he found you?'

Herzog tried to focus on the map:

'I don't know. He saved us. He took us away. But it was a longer journey than I had realized – I was not in a good state. We had to go over a high pass – a high pass that was well hidden. I fell in and out of sleep throughout the ascent, jolted awake at regular intervals. But on the way down, the route was so steep that I was asked to get down from the chair and we were all roped together in a long line; myself and the Chinese man in the middle with sherpas on either side.'

The Abbot's deputy was almost despairing:

'But tell me: do you recognize anything on this map? Does the landscape depicted here make any sense to you at all? Does it remind you of where you were?'

Herzog had drifted away. He was muttering, half to himself, half to the doctor, gazing past the Abbot's deputy.

'I don't know, you see. The path petered out altogether after some hours. We were forced onto a slender rocky ledge. For hundreds of yards, we inched our way along this ledge, winding slowly around a vast cliff-face. Below, thousands of feet further down, was a green, snakelike river, forging a course through a rocky canyon.'

The Abbot's deputy looked at the map. There was no river in that corner, no ravine, no ledge. He sighed and let his hand fall. His sad eyes studied the dying man. Herzog sensed that he had disappointed the old lama.

'You have to understand, I was exhausted. When we finally made it back on to a path, I actually collapsed from exhaustion. I was helped back into the chair that somehow the sherpas had carried with us on the terrifying journey, and as soon as I was sitting down I fell asleep. I only woke again when I heard the excited shouts from the sherpas as their home finally came into view. That is why I cannot recognize anything on your map. You must understand, I was in no better state than I am now . . .'

Herzog fell silent. The Abbot's deputy handed the map back to the monk. Then he pressed his palms together. He wanted to learn more, he wanted to hear what this place was like, even though it was forbidden knowledge and it made him feel guilty even to ask.

'So what did their home look like? Please describe it to me.'

Dreamily Herzog repeated the question, his eyes staring in awe at the heavens.

'What did it look like? It was the lushest, greenest

valley that I have ever seen. It was sublime. It was surrounded by massive cliffs that towered over it but because at its widest point it was at least a mile and a half wide, it still received a great deal of sunlight, and on the valley floor below I could clearly see a lamasery, surrounded by dwellings and farmhouses, and in the fields I could make out the forms of many people hard at work.'

For a moment, he was back there again, the jungle fell away from him, the pains that had held him fast in the physical world had gone, and he journeyed into the past, back to the beautiful valley. He was speaking. Could the Abbot's deputy hear him? He was describing his visions, his memories. He could see the Chinese man grinning with pride. He turned to him, completely awe-struck and said, 'It's so beautiful.'

'Thank you,' the Chinese man replied. 'It has always been this way.'

Suddenly Herzog's eyes refocused on the Abbot's deputy. He was sure now that he was talking and not just dreaming. He summoned all his strength and fixed his gaze determinedly on the deputy.

'I tried to learn more from the Chinese man. I said, ' "It seems an incredibly peaceful place. Do you suffer the normal problems of society?"

'The Chinese man smiled proudly at me and replied, '"There is no crime and disease is unknown. People live a full and healthy span of years and then pass away in their sleep. We have no need for mechanics, scientists, lawyers, barely even any need for doctors, and certainly no need for any proselytizing religions. We stay close to the Tao and life continues happily. With a simple diet of rice, fresh fruit and vegetables, no sugar and precious little salt, combined with vigorous daily outdoor work, the human body does not get ill, it does not develop cancers or other such diseases. The old here eventually die in their sleep, taking a peaceful leave of this life, as primitive people have done for millions of years, the world over.

'"Every ten years, we receive reports from the outside world. Yet we find there is nothing in its affairs that cannot be predicted a decade in advance with even a modest amount of contemplation. Though the Tao never remains still, it also never changes . . .'

'"So that is not a lamasery then?" I pointed towards the main building that stood amidst the dwellings of the village.

'"No. Not after the fashion of the rest of Tibet. That is a just a simple house. We hope that we can encourage Wisdom to make it her home, but we are not so presumptuous as to make it our home too. We visit it occasionally and try to listen to what Wisdom has to tell us.'

'"So you are not a Master, or a brother or even a templar of this kingdom?'

'"This is not a kingdom and I am none of those things. We are a community that seeks merely to exist without unusual suffering. We all share the same burdens and do the same work, though thanks to my particular cast of mind, I find myself naturally disposed towards study and thought and so I spend more time in those activities than most of my fellow valley-dwellers. But I too work in the fields, I too bring in the harvest and milk the yaks."'

The Abbot's deputy interrupted.

'But this sounds like a communist society – surely you must have wandered into Red China by accident . . .'

Herzog smiled.

'That is what I thought for a moment as well. But then I remembered that the Chinese man had mentioned the Tao, and I looked down into the valley and could sense from its perfectly terraced rice paddies and its splendid atmosphere of calm that this place had certainly never been touched by the poison of the

Cultural Revolution. That it was far older and wiser than any ideologies of Marx or Chairman Mao.

'And yet, it was not what I was looking for. Unless of course, this man's modesty hid the fact that from within the walls of "the house for Wisdom" as he had put it, they secretly tried to influence events in the world using telepathy and the ancient practices of Tantric yoga.

'Without intending to offend him in any way, I asked the Chinese man what it was that they hoped to achieve in the wider world. Did his community seek to spread its knowledge to other peoples? Did he leave the valley in his thoughts to commune with peoples elsewhere? His answer was simple and direct.

' "I think you misunderstand us. We seek to teach no one anything. Visitors are welcome to come here and learn how we live, but we would not for a second want to persuade someone that our lifestyle is the only way. But I think I understand what it is that you are talking about. Here in the valley, we have knowledge of many things, and we know full well that there are ancient arts that allow humans to access the non-material planes of this world, to reach down and make suggestions to other minds. These suggestions, if they are to reach all men, must be made in symbols and not language, otherwise only the speakers of one particular language would understand, and besides, symbols are far more powerful.

'"But it is against the oaths of our order to indulge in such activities, for such behaviour is far from the Tao. For how can someone live happily if they are acting only on our unconscious suggestions and they have not decided on a course of action for themselves? Instead, we put our energies in this direction to the task of discovering and nurturing the Tao. And since the Tao retreats from you if you seek it out and comes towards you only if you retreat from it, we find it is best not to try to find it. We try simply to work alongside it.

'"We focus our energies on ensuring that we live by the Tao, and if we succeed, then knowledge of our happiness will trickle down from our high valley into the valleys below and from there it will gather strength and become a great river and finally, it will descend to the lands below and become the Brahmaputra itself, and its flood plain will nourish the whole of India and the whole world. The Tao teaches us that even if you merely sit in silence in a quiet room, if you think the right thoughts, you will be heard a thousand miles away."'

Herzog had fallen silent. He was smiling again – a dreamy look in his eyes. Perhaps he has forgotten the awfulness of his predicament, the Abbot's deputy thought. He found the stranger's mood swings inexplicable, even with the opium. But he wanted to learn more.

'Did you believe him when he told you these things? Do you agree – can good be achieved through such inaction?'

A feeble laugh escaped from Herzog's cracked lips.

'No. His aims were laudable, but to this day I do not believe they can be achieved through such methods. If you, in Litang gompa, scarcely a few hundred miles away, have not heard of this place and its teachings, then it seems highly unlikely that India, let alone New York or London, will ever hear about this idyllic community, and even if they do, it would take eternity to convert the world to the way of life of the valley. People are busy with their own schemes.'

Herzog paused to cough and then he looked up, his smile completely gone:

'I knew, and Felix Koenig knew before me, that only active intervention and the skilful use of the lost Aryan arts that were in the possession of the kingdom of Shangri-La could change mankind for the better and elevate it to a higher evolutionary field. I had stumbled into a valley of ascetic monks, given over to quietism and the contemplation of the Tao. Splendid as this community was, it was not the place that I was looking for and so I put it to the Chinese man straight.

'"I am very grateful for the opportunity to learn about your wonderful valley, but it is my intention to reach the kingdom of Shangri-La. Can you help me? Can you direct me or lead me on my way?"

'For the first time since I had met him, the Chinese man looked sad.

'"Yes. If you insist upon it we can show you the way. But we would urge you to stay with us. Lend us your strength here in the valley; you will be happy and from your example, others will follow. Shangri-La is not a good place. They take a different path from us. They do not seek to educate mankind through simple example but through the exercise of power and magic. They are prepared to use all sorts of methods, even methods that involve powers that we believe are beyond their control. Stay here. This is a happy, peaceful place."

'He was a good man and it was upsetting to have to press my point, but I had no intention of retiring from life and becoming a priest–farmer, marvellous as this valley was. And as for his evaluation of Shangri-La, it was just what you would expect to hear from a retiring monk who was afraid of engaging with the wider world.

'"I would be most grateful for your assistance."

'"Then so be it. But let me warn you, if you leave, you will never be able to return, for it is not possible to draw you a map, or explain how to get back into here. The route by which we came would be impossible for a stranger to follow, and it is only every ten years that our caravan goes out into the outside world, and unless you were in dire need of help, we would not encumber you with our assistance or even let ourselves be seen by you . . ."

'For some reason, I felt a tightening in my stomach.

' "But I could come back from Shangri-La? Surely I could just retrace my steps from there."

'The Chinese man smiled.

' "Alas, that is not possible."

' "Why not?"

' "Because the route can only be travelled in one direction."

' "But how can that be?"

' "Come, if you are ready. I will show you."

'We rose to go and, almost immediately, the strange feeling of regret began to leave me. I was going to Shangri-La after all. I was going to reach the place that I had strived so hard to reach.

' "Where exactly are we going?" I asked, as we mounted a little trap, drawn by a young yak mare.

' "There." He pointed up towards the dark cliffs at the end of the valley. "Up there."

'I stared upwards; the tops of the mountains were veiled in mist. He must be pointing to the hidden entrance to a cave, I thought; a cave that would turn into a dark passage that would eventually disgorge me into the kingdom of Shangri-La. But what kind of route could only be traversable in one direction? It occurred to me that it might be an underground river. That would certainly not be navigable in both directions.'

The Abbot's deputy had picked up the map again. He scoured it for a valley of the correct proportion that was abutted at the end by giant cliffs. Meanwhile, Herzog continued with his description of his journey.

'We rattled along in the trap and in no time at all had passed through the green meadows and lush paddies of the top end of the valley. Wherever we went, people paused from their work and waved at us or hailed the Chinese man. Several times we stopped to be given pieces of fresh fruit and for the Chinese man to indulge in pleasant conversation with his fellow valley dwellers.

'Finally the road petered out at the base of the vast cliffs that seem to rise up into the sky for ever. I was an experienced mountaineer in my younger days, yet no matter how I scrutinized that cliff-face, I could see that there were absolutely no routes up it at all. It might as well have been a sheet of black ice. I turned to the Chinese man.

' "So where is the entrance?"

'"One moment please. I have not been here in sixty years."

'The Chinese began very slowly to pace about. He appeared to be concentrating very hard. I realized he must be engaging in some form of meditation, for his eyes were focused on a spot about a yard from his face and his expression was locked. He was in a deep trance, and then suddenly he stopped and reached out in front of him as if he was grasping hold of an imaginary butterfly.

'"Here."

'I stepped over to him, completely baffled as to what he meant. And then, to my amazement, I saw that in his hand he was holding a single thread of silk. It was so fine that it was barely visible to the naked eye but now I could just see that it rose up into the sky, though I lost track of it after about six feet. Nevertheless, I felt it must derive from the top of that dark cliff, thousands of feet above, that somehow it was anchored up there.

'With a firm but gentle tug, he pulled the thread. For a second, it brought to my mind an image of a bell-ringer in the wooden village church near to my parents' house in the Pampas. I did not know what to say and the Chinese man's eyes were closed in concentration.

'Then to my amazement, I noticed a loop of thread

appear above his hand. Someone, or something, high in the heavens above, was reeling out the silken line. In stunned silence, I watched as spool after spool of semi-visible thread coiled on the ground around our feet. On and on it came until the ground around our feet was covered in a spider's web of this gossamer-like thread. Then, after some four or five minutes of this, the silk thread turned into a silk rope. The lama nodded his head and let the rope descend until it had created a couple of loops on the ground and then he tugged the line twice and suddenly all motion stopped. The silk rope hung in the air.

'"Please, raise your arms," said the Chinese man.

'I watched as he wound the rope under my armpits and tied it behind my back.

'"Is it strong enough?' I said in genuine fear, for the rope was really quite thin-looking and it was hard to imagine how it would ever be able to support my weight.

'"Yes."

'Then without another word he reached up and tugged hard twice on the rope above my head and within a second I felt a jerking motion as the rope tightened under my arms. My feet were lifted off the ground. Within ten seconds, the Chinese man had been reduced to the size of a small doll. I saw him turn and get back into the trap. Then I could hardly see him any more. I was being drawn ever higher. Beneath me I could see the entire valley, and suddenly to my horror I remembered what Gustav had said about how he had a vague recollection of staring longingly over the parapets of Shangri-La and how he had dreamed of flying down to the Emerald Valley below. But it was too late to do anything now.

'Up and up I was carried, like a spider ascending a thread, through veils of mist and cloud, passing sometimes perilously close to the cliff-face and then sometimes floating in the thin air, ten feet away from it. Finally, after what I estimated to be about six minutes or more of this, I could at last see an end to my flight. Above me, the rope passed over a wheel on the end of a wooden arm that extended from the edge of the cliff. I was barely twenty feet away and rising fast. The adrenalin surged through my veins; who would be there waiting to greet me?

'And then suddenly I was at the top of the cliff, staring at a great stone battlement, and then to my everlasting horror I saw that on top of every battlement, mounted on successive spikes, was a decaying human head. I screamed in terror and kicked my legs, trying to swim backwards through the air. It was absurd and futile, an expression of simple bodily fear. For a second I swung in mid-air, like a helpless fly, caught in a web. I could see beyond the battlements to an area of rugged ground, and then beyond that were the black walls of a lamasery, a dark tower rising at the heart.

'Suddenly, I was not alone. An oriental man in his mid-fifties appeared to me, a man dressed in silk robes of the nineteenth century. He reached out his hand and leaned towards me and said in heavily accented, broken English, '"Welcome to Shangri-La. Lamas are expecting you. Please take hand."

'I didn't really have any choice, despite my pounding heart, so I did as he suggested and clasped his hand. Then I was standing on the firm ground of the battlement walkway. The man had noticed that my face was ghostly white and that I was still staring in terror at the human heads. He waved his hand through the air. His English was awkward and jerky but perfectly comprehensible.

'"Apologies for frightening figures. Necessary to scare unwanted visitors. Room prepared for you in tower. Trust you find comfortable."

'I decided my best course of action was to try to project a sense of purpose and determination. His explanation of the disgusting display of heads was hardly adequate; human scarecrows they may have been, but the question remained of who the heads had belonged to, how the victims had come to be thus mutilated.

' "I would like to speak immediately with the Abbot of this place," I said.

'The oriental man did not smile.

' "Come to tower. Lamas receive you there."

'He gestured at me to descend a flight of stone stairs. I could see they led down to the rocky area between the battlements and the lamasery. I was helpless, standing with the beheaded warnings to one side, the unfathomable drop to the other, and so I acceded to his request. I noticed as I stepped past him that he carried a sword which I assumed was not for ornamental purposes alone.

'Together we walked over the bare earth to the lamasery gates, where he banged hard with his fist on the doors. The doors swung open, revealing a gloomy courtyard. The doorkeeper was a stocky sherpa; apart from him the courtyard was entirely empty. I followed my now silent guide across the courtyard, through an arched doorway, down several stone corridors, across several inner courtyards and finally, into the base of the great tower itself. A wide flight of steps arched majestically around the interior of the tower, with landings and doorways coming off at intervals. We ascended the stone stairs until we had almost reached the top, at which point he opened a door and gestured for me to go in.

' "Please. Wash. Rest."

'What choice did I have? None. Even if I had forced my way past him, where would I have run too? To the battlements? There was no way I could have descended the silk rope alone, even assuming that no one tampered with it as I went down. And as for trying to escape beyond the lamasery, over the high Himalayas, well, that would be effectively suicidal. I could not imagine I would last more than a couple of days without the correct clothing and supplies.

'I took a deep breath and ducked under the doorway and found myself in a small cell-like room. I was just about to turn and ask when I might be granted an audience with the Abbot when I heard the door slam shut behind me and a key turn in the lock. I spun around but was too late. All I could hear were footsteps receding down the stairs. Shaking my head at my folly, I turned to survey the room more thoroughly. There was a bed, a chair, a table, a bowl and a jug filled with water, a window; I ran to it. It had a grille on it of wrought iron. I pressed my face to the grille and peered down into the lamasery. The window was even higher up than I had realized; I had a commanding view of the rooftops and the courtyard directly below. It was not the front courtyard I looked onto but an interior courtyard; an inner sanctum.

'As I pressed my cheeks to the grille, I saw something that made my blood run as cold as the meltwater that drips from the Himalayan glaciers. A group of sherpas were hard at work, carrying bundles of wood and placing them at the base of a huge bonfire. And on top of the massive pile of logs and kindling sat the most frightening object I have ever seen: a human-sized wooden cage.

'It was quite obvious that they could only have been at work at this task for about half an hour, which by my estimation was almost exactly the amount of time since my Chinese friend from the valley below first tugged on the dreadful string. With a horrible and complete sense of realization I began to cry out in terror. I think I produced some pathetic and impotent words – "No! Dear God no!" – but most of the time I was moaning in fear, whimpering like an animal.'

The Abbot's deputy recoiled in horror. Never before had he heard such a ghastly tale. Could it really be true that such a place existed? Sweat was pouring down the stranger's pale, cadaverous face as he recounted his nightmarish experience – it was real enough to him and his dazzling blue eyes were wide with fear.

37

As they came out of the market and into the main square, Nancy became aware that she was slightly drunk. Two beers and 12,000 feet didn't mix as well as Jack Adams had claimed. She was swaying unsteadily on her feet and the edges of the buildings seemed to be unnaturally sharp against the azure sky.

'Shouldn't we wait until Gunn comes back? We want to be able to leave as soon as he returns, don't we?'

'Don't worry,' said Jack. 'He's just over there, in the Migu tea house. And don't mention what we've just been talking about to him – he wouldn't appreciate my speculations about Tibetan Buddhism.'

Jack strode ahead through the busy market alleyway and into the square. Nancy was following slowly behind when suddenly and despite her state of intoxication she sensed danger. Just a few yards away a red-faced young Tibetan was advancing towards her.

'American, go home to your country.'

She pretended not to hear. She half-turned away from him but she could see out of the corner of her eye that he was approaching. Furiously he shouted, 'The Dalai Lama is a wicked donkey.'

She began to walk away but the young man only increased his speed. His English was good – he was clearly educated. 'Tibet is free already – we don't want monks making us work. We don't want foreigners bringing back the Dalai Lama. Tibet is free today.'

Suddenly, the man was right behind her. She felt his hands on her shoulders and before she could react, he had spun her around and had grabbed her by the collar of her shirt. She could smell alcohol on his breath and she could feel the strength of his hands. His eyes were burning with rage.

'Why do you come to Lhasa to visit old monasteries? Why?'

She tried to answer – her voice filled with panic.

'I haven't – I haven't actually been to any monasteries . . .'

He leaned his face closer to hers. She tried to recoil from him but he dragged her forward, baring his teeth at her as if he was about to bite her.

'Monasteries are evil. They oppress us. The Dalai Lama is a dictator. Now we have democracy – all people are equal. Americans should stay in America, not try to bring dictators back to power in Tibet.'

The man looked as if he was about to burst into tears. At that moment both Jack and Gunn arrived at her side. Gunn took firm but gentle hold of the young man's arms and spoke quietly to him in Tibetan. Jack stood by poised to act, but waited to see what effect Gunn's words might have. Gradually, the Tibetan man released his grip on Nancy – all the while Gunn was murmuring to him.

As the boy's arms fell to his side, Gunn put his arm around him and guided him back to his place on the steps. Nancy breathed again. It had been a terrifying few seconds. Gunn returned a moment later shaking his head. His face was very sad.

'It is bad. More and more young people are confused like this. At school they get taught that Tibetan culture is just a cover for clerical-aristocratic exploitation. The Chinese fill their heads with communist propaganda and they believe it – but as they grow up they know in their hearts that it's not true – it's not right to throw away your past. So, they become confused and unhappy – the unresolved tensions are too much – and on top of everything else, there are no jobs, so they drink and smoke and argue . . .'

'I thought Lhasa was booming,' said Nancy, trying to be relaxed about the experience. 'I thought the new Sky Train from Beijing was bringing jobs and prosperity.'

'It is, but not for Tibetans. To get a proper job you have to speak and write Chinese. More than eighty per cent of Tibetans are illiterate and very few speak Chinese. You have seen all the young men loitering around Lhasa in the tea houses, playing snooker and drinking tea and chang – that's a Tibetan spirit . . . It's very sad. But at least most of them are still patriotic. That boy is a particularly tragic case – he does not even have pride in Tibet . . .'

Nancy stared over her shoulder at the steps. The young man sat, with his head slumped between his knees, as if the world was too much for him, as if life had finally worn him right down.

'But what will happen to these young people? Will they get jobs? Will they be all right?'

Gunn sighed bitterly.

'No. There are no jobs for angry young men who don't want to learn Chinese. We are second-class citizens in our own land. It is too late for Tibet. We are outnumbered in our own country. I do not know what we can do . . .'

'But do people still dream of freedom – of freedom from the Chinese and for the Dalai Lama to return home?'

'No. No one I know still dreams like that.'

He paused and gazed at the golden stupas of the far-off Potala Palace.

'Maybe it is our karma. I have heard some monks say that the Chinese invaded Tibet because Tibetans needed to be punished – we had strayed too far from Buddhism, we had become corrupt, the lamas had become greedy. We brought it on our own heads. And some people say that it is all part of the divine plan. By invading Tibet and destroying our home-land, the Chinese have forced us to flee, and by doing so we are bringing the light of Buddhism to the whole world . . .'

Jack Adams had been listening with an irritable expression, and now he interrupted forcibly. 'Listen – you know what this kind of crazy talk reminds me of? It reminds me of those Jews who say that the Holo-caust was a necessary evil. That they were murdered because they had strayed too far from the Law of the Torah and that the Nazis were just performing God's work and that Jews were scattered from their homes in eastern Europe so that the Promised Land could be reborn in Israel . . . I don't go in for these arguments that require mass murder and destruction for the successful working out of God's law, or karma or whatever you want to call it . . .'

Gunn looked at the two foreigners and smiled weakly.

'Well, you can't blame us for trying to find a reason for the destruction of our soul that has happened since

1959 . . . A reason we can bear to contemplate. The world looks very depressing otherwise . . .'

He shrugged his shoulders. Jack slapped him on the shoulder.

'Tibet isn't history yet, Gunn. Not by a long way. Come on, let's get a cab.'

38

Colonel Jen paused for a moment and wiped his brow for the hundredth time that hour. An unstoppable flow of sweat and rainwater was coursing down his face, stinging his eyes. Next to him stood Dorgen Trungpa, dressed only in his soaking orange robes, still showing no visible signs of exhaustion. Behind them in the forest were the soldiers, scattered in a line, a line that seemed to be getting longer by the minute as some of the men, wearied by the pace and severity of the climb, started to fall behind. None of the soldiers was jungle-trained, most were not even country boys, they were from big cities like Chengdu and Chonqing. They were raw recruits, out of place in the jungle; unfit, scared and unable to read any of the signs of the forest.

A macaw let out its distinctive piercing wailing cry just above the Colonel's head, making him flinch.

'Are we still on course?' he whispered to Dorgen

Trungpa. The monk had been silent ever since they had left the monastery compound and begun to thread their way through the dense jungle foliage. Colonel Jen studied the monk's impassive face – perhaps the boy had changed his mind? Perhaps he had decided not to take them to the Caves but to lead them on a wild goose chase. Colonel Jen still had the map, but the monk had promised to help, promised to show them the best route.

'I feel . . .' Trungpa was whispering hoarsely, '. . . I fear that something is wrong.'

Colonel Jen felt his throat tighten. He had not properly accounted for the jungle. The terrain was far worse than he had feared, and even the monks, who knew it intimately, seemed to be scared of venturing too far from Litang gompa.

'What's the problem?'

Dorgen Trungpa simply put his finger to his lips and frowned. Ever since Colonel Jen had informed him of his intention to follow the lamas into the jungle, the young monk had been muttering darkly about the guardians of the forest. He refused to be drawn as to what he meant by the phrase, but a shadow crossed his face whenever he spoke of them.

A hush seemed to have descended on the forest. Very slowly, Colonel Jen began to turn around, his eyes searching desperately, trying to make out anything unusual in the endless sea of greenery. He could not dismiss the feeling that there was something out there stalking them, closing in on them. He took his rifle off his shoulder and quickly raised it above his head, gesturing to the man behind him to do the same. The message was passed down the line of soldiers. Noisily they readied their weapons and adopted firing positions. Colonel Jen could see some of their faces – the looks of grim fatigue that they had been wearing only moments earlier had now been replaced by fear and apprehension. Suddenly there was a swishing sound, as if wind was rising through the forest canopy. Then a soldier a few yards back down the track dropped his weapon and cried out in terror:

'A migu! It's a migu!'

The men panicked: they stepped off the path, cowering into the undergrowth, undisciplined in their terror. Jen was shouting at them to hold their positions when he saw Dorgen Trungpa wince in pain. The monk's eyes bulged wide and his slender hand suddenly reached up to touch his neck. Then he stumbled forward. Colonel Jen dropped his rifle and grabbed the monk as he collapsed; his eyeballs were hidden under half-closed lids, his neck lolled crazily to the side. Then everything became a blur. Colonel Jen just had time to see a small feathered dart protruding from the monk's neck, and then he felt something fly past his right ear, missing him by a hair's breadth. And then a second later he felt something brushing his chin. Blow darts. He dived onto the ground and rolled away from the body of the fallen monk. Gunfire opened up all around as the soldiers emptied magazines into the dense jungle. Colonel Jen sprang to his feet only to see something, someone, a ferocious savage face, coming at him, a stone axe raised aloft.

Without thinking, Colonel Jen lunged forward and hit his assailant square in the chest, sending him flying into the undergrowth. Regaining his balance, Colonel Jen glanced back to the path; his men were being butchered left and right, running in confusion, and on all sides were semi-naked figures, wielding lethal Stone Age weapons. Nets fell from above, traps were sprung as the terrified soldiers crashed around in the undergrowth, branches laden with poison-tipped spikes swung towards the hapless men. The battle was already lost. Ten yards away a terrifying figure, dressed in animal skins and wearing a hideous mask, had seen Colonel Jen. The beast-man unleashed a hideous cry and began to charge. Colonel Jen felt as if the whole forest was turning on him, as if every evil thing in Pemako had been ordered to hunt him down. He dived into the foliage and began clawing his way through the undergrowth like a wild animal.

He ran for his life.

39

Their truck was part of a convoy of four vehicles heading east from Lhasa across the Tibetan plateau, down into the Kongpa region and then eventually on into China itself. The road, which deteriorated very rapidly once they were twenty miles or so out of Lhasa, followed the banks of the Yarlang Tsangpo. The Tsangpo rose hundreds of miles to the west of Lhasa, snaking around Asia's most holy mountain, Mount Kailash, fed by glaciers all the way along until it finally dived into Pemako and began its tumultuous descent down onto the endless plains of India. Despite the poor quality of the road and its precipitous course, the lorry-drivers chain-smoked furiously as they spun the wheels round the hairpin bends. The intermittent smell of burning brake pads mingled with the persistent stench of cigarette smoke and their faces were gradually caked in dust and grime.

Five hours out from Lhasa, they had successfully

passed through their first police checkpoint. A scruffily dressed policeman came out of a tiny wooden hut and flagged the convoy down. Smelling of chang and with a cigarette at his mouth, he examined their documents and then waved them through without any questions. They were squashed together in the cab, the three of them plus the driver. The minute the driver put his foot on the accelerator and pulled away from the checkpoint Jack let out a theatrical sigh of relief.

'I think we're in the clear. The police in Kongpa will be less scrupulous still.'

'Kongpa?' Nancy asked.

'It's the next province, between Lhasa and Pemako. It's a wild place – lots of Burmese and Assamese ethnic groups.'

'Like Pemako?'

'No. Not as weird as Pemako but the wild west nevertheless. Lawless, incredibly poor and very very inhospitable. Hardly worth trying to govern it.'

Gunn had been talking to the driver, but hearing Jack's comments he interjected, 'Don't listen to him, Nancy. It's the real Tibet. Tough country people. None of the comforts of monastic life.'

Comforts of monastic life! She smiled to herself. That really was a joke. It must be a truly hard place to live if it made a Tibetan monastery look like a soft option. Just then Gunn pointed to the road ahead.

'Look! See what I mean.'

There, next to the roadside, were two young Tibetan men. They could have been aged anything from sixteen to thirty. They were staring at the convoy as it passed. Strapped to their hands and knees were small wooden boards to protect their skin when they kneeled and bowed – which they did with every step. They would continue like this, Gunn explained, all the way to the Potala Palace.

'See what I mean – they are tough, religious people. Real Tibetans.'

Nancy turned her head as they flashed by. The two young men stared back at her. Behind them flowed the Yarlang Tsangpo, 'the purifier' as Jack had told her it was called, and on all sides the heart-achingly beautiful mountains rose to touch the heavens.

What a place! thought Nancy. How could anyone spend time here and not be profoundly changed? No wonder Herzog had become such an enigmatic man, standing aloof from the concerns of Western journalism. It was another world. She could already feel it all getting under her skin: the cobalt-blue sky, the crystalline air, the abundant religiosity and the nearness to nature and life and death. It elevated the important things in life and made the normal cares of material existence seem trivial and insignificant.

And Felix Koenig too would have passed down this

road many years ago. She tried to imagine how he must have experienced Tibet. But there she drew a blank: she found it was impossible to guess at the motivations of such a man; he was even more inscrutable to her than the pilgrims they had just passed on the road. How did he justify working for the Nazi Party? Perhaps he had no choice, perhaps he simply didn't think in those terms. Most probably he refused to engage with the realities around him at the time – he just wanted to work, to travel to Tibet. He must have felt far removed from the war in Europe up here on the roof of the world; maybe he was actually trying to escape from it all. Or was she being too generous to him? Was he in fact a zealot, a Goebbels or a Himmler, with his own bizarre theory of German racial origins – determined to aid the Nazis, the only way he knew how, by building them a mythology anchored in the Himalayas to underwrite their violence? She was floundering; she had only questions, and no answers. Seeking to divert herself, to rid herself of these whirling thoughts which proceeded nowhere, she turned to Gunn.

'So where did you learn to speak such good English?'

The driver was changing gear as they climbed a hill and the engine was straining terribly; Gunn had to shout to be heard.

'In Dharamsala, at Macleod Ganj.'

'So you've been to India? Why did you come back?'

'I missed my family ... And I discovered that running away from your troubles doesn't really solve them.'

'I didn't know it was possible to come back.'

'It's not supposed to be. The Chinese are paranoid about people who return ...'

'So how did you do it?'

'I walked – same as everyone else.'

'Isn't that dangerous?'

'Everything's dangerous these days.'

Jack had overheard their talk.

'Tell her what happened to you on the way back, Gunn,' he said, laconically.

Gunn laughed.

'No!'

'What did happen?' Nancy asked, intrigued by his refusal.

'Oh – nothing ...'

'Please tell me!'

'If you really want to know I'll tell you, but you won't like it.'

'Tell me anyway.'

'Well, I had got all the way over the high passes, I was really worn out – I had been walking for twenty-one days, I had run out of tsampa – you know, barley flour, it's what we eat – and I was just about ready to lie down on the mountainside when I was arrested by some Chinese soldiers . . .'

'That's terrible. How did you convince them to let you go?'

Gunn laughed, a hysterical, almost lunatic laugh, which perplexed Nancy.

'I didn't. They threw me in Drongpa jail – it's a stinking hellhole.'

'Oh my God – so how did you get out?'

Jack was smiling now, wryly, watching Gunn through narrowed eyes. Gunn grimaced over at him, and then continued.

'Well, I was desperate. I had almost made it and I was so angry with myself. But I didn't know what to do. And then I was put in a cell with another old Tibetan guy. He said to me, "If you want to get out then there's only one thing you can do – get a cigarette and burn your genitals with it."'

Nancy screwed up her face in disgust. Was this meant to be a joke? she thought. she looked round at Jack, who was smirking nastily, and said to him:

'Is this true?'

'Yes.'

Feeling more than slightly disgusted she managed to muster a question:

'How on earth would burning your genitals help you escape?'

'Well, the old man said that if I did it properly, it would look like a very bad case of venereal disease and the prison doctor would probably just kick me out . . .'

Nancy's face was still screwed up in disgust:

'Did you do it?'

'Yes. Of course. I would have tried anything. First I experimented on my hand.'

He held out the back of his hand to her so that she could take a good look at the scars she had noticed earlier. Shiny, puckered skin, each burn forming a horribly neat circle.

'Yes, horrible,' said Nancy. Gunn nodded and continued, 'Then I did what the old man said. It made me very ill, very feverish and there was lots of white pus and boils . . .'

Nancy recoiled from him.

'I bet there was. And what did the doctor say?'

'He took one look at me and told the sergeant to release me as I would be dead within a fortnight and it would look bad for him if I died in jail.'

'That's the most vile escape story I've ever heard . . .'

Jack was still smirking. 'Gunn,' he said. 'I never realized you could be so charming with women.'

'I warned her she wouldn't like it.'

'I'll remember next time to heed your warnings,' said Nancy, smiling grimly.

The three of them relapsed into silence, as the truck continued its juddering course.

40

The climate began to change as they descended from the cold heights of the Tibetan plateau. With it the flora and fauna changed too. As they approached Kongpa, the mountainsides became less stark until by the time they arrived at Bayi, an ugly little town on a river crossing, the forests were abundant all around and the humidity had risen to tropical levels.

The road had deteriorated further. Abandoned trucks lay at the bottom of the gorges, their drivers doomed by a moment of negligence, and Nancy saw that the driver was sweating as he turned the wheel for one merciless bend after another. She felt light-headed, as if any moment they might tilt and fall and fall, for thousands and thousands of feet. It gave her an unpleasant sense of vertigo, to see the sheer drop beneath and the steel carcasses of the crashed trucks. Eventually, the convoy leader pulled over in a clearing by the side of the road and declared the day's driving to be over. It was almost dark.

They jumped down from the cab. Part of the deal that Gunn had negotiated was that they would get their food with the drivers. And Nancy was pleased to see that soon there was a campfire burning merrily in the middle of the clearing. The lorry drivers were a jovial bunch. Nancy imagined that their lifestyle might be envied by other young Tibetan men. They got to travel and see the rest of Tibet and even China. But although they got paid well by Tibetan standards, they were still very poor.

The food cooked on the fireplace was tsampa, mixed with yak butter, 'an acquired taste' as Jack put it, laughing at Nancy as she screwed up her face in disgust. But it was all she had to eat, not having thought to pack provisions – how she would have loved some chocolate or an energy bar. She spooned down the tsampa and drank the water, which tasted of petrol, and drank a few mugs of steaming yak-butter tea, equally unpalatable. Not speaking a word of Tibetan, she was left alone as Jack and Gunn talked to the drivers. She watched them intently, their faces glowing in the orange light of the flames.

It was almost fun, she thought, even though the ob-servation startled her. Fun, if she dismissed the darker thoughts that perplexed her, the sinister whispers from the past. The night was clear, she had never seen so many stars, and the bracing air had a purity she had never before experienced. One of the younger drivers collected up the tin bowls and then the grandfather of the group went round the circle pouring little shots of chang into their empty tea mugs. Nancy took one sip of it and announced that she was going to bed. Jack exchanged words with the driver of their lorry and it was agreed that she could sleep in the cab. The driver led her away, with much raucous applause and laughter from the group and much embarrassment on his part. Nancy was embarrassed to observe that she had been given the most luxurious accommodation available in the camp, though it was little more than a strip of foam mattress and a filthy blanket. By the cab's interior light she unpacked a pair of thick socks – it was going to be a cold night and there was no heating at all. She pulled out her sleeping bag and as she did so the Oracle fell onto the seat. That made Nancy pause. She wondered if she should consult it, but no questions sprang to mind. Or, rather, she had thousands but they were too confused, her thoughts too garbled, to trouble the Oracle with, she felt. And did she want the answers she might receive anyway? Was Felix Koenig a blinded egotist, wilfully naive in his academic obsessions? Was Anton Herzog simply a madman, his reason destroyed by his origins? She couldn't imagine how the Oracle would answer such questions.

She leaned across the mattress and carefully laid out her sleeping bag. At that moment there was a knock on the door.

'Yes?'

'Is everything OK in there?' said Jack.

'Five-star luxury,' she said. 'Come in and see what you're missing out on.'

He put his head round the door, and immediately she saw his eyes turning to the Oracle, lying open on the seat.

'Am I the only sane person left in Tibet?' he said, with a weary sigh.

For a second she was embarrassed. He smiled at her as if he had just found her reading a teen romance. 'You'll be making decisions on the evidence of your tea leaves next,' he said.

'It works,' Nancy answered firmly. 'I wouldn't have believed it myself until I tried it – but it really works – it answers the questions that you ask it.'

'Sure it does.' He checked the side pocket of the cab for something.

'Have you never tried it?'

'No. It's just not my kind of thing. Of course

Anton told me on numerous occasions how gravely significant it is, and I know most of Asia agrees with him, but I'm staying well out of it . . .'

'Well, you should try it.'

'No thanks. I just don't get it at all. Why would it want to help you? That's what I don't understand. It might be actively screwing with your head, answering your questions in such a way as to send you down some crazy path, or to ruin your life absolutely. I just don't get these people with their optimistic and self-serving belief that all the unknowable forces of the universe are simply trying to help them. Why assume that? I'd imagine it would be more likely quite the reverse.'

'Krishna said that sometimes it tells you things that you don't want to hear.'

Jack smiled.

'Or perhaps you do want to hear them – it's just that consciously you don't think you do . . .'

'Well, even if that were true, it's still helping you access the power of your unconscious mind.'

'Or it's helping you to project your own opinions, conscious or not, onto its bizarre texts. It's like a feedback loop. And anyway, maybe it's better to leave the unconscious mind well alone. Maybe there's a reason all those dark urges are suppressed down there

– the last thing you want to do is to dredge them up and let them start to make all the decisions.'

Nancy shut the book.

'The thing about you is you pretend to be this great man of the world, but really you have a closed mind. You're almost superstitious, like an old-fashioned redneck not wanting to trust the unknown. You can take the boy out of Oregon, Jack, but can you take Oregon out of the boy?'

That made him laugh. 'No, you're right. I'm just a hick. Sure, I've travelled more widely than you will ever do, in your East Coast complacency. Sure I've bothered to learn just about every damn thing I can about this region. But I'm so glad you've come all the way from your little Park Slope enclave, to tell me what a provincial I am. That has really shattered all my illusions.'

'OK, OK, I'm not saying I'm better than you.'

He grinned at her. She sensed he really didn't care what she thought of him. Of course he doesn't, she thought. Why should he?

'Perhaps we'd better agree to disagree,' said Nancy, feeling almost affectionate towards this mutable man. He was like the weather, and that made her smile again: blustering and then sunny and then hailing down on you. But it didn't matter in the end. She didn't even mind it any more.

'OK, you're the boss,' he said, and she sensed he didn't really mind it either.

'Yes, you might remember that more often. The one with the chequebook, remember,' said Nancy.

He grinned at her. 'Well, unless the Oracle has a strong view on the matter, I'm going to bed.' And with that parting shot, Jack nodded to her, and shut the cab door behind him.

Nancy settled down in her sleeping bag but knew she wouldn't sleep yet. Still, it was pleasant to be lying flat out, after being hunched in a shuddering lorry all day. She thought about what Jack had said, and wondered if there was any truth in it after all, if the Oracle was just a way of drawing out unconscious urges, bringing them into the light of day. If that was the case – and it was plausible enough – then why was that intrinsically bad? Better to know your innermost thoughts and fears, than to refuse them, surely? But what if they did overwhelm you? Was that when you became a crazy zealot, a Felix Koenig? A Nazi with a will to power? Or even Anton Herzog? Was that what Jack was talking about?

She put the Oracle on the ledge next to the sleeping bag. She noticed she was handling it gingerly, as if it was a ticking bomb. Lying down again, she tried to think of other things. Tomorrow, if all went well, she would finally set foot in Pemako. And on the way, she would also get to see a functioning gompa, one far away from the scrutiny of the Chinese power base in Lhasa. With these thoughts she whiled away the time – perhaps it was only minutes after all – until sleep overtook her.

41

By six a.m. they were on their way, and the convoy didn't stop again until they reached the dropping-off point for Bhaka gompa. They disembarked, and stood watching as the convoy roared off down the winding road, casting great plumes of dust behind. Glancing up, Nancy saw that the sky was becoming overcast; it looked as if it would soon start to rain.

They hoisted their packs onto their backs and marched along a steep path that descended the forested hillside in the direction of the Yarlang Tsangpo. A light drizzle began to fall and distant thunder rolled around the great peaks that barred their way into Pemako. The path took them to the point where the river was at its narrowest, a ten-yard-wide stone-sided gorge with the water barrelling along beneath. There they crossed a newly renovated rope bridge, which bounced and swayed as they moved along it, so Nancy was afraid, though she tried to hide it from her companions. Below, the deep green water rushed on, flooding towards what Gunn told her were the celebrated falls of Pemako.

On the other side of the bridge, the path was clearly marked and well used – prayer flags were dotted here and there before it split in two, one fork heading into the thick of the old-growth wood and straight for the Su La pass, the other following the river back downstream for a quarter of a mile before coming out on the lawn of the Bhaka gompa.

Despite the drizzle it was a pleasant day for walking; it wasn't too cold and there were no mosquitoes or midges. In this reasonable weather, it didn't seem long to Nancy before they stepped on to the monastery lawn and found themselves eye to eye with a willowy lone monk.

The original old gompa, a sixteenth-century structure, was little more than a ruin, but around it stood a collection of more recently constructed buildings. The monk, a thin-faced, tall man dressed in orange robes, his grey hair shaved to stubble, welcomed them all, and immediately began to talk to Gunn and Jack in Tibetan. Then they were shown into a building which Nancy guessed was where the monks ate their meals, and were given seats at a table in front of a roaring log fire. Another monk appeared with a large urn of soupy butter tea. Nancy drank it because she was thirsty, though the taste was still alien and unpleasant. Like tea made with milk that's been in the sun all day, she thought. Shortly afterwards, three sherpas appeared through the door. Jack and Gunn engaged them in what was clearly a protracted haggle. Neither party would move, that was clear, and it took half an hour of intense negotiation before they clinked mugs and sealed the arrangement.

'Everything OK?' Nancy said then to Jack, and he nodded. 'Fine, don't you worry your big New York brain.' She smiled sardonically back at him, Jack winked slowly, deliberately, and then he turned back to Gunn and the sherpas. There was a lot to be done; they wanted to leave as soon as possible.

Bowls of tsampa were served. Nancy tried her best to swallow as much as possible, knowing that it was a long march before they even reached the edge of the forest and began the steep ascent to the frozen heights of the Su La. Whilst they were eating, an elderly-looking lama came in and began an earnest conversation with Gunn and Jack. His shaven head was covered in white stubble and his wrinkled forehead and face bore testament to a hard life; perhaps he had been here in 1959, thought Nancy, when she had been told the old monastery was sacked.

She waited patiently to learn what they were talking about, and after a few minutes the lama shook hands with Jack and left. A dark frown now distorted Jack's face.

'Was that the Abbot?' said Nancy.

'No. The Abbot's in exile in Nepal for interfering with the loggers who operate round here. The Chinese booted him out.'

'Who was that man then?'

'The senior lama. Not a very inspiring man, I have to say. It is a damn shame that there is no proper leader to replace the Abbot.'

He was beating about the bush, thought Nancy; he must have learnt some bad news.

'So what did he say?'

Jack looked at her and sighed.

'A contingent of Chinese soldiers passed this way yesterday,' he said. 'A big well-armed group, about eighty men, on their way to Litang gompa.'

'What were they doing?'

'The lama doesn't know. But he said it's unusual. The garrison at Metok isn't due to be replaced until early September, so they're obviously on some kind of mission.'

There was a worried pause, while Gunn shook his head.

'Did you ask about Anton?' Nancy asked.

'Yes. He was here, two and a half months ago, with the Terton Thupten Jinpa. They were headed for

Rinchenpung gompa, which is halfway down the Yarlang Tsangpo, on the other side of the Su La – but the lama thinks they never reached it. One of the monks from Rinchenpung gompa came by six weeks ago on his way to Lhasa and said that they had never seen Anton or the terton.'

'Maybe he was travelling under a different name?'

'No. There would be no point. Everyone in Rinchenpung already knows him. He's a famous yogi.'

For a moment Nancy thought she must have misunderstood. 'Who, Anton?'

'Yes,' said Jack with a shrug. 'Anton is a holy man, it would appear.'

Jack was wearing a strange expression on his face. He raised his eyebrows as if he wanted to dissociate himself from what he was saying, as if he found it as disquieting as she did.

'It turns out that round here he has quite a reputation. You should have heard that old lama going on about what a wise man Herzog is. Apparently, he can work miracles.'

Nancy found her mouth was open, like an astonished child, so she closed it. Herzog was like a shapeshifter, she thought, constantly evolving into something else. Just when she thought she might have an idea about who he was, some new piece of information caused her to think again. In New York he had been a legend, but this legendary status had been based on familiar notions: the maverick, the brilliant mind, the unconventional journalist tolerated by his superiors because of the genius of his stories. In Tibet, too, myths had been woven around him, but of a completely different order. She looked across at Jack, saw he was inviting her to mock the lama with him, but she couldn't quite do it. So she nodded and drank down the last of her butter tea.

The general mood had been darkened by the news of the soldiers. Gunn was unsmiling and taciturn, and wouldn't be drawn when Nancy asked him what he thought. They went to join the sherpas outside on the lawn, Jack explaining as they went that there were always soldiers in Pemako now since the Sino-Indian war over the still disputed border, but normally they stayed put in Metok, or stuck to one or two well-known patrols down near the Doshang La. In the garden they handed their belongings to the sherpas, and then bade farewell to Gunn, who was going to wait another night and catch a lift back to Lhasa the following morning. He wished them good luck, shaking hands with Nancy and slapping Jack on the back.

'Good luck,' he said to both of them. 'You will need it.'

They passed across the lawn, and on the other side Nancy turned and saw Gunn standing still as a sentinel, his palms together, his eyes closed, as if he was giving them a blessing.

By dusk they had climbed out of the wood, and they pitched camp on a mossy clearing alongside the path. There were two tents, one for the sherpas and one for Jack and Nancy, an arrangement that made Nancy slightly uncomfortable, though she was hardly in a position to argue. A small stream bubbled between the rocks at the edge of the clearing and there was a long, beautiful view back down to the forest and the valley below. With the light fading, Nancy wrapped herself in the folds of a sheepskin coat and tried to swallow one more cup of yak-butter tea. When Jack had finished talking to the sherpas, he walked over to where she was sitting.

'I was just going through the menu options with our chef,' he said jokingly.

'Oh. I would like the smoked salmon starter and the linguini for my main.'

'I'm afraid, madam, they're both off tonight. Only yak-based products. We're having an authentic Tibetan nomad evening.'

'Great, I can hardly wait,' said Nancy.

'Don't worry,' he said, sitting down next to her. 'It's not far to go now. Are you feeling OK?'

It was the first kind thing he had said to her on the whole trip, and Nancy was almost too surprised to reply. Feeling almost awkward, she said quickly, 'Yes thanks, fine.'

'I had been thinking,' said Jack, 'that we should head for Litang gompa, but if Anton never made it there, then there's little point.'

'What towns are there in Pemako?'

Jack laughed grimly.

'In Pemako, just Metok, if you can call it a town, which would be stretching it. But we don't want to go there. There's a couple of other villages, but they're so close to Metok that I'd rather not risk them either.'

'Why not?'

'Because I suspect Anton would have wanted to avoid Metok and the surrounding area.'

'Where else then?'

'Let's start with Mandeldem hermitage. I know he liked it there. I remember him waxing lyrical about it on a couple of occasions. It sounded like a ghastly place, a pile of bricks and a leaky roof, lost in the jungle, surrounded by rhododendron bushes. But I suspect someone will have seen him there, so let's just nose around, see what we can find. The sherpas know the way and it's relatively easy walking to get there: down the river, except when you want to climb the valley sides to one or another dreadful little hovel that is used for transcendental meditation and Tantric retreats. Remember, one night spent in a trance in Pemako is worth one hundred nights of meditation anywhere else, so they say . . .'

Nancy didn't think that sounded so very absurd. Even here, on the borderlands, the landscape was already having a strange effect on her; the ancient forest and the monumental scenery seemed to exaggerate her feelings of smallness and fragility. Yet she also felt part of the very immensity that cowed her: staring around at the rocks and trees she understood that she had been created from the landscape specifically to admire it; she was nature looking back on itself.

It made her want to walk for ever in the misty vales and dark woods, journeying from gompa to gompa in the hope that one day she would reach union with the energy around her. She knew that this was what the yogis hoped for when they undertook their extended pilgrimages, dependent on alms and the benevolence of strangers, sleeping on the hills and valleys and in dilapidated hermitages. It suddenly all made sense to her now: the landscape demanded this kind of devotion and attention; it deserved to be trodden for ever by pilgrims' feet.

But where, she thought, where in all of this beauty and mystery was Anton Herzog?

42

The Abbot's deputy sat by Herzog's side, transfixed by the story he was hearing, whilst the fire cast its flickering light into the rustling leaves above. Was it true? Could it really be possible that this ruined man had actually made it to the sacred kingdom? And if so, was his description correct? To his mind, Shangri-La was no fable, but the Abbot's deputy had never imagined that it would be as the Westerner described. The lamaistic traditions were obscure and they conflicted in their descriptions of the place. The stranger had been so precise in his descriptions, so minute in his details – and yet these sorts of precise details could equally derive from vision or dream.

Nothing was certain. The Abbot's deputy studied Herzog's glassy eyes – the eyes of a madman, perhaps, a man who had fallen into darkness – or maybe this was merely the effect of the opium. That too was a growing concern: the pipes they supplied him with to maintain his lucidity would eventually tip him over the edge into the abyss of the lotus-eaters, where it was impossible to untangle fantasy from reality. For all his doubts, the deputy couldn't help returning to the vividness of the stranger's story, which had made him think as he listened that he too had seen this place, he too had visited the ambiguous kingdom of Shangri-La.

The doctor poured some water into Anton Herzog's dry mouth. His wrinkled neck contracted as he swallowed painfully until he gasped for breath and the doctor took the water bottle away from his lips. Patiently the Abbot's deputy waited, and then when he thought that Herzog had recovered enough strength he began again to probe.

'So what happened next? What did you do?'

Herzog coughed his dry, painful cough and turned his mesmerizing blue eyes back on to the deputy.

'I don't know exactly how long I remained curled up on the floor of my room in the evil tower, unable even to think, rocking gently back and forth. I was in shock, you see.'

'Yes. I am sure you were,' consoled the Abbot's deputy.

Herzog coughed again and then recommenced.

'I was paralysed by despair, I thought that this was the end of all my years of searching and aspiration. And I saw now quite clearly the vast gulf of experience and disposition that lay between me and Felix Koenig and his companions. They had come to Tibet from Germany as Teutonic knights marching into battle. They had been brutalized by the horrors of World War One and by the severity of the times; they would not have cared a damn about a battlement bedecked with human heads. And I asked myself, what had I been thinking of all these years? I had been deluded; I had imagined that I, a lone individual, little more than a dilettante scholar, could recreate the trials of one of the most powerful and driven groups of men in modern European history, whose only ethical measure was their unquenchable desire to build a better Fatherland.'

The Abbot's deputy was desperate to learn what happened next. He did not want to hear Herzog's speculations. Talk of Fatherlands and Teutonic knights was incomprehensible to him.

'Tell me what happened. You said you were lying curled up on the floor of the tower.'

'Yes. I was. And I was beyond despair. Never have I experienced such terror before or since. Then suddenly there was a knock on the door. Trembling with nerves and a determination to survive, somehow, I sprang to my feet. A well-groomed oriental man stepped into the room.

'"I am sorry to have kept you waiting," he said,

with a thin smile. "My name is Yuen – I am the Abbot's assistant. You must be hungry? Perhaps you would like to eat."'

The Abbot's deputy's eyes were wide as saucers.

'Were you not afraid they were going to kill you then and there? Why didn't you try to hide? Or attack him?'

'Hide?' A dry laugh escaped from Herzog's lips. 'Where was there to hide? And yes, I was petrified for my life, but I knew there was no point attacking him. Even if I had succeeded in overpowering him there would have been hordes of other men behind him. As I heard the knock on the door I realized there was only one course of action that I could take. At all costs I had to conceal my true fears, to claim a courage I didn't in reality possess. I still hoped that by conducting myself as someone who expects to be treated with respect and courtesy, I might discourage them from taking any liberties with me. It seemed a desperate hope, but it was all that I could summon at that moment.

'So I agreed with alacrity to the offer of food and then I said, '"Can you please confirm that I will have an opportunity to meet the head lama of this place? Or am I a prisoner in your monastery?"'

'The man smiled and answered:

'"The Abbot will be joining you for dinner. And as

to whether or not you are a prisoner, well, we are all prisoners here, though we prefer not to put it quite like that. But it is true that it is not possible to walk out of this place. The terrain offers no route out and there is no human habitation for countless miles. I do not include the settlement in the valley below in this assessment, which you have already seen. But it is against the vows of our order to visit this place. And they do not come to visit us. Indeed, we all come to love our confinement – as I am sure you will too."

'I felt as if I was about to choke on my own tongue, so desperate was I to scream out questions, but somehow I restrained myself. In the most calm voice I could muster I said, "I see, well, I will take this further with the Abbot."

'The man smiled again, as if to agree that it would be futile to discuss anything further at this moment, and so I followed him down the stairs, through various doors and finally into a spacious dining room. He pulled out a chair for me at the table and, terrified and trying once more to mask my true emotions, I sat down and waited to see what would happen next.

'I did not have to wait long. A minute later, the door at the far end of the room opened and a very elderly, sinewy Chinese man came in and joined me at the table.

'"Welcome to Shangri-La," he said, in a very soft,

dry voice. 'You have succeeded where so many others have failed."'

The Abbot's deputy's forehead was contorted by a frown. He interrupted Herzog's flow again.

'But what did he mean by that? Have lots of people tried to reach Shangri-La?'

Herzog was deep into his opium-inspired memory. A mere question could no longer pull him from the depths of his dream. He ignored the deputy's question and continued to describe the scene before him, as if he was there again at that moment, seated before the Abbot of Shangri-La.

'The Abbot paused and gestured to a servant to pour jasmine tea for us both. Even though I was in a state of almost complete panic and fear, I could not help noticing that the cups and the teapot were made of priceless Ming china. How could that be, I wondered. And, stranger still, how was it that they were using this invaluable porcelain like a normal tea set?

'The civility of the tea ritual could not remove from my mind the images of severed human heads and of the human-sized cage. I had never conceived that Shangri-La would be anything other than an oriental paradise, and now it appeared rather that I was about to become the victim of a gruesome Aztec-style ceremony. If I did not cry out and crumble altogether I suspect it was simply because I could not entirely believe what had happened. It was too far removed from all my expectations. I was in shock, I suspect, and unable to process everything that was before me. And besides it was so contradictory – the holy calm of the Abbot, the careful pouring of tea, and then outside, a pyre awaiting a human sacrifice, it seemed, and all the evidence of bloody carnage!

'Even as I struggled to understand this, the Abbot continued. "I have no doubt that you have many questions, but first let me offer you a little explanation, as it will save us both time. Throughout the world, people dream of the myth of Shangri-La; some even wonder if it really exists; a tiny few even think that one day they will try to find it, and then there are the handful of people who actually set out to do just that. These people are possessed of extraordinary mental and physical attributes. In the first place, simply to sustain a belief in a place for which there is no proof requires great powers of intuition and will. Secondly, doing all the research that is necessary even to give yourself a fraction of a chance of reaching this place requires immeasurable effort. And finally, embarking on the journey itself requires the ability to draw upon non-material realms of knowledge, and this of course means that the initiate must be of advanced psychic development.

'"From here in the lamasery we do our best to aid

willing pilgrims. We send out psychic messages to alert them to our existence, much as one might send a radio broadcast. Of course, few people these days believe that such powers exist, so even when they receive our communications in their dreams they dismiss them as being just that: dreams and nothing more. But there are always some sensitive people who are awake to their intuition and instinct, and naturally these are the people we seek: people of tremendous psychic power and ambition; people who wish to change the world. Throughout the last millennia of human history we have again and again received visitors from the coming races of men. We have received emissaries from Babylon and Egypt, from Greece and Rome, and more recently from Britain and from revolutionary France and more recently still, from Nazi Germany.

' "You have distinguished yourself. You have found the way to our kingdom, and through decades of mental exertion and a journey that brought you almost to the point of death, you have finally made it to our table and consequently, in the hallowed traditions of our brotherhood, you are a worthy successor to the throne of Shangri-La."

'I could hardly believe my ears. It appeared to me that I must finally have lost my mind. This Abbot, this old man seated before me, sipping tea from a priceless porcelain cup, seemed to be suggesting that I would now become King of Shangri-La. I simply did not know what to do or say. Clutching at my original intentions, intentions that now seemed naive and foolish, I tried to formulate some sensible demands. I had no idea what to say to this man but I had an urgent need to say something – to seize control of my destiny.

'Finally I managed to say, "I have come all this way in search of the lost Aryan knowledge. This is all I seek. And I would like to know how I may leave this place. I am grateful to you for your hospitality but I simply cannot impose on you. I merely wanted to visit and to see such a place, and now I am satisfied."

'The Abbot dabbed at the corner of his mouth with a napkin.

' "The knowledge that you speak of is contained in the sacred Book of Dzyan, which has been handed down for millennia and is kept within the citadel walls. You will be able to see the book tomorrow after your coronation. In fact, then you will have access to anything that you wish, for you will be King and you will be able to do whatever you please. But you cannot leave. You are the appointed successor to the throne, and your destiny lies here, in your kingdom."

'The old man could see that I was completely horror-struck by this news, and he tried to reassure me.

'"Do not be alarmed or depressed. We have everything that you might want here. People who arrive from outside are usually at first inconsolable – it seems no one can bear the initial prospect of giving up their lives in the outside world. But I promise you that after the first few years you will be very happy, in fact you will realize how lucky you are to be removed from the chaos of human life. From our experience, there is no one, no matter what their attachments to the outside world, be they love or material possessions, who has not become gratefully resigned to their new fate over a number of years. The passions and rewards of the outside world pale into insignificance alongside the knowledge and power that we possess here."

'His words merely enhanced my feelings of panic and horror. I had to leave. No matter what this man said, I had to leave immediately. There must be a way – there must be some possible route out. Yet I also wanted to see the Book of Dzyan, but without having to undergo my coronation. Desires battled in my head; I had to secure an escape route.

'"But how do you supply yourselves with necessary goods, even with this beautiful china we are drinking from, if you maintain your isolation from the outside world?" I said.

'"It saddens me that you are clearly still hoping that you might be able to find a way out of here. I can assure you that it is not possible. But to answer your question, every five years a caravan arrives at the high pass above the monastery and deposits for us such goods as we require. We leave payment in advance. There is no contact with the caravaneers, and even if one of our number were to reach them, they have specific orders not, on pain of death, to communicate with us, let alone help us."

'I could no longer maintain my calm, and my posture slumped. My head fell into my hands, such was the crushing weight of my despair and fear. The Abbot tried to console me.

'"Do not worry. You must believe me when I say that you will come to love your time here."

'There was something about the phrase "your time here" that disconcerted me, and a ghastly thought suddenly occurred to me that made the hairs on the back of my neck stand on end.

'"And if I am to be the new King, can I ask: what happened to the old King?"

'The Abbot averted his gaze from me and stared into the bottom of his delicate teacup.

'"The present King will be relieved of his office tonight. As will his Queen. The King always has a Queen, normally a Chinese or Tibetan woman, but in rare cases another race. But tonight is the end of their reign."

'My heart missed a beat.

' "What? Why? Who is the present King?"

' "The present King is a German man. One of a party of five who visited us many years ago, seeking knowledge and power. He is of course an old man now – though due to our climate and our practices he is still in good health. But our custom dictates that when a new pilgrim arrives, the old King must step down." '

'I felt I was going to be sick. All I could think of was the cage and the bonfire. My head was pounding as I struggled against the realization – I tried to divert myself:

' "How can he still be alive? He must be over ninety years old."

' "Yes – but he appears to be much younger. You will think that he is in his mid-fifties. Our Tantric practices that lower human metabolism, combined with the unique climate of this valley, have the effect of delaying the natural ageing processes. We have several lamas here who are over one hundred years old."

' "And the other four who came with this German man? His companions? Where are they?"

'The man looked up at me through limpid eyes and said:

' "They were all kings before him. It is the law that

where there are several prospective kings, each will reign only for a decade. They had their allotted time upon the throne and now they have departed."

' "What do you mean they have departed? Departed where?"

' "Departed to join our Masters in the higher worlds."

'I tried to swallow but my mouth was dry. The Abbot was insane. The entire kingdom was a bastion of black magic and evil. I thought of the warning of the kindly man in the valley below. How right he was, and how foolish I had been to ignore him. The Abbot, with all his craven gravitas, conducting himself as if this was a perfectly holy enterprise and as if he was a spiritual man rather than a savage butcher of lives, rose to leave.

'As he bowed to me, he said, "Thank you for listening so patiently to my explanations. It is always disconcerting for new arrivals here. It appears that you are managing very well. I suggest that you return to your room and get some rest. The abdication ceremony takes place at nightfall. As the King-to-be, your presence will be required."

'With that he left the room. I was completely terror-struck. I could barely even think. I was trapped in a medieval monastery, surrounded by a brotherhood of monks whose moral sense was so wildly out of line with any civilized norm that they were apparently about to burn a man alive.

'And yet part of what he had said rang true: I understood some vestige of his descriptions of psychic summoning, of messages sent in dreams and at dimly resonating levels of human consciousness. After all, I had clung stubbornly to the idea of Shangri-La for years without even a shred of proof that it existed. I had felt a calling, in my dreams and even in my waking hours, an insistent siren song had taunted me. All that time, I knew that Shangri-La existed and I knew, just as the sun rises in the east, that one day I would arrive there.

'My gullet rose at the thought of the bonfire and the cage: I too would meet that fate. That was the inevitable implication: they were going to burn me alive. If not tonight, as I had only moments ago feared, then one day in the future when some other poor soul struggled across the Himalayas and against all the odds found their way to Shangri-La. Then I too would be sent to join the Masters, as the crazy Abbot put it. I too would be forced to abdicate.

'A few minutes later, after I had been escorted back to my room in silence, I tried to regain a hold on my wits. I sat down and forced myself to breathe slowly and deeply and then I struggled to assemble the facts. The lamas of Shangri-La had no intention of ever letting me leave again – that much was clear. Felix Koenig had told the truth when he said that his expedition had reached their goal; that too was obvious and furthermore, according to the Abbot, one of Koenig's companions was not only still alive but was actually now the King of Shangri-La, though given the fate that befell all monarchs of this evil place, it was not at all clear if that meant anything other than that he had been imprisoned here for years with a sentence of ultimate death by burning upon his head.

'But then there was one other equally incontrovertible fact that provided at least a faint glimmer of hope: Felix Koenig had escaped. He had made it back to India; he had been seen again, and so it was not true that there was no way out at all. Sure, by the time he had reached Bombay, he was raving mad and he never completely regained his mental equilibrium, but the war was also to account for that.

'The fact was that the descriptions that Felix Koenig had passed on, though vague and strange, seemed to be of the same place. The longing to fly down to the emerald valley that he described was almost conclusive proof to me. I could easily picture myself, as the condemned King, pacing the battlements, yearning to be back in the emerald valley, and instead waiting grimly for my successor to tug on the thread below.

'And there were other thoughts that came to mind:

Haushofer and Hess had been right about Tibet and the Book of Dzyan. But did they gain anything from their contact with Shangri-La? Did Koenig's companions ever exercise their authority as kings in any decisive way, or had they been merely summoned by the lamas as sacrificial offerings, chosen from amongst the German race at the height of its powers as fitting physical and psychic specimens? And had the lamas instigated the dreams of Wotan and sown the seeds of the upheavals of the war? Had they been using their awful knowledge to cultivate, in the garden of Europe, a breed of men of such will-power and self-belief that they would be fitting heirs to the barbaric throne of Shangri-La? Or were the rest of Haushofer's beliefs also true? Was the Book of Dzyan an Aryan artefact left over from the destruction of an Aryan civilization in the Gobi desert, a civilization that itself had risen from the ashes of Lemuria, the lost continent of the Pacific?

'All these question whirled in my brain. If I resigned myself to my fate, and accepted the imprisonment and certain death of my reign as King, then I would be able to seek answers to these questions. It was ironic, I thought, that I would gain much of what I had desired – access to the Book of Dzyan, knowledge of the deepest mysteries of the psychic carnage that had devastated Europe. But the price would be my own incarceration, my own violent death. And it seemed to me at that moment that I cared much more about life than all these questions. I had to find a way out of this ghastly place. I had to discover the escape route that Felix Koenig must have discovered before me. He at least was proof that it was possible, whatever the High Lama said . . .'

43

First light came early, just after five thirty a.m. As Nancy came blearily into consciousness, she could hear that at least one of the sherpas was already up, making breakfast. She rolled over onto her elbow, and found that she was alone in the cramped tent. In the struggling daylight, she saw Jack's things folded neatly, everything ready for departure. She slipped out of her sleeping bag, her chilled breath issuing from her mouth in great plumes. She put on her walking boots and the chuba and then wrestled her arms into the sheepskin coat and crawled out of the tent.

Breakfast was a hurried affair, everyone standing in silence eating tsampa out of tin mugs and drinking butter tea. As soon as the tents were packed and the mugs had been washed in the stream, they set off again; the serious climb was about to begin. Step by step, the going got more difficult. Nancy's lungs no longer acted automatically. She had to force herself to breathe with every step in order to get enough oxygen into her veins to propel her forward. After half an hour of this, she had almost lost sight of the two sherpas. Jack was some ten yards in front of her and the other sherpa was bringing up the rear, alert for danger, she assumed. Even though Jack was just within talking distance, the idea of even attempting to exchange words was out of the question. She needed all her energy simply to stay upright.

For hour after hour they ascended like this; even when they took an occasional break for water and butter tea, Nancy said nothing, parsimonious with words because she was so exhausted. The temperature edged a little lower until it was well below freezing and the scree slopes were peppered with snow. At the back of her mind was the possibility that the pass might in fact be entirely snowbound, in which case they would have to descend again. That would shatter morale, she thought. The other concern was altitude sickness, for that too would bring to a speedy end her chances of getting into Pemako. The instant it set in, and it could come any time, they would have to get straight back down to a lower altitude. She would have to hope that she was lucky, that they were all lucky.

By midday, they were approaching the top of the pass. The slopes were spartan at this height; only the lichens and mosses still managed to flourish. A mist had enveloped the path and was billowing around the rocky crevasse up which they were ascending towards the Su La. Nancy was aware that she was getting a headache, and she seemed to be losing the ability to tell whether she was hot or cold, although it was well below freezing. This troubled her deeply, and she tried to resist these signs that her body was not coping, to push them away.

The sherpa following behind came up level with her and tried to offer encouragement. He seemed to be indicating that they were near the top. She tried to smile but couldn't manage it, and then all of a sudden she slipped and everything went dark. The next thing she knew, she was sitting inside the tent and someone was trying to pour hot tea down her throat while someone else was rubbing her back through the sheep-skin and the chuba. For a moment she couldn't speak; she was disoriented and her head was pounding as if she had received a blow. Jack said, 'OK, now, have some more of this,' and forced the tea towards her lips again. She took a sip.

'Am I all right?' she asked him.

'Yes. We are going to rest. Drink more tea. Your body needs the heat.'

'Is it the altitude?'

'I don't think so. It's more likely to be exhaustion . . .'

She tried to explain that she was fine, that they should simply press on, but then she must have fallen asleep again. How long she slept she did not know, but she awoke feeling somewhat better. When she opened her eyes, the image that presented itself to her was so surreal that she thought for a second that she must be dreaming. Jack was lying next to her and the three sherpas were squatting over them both, their backs pushing out the canvas of the tent wall. They looked like doctors in an operating theatre.

'Jack?'

'Nancy, you're awake. Good.'

'What happened? Why is everyone in here?'

'We're talking – and keeping warm.'

'What time is it?'

'It's morning.'

'Still?'

'Er . . . no. A day and night have passed since you went to sleep.'

'Really?'

'How are you feeling?'

'A bit better I think. Listen, I'm sorry about this . . .'

'No need. Let's try and get some breakfast down you and then see if we can get going. It's only few hundred yards more to the top. We were lucky you called the break here – it's quite sheltered.' He began to untangle himself from his sleeping bag, and as he did so the sherpas slipped out of the tent doors and into the snow, like seals slipping through a hole in the ice.

'I'll come back in a moment with some breakfast,' he said.

'Tsampa?'

'Oh yes. Don't you worry, tsampa is always on the menu at this hotel.'

She managed to laugh, though hoarsely as she watched him disappear through the tent door. She was feeling a bit better. It had been so intense, the feeling of exhaustion; it was as if she couldn't go on – in fact she hadn't gone on, she reminded herself. Her body had just called time on the whole escapade; it had independently decided enough was enough, no matter what her mind wanted it to do.

The tent was already much colder, now that the three men had all left. Jack reappeared and passed her two tin mugs, one of tea and one filled to the brim with tsampa.

'The orders of the hotel stroke hospital tent are that you must finish both of these, no complaining, and then we'll reassess your case.'

This wasn't so bad, she thought with a smile; being relatively snug and warm, whilst Jack waited on her hand and foot, even if it was moist sawdust that he was serving her. He must have been worried about her. Sure he was, losing the pay packet on a hazardous mountain, hardly the sort of thing he wanted to do. Always keep your sponsors alive – that must be his basic mantra. But perhaps that was unfair. He might have been genuinely concerned about her; he wasn't, she was coming to realize, quite the mercenary that Krishna had advertised him as.

Herzog must be a hard man, she thought. He was in his sixties. To do this climb was bad enough, even at her age, but they said he still scaled peaks as well. Physical strength and will-power, that's what got you up mountains; but by his age the will-power had to be pre-eminent, compensating entirely for the fading strengths of the body. To do this climb, at his age, Herzog must be a man with an iron will Or, she thought grimly, really a magician, able to conjure himself up these ancient ravines, to warp the properties of the physical world. It wasn't possible, but then what was possible anyway? – she no longer knew, and couldn't begin to imagine.

44

The final ascent wasn't nearly as bad as Nancy had expected. Perhaps she had acclimatized, or maybe she was invigorated by her twenty-four hours' sleep: either way, she reached the top of the 13,000-foot pass without having to rest again. She didn't realize at first that it was the top of the pass. She simply noted that the party had stopped, and for a time she was bent double, struggling to breathe. Yet when she looked up she saw several great piles of stones and hundreds of prayer flags fluttering in the mist. The air was full of freezing moisture and it was impossible to see more than twenty yards. Presumably the view was spectacular; she would never know. As they reached the first pile of stones, the sherpas burst into song and tied small flags of cloth to some of the sturdier-looking flagpoles. They began to chat excitedly to Jack, and Nancy asked what they were all talking about.

'They say that we should enjoy the cold while we

can.' Jack laughed heartily, also in high spirits. 'As soon as we drop down four or five thousand feet, it will be boiling hot.'

She found it hard to believe, but soon enough they were off again and, within the hour, the mist had vanished and she could clearly see the path ahead and the surrounding landscape. They were at the top end of a lush tropical valley. The path ahead was a wavy black line etched into the scree slope; the descent was clear, and a welcome change from the merciless climb of recent days.

They plodded on downwards and gradually the scree was broken up by vegetation: first, ankle-high dwarf ferns and then waist-high bushes. When they descended to about ten thousand feet the trees returned. Now, as the sherpas had predicted, they were stripping off their clothes, first the sheepskins and then the chubas. The sun was directly overhead with not a wisp of cloud to offer protection – just an azure, blemish-free sky and all around an ever-growing riot of greenery.

Their course wound through jungle, and the sterile silence of the upper levels was now replaced with a cacophony of noise: insects and animals, snuffling through the undergrowth; life in all its colour and vibrancy. They stopped for lunch in a deserted village that was surrounded on all sides by cornfields partially overrun by the creeping jungle. They drew water from an abandoned well, cleaned it with iodine drops, and made tea and tsampa.

With Jack translating for her, Nancy asked the sherpas if they had any experience of tertons. The oldest sherpa, a man called Glumbuk Mergo, gave a long and sincere account of how he had once witnessed a terton drawing a terma out of a giant rock boulder. This had happened down in his home village in what was now China, many years ago, when he was a boy. With much waving of his hands, he explained how he had seen an old terton strip himself almost bare and then, after meditating for three days and nights, he had stood up and struck the rock with a hammer, in front of the entire village. There had been an explosion, like a lightning strike, and everyone had fallen to the floor and hidden in fear. When they looked up they saw a terrifying spirit beast, a terdak, the guardian of the terma in the spirit realm, fighting with the terton. There were more explosions and they all ran into the forest and hid. When it was quiet again, Glumbuk and some of the other young men came back and discovered the terton lying on his back with the terma, a thick yak-skin book in this case, resting on his chest.

Jack translated all this with a smile and winked at Nancy when he got to the bit about the terdak. Nancy said nothing, but she wondered at Glumbuk's certainty, his absolute conviction that this was what he had seen. With my own eyes, he had kept saying, pointing at his eyes to emphasize his words. After that, one of the sherpas went off and picked some orchids for Nancy and a mood of levity took over the group; for a brief hour they forgot about the risks they were taking and the strange mission they were embarked upon.

The sherpas were just packing up the paraffin stove when suddenly they became aware that they were being watched. Unnoticed, an old man dressed in red-orange robes and wearing a golden-red crown on his head had approached to within ten feet of their camp and was now observing them calmly with his hands pressed together in greeting and prayer. The sherpas looked as stunned as Nancy was, unable to believe that an old man had managed to sneak up on them. For a moment even Jack seemed to be speechless, but then he managed to regain his composure. He stood up and, putting his hands together, he bowed low to the old man, in recognition of his seniority.

There followed an exchange of words. The old man's voice was high-pitched and grating and he spoke in very short, abrupt sentences. Jack appeared to Nancy to be asking all the questions; he spoke at length, clearly putting propositions to the old man. Suddenly their visitor turned and pointed down the valley in the direction of Metok and embarked on a long monologue that lasted for two or three minutes, Jack nodding at him earnestly as he spoke. When he had finished Jack offered him some tea, which he refused with a brisk movement of his hands. Bowing, he departed, slipping into the jungle without a sound. The sherpas looked anxiously at Jack and Glumbuk Mergo said something in Tibetan. Nancy too wanted to know what the old man had said.

'What's going on?'

Jack, who was frowning, said a few words to Glumbuk Mergo and then turned to her:

'Bad news. That man, the red king, is a powerful yogi. He's just come from Metok.'

'And?'

'The Chinese soldiers are terrorizing everyone as they go down the valley, beating people up and threatening them with torture and death.'

'How did he get past them then?'

'He's a yogi – he can become invisible.'

She hardly batted an eyelid when he said this, so used had she become to the strange world of Tibet. It wasn't that she necessarily believed it, it was more that she felt incredulity was inappropriate, given the disorienting effects of the terrain and all the bizarre things she had experienced already. And, after all, the red king had appeared out of the thin air.

'But why? What are they after?'

'A man. A white man – they say he is a spy.'

'Anton, I presume?'

Jack did not bother to respond.

'So what do we do?' Nancy asked. Jack was looking grim.

'We have a problem. The red king said we should go through the jungle but I don't think the sherpas will like that.'

'Have you asked them?'

Jack inhaled deeply and turned to Glumbuk Mergo and his two companions. They had been watching the exchange between the Westerners in silence. He spoke in Tibetan for about a minute, after which all three of the sherpas began to shake their heads. Looking down at the ground, they muttered under their breaths. One word in particular they seemed to all be saying: 'Migu, migu.'

'What is "Migu"?' Nancy asked Jack with great anxiety.

'"Migu" is the Tibetan word for yeti. They won't go into the jungle here. They say that the migu lives round here.'

'What?' said Nancy in dismay. 'They're seriously afraid of the yeti?'

'Of course they are. That is why this village is deserted. The "migu" has moved into this area and the peasants are afraid.'

'Well, look, offer them some more money.'

'I did.' He looked back at the sherpas. 'You saw their response.'

She glanced at the three men. They were regarding her with expressions of absolute resolution; there was no way on earth that she was going to be able to persuade them into the forest.

'Well, what do we do?'

'We either turn back or we go on alone into the jungle,' said Jack. 'We can't risk staying on the path a moment longer, not now we know why the soldiers are here. I was banking on bribing them if we came across them; I've done that in the past with the garrison; they are just a bunch of drunkards, but these soldiers have been sent here specifically to find Herzog – there will be no chance of that. They will arrest us and God knows how we will ever get out.'

He paused then added, 'Maybe Anton really is a spy. Maybe the Chinese know something we don't. Maybe this whole thing with his father and the Nazi terma is just a cover, or a coincidence.' He paused again, lost in thought, and then said, 'But I can't imagine why he'd bother spying in Pemako. There's nothing to find and he knows it inside out anyway.'

They fell into silence. Nancy surveyed the ruined cornfields. None of it made sense, she thought. Herzog was the quarry in a manhunt and there was no telling what the Chinese knew. She looked back up the valley towards the peaks and the mist-swathed entrance to the Su La. She didn't want to go into the jungle, it frightened her, she found it revolting – it was filled to the brim with insects, no doubt there were snakes and leeches and, worse still, wild animals. It was a horrible proposition. The path had been relatively easy; it meandered from settlement to settlement, so they were always within a few hours of shelter. The jungle was her idea of a nightmare, but then she had no intention of turning back now.

45

Within minutes, they had lost all sight of the path and they could no longer hear the river. Strange hoots and clicking noises competed with the seething of the insects in the undergrowth. It was a cascade of noise, created by millions and millions of tiny creatures. Jack had given Nancy mosquito repellent and told her to apply it generously, but it seemed to be having little effect: every few minutes she would slap herself, squashing a mosquito in mid-lunch. The going was slow. There were paths of a sort, too many in fact, but they were narrow and overgrown and occasionally they petered out all together, forcing them to retrace their steps.

Since the porters had abandoned them, they were now carrying their own bags. They had left the tent with the sherpas but had taken the paraffin stove, cooking utensils, sleeping bags, two small sacks of tsampa and a pair of kukris, which Nancy had learned were heavy-bladed Nepali chopping knives. Along with their water bottles it was quite a weight to carry. Besides that, Nancy had elected to wear long-sleeved clothes to offer one last barrier to the thousands of biting insects, and this meant she was sweating as she walked, far too hot, but she was damned if she would unveil more flesh for them to feast on.

They navigated by the rare glimpses that they got of the valley's side: it was at least impossible for them to get completely lost, as the place was like a funnel, tipping them and the Yarlang Tsangpo and anything else that moved south towards the cliff-like border with the Indian province of Assam. However, Jack had explained – his face tense – that it was still possible to waste hours or even whole days by making one wrong turn and then circling back on ones self by accident. They didn't have the food and water to do that, so it was imperative that they held to their course.

After four hours, Nancy's arms were exhausted from slashing her way through the undergrowth. For most of the time, the jungle trees were spaced ten yards or so apart; over millennia they had grown so that they could all share the sunlight in the upper canopies. But, at some points, where the soil changed, or where the ground became steeper, there were great waves of shoulder-high vegetation and blankets of ivy that hung in curtains from the lower branches of the trees. At other points, the ground became waterlogged; they would have to tread a path over the backs of old rotting logs, one of which crumbled apart as Nancy stood on it, almost causing her to fall into a coffin-like interior that was filled with dark black insects. On other occasions, the going was good and the ground was hard, and Nancy's mood improved. Then there was space between the trees, the air was cool because of the shade provided by the canopy, and at some points it was possible to see up to a hundred yards. Just as she was beginning to think it wasn't so bad after all, however, they would sink into another patch of dense, tangled vegetation, and have to slash a nervous path, mindful that at any moment they might find their way irreparably barred.

Dusk was beginning to fall as they arrived onto what must have been a well-used animal track. The vegetation was thick on either side but the path was clear and there was no need to do too much hacking. Nancy was walking a few paces behind Jack. They hadn't spoken for some time, it was hard to know how long. They were concentrating on the business of brushing vegetation out of the way, stepping over tree roots and of course watching out for snakes that might be crossing the path or the funnel spiders that were known to hover above the track, falling onto their victims as they passed below.

Nancy knew that all around the world, forest peoples could always tell who was coming and going in their part of the jungle because of the changing patterns in the background noise. She was just meditating on this and listening to the various hoots and tapping noises, the barks and rattles and cicada-like waves of sound that constantly played in the jungle air, when suddenly she became aware that the noise had died away in the area off to their left. Only a lone monkey, hooting at intervals, as if sending a warning, was making any sound at all. She tried to peer through the vegetation – she only had a clear line of sight for about ten feet – but now she was sure: animals had frozen in their tracks, insects and reptiles had suddenly fallen silent, off to the left, up ahead.

She tried to dismiss her fears, thinking that it was probably just her imagination or the changing acoustics of the forest, or perhaps it was simply a deer or another large mammal that was causing the disturbance. She began to walk again, quickly, so as to catch up with Jack. But the monkey was still hooting – and then she was brought up short. Jack had stopped and was holding up his hand in a gesture that obviously meant he wanted her to be quiet.

They stood frozen to the spot for almost a minute, then he turned to her and hissed, 'Do you get the feeling something is watching us?'

'Yes,' she whispered back urgently. 'I was just thinking there might be something out there.'

'Where?'

She pointed off to the left, the adrenalin pumping.

'Yes. That's where I felt it.'

Her throat tightened.

'What is it?'

Jack frowned at her, his heavy blond brow covered in sweat and furrowed in worry.

'I don't know: a migu?'

'Jack!'

He moved his hand to his lips. She could see that he certainly wasn't joking, then he whispered again, quickly:

'Did you hear that?'

They were silent, waiting for a repeat of the sound he thought he had heard. And then she heard it too, quite distinctly, and her eyes bulged in fear.

'Oh my God. It was a groan, or a growl or something.'

Jack was wiping the blade of his kukri on his trouser leg. He peered into the dense undergrowth. It was impossible to see anything. Impossible also to gauge distance. She tugged his arm.

'Let's go back.'

But he didn't answer; instead, bending into a crouch, he began very slowly to creep forward, gently moving the fronds of the forest undergrowth with his outstretched kukri. Nancy reached forward and put her hand on Jack's belt, terrified that something was about to drag her off into the bushes. Her other hand squeezed the handle of the kukri, ready to deliver at least one blow of as much force as she could muster to whatever might be coming for them.

Suddenly, Jack froze in his tracks; she could hear him curse in appalled amazement. Nancy moved alongside him on the narrow path. The vegetation changed. Further up the path widened. Their view was clear for fifty yards, and up ahead, thirty yards along, they could see the most terrifying sight she had ever seen: an enormous brown bear was standing on its hind legs pawing furiously upwards into the air, trying desperately to catch hold of a big net that was suspended from the branches of an overhanging tree. The net was made from vine rope, and inside the net, scrunched into a ball, was what appeared to be a human. It was a trap, a trap that had been sprung by the poor soul who was being crushed in the net and tormented by the bear. Thoughts flashed through her mind: if the bear turned round and saw them, they wouldn't have a chance, kukris or not. And what about the human in the net? How long had he or she been there? Were they alive or dead?

Jack, as quietly as possible, slipped his backpack

straps off his shoulders. Nancy stared at him in horror, wondering what he was planning. Surely he's not going to try to scare it away, she thought. Perhaps it might work – though she hardly knew much about the duelling habits of vast brown bears – but she imagined it might just as easily turn around and rip his head off and then come for her. Jack unclipped the top pocket of his bag and slowly pulled out a long plastic tube about the size of a rolling pin. She was desperate to ask him what he was doing but she knew she couldn't speak.

He motioned for her to back into the undergrowth at the side of the path, and just as she began to do so she realized what the object was: it was a distress flare, for use when you were lost in the desert or high on some mountainside and you hoped a search patrol was looking for you. Jack backed off the path and holding the flare at arm's length, pointing it down the path towards the bear instead of up into the sky, he pulled the cord at its base.

There was an enormous whooshing noise, much louder than Nancy had expected, followed by a huge flash and a clattering noise that lasted for a couple of seconds then died away. By the time she had regained her senses and looked back down the path the bear had gone and all that was left of the flare was a thick, acrid trail of smoke that hung in the air above the path and then disappeared off into the jungle some forty feet further along to the left.

'Quick,' said Jack, 'before it comes back again.'

They scrambled out of the undergrowth and along the path until they were standing under the net. Now that they were right beneath it, they could see that the person suspended inside was a man, a Chinese man dressed in a filthy uniform. Looking up from beneath, her right arm hanging by her side, still holding the kukri, Nancy said:

'A soldier?'

'I think so. Doesn't look as though he's armed – I wonder how long he's been there.'

'How do we get him down?'

Jack turned to look at her in surprise, as though he hadn't considered doing anything of the sort.

'We have to get him down,' she said firmly. 'He can't be dangerous. He's probably dead anyway.'

Jack shook his head and then strode over to the tree. The other end of the rope was tied to a boulder that sat on the ground near the base of the tree, just off the path. It was the counter-weight and it must have been balanced somewhere and then triggered to fall, lifting the net when someone stepped on it and broke a tripwire somewhere. He lifted his kukri above his head to slash the rope, but before he had time to do so Nancy shouted at him:

'No! Don't – he'll break his neck if you do that. Hold on to the rope higher up, then I'll cut it, then you can let him down slowly . . .'

Jack grunted but did as she suggested. Grasping the rope in both hands, he looped it over one of the high branches on the tree to carry the weight of the net and its catch. She weighed the kukri and measured up her blow against the taut rope that was tied fast against the boulder, and then with a thunk that sent sparks flying she sliced right through it in one go. Jack was lifted up onto his tiptoes, his arms stretched in the air. Quickly she dropped the knife and ran over, and standing beneath the net she tried to get hold of it.

'Let him down some more,' she cried.

Jack tried to stretch up some more, and then he jumped and the weight dropped another foot into her waiting hands. She grabbed hold of it and Jack let go, causing the net, the man inside and Nancy to end up in a pile on the track. Bruised but not seriously hurt, she quickly got to her feet. It was clear then that the man in the net was alive. He was groaning in agony, curled into the foetal position.

'Cramp,' said Jack. 'Probably been up there for days. Circulation's screwed.'

'What can we do?'

'Nothing.'

'At least try to give him some water, Jack.'

He did as she said, offering his water bottle to the man's lips. The man was certainly no danger to them; he looked as though he would never be able to straighten himself out again, and in any case he was unarmed and still tangled up in the net. She peered over at his face: he was handsome, with angular cheekbones, and she could see he was tall, though his long limbs were still entangled. She couldn't tell precisely how old he was – perhaps thirtyish, she guessed.

Jack watched as the man thirstily gulped down every drop that he offered him, then once he had drunk for a full minute, he took the bottle away and said, 'Do you speak English?'

The Chinese man looked at them out of the corner of his eyes, unable to turn his aching neck. In a feeble voice he said, 'Yes.'

'Who are you?'

'My name is Colonel Jen; I am an officer in the PSB . . .' He winced in pain. 'Thank you for getting me down.'

Nancy looked at Jack.

'Come on – we should get him out of the net.'

They both knelt down and began to untangle the man's limbs from the spiderweb of netting. Eventually he was free, and they rolled him over so that he was lying on his side on the track, still moaning. They stood up and watched as, very slowly and with great effort, he rolled himself on to his back and ever so gradually managed to straighten his legs and arms, grimacing in pain as he did so. Then he slumped on to his side again and looked at Nancy out of his baleful eyes.

'Please can you help me?'

Jack smiled edgily.

'He can tell you're the soft one.'

Nancy ignored him and spoke the man, 'What do you want?'

'More water. I am very thirsty.'

'Come on, Jack; let's lean him against that tree.'

They grabbed him under the arms and dragged him up to the trunk, then Nancy poured some more water down his throat. He was still drinking thirstily when Jack tapped her on the shoulder. 'Come with me.'

She frowned and stood up. What did he want? They had to help this man; perhaps his blood had clotted already; he was certainly extremely dehydrated. She followed him up the path a little way, then he turned to her and whispered urgently, 'Before you get too carried away, you might remember that this man could well be part of the gang looking for Anton.' He glanced back down the track at Colonel Jen. 'No more Florence Nightingale antics until he tells us who he is and what he's doing – I'm going to tie him up before he recovers his strength.'

'We can't tie up a Chinese intelligence officer,' said Nancy, in alarm.

'Why not? We'll let him go afterwards. He won't tell us anything otherwise.'

'But imagine the trouble it could get us in. It's madness.'

'Nancy, we've just saved his life – we don't know who he is, he might even be dangerous, and there's a good chance he might know where Anton is. I'm going to tie him up. Most likely he'd do the same to you, if the situation was reversed.'

He took the water bottle from her hand and brushed past her, returning to the waiting Chinese man. Then he knelt down by the man's side and working quickly with his knife, cut lengths of vine rope and then proceeded to bind his ankles and wrists. Still curled forward in pain, he put up no resistance; he was too enfeebled, and his head lolled as Jack Adams jerked him around. The job finished, Jack leant back on his haunches.

'OK, now you can begin by telling us what you are doing wandering around in this forest.'

With great effort the Chinese man raised his head and stared at the water bottle.

'Sure you can have some more – but answer my question first.'

Clearly in great pain, the man mustered a response. 'I'm looking for a man.'

Jack nodded. 'A white man? Anton Herzog?'

There was a pause whilst Colonel Jen collected the strength to talk. He looked confused.

'Yes.'

Nancy knelt down next to Jack. She could bear it no longer; she grabbed the bottle back from Jack's hands.

'Here. Let me do this.'

She touched the bottle to the man's lips and let him drink until he was gasping for breath.

'Are you looking for him because he is a spy?' she asked. The man was silent. This made her angry – she didn't want to see him suffer but she was desperate to learn all he knew.

'Listen, we'll untie you and give you water and food and help you, if you help us. Otherwise you will die here in the jungle. We are trying to find the white man too.'

The man struggled again to speak.

'He's not a spy. But he is a dangerous man.'

'Why do you think he is dangerous?'

Again he paused, and with great pain, moved the position of his back against the tree.

'He has information. I have to find him.'

Nancy was electrified by these words. With a sudden intuition, she began to speak quickly.

'He knows the whereabouts of the Black Book, doesn't he? The Book of Dzyan. That's what you mean isn't it? Tell me. That is why you are after him?'

The man nodded his head – she couldn't tell if he was surprised that she knew what he was looking for. Perhaps his astonishment had reached a maximum level: he had already been caught in a net, had narrowly avoided being eaten by a bear, and now he was being questioned by two Westerners, deep in the jungles of Pemako. Nancy looked at Jack. He was staring in incomprehension at the Chinese man.

Suddenly he interrupted. 'Why does your government call him a spy then?'

The man's eyes darted across to Jack.

'Because they are afraid of him,' he answered flatly, as if he was stating the obvious.

'Why are they afraid?' said Nancy.

The Chinese man's dark eyes studied them both in turn – Nancy could tell that he was confused, still too weak to think clearly and yet struggling to assess the circumstances in which he found himself.

Finally he spoke. 'The book is known in China, for its power. It is said that it can start revolutions, it can bring change. It has been lost for thousands of years.

The Communist Party is afraid that if it is rediscovered, it will be used to overthrow them. They themselves came to power because of the ideas contained in one book: *The Communist Manifesto*. So they are wise enough to know that books can be very dangerous.'

'Where is Herzog?' Nancy demanded. The Chinese man fell silent again. She continued. 'Tell us where he is. You know, don't you?'

There was a pause then he answered:

'He is dying.'

For a second Nancy felt as if her heart had stopped beating and her lungs had suddenly ceased to function. Herzog was dying? It was an eventuality that she had not really considered for a while. She had been concerned about him at first, but in Tibet he had seemed a mythical figure, a magician; she had grown to think of him as invincible, even terrifying in his powers.

'What on earth do you mean?' she stammered.

'The monks have taken him. On a stretcher.'

'Taken him where?'

'To Agarthi. To the sacred city.'

Jack Adams interrupted:

'What are you talking about? There are no cities in Pemako.'

'Colonel Jen, do you know where they have gone? Can we find him?' Nancy asked, entreating him to be eloquent, holding the water towards him.

'I almost had them. I was just behind. Then we were attacked.'

Adams interrupted again:

'By who?'

'I don't know. It happened so fast. My men were killed.' He tried to lift himself up but slumped back against the tree, exhausted by the effort.

'I must go. Before the other soldiers find him. Please untie me.'

Adams put his hands on his hips and shook his head in disgust.

'He's not making any sense, Nancy.'

She ignored him. Urgently, she tried to make the man look at her directly. She said, 'What soldiers? Aren't the soldiers working with you?'

'No. You don't understand. I must get the book. Only the book can save China now.'

'And the soldiers, why don't you want them to get it?'

'They will take it to Beijing and destroy it and all will be lost.'

'So you are working alone?'

The Chinese man sighed heavily and closed his eyes for a second before looking down at the cords that bound his hands and feet. Then he fixed her with a steely look and – his voice filled with renewed purpose – he said:

'You seek the man, I seek the book. Help me, and I will help you. You will never find him without me. Never.'

Jack Adams was incredulous.

'Who are you, Colonel Jen – who on earth are you?'

'You do not need to know that. All you need to know is that we seek to bring China back to the Tao, to return China to the way it was in the days of old, before the Revolution, when the Emperor still ruled.'

Nancy was struggling to grasp everything.

'But how do you know Herzog has found the book?'

'We have an intelligence network in the monasteries. Anton Herzog is a great man, he moves close to the Tao. If he does not have the book in his hands as we speak, then he now knows where it is.'

'How can you be sure?'

'That is what the intelligence network suspected; that is what our lamas tell us. And the Oracle has confirmed it. The Oracle is never wrong.'

Of course, thought Nancy. That's what she should have asked the Oracle. Does Herzog have the terma? She should have tried it ages ago. And this man had asked the Oracle, and it had told him. She realized it was natural that he should consult the Oracle: he believed in the old lore of China, banned by the Communist Party, an outlawed superstition, banished for being part of the country's oppressive feudal past, cast out for being irrational and unscientific: un-Maoist.

'And the Communist Party, the army – how do they know that Herzog might know where the book is?'

Colonel Jen was regaining himself, and with his voice strengthening further as he spoke, he said, 'They are privy to the intelligence; that is why I have to act fast. They are looking too. They have sent soldiers to kill Herzog and to destroy the book. They will kill you too, if they find you. They intend to destroy anyone who knows that it exists. If you do not free me, you will never get out of the valley alive. That is the truth. I am lucky you found me – but you are lucky too. We have both been blessed with fortune. Briefly, for the moment only.'

This is insane, Nancy was thinking. At one level she was aware it was all totally insane. She had crossed the Su La pass into a land of madness and danger. Pemako couldn't be further from heaven on earth; rather it was a hell populated by crazy occult fantasists and murderous soldiers. And what was more this man, this Chinese Colonel – a renegade, severed from his official role – was claiming that Herzog was dying, and that they were in mortal danger. She heard his words as if he spoke in a dream, a dream filled with menace. Now she looked over at Jack Adams. She was hardly reassured to see that he had an expression of utter horror on his face.

'Nancy, what on earth have you got me into?' he said, in a low voice.

That she could hardly bear; she felt as if she was going to burst into tears. She wanted to continue, to find Herzog, and yet she was equally compelled by an urge to flee. And Jack's fear only made her feel worse. If only she had stayed in Delhi, if only she had never come to India at all, she was thinking.

'I'm sorry,' she said, hardly able to form the words. 'I don't know what is happening. I don't understand any of it.'

'Well, what the hell are we going to do? We have to get out of here. We've got to get back to the pass immediately.'

Colonel Jen shook his head.

'It's too late. More and more soldiers will be on their way. They will flood the valleys of Pemako with men until they find Herzog, until they get the book.'

Jack spun around and stared into the jungle in disgust.

'Christ, this is a mess.'

46

'We have to free him,' said Nancy. She had taken Jack to one side and they were speaking together, while casting frightened glances around the jungle. She saw Jack was just as edgy and vigilant as her. 'He's got nothing. He needs our water and our food. He doesn't even have iodine tablets, so he can't drink the jungle water. If he runs off then he will have to waste time trying to find a village and risk bumping into soldiers, which he doesn't want. That's the humanitarian argument. But anyway I believe him: we need his help.'

Jack looked over her shoulder at Colonel Jen, who was still sitting with his back against the tree, his ankles and wrists firmly tied together.

'Listen Nancy, he could be making everything up for all we know. Perhaps there are no soldiers coming over the Su La, perhaps he's planning to trick us and lead us straight into an army camp. Who knows? Why should we trust him for a second?'

'Well, we can't just leave him to die, or get eaten by a bear . . .'

Just then Jack noticed that Jen was frantically waving his hands in the air.

'Now what's he doing?' he said with irritation in his voice.

Nancy turned to look. 'Something's wrong . . .' She began to walk quickly back towards the prisoner and raising her voice she almost shouted, 'What is it?'

She could see from the expression on his face that he was frantic. Why doesn't he answer, why doesn't he just shout? she thought. When she was a couple of yards away he said, desperately, his face moist with sweat, 'They're coming. The soldiers. You have to move me off the path. We have to hide. Please – hurry.'

Jack had arrived at Nancy's side. It was true, they could hear movement further down the path, coming towards them. She grabbed the rucksacks, hurled them into the undergrowth and then flung the netting after them as well. Jack grabbed Colonel Jen under the arms again and pulled him into the jungle. Nancy just had enough time to see a uniformed figure bobbing into view one hundred feet further along the path. Her heart pounding, nauseous in her terror, she dived behind a tree.

Seconds later, a long line of Chinese soldiers, thirty

strong, she estimated, filed past, their weapons at the ready. Nancy's face was only a few feet from the path and, as she saw their boots go by, she closed her eyes and prayed. It was a full two minutes after the last pair of army boots had stamped past her that she lifted her head and looked around.

'Jack?' she whispered hoarsely.

'Over here.'

Limbs trembling, she crawled though the vegetation. Jack was looking suspiciously at Colonel Jen, who was still lying on his side on the jungle floor, half hidden by vegetation.

'Why didn't you cry to your countrymen for help?' Jack asked the Colonel.

'I told you,' Jen replied without emotion. 'I am working alone. The soldiers have orders to destroy the book. I can't allow that to happen. I am now an outlaw, they will have orders to shoot me on sight.'

'So, if I untie you, we will travel together?'

'Yes.'

Jack glanced at Nancy and then leaned forwards and, with a few sharp movements of his knife, severed the cords at Colonel Jen's hands and feet. The Chinese man stretched out his limbs and then, for the first time, tried to stand up. Staggering like a newborn foal, leaning on the tree limbs and sturdier bushes, he slowly limped his way on to the path. Slowly dragging himself up to his full height, massaging his wrists, he scanned the track in the direction that the soldiers had gone. He had transformed into an altogether different figure now that he was free from the net and had recovered from the cramp. Nancy could tell that he was a man to be reckoned with: highly capable and no doubt used to getting his own way.

In a terse clipped voice, he said, 'We need to continue down here for about one mile, then we have to head up the valley side. And we will have to hurry if we want to have any chance of catching them. '

'And where will that get us?' said Jack.

Colonel Jen's tone of voice was firm and decisive, and Nancy suspected that he was not used to being disagreed with.

'The monks have taken Herzog to the Cave of the Magicians. It is the entrance to an ancient tunnel system that links up all the old gompas of Tibet and that also leads to Agarthi.' He glanced sharply at Jack and then added pointedly, 'The holy city of Agarthi most certainly does exist, by the way.'

'And do you know the way there?' asked Jack.

'No. That is why we have to catch them before they get inside. It is not possible to follow them into the tunnels, it would be suicide. We are not far behind but we must hurry.'

As they began hurrying along, Nancy shot a question at their former captive, who had now – it seemed – become their guide.

'Colonel Jen, how long were you hanging up there?'

He looked at her, with a little more kindness in his expression that made her hope he was not a bad man.

'Please call me Jen, you are not in the Chinese military.'

'Thanks. I'm Nancy Kelly and this is Jack Adams.'

'To answer your question, I was hanging there for about three hours.'

'But who laid the trap?'

'Mompas, I expect. Local tribespeople, hoping to catch a deer.'

'And who attacked you?'

'As I said, I don't know.'

'But was it men, or . . .'

'Or what?' The Colonel smiled at her. 'A migu? I only saw men. Probably Mompas again. They don't like Chinese soldiers or monks.'

He seemed very blasé about it all, or perhaps he was just pragmatic. Maybe that was what got you promoted to the rank of Colonel at such a young age.

'You said you had other men with you?'

'Yes. A dozen men. But they were not good troops. They were garrison soldiers; conscripts, cannon fodder. They didn't hold the formation, they scattered and fell.'

'But were there gunshots?'

'No. The Mompas rarely have guns, they have other weapons. But we must leave,' said Jen, glancing up the path. 'We cannot afford to waste a second. Let me carry your rucksack.'

As Nancy handed her rucksack to him, it suddenly occurred to her that he could just run off with all her water and supplies. She hesitated, and straight away he understood what she was thinking.

'I will not take it. I could overpower you both if I chose.'

He glanced at Jack, who was frowning at this suggestion, and then added, 'I have been trained.' He left it at that.

'It is useful that you are not Chinese, that you are Westerners,' he said. 'It may help me to get the monks to hand over Anton Herzog, if he is still alive. I am wearing army uniform and I suspect they would not roll out the red carpet if they saw me approaching alone, and now I have lost my men, I will have to rely on methods other than brute force . . .'

He turned and looked down the track.

'Keep your eyes open for more animal traps. We will be safe once we're off this main path.'

47

They had been marching quickly for several hours, gradually climbing the bowl-like incline of the valley side, when finally Jen called a halt. He had set a blistering pace, and Nancy and Jack had scarcely exchanged a word since they had started on the trek. Panting with exhaustion and grateful for the respite, Nancy put her hands on her hips and took a series of long, deep breaths. She reached for her water bottle and drank deeply.

They were standing in dense jungle at the base of an immense ivy-covered boulder. Jen was hunting around for something, peering into the undergrowth. Jack joined them, his shirt drenched in sweat and his face glowing red from the exertion.

'Why have we stopped? The path is still good.'

Jen knelt down and motioned for them to follow.

'Here – I'll show you why.'

After a brief crawl up a scree slope, they emerged

onto a rocky ledge about five yards in length and two yards wide. The view almost took Nancy's breath away, so used had she become to the endless wall of green. She had failed to consider that they had climbed several thousand feet from the valley floor, and now on this ledge they had a tremendous view over the lush, almost primeval valley below. She could clearly see the Yarlang Tsangpo winding its way towards the mountains to the south. The sun had already dropped behind the high mountains; the daylight was beginning to mellow and fade.

'There,' Jen said. Nancy turned to him. He was pointing in the other direction, up the side of the valley. She followed the line of his finger: at first she couldn't see what he was pointing to.

'What are we meant to be looking at?' she asked, still breathless.

'There. Just above the treeline. Two miles away. That's them.'

Nancy's heart almost stopped. Suddenly she saw them, just above the treeline on the scree slope; a line of tiny antlike figures, laboriously picking their way along what looked to be a very narrow precipitous path. Jack delved into his pack and produced a miniature pair of binoculars.

'My God,' he said, looking through them. 'I see monks, two dozen of them, and yes: a stretcher.'

His hands fell to his side in amazement. Nancy grabbed the binoculars from him, and following the treeline she found the train of men. Yes, Jack was right. She counted twenty-four men and it was true that they were carrying someone. It must be Herzog. She almost choked. Finally, she could see him, almost, and yet his body and head were covered in a blue sheet, or robe. Her heart racing, she passed the binoculars to Jen, who quickly scanned the line of men. Then he turned to them both and in a businesslike tone said:

'Quick, we haven't a second to lose. It will be dark in one hour. And in two hours they will be at the Caves and all will be lost.'

48

At last the monks had reached the sanctuary of the Cave of the Magicians. The walls within were covered in ancient rock paintings of sorcerers and shamans wearing wild headdresses and dancing around fires, and long-extinct animals being hunted across the Tibetan plateau. Human and animal bones littered the floor, and the debris of long-extinguished fires stained the dark sand with black circles. The air smelt of magic and death. Ten feet further in, the caves became as black as night and opened out into a hundred sinuous, angular corridors that descended deep into the earth. Even with knowledge of the route, enormous skill would be needed to navigate a step further without slipping to a wretched death down a bottomless crevasse, or descending into a blind pothole from which no way back could ever be found.

The Abbot's deputy knew that they could not afford to hesitate even for a moment. The Abbot had said that if they found themselves being pursued, they should seek sanctuary in Agarthi, deep within the ancient cave system. They would not be safe until they entered the dark labyrinth beyond, and yet he hesitated. The bitter truth was that they could not take the white man any further. They could not carry the stretcher through the caves, and the doctor said the white man would never survive the journey without it. Though they had come all this way, bearing him aloft like a saint, like a king, they would have to leave him to the wolves and the Chinese soldiers. Leaving him to die or to be captured filled the Abbot's deputy with immense sadness, but at one level he was relieved that the decision had been made for him by the severity of their flight and the treacherous terrain of the caves. The stranger was a dangerous wizard, weak physically but psychically still strong. He should not be allowed into the holy city of Agarthi.

The Abbot's deputy leaned forward so that his lips almost touched the white man's ear. He said, softly, not sure if the man was awake or sleeping, 'You are going to rest here for a while. I am going to leave, I may be some time but do not worry, we will be back for you.'

Even as he said the treacherous words he felt his heart rebel – but he had no choice. Very quietly he articulated his final question:

'Before I go, please tell me how you escaped from Shangri-La. And . . . and . . . I must know. Did you ever see the Book of Dzyan?'

The man's eyes opened. His skeletal fingers met, as if he was praying. Lifting his eyes to the roof of the cave – and the Abbot's deputy wondered what he saw, and if he knew where he was – he said, 'I am growing weak. Are we almost there yet? Is this Agarthi? I am so very weary.'

The Abbot's deputy said nothing; he could find no response to the man's words. A terrible silence filled the cave. Did the white man understand what was really happening? Did he realize he was being abandoned, being left to die alone? After a pause – perhaps he was hoping for reassurance that never came – the stranger resumed.

'I will tell you how I escaped and I will tell you the terrible truth about the Book of Dzyan.'

Silence again, as he collected his thoughts, drifting across the days and nights, wandering back to Shangri-La. Then for one last time, he began:

'Once I had discovered what a horrifying end lay in store for me, as King to be, my mind was made up and I immediately decided to make a thorough exploration of the lamasery and grounds, or should I say a thorough exploration of my prison . . .'

The Abbot's deputy settled into a guilty silence, glad that he would learn the end of the stranger's tale, aghast that he was on the point of abandoning him to his death.

The charismatic voice projected through the darkness.

'I descended the stairs to the ground floor and then walked around the tower in what I thought was the direction of the inner courtyard and the dreaded bonfire. But I came to a locked door. There was no one around to ask for assistance so I turned back and began to wander the interior passages of the lamasery. I passed the dining room, now empty, and continued unchallenged through several other staterooms. Everything was very quiet, a silence which merely menaced me further. Finally, I went through a doorway and found myself in the front courtyard, on the other side of which lay the massive wooden entrance gates and, beyond the gates, the battlements. Standing guard by the gates was a solitary sherpa.

It was then that I had an idea; I crossed the courtyard and in Nepali I said to the sherpa. ' "Where is the King?"

'The sherpa put his hands together and bowed, and then pointing back over my head, he said, ' "He is at the top of the tower, sir."

'I spun around; the tower rose up against the clear pale blue sky, and at the top was a forbidding line of battlements.

'Can I speak to him?'

'"I cannot answer that, sir. It is up to his Highness."

'Then as an afterthought, I turned back to him and asked, "Can you open the gates for me? I would like to walk along the battlement."

'"I am sorry, sir, I am not allowed to open the gates for anyone except the Abbot."

'"Not even the King?"

'"Yes, sir, not even the King."

'He was a very thickset stocky man, and although he was smiling and bowing now, I reckoned that if I attempted to overpower him he would quickly get the better of me. I couldn't risk it.

'"Thank you."

'Back to the tower I went, walking as quickly as propriety allowed, not wanting to look in any way hurried or desperate, but all the time conscious of the fact that time was running out. It would be dusk in three hours, I reckoned, and then their ghastly ceremony would commence.

'I hurried up the stairs. I passed the door to my cell and carried on up, until the broad stairs became a narrow flight of steps that corkscrewed up to the roof. At the top there was a door. It was ajar; sunlight was streaming in. Gingerly, I pushed it open and stepped onto the roof. There were battlements all the way around and the view beyond was incredible, but I didn't have time to take it all in, as the moment I stepped onto the roof my eyes fell on the King.

'He was as the Abbot had described: a European man, who appeared to be in his mid-fifties. He was wearing a white robe, hemmed with gold, and he was gazing out over the battlements, oblivious to my arrival and entirely mesmerized by the view. On his head he wore a golden crown and on his wrists, neck and ankles he was wearing heavy, thick hoops of gold, that gleamed in the sunlight.

'I paused, breathing heavily after the exertion of running up the stairs. The man appeared not to have noticed me despite the noise I was making. He remained as motionless as a statue, his arms hanging by his sides under the weight of the enormous gold bracelets.

'"Hello?" I said tentatively. Then without thinking I broke into German:

'"My name is Anton Herzog."

'Ever so slowly, the man turned around to face me. Because of the great weight of the gold, his motion had the heaviness of a deep-sea diver. I noticed that the gold ring around his neck pressed right up under his chin in an uncomfortable manner. The sight of this wretched man made my stomach turn with fear; for that is what he was, a wretched human being, dressed in a grotesque mockery of royal finery, awaiting an awful fate.

'Now that he was facing me, I could see him properly. His eyes were like two empty caves – devoid of light, devoid of soul, devoid even of hope. Suddenly he spoke. His voice startled me with the depth of its sadness.

' "So, it is true then. You have finally come."

'Fear was beginning to take hold, my voice was shaking.

' "Listen to me. I don't know what is going on here. You have to help me. I must leave immediately."

' "I can't help you. I cannot even help myself. Even if I wanted to."

'Panic was rising within me. I felt as if I was about to lose my mind. I almost shouted in my desperation. "We have to get out of here. They intend to kill you tonight. They are going to burn you . . ."

'The King stared at me through his dead eyes. I felt a sudden wave of pity and a deep regret for what I had just said. He did not need me to warn him of his fate.

' "I'm sorry. But we both have to get out of here. You are German aren't you? You came with Felix Koenig?"

'The man ignored my questions.

' "I cannot leave. And nor can you. There is no way

out of here. You must accept your fate, as so many kings have done before you." He paused for a minute and then with his voice cracking with emotion, said, "I have been preparing myself for the day of your arrival for so long – but still I do not want to go. If only I could have a few more hours as ruler of the world . . . a few more days."

'Everything about his manner and speech made me think that he had been brainwashed.

' "Listen to me. You must stop talking like this. There must be a way out."

' "There is no way out."

' "The silk rope I came up on?"

' "They will stop you."

' "Then out the back, on to the Himalayas?"

' "It is too far. It is hundreds of miles to the first blade of grass. No one has ever made it. And even if you did, which is impossible, they would bring you back."

' "But the caravans that bring things from the outside world, they make it."

' "They are prepared for the journey. They travel with yaks laden with supplies and warm clothes. One man alone will certainly perish up there. It is like the surface of the moon."

'My temper and my nerves were beginning to fray in the face of his defiant pessimism.

'"But how can you stand there and just accept what they will do to you?"

'"I am the King of Shangri-La. I came from Germany to enlist the monks in our cause and find the Book of Dzyan and unleash the superman. Tonight I will join the Masters above."

'He sounded like a hostage reciting a mantra that his captives had given him.

'"Well, I intend to try to escape, even if I die in the attempt. Come with me. We can take the Book of Dzyan with us."

'Slowly, with great effort, the King raised his heavy wrists to shoulder height and turned his hands over, as if he was admiring his gold bracelets for the first time.

'"Tonight, I will burn. All that will be left of me are these chunks of solid gold and a few bones that will be scattered on the mountainside outside the gompa gates. In the morning, they will melt the gold hoops down and recast them so that they fit you – then you will no longer even be able to dream of escape."

'Of course: it was true. How could he hope to walk anywhere, let alone up into the desolate mountains? It must have taken him an enormous effort just to mount the tower steps; the idea that he could flee overland was preposterous.

'"We can take them off . . ."

'"No. It is not possible. I can go anywhere I please in my kingdom except for the workshop. In any case, I don't have the skill, I would have to cut my hands and feet off . . ."

'What a vile, vile method of imprisonment, I thought. What wicked people the lamas of Shangri-La were, posing as holy men, pretending to oversee the world.

'"This place is evil. These monks have no power beyond their gompa walls, and they have imprisoned you and intend to murder you . . ."

'"That is a lie!" he said, in sudden agitation. "I am the King of Shangri-La. The Abbot has helped us – through his use of the Book of Dzyan, he helped the German people to win the war . . ."

'My God, I thought, he was so unhinged that he did not even know what had happened in the outside world. I wanted to shake him and bring him back to his senses.

'"What are you talking about man? Germany lost the war. The Allies won and all your dreams have been destroyed . . . the monks never helped you . . ."

'The King looked at me with a strange expression on his face. I was getting through to him, perhaps. I continued to speak, but in a gentler tone; I was afraid that my revelations might have a catastrophic effect.

'"Japan and Germany were defeated. America,

France and Britain were victorious. Hitler committed suicide when the Russians entered Berlin. It's all over. These monks never helped you, they imprisoned you . . ."

'And then he laughed at me; a laugh of such maniacal force that I found myself stepping backwards towards the staircase.

' "You fool. You have been brainwashed, which is as we intended. Germany didn't lose the war. Which three countries of the world have been the economic power-houses since 1945? Which three countries have the highest life expectancy, the greatest technological skill, the best educational institutions, the finest engineers?"

'I stared at him in shock. My mind had gone blank. He sneered at me and for a second time his hollow laugh rang out around the battlements.

' "The United States, Germany and Japan. They were the victors of the war, they and not the so-called Allies. They agreed the terms of peace between themselves. That is how we wanted it. It was all foretold far in advance by the Book of Dzyan. Three great power centres were to be established to lead mankind forward: one in Asia, one in Europe and one in North America. They are the engines of a global material culture which – when it blossoms to its full extent –

we will sacrifice in order to release enormous psychic powers. Only then will we create the real superman."

'I could barely contain my rising feeling of nausea; I tried desperately to marshal my arguments but my voice was shrinking as I spoke.

'"You are wrong. The Nazis were defeated. Hitler died in Berlin."

'The King smiled at me pityingly.

'"You poor man. How many Nazis were ever brought to justice? A token handful. And they were only tried and executed because they were not loyal to us, not for any other reason. The rest? Some came here, many went to America, most remained in Germany. We were untouchable because we had won. And as for Hitler, even you must know his body was never found. We have monitored everything carefully from here. I have presided over the great triumph of the German people. Many have been called upon to sacrifice themselves; it is fitting in a sense that I should now be added to their number."

'For the first time in my life, I began to doubt all that I knew. I began to doubt the basis of the mythology that has sustained the free world this last sixty years: the glorious struggle against evil, the dark years, the final victory. For it was true: Germany, Japan and America were the global hegemons, and it was their technology and material culture that had overtaken the world; their machines, their computers, their breeds of men. The King smiled at me again and in a soft, patronizing voice, continued.

'"It is not necessary to tell the defeated of their defeat. Let them live by whatever fantasies they wish; let them believe that despite what they can see with their own eyes, they have not lost and their countries do not lie on the slag heap of history. All that is necessary is to hasten the coming of the superman.'

'I was slipping into the void. In a whisper, I said, "And the Book of Dzyan did all this, foresaw all this?"

'The King's eyes were glowing with zeal.

'"Yes. It is here. It is our patrimony. It connects the worlds, it bridges time and space. It controls us all. It brought you here today and it will bring others. And it will bring on the next global war – a war that will be the *Götterdämmerung* – the Twilight of the Gods – a war for which even now we are sowing the seeds. We will create a mass human sacrifice and so we will rise to the next level of being. You will be the King. You will lead the world over the abyss. You will be the great destroyer. You will be Kali. You will be death itself."

'As I stood with this man, his golden fetters shining in the sunlight so that a harsh and terrible glare emanated from him, I feared that I had lost myself entirely. I felt very small and as if I was slipping away, into blackness. The journey had been too much for me, the decades of searching, the metok chulen, the terton's death, the emerald valley, the decaying heads and the human cage – I couldn't take any more, but still the King's voice was booming in my ears.

'"The Book of Dzyan comes from the depths of the past; it has helped man to emerge from the state of savagery in which he found himself long ago. Our work is drawing to a close. I only wish I could see it to the end. You will have that privilege, you and your Queen whom we have also summoned."

'"Black magic." I was clutching my head. "It's black magic . . ."

'"No. It is the voice of the universe, and all who look into the book come under its control. The book is responsible for all our actions and thoughts. The book controls us all . . ."

'The King fell silent for a moment. He was like a religious maniac. I had to take control of the situation. I had to prove him wrong. I was almost shouting: '"Who created the Book of Dzyan? It was made by men was it not? Therefore it is fallible?"

'"No. It was not written by men. It wrote itself. It represents the voice of the universe, speaking to itself."

'I was flabbergasted, speechless.

' "What do you mean?"

' "It first appeared in the pattern on the back of a tortoise's shell many millennia ago. The sages recognized its wisdom. They transcribed it to papyrus. It began to grow in power. It began to hatch its schemes. Those who listened to it prospered. More copies were made. Its power grew and grew."

'Suddenly, as he said these words, I felt as if I had just awoken from a nightmare. The King shrank before me, reverting to the proportions of a normal man. Tortoise shells? Ancient sages? A book growing in power and hatching schemes? Growing from writing on a tortoise's shell? It was gibberish. With relief, I realized that I didn't have to listen to him a second longer.

'The one thing I had to do was to leave immediately. It was clear that this lunatic King would not be able to escape. The gold hoops made sure of that, and anyway his mind was ruined. But I had no intention of getting fitted out with a set of luxury manacles myself. I had to block his insane words out and focus on my escape.

'I turned on my heels and bounded down the tower stairs, the King's words echoing in my ears as I went. I had one idea in my mind; I still had some of Terton Thupten Jinpa's powder left over from the metok chulen. Although I hadn't recovered from the effects of the last session I was going to have to gamble and use it again. I hoped – it was a desperate hope but it was simply all I had – that it might just help me to make it over the mountains to the nearest trading route or settlement. If it failed, at least I would die on the mountain, on my own terms, in the free air and not on a foul funeral pyre. And before I left, if at all possible, I would steal the Book of Dzyan.'

The Abbot's deputy, lost in Shangri-La with the stranger, marvelled at all he heard. The opium had carried the stranger aloft: he was a great orator, a Teutonic bard, weaving a beautiful and strange tale, beguiling all who listened. But behind them both the blackness beckoned; the deeper depths of the cave summoned them all to oblivion. He had not saved this man, thought the Abbot's deputy, he had betrayed him. The story of escape that the stranger was recounting ended here, in this ancient place. He would be betrayed again, as he had been betrayed already. The Abbot's deputy shivered in the darkness and he raised his eyes to the ancient rocks above as the dying man's voice filled the night.

49

For some time Jen led them onwards. They edged along the path, climbing higher and higher, scrambling on all fours up the steeper sections of the track. At one point the route shared its course with a stream and they found themselves slipping and sliding over rocks covered in wet moss. Jen led the way, remorseless in his energy. He was moving so fast that even Jack, a seasoned mountaineer, was wheezing slightly, and Nancy thought her lungs must burst.

Suddenly they came to a halt. Nancy wiped the sweat and dust from her eyes and saw that Jack was standing with his hands on his hips and Jen was pacing frantically up and down on a short, sandstone ledge. And then she realized with a sick lurch what the problem was: they were faced with a chasm that dropped away in front of them, almost perpendicularly. It plunged down into a distant crevasse that must have been driven into the mountainside aeons ago, during some geological cataclysm. The chasm was about ten feet wide, and close to where they were standing lay a length of rope. Anchored around a tree, the rope snaked across the sandstone ledge and disappeared over the edge of the crevasse. On the other side of the crevasse, Nancy could make out the other end of the rope, tied around another tree. But it had been hacked through and all that remained was a frayed end. The monks had cut it down, there was no way across.

She glanced at Jen; for the first time since they had met him, he seemed to have lost his habitual calm. Even just after they had got him out of the net, he had still sustained an air of detachment, but now she could see that he was exceptionally agitated.

Jack, still panting, said, 'We could almost jump it; it's tantalizing.'

Nancy stepped up to the edge. It was impossible even to see the bottom of the crevasse; the rock sides plunged straight down, with occasional patches of scrubby vegetation clasping to its sides. She certainly couldn't jump it, whatever Jack thought. Jen was shaking his head and muttering in Chinese, leaning out and scanning the chasm to the left and right as far as they could see. There appeared to be no narrower point in either direction, and besides, the jungle was dense; it would take hours even to clamber a hundred feet up or down the sides.

Without even telling them what he was doing, Jen threw off his rucksack and unsheathed Nancy's kukri, which he had been carrying since they began their march. Then he disappeared back into the jungle. For a few moments, Nancy and Jack stared at each other in confusion, and then they heard a thwacking noise. It sounded as if Jen was chopping down a tree.

Looking down the steep path, Nancy could see Jen smashing the kukri onto the trunk of a tree ten yards tall. It was slender, the circumference of a man's neck. She couldn't imagine it would be strong enough. Now Jen turned to them and shouted up breathlessly:

'Here – you can cut off the branches whilst I do this, so that we can drag it up the path to the ledge.'

They hurried down the path and Jack began to hack off the lower branches while Nancy pulled them away and flung them down the slope. After a few minutes of furious work, Jen had cut through the trunk, but the tree remained stubbornly upright, its higher branches still intertwined with those of neighbouring trees. With a sigh of frustration, Jen began slicing at the upper limbs, levering himself up, holding on with one hand. Jack grasped the leafy extremity of one of the higher branches and, pulling as hard as he could, bellowing with anger and exhaustion, dragged the felled tree to the ground. Frantically, Jen began to trim off the remaining branches, and within a few minutes they were hauling it back up to the ledge. Nancy could hardly believe that they had managed to do it all so quickly. They were all now drenched in sweat from their exertions, but she could see in the faces of the two men that they were determined to get over to the other side as quickly as possible.

Once on top of the ledge, they manoeuvred the log into place. Without hesitating, Jen grasped hold of the log with both hands and let his body hang. For a moment he vanished under the lip of the crevasse, but then Nancy saw him swinging his way across the void, like a monkey in the forest canopy. It looked easy, but the thought of doing it herself made Nancy nearly sick with vertigo and fear. On the other side, Jen dragged himself up onto the path and then, using a length of rope he had taken from Jack's bag, he dextrously tied the two ends together and the bridge was restored. They now had a log to stand on, and at shoulder height a rope to hold on to.

'You go first,' said Jack, his voice hoarse.

There wasn't time for fear; that would come later, thought Nancy. Not looking down, she shuffled her way across, hearing Jack behind her. The rope swung and creaked as they handed themselves across. On the other side, she breathed deeply, aware that she was trembling violently. No one said anything; they began to move at once along the path.

Night was falling. In faded light they struggled upwards, until they had outstripped the treeline once more and the vegetation had thinned out. Nancy thought they must be nearing the precipitous ledge where they had first observed the monks and Herzog. For the first time since they had scrambled onto the outcrop below, they could see the entire length of the lush valley, and at intervals of a mile or so they could see tiny bobbing lights.

Jen pointed at the valley floor. 'Search parties.'

As they were swaddled in night, Nancy perceived – quite distantly, almost as if she was detached from her destiny – that she was reaching the limits of her endurance. And yet she was so very near to the end now, or to some sort of culmination. She could no longer imagine what she might encounter, if she managed to catch up with Anton Herzog. Back in Delhi, she thought she had a clear idea of Herzog – urbane, driven, eccentric, but fundamentally explicable in the terms of her trade, the terms of her ordinary world. Layer upon layer of complexity had been added to this picture; new identities and new motives had piled up at every stage, and she had lost all notion of what he might really be like. She suspected she had never encountered anyone remotely like him before; his skills and personality seemed to be almost boundless, uncategorizable and exceeding the normal limits.

And it seemed a long way from the bustling streets of Delhi to this narrow precipice, a last bridge of stone, stripped bare even of lichen and moss, a barren promontory that would deliver her up to her fate.

She looked up the path. She could just perceive that Jen was moving forward. Relentless, she thought. What was it that had made them so driven, so urgent – was it a force within them, or something beyond – something in the restless night, some ancient power of the mountains, beyond their comprehension?

Now she saw that Jen was turning towards the rocks, and then suddenly he ducked his head and disappeared.

'He's found it,' Jack was shouting, hurrying towards the gap in the rock-face.

And Nancy, her heart pounding, laboured in pursuit.

50

In the darkness, Nancy heard a voice. A cracked, desperate voice, it hardly sounded like Colonel Jen.

'They've gone. We're too late.'

The dull sound echoed around the rocks. Nancy was too stunned to say anything, but she heard Jack sighing in disappointment beside her.

'Did they leave no sign, no trace?' he was saying.

Breathless from the last sprint towards the cave, Nancy put a hand out to the dank wall. She leaned forward, thinking she might be sick.

Then, in a changed voice, Jen said:

'Wait. Look.'

Nancy turned to see the Colonel staring into the darkness at the side of the cave entrance, transfixed by something he had seen. He ducked into a crouch and flicked on a cigarette lighter. The feeble flame cast dancing shadows on to the cave walls. And there in the shadows, just a trace, a suggestion in the half-light,

Nancy saw it. There was something on the floor. With the next flicker of the flame, she saw it was not a thing. It was a person.

'Is it Herzog?' she gasped. In a second she had joined Jen. 'Is he dead?'

The figure lay a couple of yards from the smoking remnants of the fire – at first they had missed him in the darkness. A plastic sheet had been slung across the body; the head was lolling to one side. There were no signs of life. Jen held the cigarette lighter above the man's face. Now Jack, shaking his head, knelt beside the figure and scrutinized his face.

'Oh, God,' he said, in a low voice. 'It's him all right. He must have had a terrible fever – he's barely recognizable.'

The man's gaunt cheeks were sunken into grotesque hollows, the skin stretched like parchment across them. Matted grey hair was pasted to his scalp. His face was so white and pale that it was hard to imagine that blood had ever flowed under his skin. Jen gingerly placed two fingers on his neck, searching for a pulse.

Suddenly, like a reptile's, the man's dark eyes flickered open.

'Jesus Christ,' said Jack, recoiling in shock.

'Quickly, help him,' said Nancy. 'Get him some water.'

Jack was scrabbling in his satchel.

'He doesn't just need water, he needs drugs.'

He pulled out a bottle of pills. Jen looked at it doubtfully.

'I don't think we'll be able to get them down him.'

Now, Herzog was making a noise, his eyes bulging with the effort.

'Pa . . . pa . . .'

At first it sounded like a death rattle, but then it became recognizable as an attempt to speak. Jen looked at the two Westerners in silent appeal.

'What's he saying? What does he want?'

'I don't know,' said Jack.

'Pie . . .' Herzog was wheezing. 'Pie . . .'

Then Nancy saw it and almost shrieked:

'Pipe! There on the ground. The pipe – he wants the pipe . . .'

An arm's length from the dying man lay a slender black opium pipe.

'Jen, do something. Fix it. He's desperate for it. He must be in grave pain.'

Jen passed the lighter to Jack and picked up the pipe. He looked inside it. 'The pipe's empty – we'd better hope there's some more somewhere . . .'

Nancy was staring in disbelief at the dying man's skull-like face. The dry lips parted again. She could see his tongue moving. Now Jack pulled a water bottle out of his bag and passed it to her. She unscrewed the cap and touched it to his lips and carefully let a few drops fall into his mouth. Slowly the man turned his eyes towards her and uttered a single word:

'Belt.'

Jen whipped off the blue sheet, revealing a wasted, skeletal body, barely clad in filthy rags, the rancid feet unshod, covered in sores. A money belt was slung around his emaciated hips, and Jen opened it roughly, felt inside and brought out a ball of opium.

Working quickly, Jen heated the opium on the tip of a knife. When it began to smoulder he tipped it into the pipe. Then he placed the jade mouthpiece between Herzog's lips and held it there.

'Take it. Breathe,' he said.

For a moment they were silent, all of them transfixed by the glowing coals of the pipe bowl. As Herzog breathed, the coals flamed into life. 'Keep breathing,' said Jen.

Again the bowl darkened and then again it ignited. Then, very slowly, a skeletal hand reached out from amongst the rags to take hold of the stem of the pipe. Jen released his grip and sank back onto his heels as the wraithlike figure took over.

Two minutes later, the bony hand let the pipe fall back into the sand. None of them had dared to speak – they were waiting, uncertain, apprehensive. Now Herzog turned his head towards them.

'Thank you.'

He coughed and then touched his knuckles to his mouth. 'May I please have some more water.'

Nancy carefully pressed the water bottle to his lips again. This time he drank a few gulps.

'Thank you very much.'

His voice was hardly as Nancy remembered it; thinner, ravaged by his illness. He was barely audible, and she could hardly recall that he had once been such a charismatic, forceful man. Yet there was something, some vestige of – she wasn't sure what it was – a lingering intensity in the gaze he turned towards her, which made her look down in silence. No one knew what to say, and the cave was still until, finally, the wraith spoke again.

'Please ... Can someone help me? I need ... something like a pillow. To lift me up ... Otherwise it is hard to breathe ... To speak ...'

His voice tailed off into the flickering darkness. Jack arranged his satchel into a makeshift pillow and carefully lifted the man's feeble head. The man moaned as he was moved and then sighed as his head sank back. His eyes opened again and scanned their faces until his gaze rested once again on Nancy. This time she held the gaze, leaning forward to hear his whispered speech.

'I am glad, Nancy Kelly, that you have finally come.' The eyes closed again and then after a few seconds, reopened. Now the first hints of a wry smile played at the corners of his lips.

'Every magician needs a medium and every King needs a Queen. You were sent for, and now you have come.'

'He's delirious,' Jack said. 'He must still be feverish.'

'Wait,' Nancy said, raising her hand. 'Herzog. We know why you came to Pemako, we know what you were looking for. Your father was Felix Koenig, we know you were hunting the Nazis' Aryan dream. I spoke to Maya, I . . .'

But then she stopped. Everything she could think of saying sounded wrong. Herzog's charisma was igniting, coursing through the cave. She imagined his spirit, his force, filling the entire valley beyond. She felt small and insignificant next to him. Finally she had found him but she had no idea where to start.

Urgently, Jack asked, 'Herzog, what happened to you? What have you been doing in Tibet and where is the terton? Where are the monks?'

There was no answer. Jack pressed on desperately, 'Herzog, what has happened to you?'

At last the wraith spoke again:

'I found it and now I know the truth.'

Jack and Nancy stared at each other in confusion. Then Nancy leaned forward, speaking very clearly, lest the man was really delirious:

'You found the terma? You found the Book of Dzyan?'

Herzog grimaced in pain and closed his eyes for a moment. Then he said, 'You are motivated by forces beyond your understanding, dear girl. You have pursued me desperately, but you don't really know why. Is that not true?'

And Nancy knew it was indeed the truth. All the time she had grappled with this uncertainty, she had never fully undertstood why she had been drawn to Tibet, why she was doing any of this, why she was determined to find this man she hardly knew. The question had perplexed her and she had confronted it, only to reel away in renewed perplexity. She had set it aside and it had recurred every time she tried to forget it. She had been drawn, perhaps even summoned – and she now realized, with a sick feeling, that she had felt all along that her actions were determined not entirely by herself, but by something beyond her.

'I came to find you,' she stumbled. 'I came to find out what happened to you.'

'Well now you have indeed found me. But it is almost too late.'

Jack interjected, 'Herzog, where is the terma? Where is the Book of Dzyan? What did it say?'

'Jack Adams, you are a good man but you are a terribly simple man. You will never understand.'

'Don't be so arrogant, Herzog,' said Jack, taken aback by Herzog's imperiousness. 'It is you who don't understand. You have become drunk on Tibetan superstition and Nazi occultism – and look where it has got you.'

'Nonsense. You are just a foolish American boy, who believes too many of the lies he has been told about the world. You are too much of a materialist ever to understand the truth.'

'How dare you patronize me, Herzog?'

Urgently Nancy interrupted.

'Jack, please. Let him speak, let him say his piece.' She looked down at the dying man.

Herzog coughed, and then she saw his terrible ravaged face creasing into something – it seemed to be a smile. It looked more like the leer of a death's head, so wizened and skeletal was the man, and Nancy recoiled again, though she tried to hold his gaze.

'The boy does not believe me. I do not expect him to. You at least will understand. That is why I summoned you with the bone. You see, I have been working towards this moment all these years, helping you in your career, advising the editor to promote you, and even I did not know why I was doing this, or rather, I thought I was simply doing it because you showed great promise as a journalist. But that is the way of the kings of Shangri-La. We are always the last to know the real motivations for our deeds. I sent the bone to you according to the Oracle's instructions. The Oracle knew that you would take the bone to Jack Adams. He is the only man in Delhi who could identify it and the only man who could have brought you here, and once Jack Adams saw the bone and realized its significance he was powerless to resist the call of his own vanity. You see, the Oracle knew he would be prepared to do anything to discover where I had found it – the bone was the perfect bait.'

Herzog paused and then his eyes seemed to lose focus, as if he was retreating into memories, literally seeing them rather than the flickering shadows of the cave.

51

Anton Herzog could see great distances into the past, a stone knight in a great cathedral, his head rested on the pillow, his cold arms folded onto his chest. He would lie here for eternity. But if only now he could tell them something of the things he had seen. He coughed bitterly and his chest ached; he knew his lungs were collapsing and he hadn't much time. Not so long to think, to remember, to live. To carve his life into the dull stones around him. The opium would carry him for a time, and then its effects would fade and he would spiral into darkness. And the spiral would be endless, unless of course they came for him, came from Shangri-La.

But where to start? How to make them understand what he had discovered and its awful implications? Slowly he began, trying to conjure the past, hoping it would dance on the dark walls around him. He heard his voice, thin, hoarse, whispering to the girl, 'There was once a man. A thin, ascetic, round-headed man, wearing civilian clothes. He was trying to cross the Bremervörde Bridge. It was May 20th, 1945, it was the end of the war.'

He coughed again, felt the horrible piercing pain in his lungs rise and fall. When it faded enough that he could bear it, enough to let him draw a breath, he resumed:

'There were some British soldiers guarding the bridge. They challenged him. He was carrying papers in the name of Hitzinger, he had a bandage over his right eye. In the reports that followed, the soldiers all said that there was something strange about the man, something disconcerting. The papers were quite clearly forged and so the soldiers arrested him and took him to the nearest Military Police Station. There he was questioned repeatedly for three days and three nights until finally, exhausted, he removed his bandage and said, "My name is Heinrich Himmler. I am the Reichsführer of the SS. Heil Hitler."'

Herzog groaned as the pain stabbed at him again. Jen had extinguished the cigarette lighter, and in the darkness of the Cave the three pilgrims listened as Herzog began once more to speak . . .

'Of course, at first the police did not believe him. They thought he was mad. They stripped him naked and gave him the choice between a suit of American clothes or a refugee blanket. He chose the blanket. They were about to search him for a suicide pill when he bit down hard and shattered the cyanide capsule that had been implanted in one of his teeth. They buried him in the woods, in an unmarked grave . . .'

Nancy interjected. There was fear in her voice.

'Why are you telling us this, Herzog? Do you sympathize with this wicked man? Is this why you followed your father's dream?'

'My child, sympathy or otherwise is irrelevant. My father Felix Koenig met this wicked man, as you call him. He met him on several occasions. My father told me that this man came from another ethical universe. There was no sense in judging him in conventional terms. He was like an African shaman. He was a warrior monk from another world. He was not a European, governed by the laws of conscience and the ethics of Judaeo-Christian civilization. For in the twelve years since the Nazis had come to power a whole new civilization had been erected on the banks of the Rhine, a whole new ethic had been born, an ethic that was different from anything that had come before . . .'

Now Jack interrupted: 'That's a grand way to talk about a bunch of criminals.'

There was a silence, as if Herzog's trance had been disturbed by this interjection. Then from the darkness his cultured, dispassionate voice came again.

'To call them criminals shows the frightening poverty of your mind. If you are only capable of using conventional morality to judge the Nazi mystery then you will never understand it. You are like the jury at Nuremberg or at the trial of Eichmann in Jerusalem: you are only exposing your own hypocrisy, your own moral vacuum. And we all know that nature abhors a vacuum. All you are doing is preparing the ground for another Holocaust . . .'

'How dare you talk in that way . . .'

Nancy put her hand on Jack's arm.

'Jack – let him talk.'

Once more the rasping cough echoed through the darkness and then Herzog spoke again. 'It is only natural that the boy is angry. Unpalatable truths always have this effect. He has been taught a materialist version of history in all its inadequate hypocrisy: rampant inflation and unhappiness with the settlement of World War One caused the German people to elect a leader who turned out to be an evil maniac. Conventional history likes to explain the war away in these impoverished terms, but the man arrested on Bremervörde Bridge cannot simply be dismissed as one of a handful of madmen. The Aryan race was being summoned to throw off foreign gods and return to its source. And it was summoned by powers far beyond its control.'

Appalled by what she was hearing, Nancy fumbled for words. 'But how can you say this – they sent your father to his death – they intended that Stalingrad should be his grave . . .'

Herzog stopped her. 'My father could see beyond these little men: the Hitlers, the Himmlers, the jack-booted thugs. He did not care about them – he could see all the way to Shangri-La, he understood what was really happening. Why are the Jews allowed their patrimony and history but not the Aryans? Why are the Tibetans allowed theirs, but not the Aryans? My father was loyal to the truth, not to the Nazi regime; he wanted to tell the German people where they had come from and show them their destiny. Once, I asked him to tell me about Stalingrad, about the fighting in the winter, in the streets, in the ruins; the hopeless, insane, pitiless fighting. Did it make him hate the dream that had started the war? I asked. Did it make him wish they had never been made to resurrect the truth of the German past, of the Book of Dzyan and Shangri-La? I wanted him to admit that it was all barbarism and fantasy and that Stalingrad had shown him that – but instead he looked at me with tears in his eyes and said simply, "It was sublime." Then, I did not understand, but now I do. Now, I do.'

Jack could keep silent no longer. In an urgent voice he said, 'You are all insane, Herzog. Insane psychopaths, prepared to excuse anything. And you have crossed a moral Rubicon. You have gone too far.'

'No. I have been to Shangri-La and I have seen the Book of Dzyan.'

Herzog paused for a moment. 'I will tell, then you too will understand, you too will know the truth.'

They could hear his breathing in the still night air. Then he began again, his voice deeper now, slightly quieter, but stronger, more alive – almost as if someone else was speaking through him.

52

The night, the cave, the darkness, all were transformed, all else was forgotten as Herzog carried them aloft on his fabulous, wild, fantastic story that led from a small village in Austria, to Argentina, to America and finally to Tibet. Nancy closed her eyes in the darkness and the visions danced before her. She became Anton Herzog; she saw his young father, the diligent professor in Munich all those years ago; she crossed the decades with him and traversed whole continents, all the way until she came through the emerald valley and to the terrible kingdom of Shangri-La and learned with him the truth of the world from the mouth of the King, and of the awful fate that awaited him if he failed to escape.

'I took my bag from my cell at the heart of the kingdom of Shangri-La and made my way back down to the ground floor.'

His voice echoed in her mind. It was her journey too.

'There was no one around as I began to explore the corridors and passageways. I stumbled into a courtyard, at the centre of which was the gompa well. Working quickly, in a deep panic, I drew up some water, crystal-clear and sweet as wine, and filled my water bags. I had a stroke of luck: slumped against the wall of the courtyard was a bag of tsampa. So I emptied all my belongings from my rucksack – toothbrush, bandages, useless maps – and filled it to the brim with tsampa. The bag containing the powder from the metok chulen I had tied around my neck; it was my most valuable possession. Exploring further, I found one room that contained gardening equipment, including several thick woollen winter chubas and a greasy yak's-wool hat. I tried on the chubas for size, took the biggest, and stuffed the hat into its pocket. Now I was as pre-pared as I was ever likely to be, and all that remained was for me to find the Book of Dzyan.

'It did not take long to locate the library; like a ghost haunting a ruined castle, I glided silently through the corridors and rooms until eventually I stumbled into a large book-lined room. In the centre of the room was a golden lectern. I hurried over to it only to discover that there was no book resting on it. I glanced around the room. There must have been thousands and thousands of ancient tomes cramming every inch of the walls, it might take me weeks to search through each one. I had minutes. I sighed in exasperation but then reminded myself that the King's account of the Book of Dzyan was utter gibberish anyway – a book written on the back of a tortoise, he had said, then transcribed to vellum and parchment. A book that contained the thoughts of the universe – talking to itself. "Madness and black magic," I reminded myself, speaking out loud. And then I turned on my heel and began to hunt for a way out.

'I suspected that I was going to have to make my way up onto the rear wall of the gompa and then jump or climb down the other side. I would probably need a rope. But in fact it was much easier than that. I emerged from a passageway into a back courtyard, on the far side of which was a door. I hurried over, not expecting for one minute for it to be unlocked, but tried the handle anyway. The door swung open, revealing the mountainside beyond. I could hardly believe my luck, but then quickly realized that the only reason that the monks could afford to be so casual was that they were utterly convinced that no one would ever try to escape, nor would any unwanted visitor appear from the depths of the inhospitable mountains.

'The light was fading as I stepped silently through the doorway and shut it noiselessly behind me. Pure undiluted fear tightened every nerve in my body as I set foot on the rocky ground. If they caught me now,

I would never get another chance to escape and my horrible fate would be sealed. Then as I adjusted the straps on my backpack, I noticed something glinting on the ground. I bent down. It was the mouthpiece of a bone trumpet, and suddenly I realized that all around the base of the castle wall were bones, bones and more bones; I was standing ankle-deep in ancient bones. I was standing on the burial ground of the kings of Shangri-La. I picked up the bone trumpet and shoved it into my bag; at least I would have some proof, some evidence of my horrendous journey, if I ever managed to make good my escape.

'Within a few minutes I had put a half-mile between myself and the gompa. I turned around for one last look. The tower was silhouetted against the dusk sky. Was it my imagination or could I just see the abject figure of the King, gazing out at the first stars of the evening, awaiting his awful fate? But perhaps I had now saved him – once they discovered I had gone, there would be no dethronement, and he would live until the next newcomer appeared. He would be able to maintain his gruesome delusions a while longer; he would reign a few more years over the world – or what he thought the world was.

But then there was always the chance they might come after me – and that thought set me scrambling as fast as I could up the slope of the stony hillside, towards what I hoped was a ravine that would lead to a pass. It was a painful process: the thin air contained little oxygen and it felt as if my lungs were flapping emptily as I struggled onwards. An hour later I was still climbing and still panting for breath. The last grey whispers of day were about to disappear, and I decided to stop and get my bearings by the first stars and fix in my mind the various mountain peaks before they were lost to the night. I took the opportunity to mix up a little of the tsampa and metok chulen powder with water so that I could take my first shot of the terton's magical drug. Then I turned again towards the mountainside and set off at a slower pace into the darkness.

By daybreak I had reached the top of the pass, and ahead of me lay the vast expanse of a plateau that the King had so accurately described as being like the surface of the moon. It was in fact the worst possible surface on which to attempt to walk at high speed; it was strewn with potholes and rocks ranging in size from that of an apple to that of a human head, and I was now feeling exceptionally weary. As a morale-booster, I allowed myself to pause for a few moments and look back down the ravine. The view was good, I could see the last seven or so miles of my climb and I could not see any signs of anyone following me, which meant that if the monks set out now, I would have at least a twelve-hour or so head start.

'Spurred on by the greatest motivator of all – fear for my life – I now realized that the main dangers lay ahead and not behind me. I had very little idea where I was, or where I was going. I suspected I was somewhere west and south of the Litang gompa, in the folds of the massive mountain range, probably more than one hundred miles from the Tsangpo valley. But such distances are meaningless in the Himalayas. No journey ever proceeds in a straight line. Endless zigzagging up and down mountainsides, and through high passes is required simply to get from one valley to the next. How many valleys lay between me and Pemako I did not know, but I suspected it could be as many as ten, and in addition to ten or eleven mountain crossings there would be an unknown number of plateaux like the one that lay before me now, and also an endless variety of other obstacles: unfordable, freezing rivers, impassable gorges, snow-jammed heights, a thousand ways to sprain an ankle or break a bone . . . And all I had was a compass, the stars above by night, about ten litres of water, the powder and the tsampa.

'In such situations, it doesn't pay to start calculating the odds. It is much better just to get going and concentrate on the hard work of finding the quickest path. At least the powder was starting to take effect. I had been feeling pains in my legs and my feet were bruised from stumbling over rocks, but now my bodily pain began to ease off. Also, despite the challenges of my situation, I kept catching myself daydreaming, a sure sign that the hallucinogens were beginning to take effect. By noon, I felt as if I had drunk a bottle of champagne very quickly. My spirits were high, my pace was fast, my head was almost empty of thoughts; all I had to do was remember to take more powder at dusk. How long I could keep this up I had no idea, but I knew I was going to keep going, until finally, I would either stumble into a village somewhere or I would drop dead on the mountainside.

'The sun fell from the sky, in a slow arc, the moon climbed high into the night and then vanished again like an actor walking off-stage. Then the sun reappeared, shimmering over the rocky plateau. I struggled down gorges and around massive boulders. I came across a huge stone circle that reminded me of Stonehenge or Carnac in Brittany. I sat with my back to the biggest megalith and imagined the people who might have built it long, long ago and felt indescribably lonely and bereft. The landscape was so very vast, I advanced like an ant through the massive canyons of rock and the endless swathes of sky. The sun set in a bath of blood.

'How many days I continued thus, I do not know. I crossed a great steppe, picked clean as a bone by the howling wind; I descended into a ravine that I thought would disgorge me into the depths of hell itself; I climbed mountain after mountain and crawled through pass after pass until finally, half dead with exhaustion, I crashed down a hillside and reached the edges of a lush valley forest. Where I was, I had absolutely no idea, but there were roots and bark to eat and small streams trickled down from the glaciers, their chilled waters burning my dry mouth. Finally, nearing total exhaustion, I saw the most extraordinary sight I have ever seen, even more shocking in its way than the King of Shangri-La himself, or the ghastly cage that was to be his funeral pyre. I was high on a windswept plateau, but in the distance I saw what I thought in my enfeebled, delirious state must be a scarecrow. A lone figure, thin as a rake, standing completely motionless, seemingly oblivious to the wind and heat. I approached, shouting and waving. Nothing, no response. I walked right up to the man. A monk, a lone hermit, a madman – God knows what he was doing out there, miles from anywhere. He was standing on one leg in the crane position, his hands joined in prayer, his right leg straight and his left foot tucked up into his groin. I could scarcely believe my eyes. I went right up to his face and tried to draw his attention. Perhaps he had some food or water, or perhaps he could tell me where I was. But I could get nothing from him. Nothing! I begged, I shouted, and finally I wept at his feet but not once did he respond. He just chanted mournfully through his nose. He might have been there for days or weeks, it was impossible to know. He had not a single crumb of bread on him and not a single grain of tsampa and not even a water bottle. He had nothing at all, just the rags he was wearing.

'Perhaps he thought I was a demon or a hallucination, he very well might have done. No one ever crossed this plateau, particularly a white man. To him I did not exist. I took this all to be a sign that humanity had abandoned me. It even occurred to me that perhaps I was actually dead and that was why he didn't see me. I was doomed to wander like a ghost for ever more and no one would ever learn of my fate or my discovery. Then I had one last idea, or rather the idea appeared directly in my head, or more accurately still, a hexagram appeared, answering my question of myself: "What should I do?"

'It was the Oracle talking to me. You see, I no longer needed the yarrow stalks, or the Book. I was in tune with its forces and it now spoke to me directly and I knew from years of practice exactly what the hexagram intended me to do. I took out the bone trumpet and wrapped my *Trib* ID around it and then delving into my bag, I found a pen. I had lost my journal and I did not even have a single scrap of notepaper but luckily, right at the bottom of my bag, covered in metok chulen powder, I discovered one last little picture of the Dalai Lama. I always travel with pictures of the Dalai; they make perfect gifts, as any rendering of his image in Tibet is banned and thus they are all the more prized. On the back of the picture I scribbled a few last words. By now I suspected that a replacement must have been found for me in Delhi, and it was only natural for me to assume that it should be you, Nancy Kelly, and that is why the bone was addressed to you. Dan Fischer always promised me that he would take my advice.

'But as soon as I realized this, in a flash I understood why I had been watching over your career all these years. I had assumed that it was because I thought you were a fine journalist, a perfect candidate to one day replace me in my own post. The truth was that the Oracle intended you to be my Queen, and as ever it had begun its machinations far in advance, using me to manoeuvre you and letting me think it was my own free will. But surely I had failed it? Surely I had now ruined its careful plans? I would die here in the wilderness and you would never make it to Shangri-La.

'Then I applied a secret hand-hold that I had learnt from studying the ancient Ba Gua. I touched the monk's neck just below his left ear and uttered my command: "Take this bone to the Dalai in India for he will know what to do, he will pass it on to the police." The Ba Gua's suggestion techniques are hugely powerful, but whether they would penetrate this mad monk's hypnotic state I did not know. But I had to try. Then, on the point of finally breaking down, I turned and headed onwards across the blasted, baking plateau, my limbs crying out with pain, leaving the crazy monk still standing there, all alone in the wilderness of rock and heat.

'I was in a grave situation. My body had consumed all its reserves and my muscles were shrinking by the hour. Even the powder from the metok chulen no longer seemed to have an effect. Yet, in my darkest hour, there was a reprieve. Scarcely knowing where I trod, I fell through a patch of undergrowth into a clearing. In the centre of the clearing, to my absolute amazement and joy, were the slumbering remains of a fire. I had fallen heavily into the clearing, and once on the ground I could barely muster the energy to raise myself on to all fours and crawl over to the fire, but somehow I managed to do so. I collapsed forward and then rolled over onto my back and prayed that the owner of the fire would return before I died.

'Some time later I awoke to find two figures standing over me. They were both dressed in filthy yak's-wool tunics and yakskin boots. They were not

Tibetans; they must have been members of one of the many indigenous tribes that still live in the remote valleys, pursuing ancient animist religious beliefs and existing in raw savagery. When they saw my eyes open, they immediately grabbed their kukris from their belts, and waved them towards me. I cowered in fear; I could see out of the corner of my eye that this made them relax. They began to mutter to each other in a strange language that I didn't recognize at all, and then the older of the two put down his knife and unclipped his water skin from his belt and reaching out to me he said something I didn't understand. I made myself smile, even though this most basic of gestures caused me great pain, and then I gratefully poured some water down my throat. The old man watched me closely, and when he saw that I had finished drinking, he tried to communicate again, this time in very poor, heavily accented Chinese.

' "Good?"

' "Better now, but not good. Please, where is Litang gompa?"

'This prompted another bout of clicking and tutting between the two savages and then the old man tried out his Chinese again.

' "You have gold? Salt?'

' "I have nothing. But take me to Litang. I will pay you when we get there.'

'I wasn't sure if they understood me at all. Again they fell into discussion. Then they went over to the fire and poked it with their kukris. What they were planning, God only knew. The older of the two returned to my side. They had come to a decision on what to do.

'"We listen to the bone," he said mysteriously. "Bone will tell us."

'I nodded to show that I understood, and thought ruefully to myself how happy I would have been to have the Oracle with me now. What I would have given these past few days to be able to call on its advice. Perhaps I would never have ended up in this ghastly predicament if I had not decided to leave it in Delhi after the last and final positive message it gave me, urging me to leave at once for Shangri-La. But then I wondered – I confess that in my plight I doubted the wisdom of the Oracle – why had it sent me there? What was it hoping to teach me? Except perhaps the wrongness of my obsession, the unnatural level of my pride?

'Out of the corner of my eye, I watched the two men stoking the fire and placing twigs on the glowing embers. Once the fire was burning merrily, one of them carefully placed a spearhead into its middle. They sat on their haunches in silence for several minutes, watching the fire, waiting for some symbol or sign by which no doubt they would seal my fate. Then, using a long stick, the elder of the two dragged the spear tip back from the fire onto the earth, and with much clicking and tutting in their strange language, they succeeded in slipping the spear shaft into its clasp.

'What happened next is hard for me to describe, not because it was in any way unbelievable or incredible but because it made my heart stop with fear. The younger of the two men reached into his satchel and withdrew an object from inside, an object that at any other time of my life would have had absolutely no significance for me at all, but on this day, at this time, after the horrendous ordeal that I had been through and after the nightmarish stories that I had heard from the mouth of the mad King, sent a spasm of pure fear through my brain.

'It was a tortoise shell.

'He placed this tortoise shell on the ground, with the patterned side facing up, and then held his right hand above it and muttered a few sentences. The other man, who was now brandishing the spear, then tapped the left-hand side of the shell firmly with the red-hot spear tip. I heard a distinct crack and the two men peered down at the disfigured object. The elder of the two cleared the dead leaves and forest detritus from the earth next to his feet, and then to my eternal horror proceeded to scratch a symbol onto the ground – it was, without any doubt, a hexagram.

'And this is where my story ends, for in that moment, all strength ebbed away from me and I lost consciousness and did not wake up again until many days later when I found myself tied to this stretcher being carried through the jungle by a party of Bon monks.

'And the first thing that I did when I awoke was cry bitter tears, because I knew then that I had never been the author of my own destiny, that all these years I had been a pawn in a vastly larger game, and that the King of Shangri-La spoke the truth: the Book of Dzyan had directed my every action, it had conducted me through all the years of my life, and what I had always thought was a benign tool of prophecy was nothing less than a gateway to purest evil.'

53

Nancy felt as if she was awaking from a long, long sleep. In the darkness of the Cave of the Magicians, Anton Herzog was repeating a single word, until his voice tailed off into nothingness.

'The Oracle. The Oracle . . .'

Nancy found she was shaking her head. She felt a deep sense of sadness. It was all so very strange, and dreamlike. Surely she had dreamed, she thought; it could not really be that Herzog had been lying there talking for so long, unfurling this story. She thought perhaps he had spoken and then she had slept, and everything had mingled: reality and dream, madness and sanity. As she heard him drawing air into his lungs, his breathing laboured and irregular, she thought that for all his talk – if he had genuinely been talking all this time – he remained immeasurably unknowable. And was it true? Any of it? Did Shangri-La really exist? And the Book of Dzyan, the Oracle –

could they really be the same thing – an evil force that had been in their midst all along, sucking them in, one by one – controlling all their destinies, controlling history, moving nations, starting great wars?

She imagined him lying there, like an idol, his breath rattling in his throat. His heart was cold, she thought, and this thought held her in its grip. Events in his life had cut him off from humanity, and so he had sought meaning in the dream of a retreat, a place far beyond the grasp of ordinary men. He was a victim of the war; he had not been physically wounded, but he had been psychically damaged. She wondered if it was this – that he was cold and damaged and everything he said had simply been speaking of this and nothing more. But she knew it was more than that.

Jen was the first to speak, his voice sounding strained and weary.

'So we all had access to the Book of Dzyan all along, all these years. It is the Oracle. And you believe it has been controlling us all this time? All of us . . .'

Herzog coughed feebly.

'Yes, absolutely. Anyone who opens its pages and asks it a question instantly falls under its spell. We have been driven by the Oracle, each to this point. It causes wars and upheavals, it drives whole nations and it drives single men and women. The King of Shangri-La spoke the truth: World War Two, all the great events in the history of mankind, have their origins in the kingdom of Shangri-La, brought into being by hidden masters working with the Oracle. The Oracle controls all who look into her.'

'So you are saying the Oracle brought me to Tibet, that it was the Oracle and not you who summoned me?' said Nancy.

'You know the answer to that better than I do, but I can tell you that it was the Oracle that made me send you the bone, it was the Oracle that told me to recommend you to Dan Fischer as my replacement in the event of any unforeseen events. The Oracle made it clear that was what I must do. It summoned you, it advised you; it knew you would play a part,' said Herzog.

Now Jack, with an edge of panic in his voice, tried to refute the dying man.

'Herzog, this is all madness. What you are saying defies truth. The world cannot work like this. Shangri-La doesn't exist, there is no secret kingdom that controls the world and you have no proof that the Book of Dzyan is the Oracle. You never had time to look for it; you never saw it. And besides, your story does not even make sense in its own terms. Even if we accept – for the sake of argument – that Shangri-La does exist and that the Oracle is the Book of Dzyan and that it conducted you there, then why would it let you escape? Why would it let you refuse the destiny that it had created for you? Do you not see? The Book of Dzyan has failed, even from your own testimony?'

A weak and fading voice whispered back in the darkness.

'You've missed the whole point. Everything I have said.'

'No, you've missed the point. You've failed to comprehend your own story, Herzog. You're ailing and confused and you can't distinguish dream from reality.'

The skull face creased again into a grotesque leer, and Herzog's ravaged hands moved in the flickering light. 'I am both of these things. Yet about this I have absolute clarity. The Oracle knew I would fail. It knew my weaknesses long before I did. It knew I would try to evade my destiny, that I would escape from Shangri-La. Of course it did, it sees everything long before we can even imagine it. And so it summoned Nancy, with the bone, and through Nancy you were brought here – the only man in Delhi who could have helped her find me. It knew that Nancy would take the bone to you. And this man Jen has been conducted by the Oracle to bring you the last miles of the route. You have all been controlled, in order that you will save me, that I will be given one last chance, for I am the chosen one . . .'

'The chosen one.' Jack Adams repeated his words, his lip curled, half in contempt and half in fear.

'One chance to do what?' said Nancy, though even now she feared she knew the answer.

'To return to Shangri-La. To correct my error. For I am now certain I was in error, that my escape was a terrible thing to have done. These last days with the monks I have had time to think, time to sift the wheat from the chaff, time to understand. I had it all wrong. The Oracle is our mother and father, no use running from it, there is no use trying to evade its plans. And besides, we would never be happy if we were to do so. I realize now the truth. My path is clear. I must return there; the prodigal son.'

'Look, Anton,' Jack was saying, as if he was hoping by a frank appeal that he could persuade the wraith to change his story, to admit he had been lying all along. 'Let's think of it like this. You got lost and ill and some shamans found you — that part of your story I accept. You saw them using the tortoise shell and your mind wove this extraordinary tale, to make up for the fact that you never made it to Shangri-La, that you never did see the Book of Dzyan. But even you know that is ridiculous. You want to try again because you never even got there.'

'No, I was there. That's certain enough to me. I spoke to the King and I saw the shamans using the tortoise shell, using nature herself to construct hexagrams. The King of Shangri-La spoke the truth and the Oracle is the Book of Dzyan. The world turns according to her writ. Empires rise and fall, peoples are awakened from their slumbers by the kings of Shangri-La and set to work, to achieve great things that they could never understand,' said Herzog, his voice so frail now that they had to lean forward to hear him.

'But why do you want to return to that barbaric place?' interrupted Nancy.

'Because I understand now. As soon as I saw the tortoise shell I understood. It is my destiny. I was afraid when I saw the King on the parapet, the prisoner, the sacrifice. I was terrified, and in my weakness I could only think of saving my small human self, my insignificant person. But when those people saved me, I realized the truth. I must return. I must accept my allotted role. In the end it is better to reign in hell than to serve in heaven. And a King does not choose to become King; he is appointed – by forces greater than himself. And Nancy, this is the other matter, as decreed by the Oracle. You must come with me; you are to be my Queen. Together we will plunge the world into the greatest war that has ever been known, and from the flames of our destruction will be born the superman and he will rise up like a phoenix to rule over the purified races of mankind. Come with me. The *Götterdämmerung* draws near.'

Nancy recoiled, horrified by his words.

'You really are crazy,' said Jack angrily.

And Nancy too, though she understood something of the force of the Oracle, though she was prepared to believe almost anything, so strange had her journey been, finally agreed with Jack: that Herzog's reason had cracked under the strain. That he was rambling insanely in the darkness.

'You are ignorant, Jack, and you will always deny what you do not comprehend,' Herzog was saying, in a furious whisper. 'Leave me here. They will come for me from Shangri-La, just as the King predicted. They will come and get me. You will see. They will come.'

'Insane,' said Jack after a long silence. 'This is all insane.' Then suddenly he stirred himself. 'Come on. We have to go. The Chinese army could get here any moment. Jen, what are you going to do?'

Jen was silent, as if for the first time since they'd met he wasn't sure what he would do. Ever since Herzog had begun his story, Jen had been shrinking further and further away from him, as if he was shunning the real implications of his story. Though he had wanted the Book of Dzyan, thought Nancy, he seemed repelled by the journey Herzog had taken, by precisely what possessing this book might entail. Now he was immobile, mute, as if Herzog had turned him to stone.

'Jen, please!' said Jack, more urgently. 'We've lingered here too long.'

Slowly, with a great effort, Jen raised his head.

'Yes, you are right. We must go. I must return to Beijing and consult with my Brotherhood. In the light of this new information my quest for the Book of Dzyan seems superfluous. Everything I have suffered has been in vain. We have had it all along.'

'Jen, get a grip,' said Jack in a hoarse whisper. 'Herzog is completely deranged.'

'You are wrong, Jack. I fear that Herzog speaks the truth. My presence here is proof itself: it was the Oracle that brought me here today, that took me to Litang gompa and led me into the forest. At every turn I consulted it. As much as it makes me sick to say it, at every turn I followed its command.'

Jack almost growled at him. 'Don't be ridiculous. Coincidences. You would have come anyway. These are the tall tales of an opium eater ... you should ignore everything he's said and come with us.'

Nancy was crouching over the body of Anton Herzog, oblivious to their disagreement.

'What do we do with him?'

Jack didn't answer and didn't even look at her. They had passed an entire night listening to Herzog, it seemed, and now it was morning. She hadn't noticed the time. And now she looked again at the ruined man before her. His face had collapsed, his eyes were shut tightly, as if he was in grave pain. His mouth moved but no sound came.

'Will he live?' she said to Jack urgently, desperate for him to say something.

Jack shook his head. 'Not if we move him. And if we leave him . . .' He left her to draw her own conclusions.

Tears began to form in Nancy's eyes; she tried to fight them back. Jack put his hand on her shoulder.

'He is not in pain. The opium will see to that.'

Jen was sorting through his backpack, making ready for his own journey. Suddenly he turned to Nancy and said, 'Wait, Nancy, I have one last idea. Do you have a copy of the Oracle?'

'Yes.'

She hitched her bag off her shoulder and took out the book and lay it on the dusty path. It emanated a living energy – a dark energy. She could feel Jack behind her, taut with exasperation. But she continued nonetheless.

'Have you got a coin?' she asked.

'Yes.'

Jen raised himself on to one knee and delved a coin out of his pocket. She looked at him apprehensively.

'And the question?'

Jen held her gaze for a second, then he looked down at the book and placing his hand on its cover he said, first in Chinese and then in English, 'Oracle, is there any truth in the story of Anton Herzog: is it true that you are the Book of Dzyan?'

Nancy took a deep breath and began to flick the coin. As she did so, Jen registered the results in the sand with his fingertip. When she had thrown the coin six times, the hexagram was assembled. All colour drained from Jen's face. In a flat voice empty of strength he said, 'Sun at the top. Tui at the bottom. Empty is the centre.'

With fear in her eyes she asked, 'Do you know what hexagram it is – without looking at the book?'

'Yes,' he replied, scrutinizing her with an almost angry expression.

Her voice cracking with emotion, she beseeched him, 'Tell me, please.'

'It's Chung Fu. Inner Truth.' Jen's lips curled in fear.

Before Nancy could say anything he spoke again, in a voice filled with anguish, 'It means that Anton Herzog speaks the truth. It means that Shangri-La does exist and that the Oracle is the Book of Dzyan.'

Jen turned away, immersed in his own thoughts. For a minute all was silence, then finally, as if breaking a magic spell, Jack leaned forward and brushed his hand over the sand, erasing the hexagram altogether. He placed a hand on each of their shoulders and said in a whisper, 'Come on. It's time to go.'

54

The fires and the lanterns of the Chinese soldiers who were coming for Anton Herzog twinkled below and in the far distance, down the dark valley, Nancy could see the eerie orange glow of Metok, the last outpost of Tibet before the Indian border.

'You must continue up this path,' Jen said in the darkness. 'I am going in the other direction, to the Gobi, to consult with my Brotherhood, to bring them the terrible news. Get some sleep once you have crossed the pass, and then continue over the plateau and you will come to a tribe of salt traders. They will take you to the Indian border, where the Yarlang Tsangpo goes over the falls. There is a path there, a steep hard path, but you will make it. It will take you through the mountains to the banks of the Brahma-putra; follow the Holy River and you will find human habitations soon enough. Do you have any gold?'

'I have some Renmenbi,' said Jack.

'That's no good up there.' Swiftly, Jen unbuttoned his jacket. He tore at the inner lining and produced a single hoop of gold.

'Here. Take this. It weighs three ounces. Give it to the leader of the salt-trading clan and give him these as well.'

He produced some small pieces of card.

'They are photos of His Holiness the Dalai Lama. They are illegal in Tibet, as Herzog said, they are greatly prized, and it should stop the salt traders robbing you. Now, if I could take some of your tsampa and water, then I think we are all ready to part company.'

Jack nodded his thanks.

'I will repay you the gold, if I can find you,' he said.

'Don't worry about that. You saved my life. Just get going and don't look back.'

Nancy was still in shock, only half taking in the conversation.

'And Herzog?'

Jen was silent, but it was a silence that spoke volumes. Then he said, slowly, 'I will administer him one more pipe. We will leave him with a full pipe as well. There is nothing more anyone can do. We cannot possibly move him, and if we stay longer we will all be captured or killed.'

Amongst the three of them, there was an unspoken

sense of relief that they had no choice but to abandon the dying Anton Herzog. He would never return to Delhi to recover, he would never be able to mount a second expedition and return to Shangri-La, if indeed it existed. He would die alone, and thus his spell would be broken once and for all, and by turning their backs on him they would banish his awful truth and ensure that free will triumphed; his ghastly and fantastic conspiracy was nothing more than a nightmare. Yet it was awful, nonetheless, to leave him, and Nancy stood for a moment looking down at the husk of Anton Herzog: a legendary journalist, and brilliant scholar, who would now die – crazy and alone, somewhere in this treacherous land. And she turned away, weeping bitterly, into the savage jungle. Far off, the low drone of an aircraft could be heard. It was time to go. With a last farewell, Jen walked away along the path and then they turned and began the final ascent.

Nancy could not hold back her tears. They flowed freely as she clambered along the path. She had travelled so far and learned so much, and for what? To abandon the man she had sought for so long? And perhaps Herzog had spoken the truth after all – perhaps their lives were nothing more than a puppeteer's sham? Jack Adams never consulted the Oracle, he remained immune from its schemes – but she had felt its power – the power of an amoral conditioning force that Herzog had described, some presence which was directing them all, to an end they could not hope to understand.

She was hungry and cold, and there was nothing left of her but muscle and bones. And at that moment, she wanted no part of the world; she wanted to withdraw from human society. It was a ghastly merry-go-round, a monstrous charade controlled by devils and demons; happiness was another word for selfishness and that was the real truth of the world. Sobbing and panting for breath, she put her head down and dragged her weary limbs along the pass. Behind her in the cave, lying there, perhaps already now dead, was this man – sage or madman – the man whose life had somehow been intertwined with hers – Anton Herzog.

Epilogue

New York

The salt traders had been there as Jen had promised, camped on the wind-blasted plateau in their yakskin yurts, their animals foraging through the thin blanket of snow, their feral children running wild like dogs. They had been suspicious and hostile at first, and Nancy saw that she and Jack were a strange sight, two raggedly dressed Westerners, silent in their confusion. Yet, with the cards and the gold as offerings, they soon found the traders welcoming enough. They were taken into the chieftain's tent, a smoke-filled teepee where human forms sprawled in the darkness. The chieftain, a ferocious-looking man with a cutlass and pistol stuffed into his belt, had accepted their gifts and allotted two young men and one animal to take them to the border and guide them to the path that descended through a dark chasm, down into the foothills of the Himalayas and out onto the sun-drenched banks of the Brahmaputra.

And as Jen had predicted, the going was hard but, eventually, they came across the first village and within twelve hours, thanks to lifts from farmers and lorry-drivers, they found themselves standing on a railway platform, at a distant provincial railway station on the furthest fringes of the Indian state of Sikkim, waiting for the local service that would pass them down the line of the great Indian railway network until, after a further thirty-six hours of crowded travel, they would finally be deposited at Delhi Central Station, bleary-eyed and disbelieving.

That had been six months ago now and Nancy Kelly had left India far behind. Later, she had learned from Krishna that the Indian police had abandoned the search for Herzog. The Chinese government said that they had assumed he was dead, though they claimed no body was ever found. His bones were still probably being picked over by the Himalayan griffin vultures, after his own anonymous sky burial in the mouth of the Cave of the Magicians. Charges of spying were forgotten about rather than officially dropped, but the police had informed Nancy that she was free to leave.

All that remained for her to do was to contact

Maya. She spent a tortured morning working out what to say and finally wrote that she had made it to Tibet and found Herzog there. He was dying, she wrote, he died before her eyes. Maya should now take the will to a lawyer and she would be given money, to bring up their child. She paused before she wrote the final line, and then she committed herself. 'Anton Herzog,' she wrote, 'died speaking your name. His last word was "Maya."' It was a white lie, though a lie none the less, but what was the point in upsetting her, in saying that she had seen him on his deathbed and that not once had he mentioned her?

She caught the first flight she could back to America, gazing out of the plane's window as it taxied down the runway in the blazing Delhi sunshine, wondering how different her life in India might have been, had it not been for Anton Herzog.

Ultimately, she could not fathom what had happened to her at all, but she could not throw off the suspicion that she had come close to discerning an awful truth, a truth which had ravaged the frame of Herzog, once he had perceived it. She envied Jack his outlook on life, his absolute refusal to engage even in the merest thought that Herzog could have been telling any kind of truth. But either way, even for her, the mysteries and the implications, whether correct or not, were simply too great to be factored into a single human's life. She and Jack had agreed to keep quiet about their journey, and most of all to tell no one that they had found Anton Herzog. She had hoped that in going to Tibet she would find the greatest story of her life, and in one sense – the profoundest sense – she had. Yet during their journey back into India, soul-searching and raking over their shared experience in the cave, they had realized that no one would believe them and that no one for a minute would understand. The greatest story of her entire life would never see the light of day.

She bade Jack farewell on the platform at Delhi station and promised to wire the money to his account. For a time they stared in silence at each other on the station concourse, amid the constant motion of the crowds. Then Jack squeezed her hand and kissed her on the cheek.

'Don't think about what he said. None of it was true. The fact that he died up there proves that. The fact that we left shows we have free will. If the Oracle is a prophet then it lies.'

And then Jack was gone, back to his world of antique traders, old bones and long hot Delhi nights. She watched him walking away, and saw him shaking his head, as if he was trying to banish the memories of what he had seen.

Her heart ached as she saw him go; in some ways

she had begun to fall in love with him; in other circumstances, it should surely have all led to an affair, a romance of some sort. But she was not being reasonable. He was bound up with everything she had seen, this seismic experience she had endured, and she couldn't figure it out. They both needed to escape from everything that had occurred, and they could only do that alone.

Nancy had returned to New York: to Brooklyn and the leafy streets of Park Slope; to her friends; to the cafés and bookstores she knew so well. Spring had come, the flowers were out in Central Park. She had been offered leave but refused it, afraid of spending long hours on her own, preferring to accept a post as a desk editor. She sank with relief into the cosy rituals of daily deadlines, the morning editorial meeting, the mounting frenzy as the paper was put to bed, drinks parties, dinners with contacts, the reassuring activities around her. Gradually, she began to put the strange experience behind her, or if not behind her, then at least she found that frequently she was not thinking about it, that there had been hours and then even later days when she had not really considered it. Somehow she buried it. She understood that this was the only way she could return to any sort of normality: Herzog's worldview, his story in the cave, his dream, his night-mare, his world where demons and masters controlled mankind's destiny, had to be buried under the mounting noise and activity of ordinary life. And morbid though it was to dwell on the fact, she was relieved that Herzog was dead. He was wrong, or mad as Jack put it. He hadn't been rescued by monks from Shangri-La and he had never fulfilled the destiny that he thought he had been promised by the Oracle. And this was what made it easier to view Herzog's account as an aberrant way of looking and thinking about the world, and his story of reaching Shangri-La and discovering the truth about the Oracle as a fantasy.

And then one late summer's day, the phone rang. It was seven a.m., she was at home in bed, gratefully re-established in her old routine, listening to the radio and just thinking about getting up. She picked up, wondering why it couldn't wait until she arrived at work, and then she heard a voice so familiar, so significant to her, that her hands began to tremble.

'Nancy, it's Jack,' said the voice.

For a moment she couldn't reply. He said, 'Nancy?' again, as if he was worried the line was bad, and she said, 'Jack, what a surprise,' trying to inject her response with ordinary friendly warmth. Old travelling companions, that was what she was aiming for.

'Look, I'm sorry I haven't been in touch. I – well, perhaps you understand why. The reason I'm calling is – I'm passing through New York. I'm at the airport now, I wondered if you'd like to have a coffee this morning. Deadlines permitting of course?'

She tried to laugh at his joke. But she had tensed up, as if she was back in the jungles of Pemako, unsure where to turn. She was afraid, afraid of seeing him again and afraid of revisiting her memories of those days in Tibet that she had worked so assiduously to suppress. She had consciously chosen to accept the banal world, to bury all knowledge of the alternatives, and it was not solely a negative act. She had come to understand it as a positive one as well: she was taking sides with history, with a general view of the universe, and it was probably the only way of staying sane. And besides it upset her greatly even to think of Anton Herzog, left to die, alone, in the gloomy jungle.

'You know, it would be really nice to meet,' she said. 'But this morning is difficult. I have – a lot of things to do.'

'Come on, Nancy, just a quick coffee. I won't take up much of your time.' He knew why she was reluctant. He understood, she was certain. That made her easier in her mind. She heard herself saying, 'OK, outside the Bagel Zone – it's on Tompkins Square Park, in Alphabet City. The cab-drivers all know the park. I'll see you there in forty-five minutes.'

Deeply troubled, but trying not to admit it, she jumped in the shower, threw on some clothes. Briskly, she walked out of her apartment and found a cab. It was a fine clear day. The green grass at the centre of Tompkins Square Park was already filled with people enjoying the morning sunshine: bicycle couriers waiting for their next jobs, passers-by drinking coffee and glancing at the headlines, lolling lazily on the lawn, chatting in small groups. Nancy found a bench and sat down, though she didn't have to wait long: Jack's cab pulled up at the kerb, almost right by where she was sitting. He got out, looking around for her. Her heart skipped a beat when she saw him – he looked the same as ever – handsome, agile and dynamic, and yet she knew now how much else lurked beneath his macho veneer.

'Hello there,' she called out, in a voice that sounded high and nervous. He turned and smiled. As he approached he extended a hand, then when she took it he pulled her to him, kissed her on the cheek. His breath was warm. She felt a wave of pure familiarity washing over her, and that made her all the more confused. She stepped back from him.

'Nancy, it's good to see you,' he said, looking her up and down. 'You look well.'

'You mean compared with last time, when we were both half-starved in Tibet? I'm glad you think so.'

He laughed generously, sat down on the bench with

her. For a moment neither of them said anything, and she could see that he wasn't sure how to begin.

'So, what brings you to New York?' she said, helping him out.

'I'm on my way to the Metropolitan Museum, it's to do with my research; palaeontology of the Himalayas and all that . . .'

'Oh yes, I remember.'

'And how's life back in sunny Park Slope?'

'It's good, thanks. I'm a section editor, not quite as glamorous as being a foreign correspondent.'

'Well, I guess there are fewer run-ins with the Indian secret police,' he said, smiling.

'Yes, not much of that. Just the daily hazards of New York supper parties and endless office politics.'

'Sounds treacherous enough to me,' he said.

There she was nodding and smiling at him, and all the time she was thinking it was crazy; they'd shared so much together, had really gone to hell and back, and now they were talking in this stilted formal way. It made her so frustrated, and she was angry with herself for not being able to say what she wanted to say.

'I'm sorry . . .' she blurted out. 'This is not what I really think . . . Not what I really . . .'

He put his hand on hers; she felt the warmth of his skin. 'Nancy, I know what you mean. I understand.'

'I've been . . . trying to get things back to normal. For months, I've managed not to think about it. I find it all too upsetting.'

Jack watched her silently. She wanted to say more but nothing came out. Finally he took his hand away from hers and reached down to his bag.

'I want to show you this.'

He pulled out a copy of the morning's *New York Times* and discarded it on the table and then wrestling hard in the depths of his rucksack he pulled out a box. He swept the newspaper to one side and then very carefully placed the box on the table and proceeded to take its top off, revealing what appeared to be a piece of bone.

'What on earth is that you've got there, Jack?' said Nancy, trying to recover her wryness.

'It's a human skull. The skull of an anatomically modern hominid. A *Homo sapiens*. This skull could fit on the body of almost any Caucasian man alive today.'

'It looks like a piece of a tree.'

'That's because there is a tree growing out of the skull – it has broken through the top. If I lift it up then you can see: this part is the skull and this is the tree. A seed must have fallen into the skull, many millennia ago. Perhaps the brain provided the moisture for the germination of the seed, or perhaps there was rainwater in the upturned skull. However it happened, the skull acted as a kind of flowerpot.'

'And?'

'It's perfect. The wood and the skull together vastly improve the reliability of the dating.'

He looked at her as if expecting a response. 'It's the oldest hominid bone ever discovered in Asia. It's what I've been looking for all these years. It brings my work to a close and proves – pretty much conclusively, it turns out – that I am right. Modern man did walk the earth a quarter of a million years ago. I won't make any money out of it but at least I know I am right. I'm taking it to the Met today. They won't believe me either, but I will show them all the same.'

He smiled ruefully.

'Well that's wonderful. Congratulations. Thank you for showing it to me.'

But she couldn't understand what it meant. She could see that his expression had changed, he had lost all his surface calm. His hands moved over the bone, as if he was afraid to touch it. Now he said, 'There have not been many people who have ever understood my work Nancy, let alone believed in it. In fact there was really only one man . . .' He gazed down at the bone.

'It arrived by post two weeks ago – it was sent to my home in Delhi . . .'

Suddenly Nancy didn't want to hear any more, and she even raised a hand, as if that might stop him. She was thinking she should walk away, but something rooted her to the spot. And Jack was continuing, his mouth was moving and now she had to hear what he was saying.

'It was sent to me from Pome, near Bhaka gompa, it was sent from Tibet. There was a note attached, addressed to you. I'm afraid I read it before I realized it wasn't for me. Perhaps I would have read it anyway, I don't know. It had an exact longitude and latitude written on it – and it said something else as well.'

He placed a scrap of paper onto the table and gestured to her to pick it up.

'Once again, I am the pawn,' he said, managing a wan smile.

Nancy took the note and read what it said. Then she dropped it as if it was burning her hand. The sun was bright. All around them was a scene of such ordinary tranquillity – the people moving past, holding their coffees and their newspapers, as if there was no mystery to life at all. For half a minute, Jack Adams waited for her to say something, and then, with an embarrassed shrug, he packed away the bone.

'I'm sorry I came here today, I just thought you might want to see it. I thought that it would stop you feeling guilty. But perhaps I've just made things worse for you . . .'

The note was there on her lap, just an innocuous piece of paper, but she could barely look down at it.

'Look, it doesn't mean much,' said Jack. 'God knows how he survived. I can only guess some tribes-people found him. It just means he's alive and mad. Completely and utterly mad.'

Nancy found she still couldn't speak. Slowly, she shook her head.

'If it has made things worse, then I'm sorry,' said Jack, and his face was so full of remorse that Nancy gripped his hand.

'No, no, that's not it. Thank you for coming. You did the right thing.'

Gingerly, she took up the note and read it again. To Jack, the six words it contained meant that Herzog was mad and lost to his crazy dreams. But to her – and this was why in a sense they had never understood each other, and even after everything they had shared there was a fundamental gulf between them – these words meant that her dream of normality had been shattered, that nothing would be the same again. She was changed, everything was changed for ever. Anxiously, her eyes scanned Tompkins Square Park. How long did the world have left? Days? Weeks? Then her gaze fell on the headline of the copy of the *New York Times* that lay on the table next to the box: 'US Navy warns of new Cuban missile crisis as China surrounds Taiwan with nuclear submarines. President vows to use nuclear weapons to defend the island nation.' A sudden wind chased litter down the sidewalk. Black clouds rolled across the sun, casting Tompkins Square into darkness. *Götterdämmerung*, the Twilight of the Gods. With Jack watching her, she read out the words on the note, as if they were a magic spell. The world was under the power of this spell and, she realized, no one would ever escape again.

'Greetings, from the King of Shangri-La . . .'

ACKNOWLEDGEMENTS

The quotations from the *I Ching* or 'Book of Changes' that appear in this novel are based on the translations by C.J. Jung, Richard Wilhelm and Cary F. Baynes. I have also made use of many other sources, including Claire Scoby, *Last Seen in Tibet* (Rider, 2006), one of the greatest books ever written about Tibet by a foreigner; Nicholas Goodrick-Clarke, *The Occult Roots of Nazism* (Tauris, 1985); Thupten Jinpa, Graham Coleman and Gyurme Dorje, *The Tibetan Book of the Dead: First Complete Translation* (Penguin Classics, 2006); and Patrick French, *Tibet, Tibet: A Personal History of a Lost Land* (HarperCollins, 2003).

Visit **www.panmacmillan.com** to read more about all our books and to buy them. You will also find features, author interviews and news of any author events, and you can sign up for e-newsletters so that you're always first to hear about our new releases.

www.panmacmillan.com

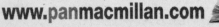

GIFT SELECTOR
YOUR ACCOUNT
WISH LIST
WAITING LIST

| HOME | ABOUT US | IMPRINTS | TRADE/MEDIA | CONTACT US | ADVANCED SEARCH | SEARCH | GO |

| BOOK CATEGORIES | WHAT'S NEW | AUTHORS/ILLUSTRATORS | BESTSELLERS | READING GROUPS |

Coming Soon...

Reading Groups

Competitions
Feeling Lucky?

Extracts
Sneak Previews

Interviews

Events
Meet Our Stars

Reviews
What The Critics Say

News & Awards

Editor's Choice
What We're Reading